www.booksbybradclark.com
You can follow Brad on Twitter @BooksByBrad

CW01498380

To Heidi, the love of my life, who inspires me to be who I am.

To all my kids, who nagged and prodded me to not only finish my books, but to get them published.

Brad Clark

Knight Fall

The Champion Chronicles Book I

***

Knight Fall

***

Chapter One

Conner had long since resigned himself to a cold night in the woods. He glanced up at the slowly falling sun that was not only taking daylight with it but the warmth of the early spring day as well. He looked through the trees, eyes searching for the fleeting doe that he knew was nearby. She was a big one, having easily survived the light winter months and would provide him and his aunt many meals and a new pair of boots or two. But first, he had to catch up to her and then bring her down.

He had picked up her trail around noon and followed as carefully as he could. Sometimes he would just sit and wait, patient as the day was long. But now with the sun heading down, his patience was following just as quickly. He could have settled for a rabbit or two. It would have at least given him a good meal, but the elusive doe was something that he really needed. So he moved through the woods carefully and deliberately, trying to get himself into a position where he could take a shot at her. But so far, whatever fates or gods were watching over him were either ignoring him or playing games.

He knew the doe was out there, somewhere nearby. He had spent the better part of the afternoon moving south, deeper into the forest, but most importantly, downwind. She wouldn't get a whiff of him, but he also needed to make sure that she didn't hear him. So he moved carefully and slowly, trying to avoid quick movements that might draw attention if she happened to be looking in his direction.

He wore a long brownish cloak that made him hot while the sun was out but would keep him comfortably warm as the sun dropped towards the horizon. His feet hurt from the small leather boots he wore. His aunt had promised him a new set, but first, he needed to bring in a deer.

He had wanted a big buck with great antlers, but they were even harder to find. He had to settle for the first deer he came across, and it was the white-tailed doe that was very adept at eluding him. The bow, which he had carved himself, was a good bow—made from a thick oak tree that grew tall and wide, deep in the woods. It shot straight and true, as a good hunting bow should. It wouldn't fell a Karmon Knight in full armor, but it would do its job on the thick leather hide of a deer.

The land had been rising slowly for a while, making his trek seem even longer and more arduous than it had been earlier in the day. He leaped across a small creek that cut into the side of a hill. In one motion, he landed and then jumped up the steep bank. His body was stiff from the long day of hunting, which made him struggle to get over the top. He stayed on the ground, panting from the effort. He was tired and knew that he would eventually have to give up and make camp for the night. But that decision was still a couple of hours off. As long as he had enough light to keep from running head-first into a tree, he would keep hunting. He rolled onto his hands and knees and pushed himself back up onto his feet. With a deep breath, he continued onward.

As he reached the crest of a small hill, he dropped into a crouch and maneuvered behind a large tree. Down in the valley below him was a swiftly moving creek snaking in and out of the thick underbrush. Although it would dry up in the summer, the creek served as springtime watering spot. She stood proudly at the water's edge, taking her fill of the cool water that had begun the long journey from the far off White Mountains and would eventually make its way to the Gulf of Taran. Conner slowly and cautiously shifted his position into one where he could launch his arrow. The bow was already strung. He just needed to pull it off his shoulder, pull out an arrow, nock it, and aim. He took in a deep breath and held it long enough to judge the distance, the angle, and the wind with barely a thought. He adjusted his aim as he had done countless times. He knew the doe was his. He just needed to release the arrow. He let out the air in his lungs and paused for one moment to still his entire body.

The doe's head twitched, and Conner knew he would miss. He released the arrow, but the deer was already moving, darting into the forest, never to be seen again. The arrow buried itself deep into the trunk of a tree, directly on line with where the deer's heart should have been. As the deer ran to safety, the sound that startled the deer came to his ears. The sound of a scream. High pitched and full of terror.

Conner gripped his bow tightly and started running in the direction of the scream. He could only imagine what could be causing someone to make such a sound, much less who might be here in the middle of the forest. The nearest village was several miles away, a good morning's hike, if you knew where you were going. Farther to the east, the Blackenwood Forest became thick with ancient trees where bears could be a problem. Occasionally, even a cougar or mountain lion would wander down from the hills to the north and cause trouble. He would even see a wolf or two in the winter when their hunting grounds were light. But winter was over, and spring was here. Food and hunger shouldn't be an issue. Regardless of what was happening, the shrieking let him know that time was important. He ran recklessly through the forest, charging through the underbrush, ignoring the scrapes and cuts that the thick brambles were causing to his face.

Fully out of breath, he broke into a clearing to find two men standing over a young woman. The scene was the farthest thing from his mind, so he was as surprised as the two men when he came crashing through the bushes. Both men were clad in the typical garb of a soldier. Or at least what he envisioned a soldier would look like. One had a dented conical helm that seemed to fit just a bit too big. The other had shaggy black curly hair. Both were armed with swords strapped to their sides and wore chainmail shirts.

No one moved for what seemed an eternity while they sized one another up. Conner looked at the girl; her large, teary eyes clearly pled for help.

Conner gripped his bow loosely at the middle, ready to nock an arrow, but he kept the arrows in their quill. "What's going on?" Conner asked.

"Be gone, boy," growled the mercenary with the dented conical helm.

Conner took offense at being called a boy. He was certainly younger than both of them, neither of whom had a good shave in quite a while. But he was no longer a boy in mind or stature.

"I heard the girl screaming," Conner said, unsure what to do, but trying to sound as manly as he could.

The two soldiers looked at one another and the one with the conical helm stepped forward, letting his companion keep tabs on the girl.

"Out hunting?" The man asked, smiling to show his crooked teeth.

"Yes," Conner replied warily.

"You best get back to it, then," the man said, his smile fading as his right hand fell to the pommel of his sword. "Don't want to see you get hurt."

Conner suddenly realized that the man had slowly halved the distance between them. Without thinking, going on instinct alone, he drew an arrow from his quill and nocked it. The man stopped, glancing from bow to eyes. The smile came back.

They both knew that Conner wouldn't fire the arrow at anyone. In one way, the man was right. Conner had never killed a man. The thought had never even crossed his mind, and if that made him still a boy, then maybe he was. He just hoped that the mercenary had just a little bit of doubt.

"Jon, take her away," called out the mercenary with the conical helm.

Jon, the other soldier, bent to take her away, but Conner raised his bow and aimed it right at him. He looked up at his partner.

"Don't," Conner said, trying to keep his voice and his hands from shaking.

"Go on, Jon, he won't shoot. He's just a forest boy. A peasant." Then he added, "We'll get him, too."

It was an accident. To his dying day, Conner would swear that what happened next was an accident. Maybe his body was tired from hunting and the sprint through the woods. Maybe he was just distracted by the girl, lying on the ground, helpless. Whether it was fatigue, concentration, or just dumb luck, as Jon took a step forward, the bow string separated from his fingers. The arrow flew straight and fast, embedding deep into the chest of the mercenary. The force of the arrow caused him to take one step back, and then he lost all control of his legs. They collapsed under him, and he fell to his knees. He tried to grip the shaft of the arrow, but his fingers wouldn't work. His eyes looked from Conner to the soldier with the conical helm. His lips quivered as if he were about to speak, but then he fell face forward, dead before he landed face first on the ground.

Conner was stunned, unable to really comprehend what had happened. The remaining soldier gripped his sword as if he were going to draw his weapon, but instead he sprinted out of the clearing, crashing through the underbrush until he could no longer be heard. Conner watched him go, his mouth still agape at what had happened. He walked slowly to the dead man and prodded him with his foot, just to make sure he was dead. The arrowhead was sticking out his back along with about a quarter of the shaft. The only blood was what was left on the arrowhead and shaft. Just like if he had taken down a deer. It was a perfect shot, right through the heart. For several long minutes, he could only stand over the body, amazed and afraid at what he had done.

He had killed many animals for food, but there had always been a purpose. He needed to eat, and his primary means of feeding himself and his aunt was what he could bring home from the forest. He had killed another man, and he felt really, really cold. It was not what he had expected. There was no joy in killing a man, even if he was threatening the girl's life. Whatever satisfaction he could have felt was overshadowed by the fact that he had taken another man's life.

It was movement out of the corner of his eye that broke him from his trance. The girl had managed to get up on her feet, even though her hands were tied behind her back and her feet were tied at the ankles. He quickly cut her free.

She tried to thank him, but her voice cracked between sobs, and she could only spit out something unintelligible. She was clothed in a simple dress—dirty and muddy, but clearly of a finer cloth than he had ever seen. Her hair was matted and tangled, but her large eyes were painted around the edges with a hint of green that matched her sparkling eyes. He had heard of women who dressed as she dressed, and made up their faces as she did, but he had never met one. His aunt had told him many stories of them. Nobles from the city who lived lives of unimaginable wealth. He looked down at her, and she looked no different than the other girls from her village. There was no magic aura that surrounded her. Other than her painted eyes, she could have been any other forest girl. Except she was more beautiful than any other girl, he had ever seen.

Shouts from a distance caused him to move. Grabbing her hand, he pulled her harshly into the brush, running as fast as he could with her in tow.

***

He didn't look like a knight, much less a fabled Karmon Knight. His polished plate armor was back at the castle, waiting for the next great battle. The enormous war mount that he used for charging picket lines of pikemen or bearing down upon hapless tournament opponents was left in the stables. He looked hardly like the son of a wealthy landowner, the seventh in a line of honorable Karmon Knights. Sir Brace Hawkden looked more like a peasant hunter, clad only in a thick leather tunic tied around his waist by a simple leather belt. A longsword, sheathed in a plain scabbard, hung from his saddle. A long dirk was stuck in his belt. He sat, however, unlike a hunter might, straight and tall, as all knights were taught. He was unmoving, as was his horse. The roan mare was fast and feisty, his favorite for hunting parties and racing through the tall grass fields. Her muscles rippled with every movement, showing off a body bred as pure as any knight or king.

He had no fear as he sat upon his mount. Maybe it was supreme confidence, or maybe it was simply arrogance. But when some might feel uncomfortable in the silence of the deep woods, he felt peace. Where the unknown would cause some to cringe, he held his head high, waiting for the next challenge. Successes were met with a simple nod, and failures with just a frown and a look of determination. He didn't get angry or overly excited. It was a coolness that he demanded of himself, as the leader of the most elite group of warriors throughout the eastern kingdoms.

His eyes shifted slightly a moment before a rustling in the trees hit his ears. He turned his horse to face the four men who approached him. Their heads were low, eyes on the ground in front of them. He had guessed from the shouts that came some time ago that they would return empty handed. It didn't take him long to notice that five had gone out.

The leader of the group, a mercenary by the name of Rogette, approached first. "There was a soldier out there. He had a bow."

"A soldier?" Sir Hawkden asked curiously.

The mercenary pulled off his dented conical helm and looked back at his companions. "Yes, sire. Some soldier."

"What was he dressed in? Chain? Leather?" Brace asked.

The mercenary shook his head. "Naw, no armor. Just a bow. He killed Jon."

Brace thought it improbable that any sort of soldier would be out in the forest this far from the city.

"But you took care of all of her guards, right?" Brace asked sharply. "Could it have been one of them?"

"Four left with her from the city. We took care of all four just as planned. It wasn't one of them. It was someone else. Who could it be?"

Brace wondered as well, but he could not dwell on it. Even if it was only one, then he could be tracked, and they would take care of him. He didn't really like the idea of having more lives lost, but it was simply a part of the bigger picture. In fact, he regretted that the Princess' Royal Guards had to be taken care of in such a barbaric manner. There were not many in the guard that he really cared for, but he also didn't like meaningless loss of life. Or murder. He pushed those thoughts away. There would be plenty of time for reflection later. The bigger picture meant that individual lives didn't matter.

"I must return to the city before dark," Brace said. "I do not have time to chase her down myself."

"The soldier?" One of them asked.

"There are four of you and one of him," Brace replied with a growl. "When I hired you, I thought I was hiring men, not cowards. Are you so afraid of one man that you would run through the forest like a bunch of little girls?"

The four looked at one another. They were mercenaries and skilled with arms. But unlike soldiers who would die for a cause, they needed to be alive to be paid. It wasn't necessarily cowardice, but it was awfully close.

After a moment, the mercenary named Rogget said, "We will find her, sire."

Brace clarified, "Unharmed. With the soldier, you can do what you want, but the princess will not be harmed or otherwise touched."

Rogget nodded his head, but the Knight Captain added to his warning. "I would rather she escape and return home than for you to harm her. For her fate will be your fate." He looked down at the rest of the mercenaries and said to them, "That goes for all of you. She is to be unharmed. Capture her as planned, but if she returns harmed, you will get twice what she got. And if you do not return, I will hunt you down, and you will regret that you were ever born."

The mercenaries were as arrogant and confident as any, but the tone of his voice, the inflection of his words, and the fierceness in his eyes caused them all to simply sulk away and return to their hunt.

Brace watched them leave, regretting everything that he must do, but knowing it was only for the best.

***

"I do not think they are chasing us anymore."

The words caught Conner by surprise, and he let go of the girl's hand. She was bent over, gasping for air. Although Conner was sweaty and tired from their sprint through the forest, he was breathing easily. He could have run faster, but the girl kept pulling him back, slowing him down. Conner knelt to the ground, closed his eyes and listened. He ignored her heavy breathing and focused solely on the forest. The trees. The wind. The animals.

All seemed normal.

He looked back at the path that they had made and frowned.

She noticed the sour look on his face and asked, "What is it?"

Conner pointed back towards the way they had come.

The girl looked and then looked again. She said, "I do not see it."

"We have made a path that a five-year-old could follow. We will need to be more careful." Then he looked around more closely to his surroundings. "And I have made a grave error!"

She chuckled. "Grave error? You do not speak like a peasant hunter. Who are you?"

Conner stood and realized he was still holding his bow and two arrows. He returned the arrows to his quiver. "Conner. My name is Conner."

She smiled. "Pleased to meet you, Master Conner. I am Princess Elissa. And thank you for saving my life."

Conner was too stunned to say anything. He knew the name as well as anyone else in the kingdom, but never dreamed that he would come face to face with the king's only child. She was as beautiful as they had said, even after being kidnapped and hauled through the forest. Her eyes were bright and full of life, like someone who lived in a high tower and never saw the pain of real life. Her blonde hair was now dull and matted, but he could just imagine what the flowing, curly locks could look like. Her mouth was turned into a smile, showing her white teeth. He could only stare back in fascination.

"You said you have made an error?" She asked.

Pulled from his trance, he corrected her. "No, I said I made a grave error. I have led us in the wrong direction. Just past those trees is a river that we must cross."

"Very well, then, lead on," she said with a flip of her hand.

Conner chuckled at her innocence. She had no idea the trouble that she had avoided, and if she did, then she had a very short memory. "It is going to be dark soon. We will need to find a safe place to hole up for the night."

She stood silently for a moment, and asked, "Should we not return to my carriage, I am sure that my guards are searching for me. If we return there, they are sure to find us."

"If they caught you, it is likely that your guards are dead. Anyway, the guys who kidnapped you are between us and your carriage. And it is getting late."

"Dead?" She said. Her eyes welled up with tears and her bright red lips quivered.

"Yes, and we will be if we don't move on," Conner said.

They moved quietly through the trees, fast enough to keep moving, but not too fast to make it easy for anyone who was following them to see their trail from far off. Conner zigged and zagged his way towards the river, mentally kicking himself for not realizing where he was. The Meadow River eventually dumped into the greater Tyre River, but it didn't take a straight course. It bent and bowed as it cut through the forest, giving water and fish to the animals of the woods. But unfortunately for Conner and Elissa, they had made straight for an almost full circular curve of the river. They were now almost completely surrounded by the river, so they would either go back the way they came and stay dry or make their way across the river. It was a cold river, and Conner had no way of starting a fire unless he was fortunate enough to find the right flint stones along the banks.

The Meadow River wasn't a fast moving river, but it had cut a big cliff into the woods right where they came out. Conner looked down directly into the water, about thirty feet below him. Another hundred yards farther downriver, the ground sloped to a small beach.

"Maybe we should head there to cross," Conner suggested, pointing down river.

Elissa had not said a word since they had last stopped. Now she had sat down and yawned. "I think we should just rest for a while. Right here."

Conner looked around, knowing that it wouldn't be long before they were caught. They just couldn't move fast enough, and if the soldiers who had kidnapped Elissa were halfway intelligent hunters, they would easily track them through the woods. "We should at least get across the river before we rest."

She furled her eyebrows and pursed her lips. "No. I say we rest right here. I am tired."

For a moment, Conner was going to argue. But the girl was clearly beaten. Her chest was heaving up and down, and her shoulders slumped. Her clothes were torn and ragged, dirty from running through the woods. He sat next to her.

"We can rest, but only for a few moments. The sun is just about to fall below the trees, and it gets dark really fast in the woods."

She nodded. The spark that had been in her eyes was gone. She looked hardly the princess she claimed to be. She looked more like the dirty peasant girls who carried the harvest from the fields to market.

"What happened?" Conner asked.

"I am not really sure, I guess," she said after a minute of reflection. "One minute we were riding through the forest, me in my carriage, and my Royal Guards leading the way. And then there was yelling and screaming. Raymond, my personal guard, pulled me out of the carriage and …I…" She looked away, a tear falling from the corner of her eye. "I tripped over Tory. I see now that he was not alive. Then I ran. There was yelling behind me, but I just ran. After I could not run anymore, two of them caught me. I think they were going to kill me. Until you came." She placed a hand on his arm and smiled up at him.

He smiled back, seeing the spark back in her eyes. Her hands were warm and sent an odd tingle up his arm. He had never been touched by such a pretty girl before, much less a princess.

"You have nothing to worry about," Conner said. "I will get you back to the city. But not tonight. It is late, and we will be in complete darkness soon. On the other side of the river are some caves where we can hide through the night."

They sat in silence for some time. Elissa sat on a fallen tree, playing with her hair, trying to brush it out with her fingers. Conner listened carefully, hoping that he would not hear any rustling of the underbrush that would signal that their pursuers were upon them. Their only route out was across the river, which would be a cold and dangerous swim. The river was deep, and the water was cold. Conner knew he was a good swimmer, but he had no idea as to how well the girl could swim. Even if she could swim, would she be able to have the strength to fight the cold water to keep from drowning? With the sun dropping below the trees, and the shadows of the forest getting longer and darker, Conner stood up to lead Elissa along the river's edge towards the small beach where they would cross.

With darkness inching through the forest, it wouldn't be too long until they were in complete darkness. He was trying to be careful, but he knew that he wasn't able to move as quietly as he would like. The fear and adrenaline that had coursed through his system were now going away, making him tired and not as sharp as he thought he was.

The odd thing about the movement was that if it had been high noon, he might not have noticed it. But the shadows and gray dreariness of dusk made quick movements just that much more noticeable. It came from the corner of his eye and suddenly the weariness was gone, and his muscles reacted without him actually thinking about it. He leaped towards Elissa, pushing her forward just as an arrow buzzed past his head. They dove into the underbrush, but away from the river. The bank of the river was still too steep and high. They could jump down into the river, but risk breaking a leg on an unseen rock. Conner kept pushing Elissa, who let out a steady stream of whimpers and whines.

Under cover of both underbrush and darkness, they made it safely to the small beach at the river's edge. Although they couldn't be seen, Conner knew that they were heard and that their pursuers were not far behind.

"Can you swim?" Conner asked.

Elissa nodded her head, her eyes wide with fear, her lips trembling.

"Go, then! Straight across. Once you get there, hide in the bushes." Conner quickly strung his bow and knocked an arrow.

"What are you doing?"

"If we both go, they'll easily pick us off from the bank. I'll stay here and keep them company."

She gripped his arm tightly. "What if you don't...?"

"I will," Conner interrupted. His eyes scanned the forest for movement. He knew he wouldn't actually be able to see them in the darkness. But he would be able to see movement. He lifted his bow towards what he thought was a body and let an arrow fly. It struck something hard with a thud. But there was no cry or the sound of a falling body. At the least, he hoped it would slow them down if they knew that he still had his bow.

She hadn't moved, so he pulled her hands off his arm. "You must go. If I don't get across, head down river. There is a village about a half days walk. Just follow the river, and you'll get to it. You can't miss it. It's where the Meadow River runs into the Tyre River." He pushed her away and pulled out another arrow. He only had five left.

Her lips moved as if she were trying to say something, but no words came out. Finally, she turned away and ran into the water. Conner turned away from her to scan the trees, looking and waiting for someone to show a face.

And there it was. It was a white face that barely visible behind a tree limb. He lifted his bow and aimed at where the man's chest should be. He let loose, and the face disappeared. Movement to his left caught his eye. A shadowed body appeared and he thought he heard the sound of an arrow flying through the air. A quick aim and then another arrow was released, and this time he heard the thud of the body falling to the ground. He crouched low, listening and watching. His eyes straining to see through the darkness, but there were no more shadowed bodies or faces visible. Knowing he couldn't swim while holding the bow, he loosed his remaining arrows into the trees and then ran into the river, diving under the cold water, swimming as far and as fast as he could.

Chapter Two

Brace guided his exhausted horse underneath the portcullis before it was fully raised up. As soon as he was through, it dropped with a crash. He glanced back, thinking the guard let it drop just a little bit too early. If his mount wasn't nearly dead, it would have been spooked and would likely have bucked him off. Instead, the horse simply lets out a snort and dropped its head. A squire took the reins as the Knight Captain slipped off.

The courtyard was dimly lit by a handful of torches hanging from the stone walls of the castle. The men that approached him were lost in the darkness, so he did not realize that the king himself was approaching until his face came out of the shadows.

"Your majesty," Brace said in greeting, forcing the tiredness out of his bones.

"Brace, it is good to see you. I see that you rode hard upon receiving my message," the King said.

"I came as quickly as I could," Brace replied. His heart was racing, and it wasn't because of his hard ride. He did not lie. At least the words that came out of his mouth were not lies. But the meaning of the words, the implication of the words, and the preceding actions could only result in accusations of treachery and ultimately death. But it was a bridge that he had long ago crossed. There was no turning back. He just did his best to hide his lying words from his beloved king.

King Reyan Thorndale, ruler of the kingdom of Karmon, was not an old man, but his hair had long since turned gray, and his beard was long and shaggy. Deep, serious eyes were surrounded by leathery wrinkles. He carried himself as a king would, with a straight back and a puffed-out chest. Even in this time of grief and anger, he was still king of Karmon. He was shorter and older than the three men who flanked him, but it was clear who was the strongest. Brace knew more than anyone that strength did not come from a length of steel, or the size of one's arms, or the number of lives that his steel and arms took. The king's strength came from the way he ruled his kingdom. He wasn't a tyrant, but he also wasn't a pushover, either. He ruled with honor and love. And the people of the kingdom returned that love. There was hardly a man or woman in the entire realm that did not love their leader.

It was painful for Brace to stand in front of this man having to lie and perpetuate the ruse. His stomach was queasy, and he just wanted to throw up.

"I thank you, although your steed may never be the same," the king replied.

Brace took the opportunity to turn away and pat the horse on the neck. "She is strong and will recover." He took a deep breath to collect himself and asked, "Now, as for what happened..."

"Thellians," one of the men standing behind the king shouted out. The man was clad in a deep blue cape, the color of the Royal Guard. His hand clenched the pommel of his sword tightly. "The murderous scum...we shall ride against them immediately!"

"Hold now, Perkins," the king said with a wave of his hand. "We know little of what happened. It is my daughter that is in danger, but we must be cautious in our assumptions."

Brace nodded visibly, agreeing with his liege. "Yes. It has been quite a while since they have done anything like this. And never have they been so bold as to go after the royal family."

"And yet, we must not discount them," the King said. "They have been quiet, and that is always something to be concerned with."

"Very well," Brace replied. "Shall we go to the hall? We can discuss this in more detail there."

Perkins stepped forward, exploding in anger. "Discuss! There is nothing to discuss. You must call your knights and head out at once. You must find these vile Thellians, kill them and return the princess to her father."

Brace stepped forward to meet the challenge. But he kept his cool and his words calm. "Perkins, I understand your anger, but you are not thinking clearly. We cannot just go invade Thell because we think that they did this. I want to find out who did this as badly as you do. But we can't make assumptions and act irrationally." He gave the royal guardsman a long stare before motioning towards a set of double doors. "Your majesty, shall we?"

Perkins took another step forward. The calmness that Brace was able to hold in check dissipated. Anger now replaced it. His own hand went to the sword sheathed at his side. Perkin's hand went for his own sword.

King Thorndale placed a hand on the chest of each man. "I do not understand this petty squabbling between you two. Rather than fighting about who is the biggest and strongest, you should be more worried about the safety of this kingdom and most importantly my daughter."

"Sire, I was only trying to express the urgency of the situation," Perkins explained.

"And not trusting decisions to those who are best able to make them," the King countered. "It is a dark, moonless night. Any trail that could be found will not be found until the morning. We will ride out two hours before first light and arrive at the forest as the sun comes up."

He let his hands drop, and the two men took a step back. "Now, we will retire to the great hall to prepare for what we will do tomorrow. Perkins, you will call your Royal Guard together and make your presence known in the city. Once it gets out about the attack, the city will be fearful. If they see you and your men out and about, then they will be reassured that all is well."

"Yes, sire," Perkins said meekly. "I would request that my men and I assist in chasing down those who attacked your daughter. It was my men..."

"That failed to protect the princess," Brace said sharply.

Before another fight could erupt, the king shouted, "Enough! And this is why I will keep you two and your men separate. Perkins, you and your men will stay here. Brace, call your knights together and prepare them to ride." He looked at one, then the other. He shook his finger at both of them, like a father chastising his children. "Your squabbling will be the death of me, I tell you!"

The king turned his back and strode strongly towards the great hall.

***

The river was deathly cold. Conner knew that it was a bad idea to cross at night with no chance of building a fire to warm them, but they had no choice. With their pursuers getting closer, their only option for escape was the river. If it were mid-day with a sun shining strong and high in the sky, he would not have worried. The spring sun was warm and sometimes hot. It would have dried them out in no time. But once that sun slipped below the horizon and darkness was upon them, it was cold and would only get colder as the night winds picked up.

Elissa's sneeze caught his attention. She was huddled in the corner of the cave shivering. He sat back from his kneeling position and let out a long sigh. The small pile of twigs sitting in front of him just would not light. For all the rocks and stones strewn about the cave's floor, none of them were useful for getting a spark. He kept himself warm by moving around trying to light a fire, but his hands were sore, and his arms were tired. Giving up, he leaned against the cold stone wall of the cave and watched her for a while. She sat with her knees up to her chest, her long hair laying across her shoulders and down in front of her face. The curls had long since lost their curl and bounce. Her dress was wet and dirty. She looked hardly the princess she claimed to be.

And then she looked up at him, and something struck him hard. The hairs on his neck perked up, and a wave of heat suddenly swept over him. Her face showed her weariness from running and crossing the river. But when her eyes caught his, she smiled. It wasn't a smile of hello, but a smile of warmth and deepness. He smiled back and locked her eyes. He wanted to look away, but he just couldn't. Regardless of her title and the royal blood that flowed through her veins, she was really nothing more than what he was. Cold and weary. Young and scared. He stood up and moved to be next to her.

"How are you holding up?" He asked.

"Wet and cold," she replied, with a slight chuckle. "What about you?"

"I'll be okay." He continued to look at her closely. He had expected her to be crying and afraid. Maybe she was afraid, but her smile and chuckle told him that there was something else behind those bright green eyes.

"Are you sure? You had to kill two of them."

Conner nodded and leaned back against the cold cave wall. "I know. I had to."

"Have you ever…" she left the question to hang in the damp, dark air.

"No. They were the first. Well, the one back when I found you was the first. But that was an accident. But the other two…"

"I'm sorry," she said, putting a hand on his knee.

He looked down at her soft, white hands, and then up into her eyes. "They were after us, and if they caught us, they would have not had a second thought about killing us."

She squeezed his knee. "Then you are my champion."

Conner let out a short, sharp laugh. "I am no warrior, I am just the son of a peasant farmer. I am nothing!"

She didn't share in his humor. Her jaw was locked firmly. "I am serious. You are my champion. I want you to come back to the castle with me."

His laughing came to a quick end. "I will certainly escort you back to your home. The forest is no place for a princess. Even without kidnappers hunting us down. Wolves and bears abound!"

"No, seriously, you should stay at the castle and be my champion!"

Conner patted her on the shoulder, doing his best to stifle a laugh. "You are a beautiful princess, and it would be an honor to serve you as a champion."

"And now you tease me!" She said, laughing with him.

"No, seriously," he said. "It would be an honor. But I am no champion. I do not know how to swing a blade or fight in a battle with knights. I would not last long as your champion."

"I think you underestimate yourself, Conner. You are brave and courageous. Two qualities that would make a champion."

"Two qualities that would lead to my quick death! Without skill with a blade, all the bravery and courage in the world would do me no good!" He was silent for some time, pondering their predicament. As long as they could survive the night and not freeze to death, they would be able to slip through the forest and avoid their pursuers. The problem would be staying warm enough. With no fire to dry their clothes or keep their bodies warm, there was a good chance they would simply fall asleep and not awaken. He had seen it before, but that had been in the middle of winter. While on a hunting trip with a friend and his uncle, the uncle fell through the ice on the river. They had struggled with a fire then, and could not get one going. Any wood they found was too wet, and the friend's uncle had the only flint amongst them. It had been lost when he struggled in the river trying to get out.

They had gone to sleep that night, and only Conner and his friend woke up in the morning.

Conner looked around the cave. It was really no more than a hole in the side of a hill. It was just tall enough for Conner to stand with a slight crouch, but it didn't go very deep into the hill. There were remnants of fires from when others who had used the cave. It was out of the wind and maybe, just maybe, it would hold the heat of their bodies in.

He moved close to the princess and put an arm around her, wrapping his cloak around the both of them. The cloak was wet and smelled dirty and musty. She protested with a groan, but her teeth were chattering too much to speak.

"The warmth of our two bodies together will be warmer," he said.

She did not make another sound. She simply rested her head on his chest and his arms pulled her in tightly to him. In only a moment, her teeth stopped chattering, and she let out a long sigh. The scent of her perfumes filled his senses. It was warming and wonderful, something that he had never experienced before. He had smelled girls before, but they mostly smelled like dirt and sweat. This was different. She was different. Her warm body was soft against his. She moved her left arm behind his back and held him tightly. His arm, draped over her shoulder, squeezed.

"How old are you Elissa?"

It took her a moment before she answered with a sleepy voice, "Last spring I had my Growing Celebration."

"You're what?" He asked with a suddenly loud voice. The response had surprised him, and his voice carried deep into the cave.

She giggled. "It is a tradition in my family."

"I have never heard of it."

"Well of course not, because you are…"

"Just a peasant?" He finished for her.

She pulled away from him and looked into his eyes. "Well, yes. But I was going to say that you were not a part of my family, so how would you know?"

"Okay. Then what is this Growing Celebration."

"When a young lady reaches her fourteenth birthday, the family puts on a fancy feast and celebration. It is a week of eating and dancing. We play all sorts of lawn games, too."

"Lawn games?"

She smacked him on the chest. "Games, you know, stick ball, bowling. A westerner showed us a game he called sock it. You play with a big ball of twine, but you can't use your hands, only your feet."

"Games," Conner said quietly. "Sounds fun."

"You do not play?"

"Games?" Conner replied sourly. "No. That is for the little boys and girls to keep them out of the way. I am a hunter. I do not have time for games."

Her joyful mood quickly dissipated and she sat back down. "I am sorry. I did not mean to make you mad."

"You did not," he said softly. "I guess…maybe I wished I had time for fun."

They were silent for a while. Conner started to feel sorry for himself. He envied the life that the princess had. Not only in doing the things that were fun but being able to do anything she wanted, whenever she wanted. She lived a fanciful life of great grandeur, and he could see in her eyes and her voice how wonderful her life was. He wished, if only for a moment, he felt the same way about his life. There was little honor in wandering the woods for weeks on end, hunting and scavenging for food.

"I miss my mother," Princess Elissa suddenly said.

"You will see her again, I promise." It was only too late that he realized his mistake.

The tears flowed from her cheeks, and she buried her head in her hands.

"I am sorry," Conner said softly. "I forgot…"

She looked up at him and smiled, her large green eyes filled with tears. "It is okay," she said. "I do not remember her. But I miss her, isn't that crazy?"

"No," said Conner. "Not at all." He said no more, for he had never known his own mother, either. He didn't even know anyone from her family. His aunt, his dead father's older sister, never talked about her. He wanted to tell her, to let her know that she was not alone in not having a mother, but he couldn't. Something inside of him was holding back. He kept his mouth closed and listened.

"My father talks about her all the time. She was very beautiful, from what everyone says. And gracious. And loving." Her lips trembled. "She is everything I hope to be."

Conner pulled her close again. Her head fell back onto his chest. "I promise you I will get you back to your father and you will grow up to be just like your mother. Beautiful, loving, caring, and a great princess for some handsome and dashing prince."

She snuggled to him and yawned. "Maybe I'll be a great queen. I have no brothers, you know."

He could not image this young, precious, delicate flower being the leader of Karmon. Small as it was, it still took a powerful and wise king to rule it. He did not want to squash her dream, so he simply let her words go. He held her close. Feeling her body close to his made him feel warm and comfortable. It was a feeling that he hoped he would have again but knew that his thoughts were far from reality. He didn't really know what love was, but he could image it was something like he was feeling for Elissa. She was likable, and friendly, and very pretty. Maybe, just maybe…

Her breathing settled down and became regular, and he knew that she fell asleep. He kept his eyes open, watching the cave entrance, ensuring that they were safe. Maybe all that he could be for her was to be her champion, to watch over her, to protect her. She couldn't love him. He was a commoner, a peasant, the lowest rung on the ladder of life. But he could love her, and he could show that love in the only way he knew how.

Chapter Three

Brace was strapping on his leather armor when the king came into the armory. The squire that was attending him stiffened and quickly fell to a knee. Brace remained standing, having long since proved his loyalty to the king.

"Rise and continue your work, young squire," the king said with a smile. The squire, unaccustomed to doing his work in the presence of the king did continue, but with nervous and sweaty fingers.

"Brace, my long and dear friend," the king said to his Knight Captain.

"Yes, your majesty," Brace said.

The king fell onto a stool and let out a long sigh. "I need you now more than ever. The Thellians have never been so bold as to attack me personally like this. They have ravaged the villages along the mountains, but never have they dared come this close. I weary of them."

"The surviving guard died of wounds soon after he made it back to the castle. Can we trust his memory of what happened?" Brace asked.

"He is absolutely certain of what he saw. He was clear in his words. He recalled their dress, their accent, and their words."

"He heard them speak Thellian?"

The king nodded. "It is fortunate that some of Perkin's men speak the language of our enemy."

"Fortunate," Brace repeated. Then he added, "Maybe too much so."

"You question Perkin's loyalty? I know that you and he do not get along, and that is personal. But you have always been able to work together professionally.

"The princess never announces her rides through the forest. Her ambushers would either have to wait for days, or they would have to be told when and where she would be."

"You suspect treachery?"

"Is there any doubt?"

The king looked down at the floor for a long time, pondering the meaning of those last words. Brace sat quietly as the squire finished pulling on his boots. With a nod, the squire was dismissed and then they were alone.

"What of your loyalties?" The king asked. His eyes looked up from the dirt floor and locked onto his Knight Captain.

Brace did not flinch, nor did he look away. He looked deep into the green eyes of his liege. He knew the king would know whether the words that came out of his mouth were true or not. It was just how the king was, and it was how the king had survived for twenty years as the ruler of Karmon.

"My loyalties are to the crown and kingdom, my lord." He had to force himself to keep the king's gaze. "Perkin's sword is to protect you and the princess. My sword is to protect the realm."

The king smiled. "It is the answer that I would expect from you. And because of you, this kingdom will last longer than me and even the memory of me." The smile faded to look of anger, the anger of a father whose daughter was taken from him. "I would have my daughter back."

Brace approached his king and placed a hand on his shoulder and said softly, "I will return your daughter to you. Unharmed. It is my vow. I shall not return until I have her in the saddle behind me."

"Begone, then," the King said. With one last gaze and nod of the head, the king left the stables.

Brace could barely stand. The guilt that swept through him was overwhelming. The princess was never to have been harmed, and even the Royal Guards were simply supposed to have been tied up. But one thing had led to another, and there were five dead guardsmen and one missing princess. He tried to think of the moment when things had gotten out of hand, and the plan had lost its way. He kept marching back in his mind until the beginning. The only moment that he could think about was that first moment when he decided to carry out the plan.

It was too late to change the past, but hopefully, he could change the future. He strode out of the stables in long strides not wanting to take the long ride north. But he had to. He had to set things right.

***

The sun was still below the horizon when they came out of the cave. Elissa was refreshed and talkative, but the night had worn harshly on Conner. Each time he had closed his eyes, the only thing that he saw was her death. Whether it was her frozen body, or an arrow-pierced body, or the worst, which was with her throat slit, the thoughts of her death kept him awake. All night she had slept, the gentle rise and fall of her chest upon his giving him thoughts of her being more than the girl she seemed. She was lithe, but not skinny. Unlike the girls he knew from his village, her bones could not be felt or seen. But she wasn't plump like many of the girls from the city, born and bred into wealth and comfort. She seemed just…perfect. He was a young man, just out of boyhood and certain thoughts were hard to suppress. But she was the princess, and he was there to protect her, not woo her. But there was still something electric about her touch.

He led her out of the cave by her hand. She held it firmly long after they had started walking south, heading towards the small village just a few hours walk away. It wasn't long before the forest began to wake up around them. As the sun peeked above the far horizon, the birds began their morning routine. The wind picked up slightly, sending leaves and branches in a gentle dance. With the sun came warmth. Their clothes, still damp from the river, were a hefty weight upon their shoulders. Soon the sun would rise high and dry them out.

Her sneeze and the scattering of birds from nearby trees sent a shock through his system. His heart stopped for a moment, thinking that for sure they were found out. He pulled her down to her knees, and his eyes scanned the trees and underbrush.

"They could still be out there," he said, maybe a bit too harshly.

Tears welled up in her eyes. "I am sorry," she whispered.

Conner let his anger fall away. He could no more be angry at the cold night than he could be angry at the beautiful face that was inches from his. Her green eyes shone brightly in the morning sun. Her face, dirtied and stained from tears that he had not seen, was still as soft as tender as the day she was born. Her hair once matted and tangled, had dried out and now flowed like beautiful locks just washed and curled. His heart pounded hard, and he could not figure out why.

He shook his head and smiled. "It is okay. We just need to be quiet. Just in case. I do not think they are near, but we cannot be certain."

As the Meadow River made its way south from the White Mountains to the Tyre River, it cut a path through woods and forests that went by many names. The locals called it the Black Woods or the Black Forest, but the map hanging in the great hall of the castle labeled it the Blackenwood Forest. The trees were thicker farther to the east and south where people were scarce, and animals roamed free without fear of hunters. In Blackenwood, the trees grew thick and tall, blanketing nearly a quarter of the Karmon Kingdom with lush greens. They were at the edge where the grasses of the plains encroached upon the forest. The ground was no longer flat and smooth, but hilly. The river cut through forest, plains, and hills. Small villages had sprouted along its banks and even a larger one where the Meadow River dumped into the larger Tyre River. Boats traveled up and down the river, transporting goods from one village to another. The great city of South Karmon was located where the Tyre River fed into the Gulf of Taran. The king's castle was located on the bluffs that overlooked both the city and the Gulf, with the city, stretched out below. Conner had visited the city once or twice, but he had never ventured near the castle, or near the waters of the Gulf

They trudged through the underbrush, across fields, up and down hills, and across little streams that were in their way. The sun did rise and warm them up, but the chill never seemed to leave, and their clothes never seemed to get completely dry. Their feet were just as cold and tired as the rest of their body. They often stopped to rest, as Elissa's strength was keeping them from walking as fast as Conner wanted. He pushed her, harder than he wanted, but not as hard as he could have. For a while they talked while they walked, sharing stories of their lives. She talked about her friends, mostly daughters of lords and other land owners. He talked about his friends, farmers, and hunters. They had little in common but genuinely seemed to enjoy one another's stories. As the day wore on, Elissa began to talk less and less. Her eyes were stuck forward, her mind forcing herself to put one foot in front of the other. Conner stopped pushing, letting her set the pace. He feared that they were moving so slow that they would not reach the village before nightfall. They ate berries, nibbled on roots, but their stomachs were angrily telling them that they needed more food. Conner feared that unless they reached the village before nightfall, they would not make it another night. *Well, she would not make it another night,* he corrected himself. He was strong and was used to the punishment that they were giving their bodies. But she was not. She was born into wealth and comfort, and simply not used to walking through the forest with little food and no strength.

Finally, she simply let her body fall.

Conner heard the thump of her body falling, then saw her head strike the ground. Her eyes rolled back in her head, and she would not respond to his calls. Her chest was still going up and down, so he knew that she was breathing. But he did not know how badly she might have hurt herself. With a heave and a grunt, he put her over his shoulders and continued walking. But now, his pace picked up. He reached deep into his strength reserves and pushed his body to make long, fast strides. His breathing became quick and shallow, but he forced himself to take slower, deep breaths, as he did when hunting. Slow the body, slow the mind, to make you faster and quicker for the kill, he had learned.

With no idea how long he walked with her over his shoulders, with no idea how much strength he had left, the sight of the village made him nearly burst into tears. His shoulders were screaming with pain. His legs had gone numb. With help just a few steps away, his mind could barely comprehend that he had reached his goal. A handful of the villagers were out and about, doing the things that they do every day when they saw him approach. Exhausted and unable to take another step, he dropped to his knees, and she tumbled onto the ground in front of him.

***

Brace kneeled down to next to the man who had an arrow stuck in his chest. He looked at him as if he were inspecting him for the first time.

"He dragged himself from the river," the ranger said.

Marik Brownbow was Brace's most trusted ranger. He was knighted as all of them were, raised from a young child to serve the king as a soldier of the forests. He had polished plate armor back in the armory, but he had only worn it once when he accepted the honor of knighthood and kneeled in front of his liege lord. Now, he simply wore a light leather armor vest that would offer only a small amount of protection in a sword fight. It was more important for him to travel lightly and silently, moving through the forests undetected. With little regard for the dead man, Marik yanked the arrow from the man's chest and looked it over carefully.

"This is an odd arrow," Marik said softly, more to himself than his captain.

"How so?" Brace asked after a moment. Marik continued to study the arrow from tip to fletching.

"It is a hunter's arrow. Straight and true enough for a hundred yard shot to take down an animal, but hardly the kind used by a soldier from across a battlefield. And the tip is stone, and not steel. It'll kill an animal just as easy, but it won't do well against even studded leather."

Brace took the arrow from his ranger and looked it over himself. "But well enough against skin and bone."

Marik gave a quick nod of the head. "It would appear that our princess came across a hunter in the woods."

A shout came up from near the river. Brace and Marik raced towards a group of knights scouring the river side. They had found another body. This one had taken an arrow through the throat and although he had died quickly, it had not been instant. The body was a bloody mess covered by buzzing flies. Brace stopped several feet away, unwilling to get close enough due to the horrid stench coming from the body. Marik ignored the smell and walked right up to it. The soldier was clad in similar dress to the other dead Thellians. But rather than having to pull the arrow out from the body, Marik took it from the dead man's grasp.

"Pulled it out himself," Marik observed. "Same kind of arrow. Fine workmanship, but not as good as our fletchers produce." He looked at it more closely, his fingers running through the fletching, down the shaft, and over the arrowhead. "Actually, it is very good quality for a hunter. I wouldn't want to come across this hunter in a fight."

Marik looked at the body, and then towards the river. He traced what he thought was the path of the arrow and came upon a small sandy area on the bank of the river. There were clear and obvious footprints.

"Captain, this is where the arrows were shot from." Marik then pointed across the river. "I'd guess that our archer then fled across the river. We should check the other bank and continue our tracking there."

"Very well. Take three others – Paul, Dolin, and John – and continue tracking. I'll have the rest scout this side of the river for more bodies and then collect up the Royal Guard and return them to the castle. The king will want to honor their bodies with a proper burial."

Marik looked down at the arrows still in his hands and then across the river. "If the princess came across a hunter, and he helped protect her, I think she will be in good hands."

"Why do you say that?" Brace asked.

"Those bodies haven't been there very long. Certainly not any longer than sometime last night. It is likely that the princess' defender made those shots blind, in the dark. Anyone who can make those shots is very good, or very lucky."

"Either way, if he has saved our princess, he will be well rewarded." Brace turned to leave, but turned back to say, "If you find her do not return her directly to the castle. I have made a promise to our king that I would return her myself. Although I would be grateful for her to be found by anyone, I would prefer the king not to know that I must disobey his commands."

"Sir?"

"I have some business to the north that I must attend to."

Marik nodded his understanding, but his eyes betrayed his thoughts.

"This attack, this ambush…is curious," Brace said in response to the inquisitive look Marik gave him. "I have some thoughts about who might be behind this, but it will require me to travel for a couple of days. They are questions that must be asked in person."

"I do not question your allegiance, sir," Marik said, his eyes lowered from shame.

Knight Captain Brace Hawkden put a hand on his ranger's shoulder. "You must trust me, old friend. Find the princess and meet me at our camp in two days. If I am not there in three, then you may take her into the city."

"Yes, sir. I'll do as you ask."

Brace left the ranger to continue the search, regretting he had to leave his knights and friends under this circumstance. It took him nearly an hour to retrace his route back to their horses. His thoughts were solely on the deeds that he had done and their immediate actions. He was worried sick for Princess Elissa. Like any dangerous mission, there were always risks. He knew that, but he also regretted that he had to put the princess at such a risk. But regardless of the risks that the princess was enduring, he was placing himself at much greater risk.

Like hers, his life was also in danger. But not only his, all his knights. The honor and trust that had been built up for so long now hung the balance. He was placing so many in danger, risking so much. The consolation had always been that the reward was so great. But now he doubted that there was going to be any reward in the end.

Chapter Four

Conner woke with a start, throwing off his blanket and jumping up from the floor. Panting and soaked with sweat, it was all he could do to keep his heart from exploding out of his chest. He still saw their eyes. He knew it was a dream, but he still saw their eyes. His hand had drawn the bow and loosed the arrows, striking those men down. He knew he killed one and had a good sight on two others. Maybe they lived, maybe they were dead. He did not know, but his dream told him all he really needed to know. The eyes were full of life, and then they were cold and dead. The faces stared up at him, ghostly and thin, eye sockets dark and sunken. It was by his hand that they were dead, and he knew that they were back to haunt him.

He fell to his knees, trying to keep the room from spinning so fast. If he had food in his stomach, he knew he would have thrown it up. He forced himself to not think of them as men, but as animals. To think of them as men was too much. He had killed, and he hated himself for it.

He fell back onto the floor and took in his surroundings. He was in a simple room with straw on the floor for a bed, a handful of blankets on top to keep warm, and a table with two chairs. A curtain separated his room from the rest of the house. It was open, showing a shaggy-bearded man stoking the fire in the fireplace and an elderly woman placing a plate of fresh bread on the table. They were dressed in drab clothes, stained and dirty.

"You're awake!!" The man called out. "I am glad that you are well. Welcome to our home. I am Marcus. And this is my mother, Melda".

Conner, surprised and a bit taken aback at his surroundings, barely squeaked out his name, "Conner. I'm Conner."

Marcus stood and asked. "Are you feeling okay? You were not doing so well yesterday."

"Yesterday? How much time has passed?" Conner looked around for his clothes, his bow, and his quiver. He was tired, despite having slept for almost an entire day.

"You came upon our village yesterday afternoon," Marcus replied. "You slept all day and through the night."

With a wide, nearly toothless smile, Melda said, "Your fever was strong, but it broke overnight. You look hungry, and we have bread. Come, sit." She gestured towards the bread, sitting on the table, steaming in the cool morning air.

The house was simple, not much different than what Conner lived in. There were two rooms, one with beds for sleeping and the main room. The fireplace filled most of one wall. The fire was now small, but large enough to heat the small rooms. For a moment Conner hesitated, not sure what to make of the scene. The man and his mother seemed friendly enough. They didn't appear to be threatening. But they were strangers. And the longer he waited, the stronger the scent of the bread became.

"Come, sit," Melda said. "You must be famished."

Conner was. He moved as quickly as his weary muscles allowed and took a seat at the table and began eating the offered bread. It was only after the third mouthful that he remembered what had brought him here. A sudden panic swept through him, and he stood, knocking over his chair. "Elissa?"

"Oh, the young girl," Melda replied in a reassuring voice. "She is fine. Once you have broken your fast, we shall go see her."

Conner was suddenly no longer hungry. "Where is she?"

The old woman's smile widened. "She is fine, but it is you who is not. You must eat."

Conner looked at the man for help, but he only shrugged his shoulders. Without another word, he took more bread and ate it ravenously.

***

"Sage is our village," Marcus said. "We are about a day's travel upstream for river cogs full of cargo coming from South Karmon. They stop at some of the other villages as well, but since we're halfway between South Karmon and Tyre, this village makes a good place to stop, and most of them do. We have a decent enough inn near the water's edge. And a blacksmith as well. Over there is Jessip who is one of the finest carpenters in all of the kingdom."

The man named Jessip was carrying a rocking chair across the main open area between buildings. He waved when he saw Marcus. He was not the only one going about his business. There was plenty of others moving about with purpose. There were no streets, only hard-packed lanes between buildings and the one large open area. The village buildings were constructed in a circular pattern around the central open area. A few smaller buildings, houses mostly, were built outward from the center. Smoke billowed from the blacksmith shop located near the water's edge. Nearby was the largest building of the village, an exquisite two-story building that blocked their view of the river. It was clearly labeled as the Village Inn. It seemed to be one of the central points of the village as a number of villagers were milling about the front entrance.

"A cog is getting ready to leave," Marcus explained. "Jessip, there, is trading one of his rocking chairs for a barrel of ale." A smile crept across his face. "There will be a fine festival tonight if you are inclined to stay."

"Have there been others...other strangers around?" Conner asked, ignoring the invitation.

Marcus stopped and turned towards Conner. "Others? What do you mean?" Marcus continued cautiously when Conner did not reply, "Only the cog from South Karmon that arrived yesterday evening. Were you expecting anyone else?"

"No..." Conner let his answer hang in the air while Marcus studied his face.

"Your appearance yesterday was quite surprising, even more so when the young woman announced herself as Princess Elissa, the only child of our beloved King Thorndale. It is not unusual for the nobles to make their way upstream on their way to Tyre, but they usually come by boat, or at least by carriage." He waited a moment to see if Conner would add anything. When he only received silence, Marcus continued. "It is not common to have travelers on foot come through our village from the forest. Especially tired, cold, and wet travelers."

"How is the princess?" Conner asked. He wasn't sure why he was avoiding the conversation with the man. Part of him wanted to trust Marcus and the villagers, but another part of him wanted to ensure the safety of the princess, and that meant being secretive and vague. He had wished that Elissa had not let on who she was. It was going to make things more complicated.

"Oh, she is fine. She was put up in the inn. As soon as she announced who she was, the royalty suites in the inn were cleared, and she was put up there."

"Royalty suites?" Conner asked.

"Well, we do not get much royalty here, but that is what Master Braggins calls them. They are just his best rooms." His eyes twinkled. "But royalty and nobles alike seem, well, appreciative when they are treated differently."

Unlike the rest of the village, the inn was extravagant in design and detail. It seemed as if it should have been built on the castle grounds and not in the middle of nowhere. A short stone wall, clearly for decoration, lined the front courtyard. To the right was a thatched roof stable. Where the village's buildings were mostly wood, the walls of the inn were stone. A balcony surrounded the entire second floor, but there seemed to be no staircase or ladder leading up to it. It appeared that it was only accessible through a room on the second floor.

The inside was as grand as the outside. Most of the entire first floor consisted of a great room whose walls were lined with tapestries and paintings that bespoke a culture beyond the simple villager. In the center of the room was a great fire pit with a chimney leading up through the ceiling. Scattered about the room were long tables, all filled with talking and laughing patrons. A barmaid pushed her way through the crowd, delivering mugs of ale, laughing and smiling herself.

"It seems like the arrival of the princess has caused business to pick up," Marcus observed. "During the day, the place is usually only filled with travelers. Today, I think the entire village is here!"

Marcus led Conner to a stairwell which was guarded by a large man, arms crossed, and a sneer painted on his face. The man stood in the middle of the stairwell, preventing anyone from going to the second level.

"Good day, Lawry," Marcus said, expecting to be let through. When the man did not budge, Marcus said, "Lawry, my man, stand aside. We are to see the princess."

Lawry shook his head. "No one sees the princess. By her order."

Marcus took a deep breath. "Lawry, this is the man that helped the princess. I am sure that she would like to see him."

Lawry's only response was to shake his head.

"Stand aside, man!" Marcus said in a raised voice.

The sneer disappeared, and Lawry's eyes grew large. Conner thought he saw his lip quiver. "I was only following orders," he said with a soft, whimpering voice.

Marcus patted him on the shoulder. "And you are doing a fine job. Now, please let me and my friend pass."

Lawry turned to let Marcus and Conner climb the stairs. But as soon as they were passed, Lawry returned to his position and his sneer.

At the top of the stairs, a hallway led to the end of the building with doors on either side. Only the last door at the end of the hall was closed. Marcus led them to that door and gently knocked. After a moment, a soft patter of footsteps could be heard approaching the door, then it was opened.

A young woman wearing a plain gray dress greeted them. She did not look up at them as she backed away from the doorway.

"Mary, dear, who is it?" The voice came from behind a screen in the corner of the room.

Conner stepped in at hearing Elissa's voice, but the tone and manner of her words were clearly unlike what he had heard from her in the forest. It had a slight accent, which made it sound snotty and superior.

"Mary, dear, come hither. The bath water is getting cool, it must be warmed up!"

"Elissa is that you?" Conner called out.

"Conner?" For the briefest moment, the tone and voice changed. It was the voice from the forest once again. "Oh, I am so glad that you are here! Please do come in. Mary, please see to their cloaks."

Conner glanced at Marcus. Neither had a cloak. Mary finally looked up at the men, and her eyes told the story. They were red and tired.

Marcus put a gentle hand on the young woman who was trying so hard to serve the princess. "Mary, I am sure the princess can bathe herself…"

Mary glanced back at the screen and said, "I am not so sure. She could not even undress herself." Before another request could be made of her, she quickly left the room.

"Mary? The water?"

"She left," Conner called out. "I think you've run her ragged!" He chuckled.

"What!" Elissa cried out. "Who will tend my bath?"

Conner smiled at Marcus and said, "I would be more than happy to!"

"You will not! How dare you think of such a thing!?"

Marcus held his laughter in and said, "Conner, you have your hands full. If you need anything, I will be downstairs."

Conner looked out the window to where the river cog was docked. "When is it leaving?"

"If you're thinking about heading back to South Karmon, she won't take you. She is heading up river. If you want to stay a week, she'll be back then."

"It's a hefty hike back to South Karmon," Conner observed.

"Oh, for the princess, I think we could scrounge up a horse or two."

"I would be in your debt," Conner said. "I am thinking that we should be heading out as soon as possible."

"I will see to it. Two horses it is. I'll get two of our besting riding horses saddled and ready as soon as I can."

Marcus left, leaving Conner alone to the sound of the princess getting out of her bath. While she dried and dressed, Conner walked around the room. Like the rest of the inn, this room did not seem like it should be in the middle of the forest. The furniture was finely made, carefully etched and constructed of the finest oak. A large rug lay across the floor, making the room seem cozy and comfortable. The bed was dressed with fine silk sheets and a warm wool blanket. He touched the bed and could only imagine at the comfort of sleeping on one.

"It is a tad bumpy, but it will do," Elissa said, still in her snotty voice.

Conner turned and was floored. Although she was dressed in a commoner's wool dress, she was stunning. Gone were the dirt and matted hair. Her face was smooth and perfect as if she were just carved from the finest mold. Her long blond hair, although still wet from washing, shimmered in the sunlight that fell through the window. Her eyes, green and bright, shone with a beauty that took his breath away. Words were stuck in his throat. This was no girl princess. She was all woman.

She smiled, and his heart melted even more. "What is it?" She asked, her voice no longer the snotty tone. It was her forest voice again, the one that made her seem just like him.

"You are beautiful," Conner said, unable to say much else.

Then his cheeks flushed and he turned a bright shade of red. He had to turn away, or he was going to die, but he could not fully tear himself away from her gaze. Her rosy cheeks grew brighter, and her smiled spread to show her teeth. They stood looking at one another for what seemed an eternity. Conner knew it was an awkward moment, but he just could not help himself. He had never seen a more beautiful woman, and he was sure that he would never see one as beautiful again.

Finally, Conner broke his gaze, and said, "We should get going. We cannot be sure that the...uh...whoever was chasing you isn't tracking us here."

"Can they do that?" Elissa stepped over to the dresser and took a brush. She looked at it carefully before she began brushing her hair.

"Of course," Conner replied. "We weren't very careful about leaving tracks. We were in kind of a hurry."

"We will be safe here."

"Elissa, we are in a small village. You won't be safe until you're back at the castle."

She pointed her brush out the window at the river cog. "We will take the boat back."

"It's going the wrong way," Conner said. "It's going to Tyre."

She looked at him curiously and then looked back out the window. She chuckled and said, "Well, it can turn around, you know."

"It's full of cargo and heading up river. And besides, Marcus is getting us horses."

"You shall go talk to the captain, he shall change his plans and take me back home." She turned towards the mirror, turned her head left, then right, and then smiled.

"The horses will do," Conner said. "The boat has business elsewhere."

"Horses? You have ordered a carriage, of course," Elissa said, grabbing a brush from the dresser. She looked at him and gave him a wide smile before continuing to brush out her hair.

Conner was left speechless. This was no longer the girl that he found in the forest, on the verge of being killed – or worse. This was a young woman who had little experience with life outside of her castle, and until now, it had never crossed his mind. She fussed over her looks, primping her hair and fixing her makeup, while not realizing that the very men who would kill her could be standing outside her door. Of course, they would have had to get by Lawry first. Her cares were not on her livelihood, but on her material being. She was beautiful, the most beautiful woman that he had ever seen. And yet, she was missing something, something very important.

"Do you realize how close you were to dying?" He asked.

"Of course," she said flippantly. "Those men would have done so if not for you." She stopped touching up the makeup around her eyes long enough to give him a thankful smile.

"And spending the night in the cave, almost freezing?"

"A dreadful experience for sure," Elissa said. "But if not for you, again, I would not be here."

Conner could only shake his head at her. She spoke the words, but her tone indicated that she did not understand what she was saying.

He grabbed her hand and said, "Come on, we're going for a walk."

She tried to pull away, thinking he was playing some game, but Conner squeezed tighter. She let out a sharp cry. "That hurts! What are you doing?!"

"We are going for a walk."

"No, I am not ready," she said, still trying to pull her arm from his grasp.

He yanked hard, causing her to stumble and fall to her knees.

"What are you doing?!" She screamed. "I am Princess Elissa! How dare you treat me that way?!"

Conner stood over her, unsure what to do. She was a princess, the embodiment of the ruling class. With her fine clothes and perfect grammar, she played her part in the game of classes. She lived her life pushing others around. Not necessarily by choice or purpose, but by her nature. It was the way she was raised, and it was the way the culture worked. She wasn't mean on purpose. She wasn't spoiled on purpose. She didn't demand the fanciest room in the Inn because she was purposely being a snob. It was who she was because that was how she was raised and how she was expected to act. But it also wasn't just how she was expected to act, it was how others were expected to act around her. She was the princess and others expected that they would serve her and meet her every whim because she was the princess. The culture expected it, and that is what happened. Not because she was a mean and demanding ogre, it was simply what was expected of everyone.

But as Conner looked down at her, with her face red with anger, her eyes burning with fury, he didn't see a princess. He saw a young woman who was scared, running for her life. Wet and cold. Huddled together in that cave, they were two young people fearful of dying, wondering how they were going to survive. It wasn't a princess and a peasant, it was a young man and a young woman.

He held a hand out to her, and said softly, "I am sorry, Elissa."

She looked at him for a moment before taking his hand. He helped her up and then she brushed off her dress. The floor was clean and her dress hardly had a spot of dirt, but she dusted it off anyway. The redness in her face was gone and the fury in her eyes dissipated into simple annoyance.

"Thank you," she said stiffly. Conner took a step back as she collected herself. She took a deep breath and looked directly into his eyes. "I mean it. Thank you for all you have done for me."

Conner simply nodded, unsure about her sincerity. Her voice was cold, and her tone was not full of any feeling. But her lower lip was quivering, and her eyes were filling with tears. Conner was a simple peasant boy who lived his life to hunt for food and wander the forests of the kingdom. There was nothing more to his life. The princess lived her life for the kingdom. She had all she could ever desire and more. She lived a life of wealth and prosperity, being trained in the ways of the noble and kingly so that one day she could serve the kingdom as the wife of a leader of the kingdom. And yet, she stood here, in front of him, a beautiful young woman, barely into womanhood, about to break down into tears. He didn't know why, but his instincts told him to act. They were the same instincts that saved his life in the forest. They were the instincts that would change lives forever and change the direction of their kingdom. If he had known what would come out of this one small act in the coming years, he would have turned and run. But he didn't. He could only act as he felt would be right. He stepped forward, pulling her into him, her face buried in his chest. She sobbed uncontrollably, shaking as she did when they were nearly frozen in the cave.

Chapter Five

Lord Neffenmark's castle was on the cold southern slopes of the White Mountains. They were far enough south that they didn't get the horrendous winters that plagued the kingdom of Thell to the north, but they were high enough into the mountains that it was cold more than Knight Captain Brace Hawkden liked. He was used to the more temperate climate that the sea provided the capital city of South Karmon. Even with a thick wool cloak pulled tightly around his body, he still shivered in the biting nighttime winds. Brace hated this ride for more reasons than the climate. Although they were at the base of the mountains, they were still at a higher elevation than the city, which caused his horse to suffer more than he liked. He was in a hurry and had pushed his mount as hard as he could, but he would need the horse for the ride back. Normally, he would make this trip over the course of two long days, or if he weren't in a hurry, he would take three easy days. But time was of the essence, and he had to speak with Neffenmark as soon as possible. Therefore, risking the health of one of his favorite riding horses, he made the trip with only brief stops for water.

The stars were out in full force, giving him just enough light to travel by. Brace didn't take the route that went through the small village that the castle overlooked. Rather, he took a carefully hidden path cut into the mountain behind the castle. Halfway up the steep and dangerous path, he stopped his horse and dismounted. It was too treacherous to ride any further. He would have to lead his horse from this point forward.

A few moments later, a man appeared from the darkness and blocked the path.

"It's Sir Hawkden," Brace said to the man.

"Yes," the man replied. "We've been watching you for some time. Lord Neffenmark wasn't expecting you so soon."

He snapped back at the man, "Does it matter?"

"What?"

Brace sneered at the man and replied, "I am the Knight Captain of the Knights of Karmon. I serve the kingdom of Karmon with my life. I come as I please."

"Yes, sire, of course."

Brace continued up the path, pushing past Neffenmark's man.

Even if an attacking force discovered the secret path, they would have been hard pressed to actually use it as a means of assault. The start of the path wound through the foothills of the mountains in the middle of a thick grove of trees. As it neared the castle, it was cut into the rock of the mountain just wide enough for a horse and its rider to traverse. This made it not only difficult to pass but also very easy to defend. A handful of archers could keep an entire army at bay. Neffenmark had also installed two sections of loose rock above the path. A quick knockout of a supporting beam would cause the path to be completely blocked. The final section leading up to the castle was steep enough that horses had trouble getting up it.

Two archers looked down upon them from the battlements that covered the rear of the castle. With a wave from the man following Brace, they disappeared. A moment later, a door hidden in the darkness opened, allowing them into the castle. A young boy took Brace's horse while he marched his way through the back hallways directly to Neffenmark's chambers.

"Well, this is a pleasant surprise," Lord Neffenmark said as Brace entered the chamber.

Brace bit his lip, forcing the words that he wanted to come out back down inside. He had bad news, and he didn't want to give it to the Neffenmark while he was mad. Instead, he put on a fake smile and gave a courteous nod. He was a warrior first, but as Knight Captain, he also had to play the politician at times.

"Come in," Neffenmark said with a motion of his plump hand. The rest of his ample girth was spread on top of a pile of silk pillows. It was the same place that Brace saw him each time he came to the castle and wondered if he ever moved from that spot.

"Dinner was served some time ago, but I am sure that I can scrounge up a morsel or two."

"No thank you," Brace said. "I have little time, and I will need to be heading back out as soon as I can get a fresh horse."

"Very well," Neffenmark replied with a toothy smile. "Wine to parch your dusty throat?"

Brace gave in and took a goblet from one of the lord's servants. It was a sweet wine and very strong, unlike the more diluted wines that he was used to drinking. It was the type of wine reserved for special feasts or celebrations, not the kind served to thirsty travelers. But that was Neffenmark's style, and it showed in his castle. Although it was designed for defense and served as the northwestern outpost for the kingdom, Lord Neffenmark's castle was hardly styled as a military garrison. Tapestries from around the world hung throughout the halls, adding color and energy to what would normally be cold and lifeless walls. Pillows of all shapes, sizes, and colors was the seating of choice. Hardly a chair could be found. Neffenmark served his justice not from a throne, but from a pile of comfortable pillows. The lord's soldiers were also dressed in the finest of clothes. Their tunics were silk and bright colored. Their scabbards encrusted with precious jewels. Neffenmark was a very wealthy man, and he put that wealth to use. Brace just wasn't sure it was the most effective use of his wealth.

After the first sip, Brace gulped the rest of the wine down, allowing the alcohol to swim through his body and calm him. He wanted to ease into the conversation, but he could not find the words. So he simply spoke his mind and didn't hold anything back.

"The plan has gone awry. The princess was not captured, and several of the men you provided were killed." He spent several minutes further detailing the failure, including the fact that the princess had yet to be found.

Neffenmark stiffened, his red cheeks turning a pale white. His mouth opened for a moment and then closed, keeping the words from coming out. He looked hard back at Brace, who did not turn his gaze away. After a few moments, the color returned Neffenmark's face. "The men are inconsequential. Mercenaries who got paid well."

"We will have to cancel the plans…"

"Cancel!" Lord Neffenmark shouted. He sat up, and his jowls shook as he spoke. "Never! The plan will proceed. However, due to your failure, there will indeed have to be some changes made."

It took Brace a moment for the words to penetrate. "Failure? It was your men that failed. The men you provided were hardly the professional military men you promised. They were scoundrels and thieves for all I could tell."

"Silly knight, there are no guarantees in this business and good men are always hard to come by." A wide smile spread across Neffenmark's face. "And expensive, too."

The fat lord paused to fill his goblet from a hidden pitcher. "We will have to make some adjustments to our plan. And to our arrangement."

"There is no more plan, and there is no more arrangement."

Neffenmark shuffled in his pillows as if he were trying to sit up. The effort seemed too much, so he gave up. Finally, he looked up at the Knight Captain and said, "I am afraid that you will do as I ask. You have already committed treason. A crime for which you would easily be convicted. I believe our most majestic king likes to draw and quarter traitors."

"I am no traitor," Brace growled, taking a threatening step forward.

Lord Neffenmark snapped his fingers and two guards, swords drawn, suddenly appeared from behind a curtain. "I have two crossbowmen on the walls behind you." He raised a finger and pointed it at Brace. "Do not test me, knight. You will do my bidding, or the king will know of your treachery. Yes, his favorite knight. The one who holds his counsel. You, my friend, will do my bidding and you will do it without complaint or argument. Do not be deceived by your own thoughts. You are a traitor. You have plotted against your king."

"I am no traitor!" Brace yelled out, glancing behind him for where the crossbowmen might be. "I serve my kingdom as I am bound."

"You serve a king, as well. Your duty is also to him, and that makes you a traitor."

"You are a traitor as well!" Brace shouted out, his muscles itching to burst forward and strangle the fat lord. But his better judgment held him at bay. He would gladly give his life to take Neffenmark's, but he could not be sure he could reach him before two crossbow bolts would strike him down. And if he did not survive, and the Lord did, then the fat man would be able to execute his plans. The only way for Neffenmark to be kept in check would be for him to live through the visit.

Neffenmark readjusted his pillows and settled into them. "Yes, I am a traitor. But the difference between you and me is that you actually care. While me, well...I have been called worse things. But I do not care what others think of me. My castle here..." He waved his arms about his finely furnished room. "...protects me from those who are jealous and desire what I have. My guards are loyal to me first, and our king second. I am the one who feeds them, protects them and gives them training in the arts of swordplay. I provide for the welfare of their families while they provide me with food. I have a small standing army that could hold off virtually any force that would dare come against me. It is an army that is loyal to me first. They would jump off the cliffs into the ocean if I told them to. They serve me and do my bidding. But, I do not care what they think of me. I do not care if they hate me or love me. But I give them what they desire, so I have their loyalty. Your king gives me nothing, so he does not have my loyalty."

"He is still your king as well," Brace said, between clenched teeth. The anger was continuing to boil inside of him. Yes, he had committed an act that would get him at the very least, a quick death, but most likely, it would bring him a long, slow, painful death. But he did it because of his loyalty to his king and the kingdom. His head was spinning, and he needed to sit down before he collapsed.

Smiling, Neffenmark recognized the sudden whiteness that spread across the Knight Captain's face. "You should sit." He motioned to a cushioned chair.

Brace took the seat, burying his head in his hands. He regretted every moment of the last two years of his life. He thought about ending his own life, for it would be the honorable thing to do. It would be quick and painless. He could jump up and attack Lord Neffenmark. Yes, he would be struck down, but maybe, just maybe he would get to the fat man before he expired.

"You serve the kingdom first," Neffenmark reminded the knight. "You are a Knight of Karmon, not a Knight of King Thorndale. You serve the kingdom regardless of the man who sits upon the throne. You know that. You are bound by blood to that charter. Do not confuse the man with the kingdom. Just because you are a traitor to the man does not make you a traitor to the kingdom." He paused for a moment while he let those words sink in. "That is why you came to me so many months ago."

"I thought your goal was to serve the kingdom, but I do not know anymore," Brace said softly.

"The treaty that your good King Thorndale was proposing to the Thellians is treacherous to the kingdom. It cannot happen."

"I have erred," Brace said.

"You have served your kingdom loyally," Neffenmark countered.

"I should have gone to the king right away and shared my concern with him," Brace said.

Lord Neffenmark sneered. "And he would have cut your throat at that moment for daring to suggest that he was wrong. He believes Karmon and Thell can coexist. Our history tells us otherwise. How many men have you known personally that have fallen to the sword of that wretched people? How many others that you don't know. How many in the history of our kingdoms of died at their hands? They serve a god of war, a god who tells them to destroy their enemies."

"At least they have gods that watch over them. Our gods abandoned us a long time ago," Brace reminded the Lord. "They walked our lands so long ago that no one can remember them. They are only in our minds because of the old stories that no one really believes anymore."

"Indeed, our gods have long since left us. They have left us to fend for ourselves, and that is what we must do. We must fend for ourselves and find our way in this world. And we will do so with the cold steel of a sword's blade. And if we don't, we will be overrun by our enemies. Our kingdom will be no more. We will be assimilated into the land of the Thellians. They will make us turn to their god, or we will perish by their sword."

"That will not happen," Brace said, his voice gaining strength.

Neffenmark smiled. "Of course not. That is why we must be diligent in our actions. We must stop this awful thing before it can happen."

"What now?" Brace asked.

The smile on Neffenmark's face stretched wider. He had his man, once again. "You must return at once to find the princess, dead or alive. If you find her body, the plan will continue as we had discussed. Thellian will be blamed for her death, and the first act towards war with or neighbors will be complete."

"And if I find her?"

"Then you will return the hero, of course. If that is the case, you must find yourself on the next delegation to Thell. We must discredit them and allow their actions to convince King Thorndale that they are not wanting peace with us, but are bent on destroying us."

"How will we do that?"

Neffenmark had a wicked smile on his face. "I have heard that the king is sending messengers to Thell on a somewhat regular basis."

"Yes," Brace said. "On occasion, the king has a need to send a message to their king. It is not widely known, and the king goes out of his way to hide it, but it is not a great secret."

"You will find out what are in those messages…" His smiled faded as another thought came to his mind. "No, better yet, you will deliver the next message yourself. But instead of going directly to Thell, you will deliver the message to me."

Brace straightened up and looked harshly down at the fat lord. "I am not a messenger. I am the Knight Captain." He took a step forward and raised his voice. "I am not the king's servant or even your servant. I serve the kingdom. I lead the most elite force of warriors this side of the Taran Empire."

"No," Neffenmark countered. "You are not the king's servant. You are mine." Lord Neffenmark lifted his enormous body from the pillows. He didn't raise his voice; in fact, he lowered it. But his tone was clear. "You are my servant or the king will know of your treachery. If you want to serve the kingdom, then you must serve me. And if the king is secretly conspiring with the Thellians, then it is the king who is committing treachery." The smile grew back, wide and toothy.

Brace suddenly realized what he had done. All the plans that he had put in place, all of the thought and consideration that had gone into his decisions were wrong. He had tried to save the kingdom, to keep it falling farther into obscurity. But in doing so, he had lost sight of his honor. It was true that he served the kingdom first as the king was only the head of the kingdom. Kings came and went, but the kingdom would stay forever. But he was no longer bound to the kingdom, due to his own ignorance and the naive pursuit of honor towards the kingdom. He had found himself bound to Neffenmark.

He vowed to himself that it would not last long. He would pretend to serve the Lord Neffenmark, but he would have to watch his back. He would have to ensure that his actions and motives would remain secret until he could remove any question of his loyalty towards the king. He wasn't sure how he was going to do it, but he knew that for now, he would have to follow Neffenmark's commands.

"Very well," Brace said. "I will do as you ask. But after this, no more. I am not your puppet. As long as your requests are for the good of the kingdom, I shall assist you. But if they are not, then you are on your own."

"We must know what the king is doing," Neffenmark said softly. After a moment, he added, "For the good of the kingdom."

Brace did not like the smile on the fat lord's face, but there was nothing more to say. He left as quickly as he could. He should have taken a quick nap to recover some strength for the ride home, but he could no longer stomach being in the lord's castle. He had to get out. Without another word, he spun on his heels and marched out of the room and directly to the stables.

***

Lord Neffenmark emptied his goblet with one big gulp and then tossed it across the room. "He is trouble," Neffenmark said loudly.

The man who had been hiding behind the folds of the curtains in the corner of the room stepped out. He was a thin man, dressed in long, flowing robes. A gold circlet rested comfortable on his head. His face was long, his skin seemingly pulled tightly across his bony face. Eye sockets were sunk deep into his forehead. But those eyes were a bright blue, in sharp contrast to his shadowy and dark features.

"*Di Hechen ze*," Hibold said in his native tongue.

Neffenmark cut him off sharply mid-sentence, "Stop it! I barely understand your words, and when you speak so fast, I understand nothing."

"Forgive me, Lord Neffenmark," Hibold said slowly and with a slight nod. "Your language is likewise difficult for me."

"You are in my castle!" Neffenmark shouted back. "You will speak my words!"

Hibold smiled, accepting the abuse as any proper politician would. "As you wish. I just hope that the meaning of our words does not get mixed up."

"I know enough of your language to know when you are lying," Neffenmark said. "And I know enough about your empire to know that most of the words that come out of the likes of you are lies."

The insult hung in the air for a moment. The Taran was used to verbal abuse; it was the nature of the business. He didn't care because he knew that he always had the upper hand. He only wished that he wasn't so far away from the nearest Taran garrison and its legion of centurions. It was the appearance of the lack of power that actually gave him the advantage. Neffenmark could spit and spout all he wanted. He could intimidate through words and actions as much as he wanted. But they both knew that the Taran Empire barely recognized this part of the world. But if one of its emissaries came up missing, then the Empire would take notice. And if the emissary's demise came about of even the slightest suspicious means, the Taran Empire wouldn't even bother with trying to expand into the kingdom, it would simply come in and wipe out the entire population.

Hibold pulled out a gold coin and flipped it to Neffenmark, who deftly caught it. He spun it around, studying the markings. Neffenmark fixated on the portrait of Hargon the Great, the current emperor of Taran. "Does the emperor know what you are buying?"

"Does your king know what you are selling?" The Hibold retorted. "Our fortunes and fates are tied together. Our meetings and correspondence have been well documented. So if you choose to … terminate our arrangement, it will not go well for you."

"You've thought this through," Neffenmark said.

"I've done this before," Hibold replied. "Many times. The empire does not expand on military might alone. That is expensive in many ways. The empire would much rather fold in kingdoms. Conquering is fine, but very, very messy. The emperor is also…wise with his gold. He does not like to waste it."

"You mean he is cheap?"

Hibold's thin face widened into a smile. "If he knew how many gold coins were delivered to you, he would not approve. He would probably consider the loss of some of his centurions better than the loss of many of his gold coins." Neffenmark started to interrupt, but the Hibold continued. "But he does not understand the worth of your kingdom and the devotion that his gold is buying. And if he were to find out how much gold he lost, and if he did not have complete submission of the people of the kingdom, he would not be a very happy emperor. And do you know what angry emperors do? They go on rampages. Slaughtering, nothing survives rampages."

"You do not need to threaten me," Neffenmark growled.

"I am not threatening you. I am simply stating facts. I have delivered gold, and now you must deliver the kingdom. However you choose."

"And what happens if this emperor of yours finds gold missing? Will I see centurions marching over the mountains and knocking on my castle gates when that happens?"

"Deliver the kingdom as you promised, and none of that will matter." Hibold nodded his head towards the door which Brace used to leave. "I would suggest choosing your business partners more wisely. You need men devoted to your cause. Not men devoted to your king or kingdom. He will be a problem."

"He will be taken care of," Neffenmark promised. "I can assure you that all is well."

The Taran emissary clapped his hands and rubbed them together. "Good. Now that our business is done, I understand that there is more food?"

Chapter Six

They stood at the edge of the water, just downstream from the docks. It was early morning, and a chilly wind was blowing in from the north. The ground was still wet after the morning's frost, a reminder that winter was not far behind them. The excitement of the princess in the village had lasted through the evening festivities and a late night of feasting and merrymaking. Conner had seen little of the princess for most of the night. It seemed that each and every villager had gone up to her and introduced themselves. Most of the men of the village had a least one dance with her, and many, including Marcus, had taken several turns on the floor of the Inn, spinning and twirling with a dance step that Conner did not know and would never be able to follow. He found himself jealous of the attention that she was getting. He sat alone most of the night except when someone tired of their merrymaking would sit by him and chat until they were bored and moved on.

For one brief moment in their lives, these villagers experienced the grace and glamor of royalty. They were able to see her, touch her, and talk to her. All the stories of the king, of royalty, of rich nobility, was embodied in this one lithe woman. Barely a woman, Conner realized. Hardly more than a girl, but she certainly looked like a woman. But her eyes were big as a girl's, taking in and believing all that she saw. She saw a village that treated her like she was, a princess of a great kingdom. She was royalty, of a class above them. And they treated her like it. She was showered with gifts from people that had very little, people who wanted to give her their most precious of belongings. And yet, each one was nothing compared to what was in some forgotten dusty chest in her room, locked away because it wasn't worth the time bringing it out of storage. She smiled and chatted, her form perfect and her words delicate and ladylike.

And Conner felt sad for her. She danced many dances, and when she wasn't twirling on the dance floor, she was seated in a corner, giving audience to those who begged for it. She laughed and smiled, nodded and curtsied, said all the right things. But she was being used. The villagers didn't care that she almost died. Didn't care that she cried herself to sleep, fearful of being attacked again. They didn't care that she had feelings, or might be tired of talking or dancing. They didn't care that her body ached from their long walk or from sleeping on the hard, cold ground in a cave. They used her to make themselves feel better. And a part of him understood. They lived hard lives, working for little more than food for their table. There was not much else for them. They had their occasional feasts to celebrate one thing or another. But their lives were rather mundane. The boats came and went. Cargo and goods were loaded and unloaded. But now, with the arrival of the princess, their world was turned upside down. They had a purpose, and that was to attend to this grand, beautiful princess. And so they did, tending to the princess' every whim.

Conner was glad that they were leaving.

"We cannot take the ship home?" Elissa asked again. Her eyes watched tearfully as strong oarsmen pulled the shallow hulled river cog upstream.

"It will be days before it returns," Marcus said. "I am sorry princess, but there are villages that survive only on the trade they make with the ship." He turned to her and place a hand on her shoulder. "Believe me, if you were in grave danger, I would put you on the ship and send you home, but you are safe here in our village. You are welcome to stay here at the inn until the boat returns."

"We thank you for your hospitality," Conner said. "But we do not have a week to wait. We should leave as quickly as possible."

"If you insist on heading out, I do feel that we should send others with you, at least until you return to the highway," Marcus said with a friendly smile.

"I know the forest pretty well, Marcus," Conner replied. "Fewer bodies means less sound."

"Very well, but I do wish you would reconsider leaving, though. We have a fine inn, and the people will be most happy to have her stay for a week."

Princess Elissa looked on, her eyes wide with the fear that Conner would agree. Although she really liked how everyone treated her, she was more than ready to get back home.

Her relief was evident in Conner's response, "I think the princess is ready to get back to the castle as soon as possible."

Marcus' disapproval showed on his face, but he didn't pursue the discussion further. Instead, he led them towards the inn's stables.

"We only have a couple horses available, I'm afraid," Marcus said as held open the swinging double-doors that led into the stables. "And they are not the best of mounts, either. This one is old. That one there looks tired and worn."

"Those two will do fine," Conner said sharply. "We are not looking for war horses, just two mounts to carry us through the forest."

The fussing that Marcus continued to do was starting to irritate Conner. It was almost as if the burly man was trying to keep them in the village against their wishes. It was all he could do to keep his irritation from showing. "And the princess and I will be fine. We will stay by the river away from the deep parts of the forest."

"At least let us send a rider ahead. He would be able to make the castle by morning if he rode through the night and then he could return with a proper escort, even a carriage."

Elissa glanced from the horse to the saddles hanging on the wall. She didn't mind to ride, in fact, she enjoyed it very much. But she didn't really care to do it for days on end. "That would be nice," Elissa said sweetly.

"But unnecessary," Conner countered.

"You now speak for the princess?" Marcus asked.

"No, he does not!" Princess Elissa said with a raised voice.

The irritation turned into anger, and it came out in a burst of words. "A lone rider races through the forest, unaware of his surroundings. An arrow takes out his horse, and then he is set upon by the very ones that ambushed the princess. A knife cut here and there and the man is telling everything he knows. Those riders come to the village, armed with swords and bows. It would not take them too much to find the princess and finish their job. "

"We may be villagers, but many of us have served in the king's army. We would be ready to face any threat."

"As soldiers? Or pikemen holding a line? Or as bowman behind the lines. Are you really trained well enough to go up against other men who are willing to kill?"

"And you are?" Marcus counted.

"I have killed," Conner spat, his neck muscles bulging and his face beet red. "Have you?"

Marcus turned away, unwilling to face up to the challenge.

Elissa put a hand on his arm. "Conner, you have saved my life, and I have asked you to be my protector. I believe with all my heart that you will keep me safe."

Conner turned at the touch and looked down into her eyes, getting lost in the beauty that was in them. The anger faded.

Marcus continued to press the issue. "Your highness, I cannot in good conscience let you go alone. At least let me send a couple of the village men with you. Four or five would be much better than two."

Without breaking his eye contact with the princess, Conner said calmly, "Four or five will sound like a herd of deer running through the forest. The princess and I will be able to move more quickly and quietly than any of your men could."

"The villagers here are not barbarians," Marcus retorted. "We know how to ride a horse. We are very good hunters. Why am I explaining myself to you, boy?" He threw up his arms and marched out of the stables shouting back to them, "It is decided. The princess will have an escort of the villager's best men."

Elissa, her gaze still locked onto Conner's, said, "Maybe it is for the best. They really will be able to help us."

In a very soft voice, Conner replied, "I do not want to be camping in the forest tonight. We must ride now so that we can get to the highway before the sun goes down."

"Princess," Marcus said from the doorway. "I will have your escort here within the hour, armed and prepared to ride with you." He then turned and walked quickly into the village to find the men who would be their escorts.

"We should leave now," Conner said, his voice now a whisper. "Something is not right. Marcus is trying too hard to keep us here."

Elissa slapped him playfully on the shoulder. "Our escorts will be here soon. We should not dismiss their generosity."

"I've tracked deer before, and they are very hard to follow through the woods. But if a deer is injured or lame, they are easy to follow because they are slow and make good tracks."

"What are you saying?" Princess Elissa asked.

"It wouldn't be that hard for anyone to track us to the village. I half expected them to show up here, but I realized that unless they are a small army, it won't go well for them. Unless they are already here and waiting for the right moment to get us."

Elissa looked out through the doorway. She could see the village and the towering trees of the forest behind. Nothing seemed amiss. It was quiet and peaceful.

"There is a good chance they are waiting for us," Conner said. "Maybe in the village, maybe just outside of it."

"Then an escort will be a good thing?"

Conner shook his head. "The more horses there are, the louder they are. Especially when the riders are men who don't know how to be quiet."

"Then what do we do?"

"I have spent my life living in the forest, hunting deer and rabbit for food. I know how to be quiet, because if I didn't, I would have starved long ago. And because I've hunted, I know what it is like to hunt, I know what a hunter would do. I know how to avoid them. But I could only do it if you would do exactly as I say, exactly when I say it. I can't trust that anyone else with us would do it."

Elissa's eyes were wide with fear. Conner wasn't trying to frighten her, but he had to make sure she understood their circumstances.

Conner pulled her away from the doorway. "Follow me," he said. "Out the back."

The building that housed the stables had a back exit through a small storage room. As they were moving through it, a small stack of weapons caught his eye. He grabbed a long knife and stuffed it in his belt. He was also able to replenish his quiver with four arrows. He wished that there were more, but he knew he was lucky enough to find the four. With a gentle tug, he led Elissa out into the small yard behind the inn. A decorative rock fence separated them from the docks. He followed the fence until it ended at a hedge of thick shrubs. There was just enough room for them to squeeze through.

Once through, Conner pulled her down into a crouch. The docks were directly ahead of them, but some distance away. "

"What now?" she asked.

"We cross the river and start heading through the forest towards the castle."

"Cross the river?" Elissa exclaimed. "Where?"

Conner nodded towards the river. "Want to swim?"

She gave him a sour look. "Not really."

"Me neither." He pulled her up and jogged towards the water's edge where a number of small boats were beached. They looked like dinghies used to transport people or goods to deep draft boats that couldn't get close to shore.

Conner pushed one of the boats into the water and then helped Elissa into it. He moved as quickly and quietly as he could. He knew it was only a matter of time before they were seen. With a big shove, he pushed the boat into the water and climbed in. It took a few strokes to get the hang of the oars. But in no time, Conner was pulling them swiftly through the water.

They were halfway across the river when they were spotted. At first, someone on the docks shouted to them and waved, not realizing who they were and what they were doing. Soon, others joined the first man. And then Marcus showed up, his long white hair blowing in the wind. He said nothing, only stood with his hands on his hips, watching the two of them rowing across the river.

Princess Elissa sat quietly in the rear of the small boat, a hand draped over the side, watching the approaching bank. Conner faced aft, watching Elissa sit quietly. But he also saw the commotion on the docks. As Marcus stood watching them, surrounded by a group of curious villagers, three men, clad in long black cloaks and leather armor appeared from the Inn. They walked out onto the dock, their scabbards swinging as they walked. One had a bow and lifted it towards them, an arrow knocked and ready to fire. Another of the newcomers put a hand on the bowman's shoulder, and the bow was lowered. Conner kept his face as calm as he could, doing his best to keep Elissa from noticing what was happening behind her.

Although the river was wide and the current swift, Conner knew that a good bowman could make life interesting for them. If he went in a straight line, an expert archer could easily account for their movement and strike them down. If he could go a little faster, and maybe change direction a little more, he would make it more difficult. But he still felt like a sitting duck. With more urgency, Conner put his back into pulling the oars more quickly and with more strength. He tried to hide his exertion from his face. She didn't need to know right now. There was nothing that she would be able to do about it other than fret and worry.

He smiled at her, and she smiled back. He watched her closely, studying her face. It was perfectly formed, unblemished from age or worry. She lived a life of comfort and ease. She didn't have to worry about where her next meal was coming from, or if she were going to survive the cold winter. She had as much food as she could eat, as much warmth as she desired, and as much protection as her father could give her. And she didn't know it. She had no idea that she lived such a life and that there were others that didn't. She was young enough to not know but old enough to begin to understand. These events of the past few days must have rocked her world, sending her vision of a perfect life into a tailspin. And yet, she hardly showed it. Back at the village, she quickly went from a cold and wet young girl to a spoiled princess ordering everyone around. But she barely survived the ambush with her life. And now she sat here in this uncomfortable boat, being rowed across a cold and deep river, her posture princess perfect, just as she had been taught. He realized that she was watching him, too.

Their eyes were locked on one another. She had called him her champion, and he had laughed at it outwardly. But inwardly, he took it seriously. He would protect her at all costs. It was not only the right thing to do, but it was the thing that he wanted to do. He liked her. A lot. Maybe there was something even more. But she was small and delicate and needed him, and that made him feel as big a man as he could have ever imagined. He was going to honor that duty, as long as he could.

As for Marcus, he didn't know what he was up to. He seemed trustworthy at first, but something must have happened. Most likely the guys who were after the princess got there and they were able to escape just in time. He hoped that Marcus was simply a pawn in some crazy game. But regardless, he knew he couldn't trust anyone. No matter how nice someone was, it didn't mean that they were honest. He almost laughed aloud at his thought. He was thinking of himself as so mature, so much wiser than the naïve princess. But in reality, he was only three years older than her. Yes, he lived a life much different than hers, but that really didn't make him wiser. He was still naïve himself, thinking that anyone he came across could be trusted.

"You've been staring at me," Elissa said, her smile turning into a smirk.

"No, just watching," he replied. After a moment of continuing to stare, he added. "I guess I just can't take my eyes off of you."

"You make me blush," she said, turning her eyes to the water.

"And you tease me."

"Will you come stay at the castle, now that you are my Champion?"

His immediate reply was silence. When she brought it up before, he thought it was just her talking to make talk. He didn't really think that she was serious. But now, with the way she asked the question, and with the way she was looking at him, he knew that she was serious.

"You said you would be my champion," she said softly.

"Yes," he finally said. "I will be here to protect you and help you get home."

"No," Princess Elissa said, her eyebrows narrowing. "My Champion. Normally a princess can count on her brothers to champion her cause – to protect her from everything. To stand in for her when she cannot fight. But when a princess does not have a brother, or a queen does not have a king, a champion is chosen to protect her. To be her sword arm."

He was speechless. He had thought that she was just talking about him helping her get home. He had no idea that she was referring to some formal concept of a Champion.

"I would want no one but you," the princess continued.

"I am not a swordsman or a soldier. I could never stand in your place to fight your battles."

"You could learn."

"I could," he admitted, regretting the words the instant they came out.

"Then when we get back, I shall talk to my father, and you shall come live at the castle!"

"Princess Elissa," Conner started to protest, but he could see the gleam in her eye. She was genuinely excited about him becoming her champion. He knew it was a ridiculous notion and that her father would certainly have nothing of it. He decided to not say anything, to go along with what she was saying so she could keep her spirits up for the rest of their journey.

He glanced behind him and realized that they were almost at the opposite bank. He gave the rowboat two quick pulls with the oars, and the boat rode right up onto the bank. He jumped out first, ankle deep in water. She walked slowly across the boat, using the sides to keep her balance. Once at the bow, she bent over to jump out. He grabbed her around the waist and lifted her off the boat and half carried, half tossed her onto the bank. She landed feet dry with a laugh.

The laugh was cut short when she looked across the river. "Is that another boat?"

Conner didn't need to look, he had seen it launch some time ago.

"We'll need to hurry."

"Who are they?" She asked.

Conner didn't answer. He took her hand and pulled her into the trees. His mind worked hard, trying to figure out what to do and where to go. He could head deep into the woods, but the men behind them on the boats wouldn't be that far behind. If they rowed hard, maybe a half an hour at most. They could make that up within a few hours. While Conner and Elissa needed to worry about whether they were leaving a trail, or moving too loudly, the pursuers would not care. They would crash through the forest as quickly as they could, not worrying about their trail or who heard them. At best, Conner would be able to keep just ahead of them, moving quickly without leaving too much of a trail. But eventually, they would have to rest and eat. Their pursuers would, too, but it would be a matter of who could last the longest. If it were him alone, he knew that he could push himself through the rest of the day and into the night. And if he made it to darkness, and he could continue to move through the forest, it would be nearly impossible to track him.

Suddenly he stopped. Elissa, breathing hard from the exertion of moving so fast through the underbrush, welcomed the rest. She sat on the ground, legs crossed, her head resting in her hands. He had four arrows in his quiver and a small hunting knife. He wouldn't last ten seconds in a fight, especially if the men who were following him were trained in any way. Any thought he had of standing up to his pursuers quickly left.

The trees had thinned out where they stopped. The ground in front of them dipped into a small bowl with only small bushes growing alongside tall weeds. Thick, thorny bushes blocked any chance they had of going around the bowl. Either they would have to double back and lose more time, or they would have to forge ahead. He made a quick gesture for her to follow and, reluctantly, she did. As he feared, the ground was soft and muddy in the bowl. He tried hard not to make too many footprints, but there was no way for them to pass through without leaving a clear trail. He looked around, wondering if he could find a way out of the bowl where his tracks wouldn't show as much, but the whole area was soggy. He trudged on, hoping beyond hope that they would be able to move fast enough to keep ahead of their pursuers.

Once out of the bowl and back into the trees, he pushed hard. They had to move faster than their pursuers. Any thoughts of hiding their trail were left in the soggy bowl. With one eye on the path in front, he kept the other eye on Elissa. She had fallen into silence some time ago. Her eyes were focused straight ahead, lost in thought. Or maybe just lost in nothingness. There were times when he was out hunting that his mind just cleared. There would be no thoughts about his family or where his next meal was coming from. He would only think about the path in front of him, and the trees around him. He would ignore the beauty of nature, just walking through the existence of it without acknowledging it. But not now. Now he had to focus on the trail, trying to find the best route between where they were and the edge of the forest. Because the best route wasn't the most direct route, he moved around, trying to keep to ground that wouldn't leave as clear a trail as another route. At least they weren't farther north where they would have to worry about predators. There were small wild animals such as foxes and coyotes, but they stayed away from people as much as they could. The wolves to the north, however, had found the taste of man delightful. They weren't hunters out looking for tasty human flesh, but if you ran into one, they were just as like to turn and attack as to run away.

Elissa was clearly tired, her breathing shallow and quick. Her eyes were half closed, and she stumbled more than walked. Their adventures of the past few days had worn on her and even though they had one good night of rest, it hadn't been enough for her to fully recover.

"We need to find out how far they are behind us," Conner said. He had stopped alongside a fallen tree. She immediately plopped down, her shoulders hunched over in near exhaustion.

"Okay," she said softly. "I'm not sure how much longer…."

"I'm sorry," Conner said softly, his back to her, looking back towards the way they had come.

She looked up at him, the tired eyes suddenly regaining some strength. "For what?"

"We should have taken up Marcus' offer. We should have taken the horses and just ridden for your castle."

"But the men back there in the village, maybe they would have gotten us then?"

"Yeah, but I have led you into the middle of the forest being chased by soldiers. If they catch us…"

She smiled weakly up at him. "But they won't. You are my Champion."

"Some champion. I have led you to your death."

"Conner, I am not dead. I won't be. I would have been if you hadn't come across me. You saved my life, and I know you will get me out of here."

Conner looked back at her, knowing that she was just being naïve, or maybe just trying to be strong for him. He knew what was happening, he knew that there was little chance of them coming out of the forest alive. Maybe they could outwit their pursuers and keep one step ahead of them. But eventually, they would tire. They needed to eat and sleep. There were small streams throughout the woods that could keep them alive, but without food, they wouldn't have the energy to move at the fast pace that they needed to move. Maybe they could survive. Maybe they could make it through the forest alive without being caught. Maybe.

Conner didn't like maybes. He also didn't like slow deaths. It was something he was all too familiar with. But he survived. They all did, but just barely. He was tired of just surviving and knew that it was time to do something about it.

"The ground rises a bit in another mile or so. We'll head up to the high ground and see how far behind our pursuers are."

"If we don't see them?" She asked.

"Then we move on."

"And if we see them?"

He glanced at his quiver. "If there's four or less, we'll be fine."

He marched forward, hoping that the strength of his words would reassure the princess. He knew that if she saw his face right now, she would have seen fear. It wasn't so much the fear of being caught, or what would happen to them. It would be the fear of what he would have to do to his pursuers once they caught up to them.

At the top of the next rise, Conner climbed up an old oak tree that had plenty of branches to help him get up high. As soon as he settled onto a branch and looked back down their trail, he saw movement. And then he saw them between the trees.

There were only three of them. He wished he could remember how many were in the boat. Maybe three, maybe four. But he could only worry about the three that he saw. One was in front of the others, leading them along Conner and Elissa's route. Occasionally the leader would stoop and bend, looking for signs of the trail, but mostly he moved forward, slowly and surely. Clearly, Conner didn't hide their trail well enough. But he knew that. He knew that he didn't have the time to cover his tracks. Speed was more important. He had hoped that whoever was following him wasn't a good tracker, but he knew that it had been too much to hope for. The two who followed behind were armed. Bows were slung across their backs and swords hung at their sides. Conner knew that he would have to take them out first. He cautiously climbed down from the tree while formulating his plan.

Elissa didn't ask him what he saw. She didn't need to. As soon as he was down from the tree, he strung his bow and pulled his arrows out of his quiver. With silent determination, he pulled off his cloak and quiver, removing anything that might get in his way.

"You keep moving. Just keep the sun at your back in the morning, and at your face in the evening. Eventually, you will get to the sea."

"I'm not leaving," she said. "I'll stay and fight with you."

"There are three of them," he said. "I will have to take them out, but if I don't, you have to be far from here. Maybe I can hold them off long enough so that you can get away."

Her lips trembled, and tears began to form at the corner of her eyes. "I can't," she said meekly.

He gripped her shoulders and looked deep into her eyes. "You are strong. Stronger than you can imagine. I can see it in your eyes. I can see it in the way you carry yourself. You don't complain. You just do. You might be a princess, a delicate flower in your mind, but you are strong like you grew up in a village just like me." He squeezed her shoulders. "You will survive. There are small streams all around here. Keep drinking, as much as you can. You can live without food for days, but without water, you will die quickly. There are small bushes with dark purple berries. If you squeeze them and they are juicy, they are edible. You must go on to survive. If you stay with me, and I can't kill them, then they will get you, and they will kill you."

"But if you kill them, then how will you find me?" A tear smudged her dirty cheek with a single line. "I would be lost without you."

Conner looked deep into her eyes. He heard the words and understood what she was saying, but there was something about them that had so much more meaning than just the words. He found himself suddenly fearful that if she did leave, that he would never see her again. That she would go back to her castle, to her room decorated in plush adornments, scented with perfumes from all across the world. Doted upon by her father. Cared for by servants. Given anything she desired. What could he give her? Nothing that she didn't already have or need. He squeezed her hand one last time, wondering if this would be the last time he would ever touch her, talk to her, or be around her. Regretfully, he let go and took a step back.

"I will stay here, at this tree," she said. "If you come back, we will go on to my father."

"And if I don't," he asked.

"Leave me your knife. I will not go quietly." Tears were now fully streaming down her face.

He hesitated for a moment, looking long and hard at her, seeing the strength in her that others probably had never seen. She was young, but she was strong. These two days, lost in the woods, would change her life forever. And it would either go on, and she would be a great and wonderful princess, or it would end now. Knowing what it meant, he pulled out his hunting knife and held it for her to take. It wasn't very sharp. It was old and had a bit of rust on it. But it was sharp enough that if stuck in the belly, it would kill. She took it gingerly. Without another word, he turned and walked into the trees, retracing their path.

He set up off their trail, hidden in the underbrush as well as he could. The four arrows were stuck in the ground in front him, ready to be pulled out and sent flying. Based on how quickly their pursuers were traveling, he figured it would only be a few minutes before they would appear. He settled into his position, trying to find the most comfortable position that he could stay in without moving. It felt good to rest. His mind was still in overdrive, thinking about Elissa, their trek through the woods, the men he was going to kill. But his body was able to rest, and it felt good. After a while, he yawned, and then began to force himself to stay alert. He could easily have fallen asleep, but Elissa kept him awake. Knowing that her survival fully depended upon him kept him from closing his eyes and succumbing to the pleasant wonder of a dreamy sleep.

Before he saw them, he heard them. He had kept his eyes searching through the trees, but it was his ears that had picked them out first. It could have been a deer, but what wind there came from behind him and his scent would have scared away anything as flighty as a deer. But men didn't have the nose of animals, so the direction of the breeze didn't matter. It could have been a rabbit or squirrel, but they made hardly a peep in the woods. Those small animals are seen before heard just about all the time. The rustle of bushes, the crack of a twig. It was the sound of men walking through the woods without regards for being quiet. Maybe they didn't know he had a bow, or maybe their desire for speed made them careless. Just like he was forced to do.

He took an arrow from the ground, set it in the bow, and moved into position. They appeared as shadows. Movement that he could see, but bodies that he couldn't. He brought the bow up but didn't pull back, yet. He wanted a good shot at one of them, but if he were quick enough, he would get two arrows off. That would leave just one on one. And if it was just the tracker left, he just might run away, knowing he was out-weaponed.

One of the armed men came out from the underbrush first. It surprised Conner a bit, but it didn't make him concerned. The tracker might just be sending the muscle through first. His armed companion came through second, and Conner's thoughts were solely on targeting the men. He pulled the bowstring back, closed his left eye, and aimed for the first man's chest. He could see the man's eyes. Not clear enough to tell if they were the dark brown that were common of Thellians, or if they were the blue or green that were common among his own people. But he could see eyes. He could see the stern facial expression. The man breathed, scratched an itch. Conner pulled back farther, readying to fire, but his hands were frozen. The man's chest was on target, but Conner couldn't release the arrow. He wanted to, but his hands were stopping him. It was a man who was coming down the trail. Not a deer. Or a wolf. Or a large black bear. Maybe he was just as dangerous, or likely more dangerous than the grizzlies that prowled the mountains to the north. But he was a man. He breathed. He lived. He thought. He had a father and a mother. Maybe he was married and had children. He was older with a bit of gray around the temples. He could be as old as his father would have been when he was born. It could have been someone just like his father. Or even just like himself.

He lowered the bow. He couldn't do it. He did it when he had to when he didn't have to think about it. But now they would kill him and Elissa. Probably without thought or remorse. But he couldn't do it. He couldn't kill a man this way, without him knowing that it was coming. Anger burned inside, anger directed at himself. He didn't know what to do now. He had to kill them, but it didn't happen. It wouldn't happen. He released tension on the bow and wept at his cowardice.

"Don't move." The voice startled Conner so much that he jumped and let the arrow fall to the ground. He turned to find the tracker facing him, a long, thin hunting knife held comfortably in front of him, ready to slice or thrust.

Conner knew he looked ridiculous, tear streaks down his cheeks, a bow in one hand, an arrow on the ground, and three more stuck in the dirt.

"Relax," the man said. "My name is Marik. I am a ranger and a Knight of Karmon." The man lowered the knife. "We are here to bring the princess home."

Conner was stunned. He turned to look at the two men coming up the trail, two men whose life he almost ended. He looked down at his bow and the arrows. "I almost…"

"Yes, you did," Marik said. "Whatever held your hand, I am glad it did."

Conner felt worse. He was ashamed. He knew what it was that held his hand, it was fear. Cowardice. He had the chance to save Elissa and he failed. Yes, it worked out. He didn't need to kill a man. And if he had, who knows what the ranger would have done to him. But he felt worse for his failure. He took his bow, grabbed his arrows, and followed the ranger back to where he had left Elissa.

***

Marik spent most of his time ahead of the group, scouting the best path for them to follow. But when they rested, the ranger and Elissa sat away from everyone else, talking quietly. Conner and the other two knights followed mostly in silence. They chatted some, but the two knights didn't seem to desire idle conversation. They were polite enough, but it was clear they didn't have much to say. Marik never let on what happened in the trees, never mentioned how close Conner came to shooting his arrows. Conner was glad. He didn't want bad blood to hover over the rest of their trip. He just bid his time, waiting to get out of the forest and return to his home.

They took it at a pace as Elissa allowed. It wasn't a fast pace, but she surprised them all moving at a steady pace. By nightfall, they were nearly out of the forest. Exhausted, she fell into a quick sleep while the men prepared their camp. Once the princess was asleep and a fire was going, Marik left the others to guard the campsite. He returned some time later with three rabbits that were quickly gutted, skinned, and cooked. They slept in shifts through the night, waking just before dawn. After a small breakfast of berries and the little bit of rabbit from the night before, they broke camp.

They trudged through the trees, following game trails and whatever open space they could find. Little was said other than acknowledging commands. Conner wasn't last, one of the knights was always following a few yards behind. But he was always behind the princess. The physical separation while they walked did not surprise him. She was of royal blood and should be walking ahead of him. He, the peasant, should be relegated to the back. He missed her voice and conversation. He was glad that they had been found and were heading back to the safety of the castle. But the lack of communication between them bothered him. He hoped that soon they could be back to what they were, friends who could talk. In the meantime, he just followed them in silence.

By mid-day, they reached the edge of the forest and found a small camp. There were three lightly clad knights tending the camp. As soon as these knights saw who approached, they shouted their joy. They showered the princess with praise and adoration. They practically carried her under their lean-to, covering her with blankets and shoving food and drink in front of her.

Marik and Conner found themselves outcast from the group and made themselves busy building up their fire.

"That was you on the docks?" Conner asked.

Marik nodded his head. "We came into the village just as you were rowing out into the river. By the time we found someone who would give us a straight answer about you two, you were already halfway across the river." Marik let out a soft chuckle. "You had them pretty uptight about a band of murderers chasing you."

"We thought for sure we were being chased," Conner said.

"You took care of them all way back up river," Marik said.

"All of them?" Conner asked.

"It appears so. We only found your tracks. No one else was following you."

"Then we were worried for no reason," Conner said softly.

"No, of course not. You were right to be worried. You had no idea who they were or how many there were. You did a great job of protecting the princess. You did an amazing job."

Conner shrugged his shoulders, embarrassed. "Anyone would have done it."

"No," Marik replied. "Not anyone would have. Many would never have gotten involved. Many would have not found protective shelter in a cave. Staying there saved your lives."

"Barely," Conner said. "It was really cold."

"It would have been colder out in the open without protection from the wind."

"Do you know who they were?" Conner asked.

Marik shrugged his shoulders. "Bandits. Kidnappers. They were pretty ragtag. Skilled enough to take out her guards, but certainly not real soldiers. They were too sloppy. But now she's safe, and the king will have her daughter back. All thanks to you."

Conner was silent in his embarrassment. Then he asked, "You drew on us back on the docks. If you knew it was us, why do that?"

Marik glanced over at one of the knights putting a saddle on a horse. "They thought that a couple shots might get your attention. Turn you around even. Or accidentally kill you."

"It made me think that you were from a group that was chasing us."

"Yeah," Marik replied sheepishly. "I could tell. You started going faster right after that." He slapped Conner on the shoulder as he stood up. "At least it all worked out. I thank you again for helping the princess. You have done this kingdom a great service. If the princess spoke even half truths about your adventures, you are a very brave young man." He held out his hand. Conner gripped it tightly. Marik continued, "I am sure the king will reward you well."

Conner replied softly, "I didn't do it for the reward."

"No," Marik said. "I am sure you didn't." He released Conner's hand and looked around. There was little to indicate where they were. "We are kind of in the middle of nowhere. Do you need help in finding your village?"

Conner shook his head. "I've hunted these woods before. It's maybe a day or so to the north. I can manage."

"Very well. I'll make sure you have provisions for your journey. There is plenty for lunch. Our fine knights are pretty good cooks and made a fine stew for us. You are welcome to stay and feast with us before we leave."

The princess, overhearing the conversation, pulled herself up from the underneath her blankets. "Sir Marik, Conner will be coming with us to the castle."

Marik looked uncomfortable. He clearly didn't want to argue with the princess, so he chose his words as carefully as he could. "I am sure that Conner would like to return to his family as soon as he can."

"I don't think you quite understand what happened out there," Elissa replied. "Conner saved my life. He is to be named my Champion and will return to the castle with me."

"Princess, we are all very grateful for what Conner has done to bring you back safe. It was very courageous and quite frankly, pretty amazing. And I am sure he will be well rewarded." He turned to Conner and nodded his appreciation again. "But you must understand…"

"You must understand," Elissa said firmly. "That I am Princess Elissa, heir to the throne of Karmon. And you will do as I say."

Marik smiled as if he were talking to a young girl half Elissa's age. "If you had a brother, he would be heir. You…"

"She is as strong as any boy I've ever seen," Conner interjected.

"Her strength does not change the laws of the land," Marik countered with a sharp glare. He was not used to being interrupted, much less by someone who was not of noble blood.

Elissa stepped out from underneath the lean-to. "My father is the law of the land. I think you forget yourself, Sir Marik."

Marik, recognizing a battle he could not win, retreated. "Yes, my lady. You are right. I will do as you ask. But be careful about the words that you use. Calling a man your Champion is more than just words. It has meaning and importance."

"I know what it means," Elissa said softly. "He saved my life, and he is someone that I desire to be my Champion."

"He must wish it as well," Marik replied. He turned toward Conner to give him the opportunity to reject the princess's crazy notion.

"He has agreed," Elissa said.

"He has agreed to what?" Conner asked, stepping into the conversation, suddenly realizing that they were talking about him. "You are talking about me as if I am not here. What are you talking about?"

"When a princess or queen cannot defend herself, or protect herself, she declares a Champion to stand in her stead. He is to uphold her honor and fight for her if need be. The champion is duty bound."

"Yes, I understand," Conner said. "We have discussed this already."

"Do you understand that you are duty-bound for life?" Marik asked.

"Okay."

"Your one purpose in this life is to serve her. Everything else is meaningless."

"Sir Marik!" Elissa exclaimed. "You are making it sound like he is to be my personal slave!"

"Your highness, it is an honor and must not be given, or accepted, lightly. I just want the both of you to understand what this means. Not just to you, princess, but for you as well, Conner. Whatever plans you had for your life are now changed."

"My plans?" Conner asked. "Other than spending my life hunting for food?" He looked at the princess. She had lowered her gaze to the ground. Her cheeks were flushed and once again, her eyes filled with tears. She no longer looked the princess, nor a young woman, but just a common girl, alone and afraid. Conner approached her and took her hand. She looked up and into his eyes. He smiled and said, "I would be honored to be your Champion. But I fear I cannot defend you or protect you. I am no soldier or fighter."

"You have done a fine job so far," Elissa said.

Marik watched the two of them interact. More had happened in the forest than what had been shared. Conner didn't just save her life. He became more to her. He could see it in the way they looked at one another. How her voice changed when she talked to him. A friendship had come out of the forest, and he now had the power to either squash it or to make it bloom.

With a soft voice, he added to Elissa's argument. "You don't need to be a soldier to be a Champion. You just need to be a man." He put a hand on Conner's shoulder and squeezed. "We can help train you to be the rest."

Elissa looked up at Marik and smiled. Conner, surprised at the sudden change in heart, simply nodded his head.

The sound of an approaching horse caused them to all turn their heads. The rider pulled the reins of his mount and stopped just before he was to crash into them.

"What is this?" The booming voice of the rider demanded.

Conner was still holding the princess' hand as the hulking rider dismounted from his horse and strode quickly to them. After an awkward moment, he dropped her hand and took a step back.

"Princess Elissa," Knight Captain Brace Hawkden exclaimed in relief. "Are you well?"

"We found them in the woods to the north of the river," Marik said.

"I am fine, Sir Hawkden," the princess replied. "Thanks to my Champion, Conner."

"I thank you for safe keeping of the princess," Brace said. He eyed Conner carefully, wondering how a boy like him could have helped the princess. He wasn't anything special, thin like most commoners seemed to be. His hair was long, shaggy, and unkempt. But clearly, the boy, or young man, was well schooled in the bow that he carried. Still, he was well out of his element standing among knights and princesses. But he did stand tall and confident. Conner returned the gaze that Brace gave him, never wavering or turning away.

His eyes continue to linger over Conner, wondering how this one boy could have interrupted his plans. He was glad the princess was safe, and the guilt he had for putting these events into motion was overwhelming. His heart ached, and he could tell no one. He then looked over at the princess and was ashamed for what he had done. It was all in the best interest of the kingdom, but it could have hurt so many people so badly. Maybe someday he would be able to forgive himself.

For the past day, while he was riding from Lord Neffenmark's castle, he had convinced himself a hundred ways that the plan was worth it. But when he saw the princess, standing here in the middle of the forest, his heart broke from the pain he had caused. How could he make it right? He listened carefully as Marik and the princess explained the exploits of this boy, and as the words came, the shame grew. The boy held more courage and honor than the greatest knight of them all. The boy deserved every reward he would get. And he himself deserved every punishment a traitor should get.

To the rest of the knights, Brace announced that they must leave for the city immediately.

"They are weary of being in the forest," Marik countered. "They are hungry and should feast before they ride."

Brace glanced up at the sky knowing that they would already be hard-pressed to arrive before dark. If they waited any longer, they would either be riding through the night or it would have to make camp and take another day for their trip.

"We could ride ahead and announce the princess," one of the knights suggested.

"No," Brace said harshly, maybe too much so. "I made a promise to the king that I would bring her home. I will do so, and safely. But if the ambushers are still out there, they may yet try again. I do not wish to presume her safety until we have arrived at the castle gates." He turned to Marik. "Make haste with your meal. We must ride as soon as we are able."

"Sir Hawkden, it seems as if we are short a horse." Princess Elissa said.

Brace glanced around, quickly counting his men and their horses.

Marik cleared his throat, gave a quick glance at Elissa, and then said to his Knight Captain, "It seems as though that Princess Elissa has declared Conner as her Champion, so he will need a horse to join us back to the castle."

Brace looked from the princess to Conner and then back again. He let out a long sigh, knowing what this all meant. It was likely that this little game would come to an end when the king heard of it. But the princess had the power and the authority, so the game must be played out. If she were a few years younger, he would just smile and nod, but still send Conner back to his village. There would have been some kicking and screaming and yelling and tantrums, but in the end, she would have lost the battle. But now that she was older, with power and clout, her words meant something and her orders were to be listened to. She would have to be obeyed. At least until the king heard of it. And then he would take care of it. He could handle his daughter and the anger that would ensue. His large shoulders and even larger heart would handle that burden. He also was the only one who had the authority right now to tell the princess no.

Conner stood like a man, waiting for Brace to say something. All the knights stood waiting for something to be said. Brace knew what this all meant, probably more so than the princess did. Certainly, more than Conner did. Maybe the princess thought it was a game, or maybe she really did understand what being a Champion meant. But Conner was certainly not a Champion. Yes, he was able to help her survive the forest, keep her from the ambushers and bring her back to safety. But a Champion must stand up to any who would come against her or challenged her authority. He had a hunting bow and was a good shot. A small knife hung at his side. It was unlikely that Conner had ever even held a sword, much less swung one. A Champion would have to know the skills of the blade and be ready to defend the princess. He would go along with this game for the moment, but he knew that the king would put an end to it. This boy, for all his heart and confidence, could not possibly serve properly as her Champion.

He felt sorry for Conner because he was simply a victim in this game. He didn't act proud to be called the Princess' Champion. In fact, based on the way his cheeks turned red each time it was mentioned, it was likely that Conner really didn't want the honor. But the princess asked him, and he accepted. So for at least for the time being, he was her Champion. But the king would put an end to it and then the boy would go back to his home. Maybe he'd be lucky enough to spend a night or two in the castle, but it wouldn't be long. He'd be given a decent reward and a horse to return to his home. He'd probably even be allowed to keep the horse for his trouble. But he would be forgotten in time. The princess would move on to be courted by serious men. Men who would be able to provide her with a proper bloodline, men who would be able to stand in until a male heir was able to take the crown. Conner was a commoner, and that was all that he could ever be.

"Eat quickly," Brace said harshly. "We leave soon. The boy will take Sir Esha's horse."

Chapter Seven

They arrived at South Karmon well after the sun had fallen below the horizon. The northern gates were still open, and a few travelers and merchants were on the lamp-lit road leading into the city. The Guardsmen attending the gates simply nodded as the knights rode through. They kept their eyes open for bandits and drunken troublemakers and did not bother to give their group of weary riders a second look.

They rode with authority through the city streets, and anyone in their way scattered quickly. They wound their way towards the castle, around which the city was built. A great wall separated the castle grounds from the rest of the city. The wall was higher than the wall that surrounded the city and was guarded more tightly. Conner could see bowmen walking the top of the wall, looking down upon the city, keeping the king safe. Not only was the wall massive in size, but it was also the oldest part of the city. Having been built when the Taran Empire was still expanding with reckless abandon, the small kingdom of Karmon needed as much protection as it could muster. Those walls saved the kingdom many times, having repelled countless assaults. The last time that an invading army had assaulted the walls was so far in the past, that no one alive had ever experienced it.

Upon reaching the gate that led into the castle grounds, Brace dismounted first. He walked to the rear of the line where Conner was stretching his sore muscles. "This is where we will part company," the Knight Captain announced with his powerful voice. "I am sure the king will have an audience with you in due time."

"Sir Hawkden," Elissa said firmly. "He is to come with us. To meet my father."

Brace let out a long sigh. "Yes, my lady, and he will do so. Your father is unaware of our arrival, as I wanted to be sure that we would get here without incident." He glanced around as if he were being spied upon. "Your father will be most pleased at your sight, and I believe that there will be a time for your father to meet Conner. Now is not that time. He will be put up in the barracks, fed, and when your father is ready to meet him…"

"I believe that I know my father well, and he would like to meet the man who saved me," Elissa interrupted firmly. "He will wish to meet my Champion. Now."

Brace looked around at his knights and was offered no advice. He felt sorry for the boy. Today, he was her special prize, a hunter from the woods who was lucky enough to help her survive the forest. Tomorrow, he would be forgotten as she went about doing … whatever it was that princess' do.

The portcullis opened, allowing them passage into the courtyard. Their horses were taken while they walked up the cobblestone path towards the castle. Conner walked in awe, taking in the sights that he could not have imagined. The castle grounds not only included the castle itself, but a well-manicured garden of trees and bushes that were lush and green. Statues lined the courtyard. A fountain sprayed water in the center of the courtyard. The castle itself, older than any other building in the city, sat magnificently upon a small hill, overlooking it all. The crash of the ocean against the rocks below the castle could be heard, just above the din of the city.

Conner looked around, wrinkling his nose at the odd smell. It wasn't a horrible smell, just different.

The ranger Marik was walking past and noticed the look on his face. He remembered the first time that he had come to the city and smelled that very odd smell. "It is the salt of the ocean," Marik said to Conner. "Just on the other side of the castle is the Gulf of Taran. You hear the waves? They are crashing against the cliff that the castle sits upon. It is quite an amazing sight." He paused for a moment, just as he was about to walk away. It struck him, just at that moment, that he was looking at himself, only about ten years younger. Maybe he could like the boy after all.

He shouldn't have stayed, he should have kept going. Conner was a commoner, someone supposedly beneath him. But the boy did something he never would have expected. He had saved the princess. Not only did he help her escape her attackers, but he had killed three of them in the process.

"Tomorrow there will be a great feast in honor of the princess' return," Marik said. "At some point after the ale has flowed for many hours, and it becomes dull, I shall come find you and then we will go walk the cliffs."

Conner looked shocked, and simply nodded his head. They followed Brace towards the great oaken doors that led into the king's council chamber.

***

The king was speechless, and he let his tears flow freely. He had been awoken from a restless slumber and had not taken the time to prepare himself. His thin, graying hair was matted, and his clothes were wrinkled and stained. It was the first time Conner had laid eyes on someone as noble and powerful as a king, and he was not really impressed. The king had not shaved in quite a while, leaving his face with a graying stubble.

Great proclamations were made, expanses of land were handed out, gold and jewels were promised. As any loyal and honorable Knight would do, Brace declined all that was given to him. Conner, looking on from the back of the hall, found the whole event slightly odd. It seemed scripted as if everyone was supposed to behave and act in a specific way. As each proclamation of gold and lands were rejected, he thought the king would be insulted. But the king handled it graciously as if it were expected to be declined. As word spread of the princess' arrival, the hall became more and more packed. Conner was pushed farther and farther to the rear of the chamber until his back was pressed against tapestries hanging along the back wall.

In turn, each knight who brought the princess home was paraded in front of everyone. Cheers rose up at their names, rounds of drink were promised, and the hands of pretty maidens were offered. There was much laughter and merriment all around, but Conner felt small and alone in the back of the chamber. Everywhere were noblemen and noblewomen, people that looked like him, but where not. Dresses that Conner thought would be reserved for weddings or funerals were worn as everyday clothes by the ladies and their servants. Their hair was brushed and primped. An array of perfumes filled the room as each lady wore their favorite. The knights and nobles were clad in their long silk tunics, looking all too comfortable dressed up without their swords and armor. Only Brace, Marik, and the other knights who had arrived with the princess looked out of place. And he, of course, looked most out of place of all of them.

A cheer rose up. The king had said something, but Conner had hardly heard a word that had been said for the past few minutes. Conner stretched to see what the cheering was about, but everyone else around him was stretching their own necks, trying to see. Suddenly, it became quiet, and the lords and ladies in front of him parted so that he could see directly up to the front of the room. Brace and Marik had turned towards him. Brace's outstretched arm was directed right at him. A sudden panic swept through him as if he had done something wrong. Maybe it was Brace's stern gaze or the fact that everyone else in the entire hall had turned to look at him. Then King Thorndale stepped into his view, his eyes red and still teary, looked across the hall at him. The panic that had filled him overwhelmed him, and he suddenly felt as if he were about to faint. But then the king smiled, and spread his arms wide, and gestured for him to come forward.

He was dirty, and he knew he smelled horrible. The heat of the packed room didn't help, nor did the panic that had nearly overcome him. The lords and ladies looked down at him and smiled as if a young child was being presented in front of them. Their smiles were pleasant and warm, yet still, as if he were a decoration or prize and not a man.

Uncomfortably, he walked forward. Brace looked upon him still with his stern gaze. Marik actually smiled, and his eyes showed honest warmth. The king was smiling at him as well, but Conner could not take his eyes off of Princess Elissa. She wore a white gown that hardly showed her as the princess, but in its simplicity, showed her utmost beauty. Her eyes were as teary as her father's. And as Conner neared, he could see the streaks down her cheeks that those tears had made. She sniffled, un-ladylike, but her chambermaid was nowhere to be seen to correct her.

"Is this the young man who saved my princess?" The king asked in his powerful voice.

"Yes, my lord," Brace replied. "That is Conner."

Princess Elissa took a half step forward as if to come to him, but a hand from her father on her shoulder held her in place.

"Come forward and present yourself," the king said.

Conner stopped just in front of him, at the steps that led up to the platform where the king, Brace, Marik, and Princess Elissa stood. He fell to a knee, as he knew protocol was and bowed his head.

"Arise, Conner," the king said.

Conner stood to face the king, but his eyes could not be pulled away from the princess.

"I understand that you most of all deserve my thanks," the king said, his eyes going from Conner to the masses behind him. "From my heart, I thank you for bringing my daughter back to me."

Conner did not know what to say. He could only manage a weak smile.

Princess Elissa, taking advantage of the awkward silence quickly stepped forward before her father could stop her. She put both hands on his shoulders and looked deep into his eyes. Conner now felt even more awkward. They locked eyes for some time, her smile mesmerizing him so that he no longer felt awkward, no longer felt alone in a crowded room.

"Conner, forever and always, I give this to you, that you will be my Champion, to serve and protect me and the crown that I represent." Her voice was loud and clear so that everyone in the hall could hear.

King Thorndale had moved forward and whispered into her ear, just loud enough for Conner to hear. "Come, Elissa, we should let Conner return to his family."

The princess snapped her head around and stepped back from his father. "Father," she said softly. "He was the one who saved me. He is my choice to be my Champion."

The king looked up and around, clearly not wanting to have this conversation at this time. He looked from Conner and then to Elissa, "I am not sure you understand what you are asking. A Champion is not just someone you choose because you like them." This made Conner blush, and look away. "A Champion is called upon to fight your battles, to be your sword in duel or battle, to physically protect you because you cannot protect yourself. You have the entire Royal Guard at your disposal."

"And they could not protect me in the forest," Elissa retorted as silently as she could, but loud enough for those nearby to hear.

"You also have the Knights of Karmon, the greatest warriors in all of the land to protect you," the king said loudly, loud enough for all to hear. Shouting and cheering arose.

"I trust no one with my life, but him. And yes, it is my choice," Elissa declared loudly.

The cheering rose louder until Conner could hardly breathe. The sound was oppressive and uncomfortable. He was not used to so many people in one place, much less all of them yelling at one time.

The king looked around at his cheering and shouting people let out a heavy sigh. Wars were not won because you fought every battle, wars were won by winning those that you could win. His father had taught him that when he was young, and he used that adage not only on the battlefield, but when ruling his kingdom.

He looked down upon Conner and studied him for some time. Conner could only look back, locking his eyes upon the greatest man of their kingdom. He was too afraid to look away.

"And you understand what this means," the king said. "And you accept it?"

Without thought, he replied, "Yes, your Majesty, I do."

"Then it will be so," the king declared.

The cheering grew even louder. Most did not know what they were cheering for. They just knew they were supposed to cheer because everyone else was cheering. Nobles that were nearby patted him on the back and shook his hand. Elissa stood back, watching it all with a wide smile on her face. But it was Sir Brace Hawkden who left a lasting impression on him. He stood stoically, arms crossed, and a penetrating stare aimed right into the heart of Conner.

***

"He is but a boy," Brace said. "And untrained in any sword skill or fighting skill."

The king, freshly bathed and dressed in a long brown tunic trimmed with gold lace turned from the long mirror towards his Knight Captain. "I understand he killed three of the attackers."

"Yes."

"Then he has skill with the bow."

"Which does not make him a warrior. Maybe a ranger, or a scout, but not a knight," Brace countered.

"He is not being asked to take the oath of knighthood."

"He is not of noble blood. He cannot take the oath," Brace reminded his liege.

The king strode across the room and grabbed a golden goblet full of sweet wine. He took a long drink before returning his attention back to his Knight Captain. "She is my daughter, first and foremost. She has asked this of me, and I will do this for her." He set the goblet back on the table and continued, "There are many affairs of the kingdom that require my attention. This is not the empire, and I do not have a council of governors to handle affairs of the mundane. I have only but a handful of ministers to help me govern, and you to help keep the peace. So, if I can give my daughter this, keep her out of my hair until she is old enough to win a suitor, then what harm is there?"

"Sire, you have always asked me to speak freely when we were alone, so I will do so now."

"Go on," the king said.

Brace took a deep breath and continued, "Sire, there is great harm in it. We have certain traditions that we follow to help keep the peace and to ensure that the best, the most worthy, are in positions of leadership. We cannot have just anyone serve as a knight. They must be of noble birth, with the right upbringing and tutelage."

"Again, she is not asking him to be a knight," the king said with some impatience. "She is asking him to be her Champion, to fight in her stead, so to speak."

"She does not need a Champion," Brace retorted. "No one would dare even think about fighting her. There is no need for her to have a Champion!"

Brace's voice had raised to the point where he thought he might offend his liege, but instead, the king had a wide grin on his face. "Your point is well taken, and like usual, it is correct."

"My point?" Brace asked, confused.

"The one about her needing a Champion. You are right. She does not need one, but it will occupy her time for a while."

"But in the meantime, the boy must be trained."

"And that will be your responsibility," the king said.

"He cannot train with the knights, he is not a noble," Brace said. "He would fit in better with the Royal Guard."

The king raised an eyebrow at Brace. "And what do you think your good friend Perkins will have to say about that? I am inclined to think that maybe he would be better off being trained by your men."

"He cannot, he is not a noble," Brace repeated with as much emphasis as he dared.

"Am I not the king?" King Thorndale said with a raised voice. "I do believe that not only can I make the rules, but I can break them."

"And to do so would undermine my authority and the authority of all my men. There are reasons that only nobles can be Knights. Our ancestry is pure and not diluted by the common. We are stronger, smarter. Better in just about every way. A common man will just not make a good Knight. It would be a waste of time to have him go through the process. Especially to begin at his age."

"Which brings us to another problem," the King said. "Regardless of which of you gets him, he will be training with boys who have many years of experience behind them. He should train with those of his same age, but he will be at a distinct disadvantage due to his lack of skill."

"And what would you have me do, my lord, train him myself?"

"I had thought about that," the king replied seriously. "But I have someone else in mind. Someone who isn't accountable to the politics of either the Royal Guard or Knighthood. Master Goshin will teach him."

"Master Goshin?" Brace repeated. "The outcast from the far west? What can he teach him? He is not a warrior, he is a glorified scribe!"

The king burst out into laughter. "You do not know one thing about our friend from the west. He is so much more than what you could imagine. He is a master of an ancient fighting style. One that the likes of this kingdom has never seen before."

"The bookworm? A swordsman?"

"Yes. Find him, and send him to me," the king ordered.

"If I can even find him. He always has his face buried in some book or another." Brace turned to leave but then hesitated. "Sire, when Princess Elissa tires of this little game of hers, and no longer cares to have the responsibility of a Champion watching over her, what then? What will Conner do, then? What will we do with Conner?"

The king shrugged his shoulders. "Of all the things that I worry about each day, this one will be the least of them. If my daughter never sees him, never mentions his name again, then after a few weeks Conner can return to his home, and it will be as if nothing happened. But, if I know my daughter, and I think I do, then I know she is taking this very seriously, and she will not forget about him. She will really think of him as her Champion. And for the time being, we will play along with this game."

"And if he has no skill with the blade? If he cannot swing a sword, or does not have the fortitude for battle?"

"Brace, my good friend, I think you are underestimating this young man. Elissa has told me the story in detail of how he helped her survive in the forest while being chased by men who wished to kill her. He is good with the bow, which I know does not make him a swordsman. But instead of thinking he will fail and trying to come up with what we will do when he does, let's plan on him succeeding."

Brace bowed his head and said as respectfully as he could, "Yes Your Majesty."

"Now," the king said with a clap of his hands. "If there is nothing else, then I have a feast to get ready for."

"Actually, there is one more thing," Brace said. His voice was quiet and nervous, which the king clearly picked up on.

"Go ahead, speak."

Brace cleared his throat, unsure how to start. His palms were sweaty, and he resisted the temptation to wipe them on his pants. "It came to my attention some time ago, that horses were leaving in the middle of the night from the stables."

"Oh?"

"Not warhorses, but fast messenger horses. I had one followed. To Thell." Brace let the statement hang in the air for a moment before continuing. "The rider was followed back, and upon arriving back at the city, he went directly into private audience with you."

The color had slowly drained out of the king's face as Brace spoke. He started to respond several times, but the words could not be found.

"The king's business is your own," Brace said. "But the kingdom's business is mine."

The king nodded and took a seat in one of his great cushioned chairs. He stroked his beard while he gathered his thoughts. "I had contemplated sharing with you…and others…this idea of mine. But I feared that it would not be taken kindly by some. There is resistance to any sort of communication with Thell. Some would have that just talking to a Thellian would be grounds for a charge of treason."

"And rightly so," Brace exclaimed loudly. "They are barbarians, sir, unworthy of our time, except at the end of a sword."

"They are not much different than us if truth be told, Brace. In fact, there are some stories that Thellians and Karmons have the same ancestors."

"That is all well and good, but our brothers from the north have come down here and tried to kill your daughter. Each spring, their raiding parties sweep down from the mountains and attack our villages for sport. I do not care if they came from the same womb as me, they are barbarians and have one purpose in life, and that is to fall to my sword."

"And yet, there are some that seek peace with us."

"A peace offered just before they strike us down!"

"Enough!" The king shouted, tired of the anger coming from his Knight Captain. "Yes, I have given you the right to speak freely in the chamber, but you are getting close to crossing the line from disagreement to disobedience. If I feel that we should have communication with Thell, then that is my right, and you will not question that decision. Is that clear?"

Brace nodded his head, letting his anger slowly simmer down. "But if others discover this, others that may not have the same loyalties that I have…" He let his words trail off, hoping the king would finish the thought for him.

"That is why I have you, Brace, to keep the kingdom from rebelling against me and my decisions."

"And yet you risk this by sending a messenger, unguarded and unarmed?"

"And who else would I send? You?" The king asked.

"Yes!" Brace replied. "Who better than me? I can protect the message, and no one will question me or where I am going, or what I am doing. What if your messenger was stopped by a patrol in the mountains and asked about his task? What then? What would your messenger do? Tell the patrol what he was doing? Get caught in a big lie?"

The king was silent, letting the thoughts stew inside. Finally, he said, "And if I were to send you, then it would be noticed. Your absence would be asked about. I, and you would have to answer those questions."

"It would be worth the risk to ensure the safety of the message. Plus, I often travel to the outlying garrisons. My absence for a few days is never noticed."

"Then it is settled," King Thorndale said. "You have convinced me that you should be the one to deliver the next message."

"That is a wise choice, your majesty."

"Now leave, so that I can finish preparing for my daughter's feast!"

Brace left, regretting every word he said, although he meant every one of them... He was honest in his concern over the rider from Karmon going into Thell with a message. Anyone could find out, and anyone already knew. Lord Neffenmark knew about the message, just not the contents. But through his actions and words, the fat lord would soon know what was in that message.

Chapter Eight

The courtyard was filled with tables overflowing with all varieties of food. Large casks of ale had been rolled in and were being emptied almost as quickly as they could be set up. More food was consumed in that first hour than he had ever seen in his entire lifetime. An uncountable number of pigs were roasted, large sides of deer were hung over the fire, cooking until tender and piping hot. Breads of all shapes and sizes were stacked higher than he was tall. Stewpots were full of meats and vegetables, seasoned so well that Conner's stomach could barely handle the wondrous scent. He walked slowly through the crowd, taking it all in. He watched the lords and ladies laugh as jesters worked their tricks and jokes, dancing to the pipe and fiddle, and making fools of themselves as they ate and drank more than their fair share.

He felt out of place, but at least he didn't look it. After the meeting with the king, he was quickly hauled off to a hot bath, were an old maid scrubbed him down. He was sure she enjoyed every moment of it. He certainly didn't. But after being washed and primped, his hair trimmed, and even his long nails were clipped, he was dressed in the finest silk the castle had to offer. It was a simple garment, light blue with an odd dark blue pattern woven through it. A belt was buckled tightly around his waist, helping to hold up his thick wool leggings. He looked no different than any other young man there, but he still felt out of place. He didn't know what to say or what to do. He didn't know what food was good, or what was bad. His stomach growled in hunger, but there was so much food, he had no idea where to start.

A group of loud older boys, probably not much older than Conner pushed their way through the crowd, ignoring everyone around them. They got sour looks from the revelers, but they did not care. Conner tried to avoid them, but they were oblivious to their surroundings. Or maybe they knew exactly what they were doing and where they were. Without so much of an acknowledgment of what they did, they walked right through him, knocking him to the ground. He was too embarrassed to be angry and too annoyed to do anything but stay on the ground. They kept moving as if he had never been there in the first place. While he sat on the ground, wondering what to do, a familiar face bent down to him and offered a hand.

The Knight Ranger Marik helped him to his feet. "I see you got caught by the rampaging squires."

"Squires?" Conner asked. They looked no different than him. They had no magical aura surrounding them. They were just loud and obnoxious, just like any other group of bullies.

"Yes indeed," Marik replied. "A couple of them will be knighted during the Summer Festival. They are mostly a good group of kids, but they tend to be a bit rambunctious when let loose."

Conner wiped off whatever dirt he could, taking more time than he really needed to. He hoped that the ranger would move on.

"Enjoying the feast?" The ranger asked.

"It's a bit…crazy. All this food and drink. And all the people. And they're tearing up the garden!" He pointed to the edge of the common area where drunk and overzealous partiers had crushed a line of freshly planted flowers.

Marik smiled at the observation. "There are gardeners to take care of the garden. It gives them something to work on."

Conner could only shake his head at the disasters these people were causing. Did they not see the beauty of the garden? The fresh flowers, in early spring bloom, were an amazing site. Bushes, trimmed not just round or square, but to look like animals of the forest. The chaos was too much for him. He didn't like the noise or the utter disregard for the garden and the castle grounds. He glanced about, trying to find a way out.

Marik put a hand on his shoulder, giving him a gentle tug. "Come. Walk with me."

Conner had hoped to see Elissa, but it was clear that she was occupied with more important guests and courtiers. He had seen a glimpse of her once when she came out of the castle, but it was fleeting. His only reason for being here was for her, and he was coming to the realization that everyone else was right, that he didn't belong and that this Champion idea was simply that of a young and impressionable girl. It was silly that someone like him, a commoner, born and raised in the wild, living off the land, always wondering where the next meal was coming from, could be something more than that. Yes, he did save her life, but he knew that anyone else in his situation would do that. And if you put him in the same bunch as the other nobles, he would stand out as a commoner. Not only was there nothing special about him, but there was also nothing particularly distinctive, either. He wasn't big, with strong muscles. He wasn't fast or smart. He was just Conner. And without the pedigree of noble parents, he was simply that. Not only was he trapped somewhere between boyhood and manhood, but he was also caught in a world that was confusing and foreign.

Marik guided Conner underneath an ivy covered archway, and they entered a whole new place that was, thankfully, out of his own thoughts. The courtyard was certainly very impressive with freshly blooming spring flowers and the expertly carved bushes. But deep into the garden, it was even more astounding. Just past the opening, the path was lined with delicately carved stone statues of mythical creatures. As it was still early spring, the natural flowers of the garden were either just coming up or were in the initial stages of their yearly growth. It wouldn't be too long before the garden would be fully blooming in color, making an impressive garden even more spectacular. The Gardens of Karmon were known throughout the continent. Aristocratic visitors from the Taran Empire would come during the height of summer just to walk the exquisitely manicured paths. Birds of all colors, shapes, and sizes made their home in the garden, giving life to the bushes and trees. A shoulder-height labyrinth was at the center of the garden. Marik pointed it out, talking about the hours that could be spent trying to find the prize at the center.

"And what is the prize?" Conner asked.

"It would not be a prize if I were to tell you," the ranger replied with a smile. "That is something that you will need to experience for yourself!"

Oil-fed torches marked the way, and there was enough light to peer down one of the openings of the labyrinth, giving an eerie and mysterious atmosphere to the maze. Conner paused, thinking how fun it would be to find the prize. But during the day. At night, in the dark, it actually seemed a bit spooky. The path wandered around towards the back of the castle. Torches were lit along the castle walls that seemed to have no function, other than to give light to the stone. Although they didn't seem to serve any obvious purpose, Conner found himself thinking about how the harsh yellow torchlight gave further beauty to the garden.

"It is just around the corner," Marik said. The open path had become hedge-lined, and it seemed like it came to a stop just in front of them, but the path made a sharp right turn. As soon as they made the turn, the roar of the ocean crashing on the rocks of the cliffs filled their ears.

Conner stopped several yards in front of the cliff, unsure about what he should do. The sound of the waves was deafening. The scent of the salt was overwhelming. The sight of the endless water was disconcerting. He was frozen in a combination of fear and amazement. The top of the cliff was almost a hundred feet above the water, giving him a perspective that he could see forever. With a slight grin, Marik nudged Conner to the edge of the cliff.

"Some days," Marik said, pointing across the open expanse of water to the horizon in the distance. "If there aren't any clouds, and the sun is just in the right position, and you looked carefully enough, you could actually see across the gulf to the Taran Empire."

Conner just stood, his mouth agape, taking in the sight, sounds and smells. He had no reason to dispute the ranger. It was a sight he could never have imagined, and if Marik had told him he could fly, he would have believed him.

"You will catch flies with your jaw hanging on the ground like that."

"I...I...," Conner was amazed and didn't know how to express it with words.

"I know how you feel," Marik said. "I was you, so many years ago. I grew up in Tyre, well actually outside of Tyre. My father owned quite a bit of land outside the city, so I spent my share of time in the woods hunting and living in the woods. I came here to serve the king when I was young. I will never forget the first time I stood in this very spot and looked upon the ocean. I was overwhelmed."

"I never realized...how big..." The words came out slow. His mind was still reeling from what his mind was telling him.

"What you see is just the Gulf of Taran. It is only a tiny part of the ocean. The ocean goes on for, well, forever, I guess. I have never seen the end, but I guess it must end somewhere." He watched Conner for some time before asking, somewhat awkwardly, "What about you? Your family? What are they like?"

It took Conner a moment to realize that Marik had asked him a question. "Oh...my family? I live with my aunt. She is my father's sister. He passed when I was young. About ten. I remember him pretty well. He taught me how to hunt and to use a bow."

"He did a mighty fine job," Marik said, "How did he...?"

"Just got sick one day. Got a fever and laid down to sleep. He never woke up. After a couple of days, I finally realized he wasn't waking up. The others in the village helped me bury him. After that, I moved in with my aunt. She raised me. Well, she gave me a roof to sleep under when I wasn't out hunting. I came and went, and she didn't really mind. I don't think she ever really cared for me."

Marik let the statement hang around for too long. It seemed as if there was some bitterness towards his aunt, but he didn't know how to make the conversation move along. Finally, he asked, "What about your mom?"

The made Conner smile. "I have a couple memories of her. Not a lot. Just some images in my head. I was very young when she died. My father never told me how. Maybe like so many others. Just got sick and died. I know it hurt my dad pretty hard because he talked about her a lot. He really loved her and missed her. I wish I could have known her."

"You and the princess are alike in that way! You both lost your mother early on." The sudden awkwardness of the statement was obvious the moment it came out. He quickly tried to change the subject. "I remember the Queen. She was pretty, but I don't think near as beautiful as Princess Elissa will be. But she was raised to be royalty. Raised to serve her husband and to be a wife. She was a great woman, but there is something more about the princess. She has a strength that I would not have imagined that her mother had. The Queen would have just rolled up into a ball in those woods and died. She did not know how to survive. But the princess. I like what I saw from her. I like that she is strong."

"She will make a great queen," Conner said.

Marik let out a sigh. "Only if she finds the right husband to be her king. Laws of the land, Conner. Women have their place, and the ruler of the kingdom is not one of them."

"It's silly," Conner protested.

"Maybe to you," Marik said. "But there is an order to the world that must be kept. It keeps the world from falling into chaos."

Conner fell silent and kicked a stone off the cliff, and they watched it disappear into the darkness. The more he thought about where is was and what he was doing, the more he realized he didn't belong. He was a commoner in a place meant for the noble. "I should go back," Conner said softly.

"Yes, there is still much food left!" Marik replied heartily.

"No, not that. To my home." After a moment, he added softly, "Or what I call home. This place is not for me. I do not belong here."

"The princess has called you to be her Champion! You cannot abandon her." He felt his words coming out flat and uninspiring. He didn't even believe it himself.

"Her Champion?" Conner said, turning away from the gulf and towards Marik. "I am a nobody. A commoner. I stumbled across her in the forest. I am no more her Champion than…than…"

"Then what? Then who? It is her choice. You really don't have much say in the matter!" His words were meant to be lighthearted, but Conner did not take it that way.

"Oh? I am not bound to her. I do not owe her anything."

"No. You don't," Marik replied. "But before you leave, before you make a decision, think about something. Think about your life and this world, and maybe what you can give back to it."

Conner gave Marik a funny look. "What do you mean?"

"I know you might feel like nobody now, and well, in the scheme of things, right now, I guess you are nobody. But I think you have a chance to do something that not many young men have, and that is to make a difference in the world. Think about it, what would you do if you just went back home. You would live your life. Hunt for food, maybe find a wife and get married. Raise a family. But what if you had the chance to do something more, to be something more? Why do you think the nobles send their boys to the castle to be trained towards knighthood? Mostly because they know that they have done something productive in their own lives and they are trying to get their boys to do the same. But now you have a chance to do the same. You can do more than what you could have imagined."

"I cannot be a knight," Conner said. "I have no noble blood."

"You don't need to be a knight to make a difference," Marik said. But even though he said the words, he didn't know if he really meant them. Being a knight did make a difference. Everyone respected a knight and looked up to them. They didn't have to prove themselves to anyone. He fell silent, unable to keep up the argument. How could he convince this commoner to be more than what any other commoner could be when the rest of the world would be against him?

Conner waited for Marik to argue more, but the conversation had stopped. They both knew that without noble blood, he was always going to be a commoner. He looked again out to the ocean, out to nothingness. The black sea merged into the black sky at the horizon. There were some stars, but mostly the high clouds obscured them. The moon was hidden, so there wasn't much light other than what the torches lit. He knew there was more out there than what he could see. Marik had said that the Taran Empire could actually be seen from the cliffs. And beyond the empire, what was past that? He did not know. He knew the empire covered most of the continent, but there had to be an end to it, right? He had a sudden need to see the world, to see what he did not see, to know what he did not know. He had wandered the forests and hills and woods of Karmon, but there was so much more to the world. There were cities many times the size of South Karmon. There were buildings that would make the castle here look like an ant hill. He wanted to see the land on the other side of the gulf. An itch started, and he knew he couldn't scratch it. But he would always be just a commoner. A peasant. A servant of the king.

"I am just a common hunter," Conner replied meekly. "It is who I am. All that I am."

"And there is great hunting around here. And up in the mountains. Each fall, we take a long trip up into the mountains and hunt elk. That is an amazing time. You can always do the things you like to do, but what about doing things you were meant to do?"

"Meant to do?" Conner asked.

Marik let out a long sigh, still unable to get the words out of his head. "This is a conversation best suited for Master Goshin."

"Who is that?"

Marik let a smile sneak out. "Someone you will likely meet in the near future. Someone very wise, much wiser than me. Someone who can make his words mean something."

Conner watched Marik struggle. He could tell that the ranger wanted to say more. His eyes told him that there was more to say. But he had heard the words and he listened. He knew that he was good with the bow, better than anyone else that he knew. He always had been. He could run for miles without tiring. Farther than anyone else that he knew. He was strong, even though he didn't look like it. He wasn't the strongest he knew, that would be Orag, who farmed next to his aunt. But he could chop wood as quickly and as long as anyone else he knew. He loved to hunt, loved the time alone in the woods. But was there more? If there was, what was it?

"Do you really think there is something here for me?" Conner asked.

"Of course," Marik said. "But you have to make yourself ready for whatever it is. Stay. Stay here and learn. Learn what you can, and then you can decide what to do. Even if it is for the summer season, just give it a try. And if it doesn't work out, then you can always return to your village."

"I do know now..." Conner said. He cut off his words as he caught movement out of the corner of his eye.

"So this is where you are hiding!" Princess Elissa said from the edges of darkness.

His heart stopped at the sight of her. She was dressed in a long shimmering blue gown that exposed her shoulders and lifted her young bosom. It was not the gown of girl, but of a woman, and he was stunned.

She walked to him and touched her lips to his cheek. "Thank you, again, my Champion. So what are you two talking about? You both look so serious!"

"Conner is considering leaving," Marik said softly.

Elissa stepped back, astonishment clearly on her face. "Is this true?"

Conner looked at his feet. "I do not know how to be your Champion," he said softly. "I am not worthy. I am just a commoner." He looked up and waved at the garden and the castle. "I do not belong here."

The look of horror on Elissa's face quickly went away. She stepped forward and took his hands in hers. She ignored his sweaty palms. "My dear Conner, you are strong and brave, and that is all that you need to be my Champion."

"You will learn the sword," Marik said from behind. "You are smart, and if you are willing, then you can learn to be the best."

"I am not a noble, I do not have the blood of knights in me."

Elissa squeezed his hands. "I am not asking for your blood, but your heart."

They locked eyes for a long time. He could not look away. Before this moment, he had not known what love was, but now he did. Without knowing why he tucked this moment away. It was a feeling that he would never forget, never want to forget. He was in love with Elissa, and he did not know why or how. His heart was bursting with what he felt for her, and no words could ever express what he felt. Suddenly, he knew what he could do. He knew that he could be her champion, to watch and protect her, to be for her whatever she needed from him.

Then you have my heart, he said in his head. The words passed between them without a sound, and he knew from her eyes that she heard him. He squeezed her hands, gripping them firmly.

After what seemed only an instant for them, but seemed an eternity for Marik and the guards who stood in the darkness, they released hands. "I have guests to return to," she said quietly. "But this feast is as much for you as it is for me, you should come and be announced to the city."

"I think Conner is feeling a little overwhelmed, princess," Marik said softly. "He is unused to this attention."

"Very well, then, my Champion," she said with a smile. "I shall attend my guests, and you enjoy the feast. And tomorrow, we will walk the labyrinth together. Just you and I. There is a wonderful prize at the end, you know."

Conner smiled back and replied, "So I've heard."

They watched her leave. The guards who escorted her fell into step behind. At the edge of the darkness, her head turned, and Conner could see her face and her smile.

"Food," Marik said, slapping Conner on the back. "It is time for food."

Chapter Nine

It was a cold morning, probably one of the last really cold ones until fall returned. Frost covered everything with a light shimmering glaze, reflecting the light of the full, bright moon. The sun, still yet to rise, cast a red glow on the far away horizon. As it crept up towards its afternoon peak, it would bring a pleasant warmth to the spring day. But for now, there was a chill in Brace Hawkden's body. He checked his horse over one last time. With a tug here and a pull there, he ensured that the saddle was tight. He patted the horse on its cheek, and it responded with a snort, its breath visible in the cold air. Brace wore an old brown cloak that had been stitched and patched more times that he could count. It was his favorite cloak, but too many battles had rendered it almost useless. But now, needing something to disguise his appearance, it worked for him. He wore nothing that indicated he was a Knight. But he did keep his sword, but it was wrapped in thick cloth and strapped tightly to his saddle. It was the one item that he could not leave behind. He borrowed an old hunting bow and a handful of arrows from one of the castle's cooks. They wouldn't serve well in a fight, but if he needed to bring down a deer, they would work fine enough.

"It is an early morning," Marik said from behind.

Brace turned, surprised. "Sir Marik? What are you doing up this early?" His words were sharper than he wanted as he was taken aback at being discovered. It was not that he was trying to be deceitful in leaving so early, he just didn't want to make his departure well known. The last thing he wanted to do was to be asked a bunch of questions.

"Perseus has a split hoof, and I was going to tend to him," Marik replied. "Your dress seems a bit casual."

"I have some business to attend to," Brace said curtly. Again, saying more than he wanted. Marik's appearance had really thrown him off.

Marik said nothing, he just watched his friend continue to pack provisions into saddle bags. Clearly, something was going on as Brace was not acting normal. Although Brace was not known to wear ceremonial garb like other knights, he would also never be seen in something so tattered and worn.

"It is to the north," Brace continued. "I will be gone for a week or so. I left instructions for Dell to see to things while I was gone. But I will tell you as well, as I saw you and that Conner boy together last night. The king decided that it would be best if the boy trains with the squires."

"Oh," Marik replied cautiously. "Isn't he a bit old?"

"Not the young squires-in-training," Brace said, referring to the group of young boys who were not yet truly squires. "He is to train with those his own age."

"He does not know swordplay or horsemanship!" Marik countered. "Yes, he can ride a horse, but fight from a horse? He is far from ready. They will eat him alive!"

"He is to be trained in skills that will allow him to be the princess' champion. I do not foresee him competing in jousting events, so I do not think it is necessary for him to learn to fight from a horse. But he will need to learn how to fight and be a warrior."

"Learning with boys that have already been training for five, six years?" Marik asked.

"As soon as he is awake, he will see Master Goshin to be fitted with a sword," Brace said firmly and with meaning.

"Master Goshin?" Marik repeated.

"It is the king's wish," Brace answered the unasked question. "You will see that Conner is taken care of. He is still hardly more than a boy. Young and impressionable. We must do what we can to protect him, the princess, and the kingdom."

"Conner? Yes, of course." He moved closer to Brace, interrupting the knight captain's preparations. "He is a good young man, you know. He is more than worthy of this calling."

"Worthiness will not save him in battle," Brace replied sharply. With a firm hand on his shoulder, the Knight a Captain moved Marik aside so that he could finish filling the saddle bag. "But hopefully it will not come to that."

"This conversation must go no further than you and me."

"Understood," Marik said.

"This is from both your friend and your Knight Captain," Brace reiterated.

"Sir Brace, I understand."

"Do you? If the king were to fall in battle or get sick, then the throne will be up for the taking. It would be within Elissa's right to claim the throne, but she is…well, she is a she. No woman has ever held the throne alone. And now, with him declared to the world as her Champion, it will not fall upon the Knights of Karmon to stand in her stead in battle, or in a duel. It will be Conner. He is her champion who will stand in her stead, who will defend her honor. If this Champion is not worthy, is not skilled, is not ready to defend her honor, then at best we will have civil war, and at worst, the kingdom will fall."

Marik was silent as he pondered the words. "The fate of the kingdom hangs in the balance," he said softly.

Brace laughed at Marik's serious tone. "That is why we have a job, my friend. The fate of the kingdom always is hanging in the balance. It is our job to ensure that the kingdom survives."

"Is that where you are going?" Marik asked. He did not know what his old friend was up to, but he just knew that things were not right with him recently. He was not known to disappear for days on end, and now this was the fourth time within the past few months that he left for an extended period. When Brace didn't respond but turned his head away, Marik added, "I will never question your loyalty, you know that. I have told you that countless times, and I will continue to do so. But…"

Brace hung his head. He was trapped and now caught. He was thankful for his friend. He just wished that he could share everything with him. He would, but that would also put Marik in the same danger that he was. After a moment, he said, "Kings come and go, but the kingdom must survive. If we do our jobs, then King Thorndale will rule for many more years, and our little kingdom will not only survive, but thrive. Remember, our duty is always to the kingdom first. Remember that."

Marik took a step back to allow Brace to mount the horse. Without another word and a slight tap of his heels, Brace guided his horse out of the stables. Marik watched as his friend left, waiting until he went through the gate and into the city. He didn't like where the conversation went. His trust in his friend had been solid, but now he just wasn't sure what to believe. Brace Hawkden was the bravest and most courageous man that he knew. He would never betray his king or his kingdom. But the words "kings come and go" resonated through his mind and he didn't like the impression that he was left with.

***

The king watched from his tower. He had climbed the two flights of stairs from his bedchamber to see the moon rise from the horizon before the sun did. It was one of the few chances that he could spend time alone in his thoughts without having to think about the kingdom. It was cold, but he had a warm blanket pulled around his shoulders. His chief attendant, Arpwin, a man who had also served the king's father, tended the looking glass that the king used to get a closer look at the moon. With the same gentleness reserved for newborn babies, Arpwin used a soft cloth to gently clean the glass at the end of the long tube. While performing his delicate ritual, he glanced up to see the king not looking at the moon, but out towards the garden.

Most of it was cast in darkness, but the center of the labyrinth was clearly visible. There was just a small tree, its green leaves reflecting the bright white light of the moon. Next to the tree was a simple stone marker.

"I do miss her," King Thorndale said softly.

Arpwin set the looking glass into its stand, letting his king weep silently. His heart broke for his king, sad and lonely for so many years.

"In time, she will grow up and will have no need of a champion," the king suddenly said.

"Princess Elissa?" Arpwin asked. "Yes, she will grow up to be strong, like her mother. And father."

"Not strong enough," the king said. He let out a long sigh. "If only I had a son." He turned to see the frown on Arpwin's face. "Princess Elissa is a wonderful daughter. I love her with all my heart. But this kingdom needs an heir."

Their heads both turned at the sound of a horse leaving the castle grounds. Hooves tapped over cobblestones, echoing through the courtyard and up to their ears.

"Sir Hawkden should return within a week or so with an answer," the king said. He looked down as if he were ashamed of the words that were about to come out of his mouth. Quietly he said, "And then I shall have one."

"Sire?" Arpwin asked with a raised eyebrow. Arpwin was more than just the king's faithful attendant. Although he spent most of his days tending to the king's needs, he was with the king at his most vulnerable times. He knew more than the advisors because he knew the king better. He could read his moods and many times, knew what he was thinking. But it seems that the king was able to keep some secrets to himself.

"Sire, what have you planned?" There was a bit of astonishment, a bit of fear, and a bit of accusation in his voice. He loved his king and was wholly devoted to him, but he had thought that the rash and desperate acts of his youth were long past.

"If I were to pass on without an heir, this kingdom would be torn in two," the king explained. "There's that fat idiot Neffenmark to the north. I trust him as far as I can throw him, but he has just enough of an army to hold the north and keep the Thellians at bay. To the east, Lord Kirwal has the prosperity of his city, Tyre, but no army. If Lord Kirwal didn't hate Neffenmark as much as I did, I would be afraid of them joining forces. But with no heir..." He let the words be left unsaid. He knew that with no ruler in the castle, Neffenmark would try to claim the throne as his, and ride his army against the city. There would be blood and much of it. King Thorndale had no doubt that his knights would prevail, but many good men would perish. Someday he would have to do something about Neffenmark, but because he held the north against Thell, he was more valuable as a vassal than as an enemy.

Arpwin gave his liege a stiff nod, accepting the explanation without further discussion. He had his own opinions, but it was not his place to share them. His life was devoted to the king, and it would continue to be that way as long as there was a king and a kingdom. But there were many fine women through the city and kingdom that would be able to provide the king with the heir he needed. He really didn't need to go to extreme measures to find a noble woman to bear his children. He held his thoughts and opinions to himself, knowing they would only fall on deaf ears.

The king turned back to the looking glass and adjusted it to point towards the moon. But although his eyes were looking at the moon, his mind was far away. He was selling his daughter for peace, and it did not make him feel good. He knew it was the right thing to do because the kingdom needed to remain strong. The empire had continued to stretch its boundaries and was now getting close to the eastern kingdoms that had so far been ignored. Their strength was not only in their distance from the empire's homeland but also in the peace between them. If the empire sensed weakness and strife between kingdoms, they would swoop down and swallow them up. Karmon and Thell had been bitter rivals for as long as anyone could remember. Not only would this union allow his kingdom to survive, but hopefully allow everlasting peace between their two kingdoms. But they have been rivals since the beginning of time. Their borders were always in question, and their kings were always distrustful of one another. They were not always at war, but they were never fully at peace. Peace was necessary now. They needed to settle their differences and learn how to coexist. He just hoped that the king of Thell was truly as honorable as he seemed.

After some time, the king moved the looking glass far away from the moon, towards the northern skies, up high in the sky. He carefully adjusted the position of the instrument until he had one bright light in the center of the lens. He studied it for a moment and then backed away.

"I do not understand," the king said softly.

"The new star?" Arpwin asked.

The king nodded his head. "Yes, it is still there. And if my eyes do not deceive me, I would think that it is actually getting brighter. It is even visible in the morning sky."

There was a sharp knock on the door, surprising both of them.

The door cracked open, and the Royal Guard attending the door stepped inside. "Sire, Master Goshin to see you."

"Send him in."

The guardsman stepped back out into the hall allowing Goshin to step in. He was a short man with dark olive skin that made him stand out from the rest of the lighter-skinned Karmons. His eyes were narrow and seemed as if he were always in a perpetual squint. His stringy black hair was long and unkempt as if he never bothered to wash or comb it. He wore a baggy wool tunic that hung loosely off his shoulders and down past his knees. His face was wrinkled from age, but it was impossible to tell how old he was. King Thorndale had asked him once, but he never got a good answer.

"Your Majesty," the old man said with a slight bow. "Looking through the glass?"

"It is why I summoned you," the king said.

"Oh? Is it not working?" Goshin asked.

"It seems to be working just fine," the king said. "But it is this star. It is not supposed to be there."

Goshin raised an eyebrow. He shuffled over to the looking glass and peered through the lens. "Are you sure?" The old man asked, continuing to look through the eyepiece.

"Quite sure. It is also not like any other star," the king added.

Goshin stepped back from the looking glass, looking up into the sky to where the new star was located. "How is that?"

"It does not move. The other stars, they move like you taught me. After the sun falls, the stars are in one place. Before the sun rises, they are in another place." The king fumbled through loose parchments lying on a desk nearby. He pulled one out that was well used and full of notes and other markings. "I marked them like you taught me. In fact, if my markings are correct, it is as if the stars actually circle around this one new star."

Goshin took the parchment with the markings and looked at it carefully. "You are very accurate. They do seem to circle around this one star."

"What does it mean, though?"

Goshin handed the parchment back to the king. "The stars in the sky are your gods having left the earth for their heavenly realm. Is that not what you believe?"

The king hesitated for a moment, unsure if Goshin was actually asking the question or taunting him. "Yes."

"Then your gods have added to their ranks," Goshin declared.

"But it is not what you believe," the king said.

"Does it matter what I believe?"

"You are a wise and trusted servant, Master Goshin. I do care what you believe."

"But does it matter what I believe?" Goshin asked again.

The king's eyes narrowed, trying to figure out where Goshin was going. He seemed to always want to talk in riddles to get his point across. He wished he would just say what he was thinking. The king straightened himself and said, "You are an astronomer from a land that has studied the skies for centuries. I would like your explanation as to the appearance of this new star."

"There is an explanation," Goshin said after a moment of reflection. "But it is beyond me at the moment. I know that is not the answer that you were looking for, but it is the one that you will get."

"There are times when I do not like your honesty," the king said grimly, but with a twinkle in his eye.

"And there are times when I do not like giving it," Goshin responded in kind.

The king laughed with his friend. "Can you guess? Do you not have any idea?"

"I have seen stars appear before, but they moved. Not like the other stars did, but across the sky, like the moon. They come quickly, and they go quickly. But this, I have never seen before."

"It is ominous," the king said. "As the kingdom hangs in the balance, something like this appears. I do not like it."

"The world does not revolve around Karmon. It could mean nothing to you."

"I do not believe in coincidence," the king said. "I would like to do what I can to ensure that this has nothing to do with Karmon. And, if it does, find out what I can do about it."

"I can search what scrolls I have," Goshin said. "If the library of my people were still standing, then I would be hopeful that the answers might be there. But for all I know, what I was able to salvage is all that exists. It will take some time." The old man gave the king a slight bow.

"I thank you. I hope that it is nothing, as you suggest. But I would rather have an understanding." He let his words sink in for a moment before going on to his next request. "Now, there is another matter that I must ask of you, one that is more pressing."

Master Goshin bowed again, and said, "I am your servant."

The king smiled. "I hope it is not too much to ask, but I would like to take advantage of your other skill."

***

Conner found the door after about an hour of searching. Marik had told him exactly where to find it, and it was indeed exactly where it should have been. He just got lost trying to find his way there. The castle was bigger than what he saw from the outside, which surprised him as much as it had surprised many attackers in history. The castle walls could be breached, but there were also the lower floors that greatly exceed the castle's footprint. With corridors and halls that twisted and turned, the lower floors were easily defended. Add to that the secret exits at the base of the cliff, the castle was nearly siege-proof.

Conner grasped the iron door pull and pulled the door open to reveal a lamp-lit corridor that sloped downward. With a cautious first step, he entered the corridor. The harsh light of the oil lamps made it easy enough to see by, but he still walked slowly as if he were waiting for something or someone to jump out at him. The air got cooler as he went down, but not as cold as it was outside, which he thought strange. After one sharp turn, the corridor ended at a large chamber filled with rows upon rows of swords, shields, and armor. Most of the weapons and armor were lined neatly along the walls and floor, ready to be used in battle. Others were spread across large tables, presumably being worked on. Amazed at not only the number of weapons, Conner was also astonished at the variety of weapons. There were swords of all sizes. Small swords that looked like they were for young boys, and large swords with hilts as long as his forearm. He couldn't even imagine two men being able to lift those swords. There were swords with wide blades and thin blades. Steel swords and bronze swords. There was even an assortment of wooden swords.

He looked around, seeing no one. He called out meekly, "Master Goshin? Hello?"

There was no answer, so he continued down a row of weapons of a type that he had never seen. They were each comprised of a long wooden handle, a steel ball, and a chain that connected them. Some of the balls were wooden, others were steel. The wooden balls had nails hammered in, the steel balls had spikes somehow attached. He picked one up by the wood handle, holding it carefully so that the ball didn't swing back and strike him. It was a vicious weapon that would cause a lot of damage if struck with any kind of force.

"That is mace," a voice said from the end of the row. The words spoken were heavily accented which made him barely understandable.

Conner glanced up, weapon still in hand. The man who was standing in front of him looked nothing like any other man he had ever seen. His skin was darker that his. Not tan from working in the sun like his fellow villagers, but different. It almost had a green tint to it. He was shorter than Conner and skinnier. He wore a baggy gray tunic that hung loosely off his shoulders.

Conner looked from the strange man to the weapon. He thought briefly about swinging it, but he didn't want it to come back and strike him in the leg. Instead, he set it back in its place.

"It is not for you," the old man said.

"What?"

"Mace. Not for you." He stepped forward, his eyes scanning Conner up and down. After a moment, he took four big steps to reach Conner and grabbed his hand. He turned it over, rubbed it, and then held them both while looking in his eyes. "You shoot bow, but you do not use sword."

"Yes," Conner said slowly, trying to figure out who this man was and why he was acting so strange.

"It was not question," the man replied sharply. "You are thin, with long limbs. Good for archer, bad for Knight."

"I am not a Knight," Conner said.

"Oh? Then what are you?"

Conner had to think for a moment. He didn't know who he was, or what he was. "I am Conner," he finally said. "The Princess' Champion."

The old man smiled. "Yes, I hear. And yet, you do not use sword."

"No."

The old man's smile grew wider. "Again, not question."

"Master Goshin?" Conner asked.

The old man nodded. "I am," he said.

"I need a sword," Conner said. He looked across the room at the rows of swords, resting and ready to be used. "I am to train with the squires."

"They use broadswords. They are big, wide swords that are heavy and cumbersome. Too heavy for you."

"If I am to train, then I will need one."

"Follow," Goshin commanded.

Conner did, following him down an aisle of seemingly enormous swords, most of which were taller than him and probably just as heavy. "How does anyone wield one of these?"

Goshin turned his head back and said, "Knights are grown large around here. They are trained young and eat lots."

"It must hurt to be struck by one."

"It not hurt. One strike and you would be split in two. You would not feel, you would be dead." A slight small fell across the old man's face.

Conner returned the smiled. "Unless I dodged out of the way."

"You could only dodge for so long," Goshin replied more seriously. "This one." Goshin handed Conner a sword that was not quite as long nor as wide as most of the others.

Conner went to take it, but the old man suddenly pulled it away. "Left hand."

Conner reached this time with his left hand and held it awkwardly. "I use my right hand," Conner protested.

"You will train with left hand," Goshin said. He paused for a moment before adding, "When you train with the squires, you will train with left hand. They train with clumsy weapons using clumsy techniques. You will learn strength with left hand. "

"But I shoot a bow with my right hand," Conner said.

"You will not shoot bow while you train. When you train, you use left hand," Goshin repeated. The man turned and walked away from the enormous broadswords.

Not sure what to do, Conner followed Goshin away from the racks of broadswords towards the back corner of the room. Past some shields of various sizes and shapes, Goshin came to a stop at a small rack of thin swords. He stood, looking at the swords for several moments before picking one up and handing it to Conner.

Conner clumsily moved the wooden training sword to his right hand and reached for the long, slightly curved, singled-edged sword with his left hand.

Master Goshin slapped the wooden sword out of his right hand painfully. "No! Right hand."

Confused, Conner took the sword with his right hand. He looked at it closely. It was actually lighter than the wooden sword but had a single, sharp edge that curved slightly to a pointed tip. He took several practice swings and Goshin looked on with approval.

"I have never seen a sword like this. It is so light. Will it break?"

Goshin laughed aloud. It came out as a sharp burst and lasted for several seconds. "That sword has been used for centuries by my people from the west. It is shunned by Knights as too light. But in right hands, with right training." He handed Conner a second, identical sword. "And with two swords, you become not just man, but machine."

Conner moved the two swords, one in each hand, trying to figure out how he would fight with them. "How would I defend myself with no shield?"

"Shield not necessary," Goshin replied. "With these and much training, you could dodge forever." A sly smile crept across the westerner's face. "Or at least long enough to kill your opponent."

Goshin took one of the swords back and carefully placed it back in its slot. "We will begin tomorrow. She is yours."

Conner looked around, wondering what he was talking about and then he realized that he was referring to the sword. "Mine?"

"Yes."

"Start with a real sword?" Conner asked. "The squires only use wooden swords."

"It is the only way," Goshin replied. "Squires are clumsy and will cut themselves. You are not. When with me, you train with steel. When with squires, you train as they do."

Conner slowly looked over the sword and said, "I have never seen or even heard of this type of sword."

"It is light sword that does not carry much punch," Goshin replied. "Which is why they do not use it and look upon it as if it were but a twig. A knight is strong. And slow. Which is why their broadswords work for them. One strike can cleave a man in two."

Goshin took the sword from Conner and looked at it closely. Then, with a quickness that belied his age, the old man swung the sword three quick times. "This sword, thin and light, can cleave a man in two as well. But only if you know how to use it." He then sheathed the sword in a simple leather scabbard and handed it back to Conner.

"You will teach me?" Conner asked.

The old man paused and looked closely at the young man who stood in front of him. After a moment, he replied. "Yes. I will teach. But, will you learn?"

Conner nodded, an eagerness in his eyes that told the old sword master that he did not clearly understand the question.

"I am from a village named Tobin from the far, far west," Goshin said. He turned to walk, but Conner did not move. "Come, come. You must understand if you are to learn."

Conner followed while Goshin continued. "Tobin is located on a large island. We were part of an ancient civilization with a history that exceeds even that of the Taran Empire. We call ourselves the Hurai. It is part of a race of people that are different that you. Our skin color is different. Our hair is different. The shape of our eyes is different. I do not know why God made us so different."

"Each of the gods made a different race in their own image," Conner interrupted. "That is why we are different. And the gods are jealous of one another, so that is why we fight one another."

The laugh exploded so quickly and loudly that Conner took a step back. "Oh, my young pupil you have much to learn." Then suddenly the humor in Goshin's eyes left and was replaced with steel darkness. "The first of which is to not speak when your Master is speaking."

"Sorry," Conner said meekly.

"Because we are so different," Goshin continued. "The kingdoms and empires around us thought us weaker and easy prey for the warriors. And for some time we were. Our lands were constantly being invaded. Our women and children enslaved and our men forced to fight for others. A revolution grew up some thousand years ago that freed our people from a notoriously bad emperor. We came together as a single people, ruled by a wise man, and prospered for many generations. One of the wise things that he did was to begin a school for warriors. As many of our men had trained and learned many different styles of being a warrior, we had experts of all sorts. Our wise leader took the best of all the disciplines and made a single fighting style. This school taught that fighting style and developed the Sak'hurai, master warriors of the Hurai. We have never been beaten in battle. No single man could ever stand up to a single Sak'hurai. A master Sak'hurai could easily handle five heavily armed knights."

"No!" Conner exclaimed. "That cannot be true."

Goshin ignored the interruption and continued, "It is not because one Sak'hurai is better than five Karmon Knights. It is because knights fight slow. They move slowly because of their armor. They are taught to fight with strength. A Sak'hurai is taught to fight with speed and quickness. One strike of a knight's sword can be matched by ten slashes of a Sak'turana, the sword of a Sak'hurai. Your people call our weapon a scimitar because they do not know any better. Yes, it is like a scimitar because it has a single edged blade, and it is forged with a slight curve to it. Yet, a Sak'turana is more than that. It is an extension of the warrior. It is the warrior."

Goshin had led Conner out of the chamber of weapons, down a dimly lit corridor, and to a large, open natural cavern. The scent of the ocean was heavy, and with Goshin no longer talking, he could hear the crash of the waves on the cliffs. A number of torches were lit around the perimeter of the cavern giving just enough light to see. It was clear this was where Goshin lived and worked. The cavern was strewn with every imaginable piece of equipment that a blacksmith would use. There were many swords and other weapons in various stages of production. But the center of the chamber was clear and open.

"Here you will train," Goshin said. "You will earn that sword you carry, and in time, you will earn her twin."

"I can learn from the knights who teach the squires," Conner protested, wondering what he had gotten himself into. He just wanted to learn to fight like the knights so he could be a proper champion to the princess.

"No," Goshin's replied curtly. "You will commit and sacrifice, or you will leave."

Conner remained silent, not quite understanding Goshin's meaning. "Leave? As in leave this cave?"

"I mean leave castle," Goshin explained further. "Leave the city and return to your home."

"I have committed myself to be champ…"

"No!" Goshin shouted. He took two steps and was in Conner's face. He was a few inches shorter than Conner, but his mere presence caused Conner to shrink back. "You have committed to nothing. Now. Now you must make a decision. But know this: this is not a game. You do not become her champion because it is something you want to do. You do it because you are committed to saving her life. To sacrificing your life for hers." He took a step back, letting his angry words dissipate into the shadows. After a moment he continued, "I left my country many years ago, soon after I attained the rank of Master Sak'hurai. I spend my days making weapons using just some of that which I was taught. The rest…" He tapped the side of his head. "Remains up here, but is aching to get out. The rest, I will teach you." He tapped Conner on the chest. "I will teach you that this is where your strength begins and ends."

Conner did not understand. He could learn how to be a swordsman without all of this. He could learn how to wield the swords of the knights, to be like them. He knew that he could never be one, but he knew could be as good as them.

Clearly, the confusion was written on his facial expression, so Goshin continued. "You are not much more than a slave. In fact, a slave may have it better than you as a master is responsible for his slave, where you are responsible for yourself. If you die, no one will care, save your family. If a slave dies, then the master is responsible, and may even face judgment from the king. You will forever be a nothing. You will spend your days hunting for food, trying to stay alive. And then there is nothing for you when you die."

"There is Nirvana," Conner argued. "The gods will take us to their kingdom when we die, and we will live in peace forever."

Goshin muttered something in his own language softly. "Very well, be gone, then. You should leave quietly and return to your mother's bosom. You are still a young child and should still be suckling at her breast."

"I am no young child, I am a man! I have killed."

"You have killed? How many? A hundred? A thousand?"

"Three," Conner replied, eyes dropping to the ground.

"And I have killed seventy-eight in my lifetime, and that does not make me more man than you," Goshin replied. "I see each one that I have killed still in my mind, and there are days that I am sick for what I have done. But I did it because I had to, not because I wanted to."

"So did I."

"Yes, you did. You protected your princess. If not for you, she would be dead. That is truth. And now you run, run from your princess. Because why? You are afraid?"

"No!" Conner shouted out.

Goshin waited patiently for Conner to correct his reply. "Yes."

"Then good," Goshin said. "You should be afraid. Fear will keep you sharp."

Goshin stepped forward and placed both hands on Conner's shoulders. "Knights are bred for their strength and size. When mother and father are big, their children will be big. When mother and father are small, children will be small. But sometimes, even when mother and father are small, child will be big."

Conner blinked, not understanding. "My father was just normal sized, I am sure. I do not remember what my mother looked like, either. But I am sure she was normal sized, too."

Goshin smiled and let a soft laugh escape his lips. "It is an old Hurai saying. We do not have classes like you. There are no lords and no peasants. Anyone can attempt to become Sak'hurai, but only the best will be given that honor. You do not need to be born with certain parents. You can be the poorest of the poor, and if you have the courage here." He again tapped him on the chest. "Then you will be given the right to name your Sak'turana and become a Sak'hurai."

"But I still cannot become a Karmon Knight," Conner said.

Goshen let out a long sigh. "I am not asking you to. I am asking you to become Sak'hurai. I will teach you, but you must listen. I cannot learn for you. I cannot make you courageous. I cannot make you strong in heart. Only you can do that."

"I can do that," Conner replied with as much confidence as he could muster.

"The days that come will determine if you believe you can, and that will determine if you will." Goshen stepped back and motioned to the center of the chamber. "Now, today, you will learn to stand."

Chapter Ten

Brace Hawkden sat still atop his horse, waiting for the sun to finally dip below the horizon. The castle was far off in the distance, just far enough for his bad eyes to make out the twin spires that shot up from corners of the stone keep. When he was younger, he would have been able to make out the archers that sat atop the battlements, or if the sun was behind him, he might have been able to see a soldier keeping watch from a window. But it had been some time since his eyes were that good. Now he just trusted his memory to know that the fuzzy gray building he saw far in the distance was Lord Neffenmark's castle.

He was still in the trees, covered in the shadows that had fallen some time ago. If anyone standing atop even the tallest tower had seen him, it would have been a miracle. He was on higher ground than the castle, with the peaks of the towers just below his eye level. The builder of the castle, Lord Keffenkarn, great-grandfather to Lord Neffenmark, had built his castle halfway up the side of the valley. Any attack would be uphill. With the mountain at its back, the castle was very defensible, almost to the point of invulnerability.

No invader had ever tried to assault the castle. Once, before Lord Neffenmark was even a thought in his father's head, Thell had sent a raiding party to test the castle's defenses. Only a handful of Thellians had returned home to report how well defended the castle was. The steep slopes up to the castle would have made it very difficult to bring siege engines to break the walls. But Brace had heard of great machines called Trebuchets that could sling rock and fireballs great distances. Where he stood might be a good spot for them. He just hoped he would not have to learn how to build one of those devices.

But those were thoughts for another time. Today, his thoughts were only on the mess that he was now in. The message, sealed with the king's wax, was safely inside his tunic. He could feel the parchment as it scratched his side. Each tickle, each itch, reminded him of his treachery. He had no choice but to bring the message to Lord Neffenmark, to let him in on whatever plan the king was hatching. Failure to do so would mean that he would be exposed by Lord Neffenmark as a traitor, his place in life would be forfeit, and Knighthood itself would suffer a serious scar. He could handle himself. Whether he was to be executed by the king's hand or to be exiled into the great frozen north, he did not care. But it was the thought of the downfall of the Karmon Knights that kept him from riding into Thell. Knighthood was based on courage and honor. Yes, they were great warriors. They were feared not only for what they could do with their sword but because they were fearless themselves. They were respected not only as soldiers but as men because they did all that they did with honor. Centuries of honor and respect could be washed away with this one fell mistake.

For so long he had told himself that what he did was for the greater good. He hated the Thellians with a passion that was only held for one's worst enemy. There was not one of them that he thought was worth spitting upon. But the king thought differently. He saw them not as their enemy, but as their neighbors, their brothers to the north. Brace had not understood it then, and he still did not understand it. All their plans, all their scheming, all the secret meetings to get Karmon and Thell to finally go to war was treachery. The king wanted peace, and the king represented the kingdom. If he disagreed with the king, then he should have shared it as his personal counselor, not going behind his back to an evil cretin like Lord Neffenmark. How many times had he told himself the kingdom was greater than the king? But the kingdom was the king and the king was the kingdom. They were one and the same. How he had forgotten that.

Maybe it was because he saw his king as a man. He had seen his failures as much as he had seen his successes. He had seen the man break down and cry at the birth of his daughter, and the unimaginable fury when he discovered his daughter had been taken away from him. He had seen the king act like a failed man more often than he had seen him act kingly. And that didn't make him think less of him, but it made him think more of him. Maybe that was why he had long since stopped thinking as everyone else did about their liege lord. He loved the man, but he had let his friendship overshadow the fact that the king was the king.

He wanted to scream out his frustrations, but he only sat silently, knowing what he really should be doing. He knew the king would give him mercy, but he didn't know if he wanted it or not. He would deliver the message, and let the king's decision be the king's decision. He was not the king, and he should not act like it.

With dusk now upon him and the sun below the trees far to the west, Brace Hawkden turned his horse back into the woods to find the trail leading north into Thell. A great relief was lifted from his shoulders. He was a traitor, and he would pay for his crimes. But he would do so with whatever honor he had left.

***

The archer, hidden in the trees, cursed silently to himself. His orders were clear. He could only take the shot if he knew for sure the man wasn't heading to the castle. It was a long and painful wait, and by the time the rider moved, it was so dark, he could barely discern tree from the rider. His original plan had been to hide deep in the woods and sneak up on his target from behind. With a good enough shot, the man would never even know that he was going to die. But at the time, he didn't think it sporting enough, so he hid closer to the edge of the forest, so he could strike the man from the front. They had said he was the great Knight Captain Brace Hawkden, so he wanted to give the knight a sporting chance. He hid in the underbrush, using his skill and knowledge to keep out of sight.

But the knight had never come out of the woods. He was in just far enough that he could barely see him in the failing light of the evening and now that night had fallen, he could only see shadows. A missed shot would be deadly for him. His skill was with the bow and not with the sword. Had the knight known he was being hunted, the tables would be quickly turned on him. His only recourse would be to run. And run fast. But not back to the castle, as Lord Neffenmark would surely kill him. He would make his way to the empire where he could just blend in and disappear. Lord Neffenmark did not like failure, which was why he was here in the first place.

The archer waited for a few minutes before following. It was not difficult as the knight's horse made enough noise to easily follow. But his going was slow as he had to stay with the hunter. He made steady progress as minutes turned into hours and the woods gave way to hills and hills gave way to the mountains. The knight was being careful, moving slowly enough to ensure that the horse found safe footing in the rough terrain, but just fast enough that the archer couldn't get close enough for a good shot.

But as the knight came closer to the mountains where the ground was rougher, rocks were strewn about, and crevasses and gullies began to make their appearances, the archer had the advantage. This was his land. He knew the rocks and trees as well as anyone. He knew the path the knight was taking as it was the only safe option to get to the pass that led through the mountains and on into Thell. So rather than pursue him, the archer sprinted to a spot where he knew the knight would pass by.

And sure enough, not too long after he had settled in, he saw shadows move in the night and heard the patter of horse hooves on the hard ground. Slowly, the knight came into view along the path that he predicted. The archer brought out his bow and a single long, black arrow. He would only need the one. He knew he was that good. He stood and pulled the fletching back to his ear. As he adjusted his body into position, his right foot kicked the ground, making just enough noise for the knight to freeze. The horse's ears perked and the knight pulled back on the reigns so that he could listen for more sounds. It was just what he needed. The knight was a perfectly still target. The archer released the arrow, and it flew straight and true for the man's neck. It would be a bloody and painful death.

His heart sank in the instant that he released the bow as the knight, having been tired and worn from days of travel, straightened from his hunched position. Rather than a killing blow through the neck, the arrow sunk deep into the upper chest of the knight. The archer nocked another arrow, but the knight, the warrior that he was, knew that more arrows would come. The knight slid down in the saddle, putting the horse between himself and his assailant. In the same instant, he kicked the horse into a full run.

Without a thought, the archer adjusted for the sudden movement and loosed his arrow at the large shadow that was the horse. The arrow struck deep into the side of the horse, sending it kicking high into the air, throwing the knight off its back. But to the archer's dismay, the knight didn't just strike the ground and stop, he bounced and fell, sliding down into the darkness of a deep chasm.

The archer's third arrow silenced the screaming horse for good. Like its rider, it fell down into the chasm, to be lost forever. He would have liked to have saved it for an easy ride back to the lord's castle, but the first arrow had mortally wounded it anyway. The archer raced to the edge of the road and looked down into darkness. The sides of the chasm were steep, too steep to climb down. There was no sign of the knight, but the bottom was unseen in the darkness. For good measure, he fired three more arrows into the blackness of the deep, but he knew that the knight would be dead soon if he weren't already. There was no way out of the chasm. The sides were steep and smooth for as far as he could see. For several more minutes, he waited, hoping to hear any sounds of the knight trying to climb out. But he heard nothing. Satisfied that the knight was dead, he scouted the area and found the knight's sword, just inches from tumbling off the edge of the trail and into the chasm. He picked it up, thanking the gods for their mercy. If he had no proof of death, Lord Neffenmark would not believe him and would likely kill him. There was always the option of trying to climb down and find the body, but he knew it was a one-way journey. With sword in hand and not a hint of guilt on his conscience, he began jogging back towards Lord Neffenmark's castle.

***

The archer slinked through the main gate of Lord Neffenmark's castle when the guard's back was turned. He didn't need to, but the hunter in him enjoyed the thrill of the surprise. Most of the time when he tried to sneak into the castle, at some point one of Neffenmark's minions caught him. But occasionally, he made it all the way into the lord's plush quarters. The guards were barely skilled with arms. They were pulled from the villages of Lord Neffenmark's domain and were poorly trained by other poorly trained soldiers. The archer knew that they would be inadequate in battle. It wasn't because they couldn't swing a sword or thrust with a hauberk, it was because they were peasants at heart. They were not drilled to kill or to see death. They were drilled only to have their lives taken instead of the lord's.

He didn't care, though. His devotion to Lord Neffenmark went only as far as the gold coins that he was paid with. As far as he cared, the castle could be overrun by the Thellians, and he would just sell his service to the northern barbarians. He almost regretted sneaking in because it would mean the lashing of the guards who weren't capable of properly defending the castle. But that was Lord Neffenmark's way. It meant that he didn't have to pay them very much. They were expendable.

Once inside the castle, he moved quickly through the shadows, his ears perked to listen for the soft patter of feet through the corridors. He knew the castle well, as he had been here many times. He could probably navigate its halls blindfolded. Two lefts and then a right, and he was just outside the great hall. He could hear that the lord was in audience with someone, arguing over unpaid taxes. It would tire Neffenmark out, and he would return in due time to his own chamber. He easily picked the lock of a back door and quickly entered into the darkness of the lord's residence.

Two large windows provided just enough light to see by. Night had fallen quite some time ago, and the moon had yet to rise. But the cloudless skies allowed the infinite stars to shine brightly, and that gave the archer all the light he needed. He took a goblet and poured it full, drinking the sweet wine deeply until gone. He filled the goblet again and drained half of it before his thirst was quenched. A plate of cheeses and fruits was spread out on a table, waiting for Lord Neffenmark's return. The archer stuffed his mouth, chewing as quickly as he could. In the end, he did more swallowing than chewing.

He heard the voices at the main door a moment before he knew they would open. The archer's first reaction was to duck and hide, but his mind forced his body to relax. He wanted to be in the open, to be caught red-handed. It would certainly keep him from being accidentally killed if he were found to be sneaking around, stealing the lord's fine wines.

Lord Neffenmark threw the doors open and marched in, his boisterous voice belittling his thin, emaciated servant. But the words stopped mid-sentence as soon as his eyes fell upon the archer, who was standing in the middle of the room, munching on a handful of ripe red grapes. The eyes grew wide, and his face flushed with anger. His mouth moved as if to say something, but no words dared come out. Instead, he headed straight for his sword, which hung from a peg on the wall. But before he took two steps, the archer tossed a sword to the floor. It came to a skidding stop at Lord Neffenmark's feet.

The redness faded, but the anger in the eyes did not. He turned to his servant and ordered the torches of the room to be lit. Quickly, the servant did so before disappearing back through the door.

Once they were alone, Neffenmark stooped down with a grunt and picked up the sword. He eyed it carefully before saying, "Someday, your impetuous arrogance will get you killed."

The archer smiled, still chewing his grapes. "Not until you actually find some guards that can actually guard."

With sword still in hand, Neffenmark walked across the room to the platter of food. The archer grabbed a handful of cheese and backed away, making sure that Neffenmark was farther than arms reach away. Despite his girth, the fat man was known to be an able swordsman.

"He is dead, then?" Neffenmark asked with a mouthful of food.

"He was struck with my arrow, and fell down into Krafer's Chasm. I found his sword at the edge of the trail, just before the cliff drops off."

"You were supposed to cut off his head and deliver it to me," Neffenmark said with a slight smirk.

"The body is at the bottom of the gorge. If you would like to see it, you may drop yourself down into it."

The smirk spread to a smile. "You have no fear, my friend."

"I fear many things," the archer replied firmly. "You are not one of them."

Lord Neffenmark laughed heartily causing his thick jowls to giggle. He pointed the sword directly at the archer. "And that is why I like you."

The archer smiled back. "I think I will take my money, now."

Neffenmark nodded. "And you shall have it. All that you have earned."

The archer's smile faded after a few moments when the lord of the castle did not move. Lord Neffenmark stood silently, unmoving. His eyes were bright and full of life along with something else. Was it mirth? Or maybe satisfaction? The archer glanced around, looking for someone else in the room. But he saw nothing, heard nothing, felt nothing.

Neffenmark, seeing the eyes of the archer said, "We are alone. Are you afraid that someone else is in here?"

"I do not fear you, nor do I trust you," the archer said. A bead of sweat started to fall from his hairline. The wine was tasty, and must not have been watered down, as he could feel its effects on him. He was a bit light headed and almost dizzy. He generally avoided wine or anything stronger as it had a direct effect on his aim and his senses. And this wine did affect him, although it seemed to creep up on him slowly. As he thought about it, the wine should have affected him more quickly, numbing his senses and making him feel warm and tingly almost as soon as he drank deeply from the goblet. But he was feeling something different, something that he'd never felt before. He didn't feel better, as wine would do at the onset, he felt worse. His stomach cramped, and he gripped his side.

The smile on Neffenmark's face grew wider. "We are in the endgame, my friend."

A steady stream of sweat poured down the archer's face, and his heart began to pound heartily. He looked at the pitcher of wine, sitting alone in the center of a table, a single goblet next to it. It had been set out for a single person to partake, and it wasn't for the fat lord. His face flushed, and his breathing became labored. He clutched at his chest, trying to take in more air, but it was as if someone was squeezing his chest, keeping him from breathing. He knew of poisons and knew that some weren't fatal, they just made you go to sleep. But as he fell to his knees, he knew that whatever was in that wine had killed him. If he had just an ounce of strength left, he would have hurled a knife at the fat blob of a man. He could have killed him easily, if only he had the strength. But the lord was smart, too smart.

The archer collapsed onto the ground, his limbs unmoving and unfeeling. He wasn't dead, yet. He could still hear. He could hear the door opening, the sound of footsteps, and Lord Neffenmark giving the order to dispose of his body. He couldn't breathe, and his body ached for air. He wanted to kick and scream, but his body was stiff and uncontrollable. He felt himself being picked up and thrown over the shoulder of a heavy-set man. He bounced once, then twice, and then things became fuzzy. He didn't dread the darkness. He accepted it, only hoping it would come more quickly, to end the agony. He knew he was dead, but death had not quite taken him. He wanted to cry, wanted to shout. But then the darkness did come, and he knew no more.

Chapter Eleven

Brace Hawkden moved, and there was pain. He thought, and there was pain. He tried to localize the pain, but it seemed to be coming from everywhere. There was no escaping it, he could only embrace it. With tremendous effort, he forced himself to open his eyes. The daylight burned as much as anything, but he forced himself to keep his eyes open.

He was on his back in a somewhat comfortable position. There was a thick wool blanket that covered him from legs to mid-chest. His head rested on a stiff cushion of some sort. He tried to sit up, but pain exploded from his legs and up his back. His movement seemed to cause some activity as voices suddenly could be heard. But it was in another language, one that he was not familiar with.

An elderly man, with a long, stringy gray beard streaked with a bit of black kneeled over him. The old man's steely eyes scanned up and down before finally coming to rest upon him.

The man said something, obviously directed at him, but he did not understand, so he shook his head. "I don't…" he croaked out.

The old man glanced back away as if he were looking at someone or something. Then he asked, "Do you understand me, now?"

"Yes."

"You are injured, and you must rest," the old man said. The grim face softened into something of a smile. "I am Mirfar. You?"

After a moment of clearing the cobwebs, the injured Knight Captain of Karmon said, "Brace."

Again, the old man looked away. This time, Brace stretched his neck to see what the old man kept looking at. They were at the center of a camp in the mountains. There was little else but rock and dirt around them. Three other men were huddled around a fire, which was next to a small tent. Brace could not see any weapons, but he figured there must be some within easy grasp.

"That is a name known to me," Mirfar said, his eyes still looking at the group of three men. "It is a name that many have cursed."

Brace's heart jumped. It all started to come back to him, now. He was heading towards Thell, having decided to skip Lord Neffenmark's castle. He would indeed deliver the message to the king of Thell. But then his horse suddenly reared back, knocking him to the ground and over a cliff. He fell and rolled, seemingly forever. That was the last thing he remembered. He looked closer at Mirfar. Thellians didn't look much different than Karmons, as they shared some common ancestors. But there were always little things that would distinguish one from another. He could not be certain, but Mirfar certainly looked and acted Thellian.

Sensing a change in Brace's demeanor, Mirfar placed a hand on Brace's shoulder. "Do not worry. I have nursed you back to life. I will not do anything to harm you."

Brace pushed himself up onto his elbows. "I have a message. For the king."

The old man chuckled. "You are far from your king's castle."

Brace shook his head. "Not mine. Yours."

The old man took his time thinking about Brace's revelation. After a few moments, he said. "We are far from our king's castle as well. Too far for you to travel in your condition."

Brace sat up, grinding his teeth hard at the pain that was shooting up from his leg.

"You have a broken leg. If you ever walk again, it will be a miracle," Mirfar said.

"The message must be delivered." His hand drifted up to a spot on his upper chest that was sore. He remembered vaguely getting struck in the shoulder just before falling into wherever it was that he fell into.

"You were lucky with that one," Mirfar said. "A glancing wound. The arrow did not go deep, and I was able to pull the arrow head cleanly. I have packed it with mud, so it will heal faster."

"Mud?" Brace asked.

The old man smiled and tapped him gently on his good shoulder. "It is an old remedy."

The other three men had noticed that Brace was awake and now had made their way over to where he was resting. They didn't look as old as Mirfar but had the same weathered, harsh look.

"You cannot travel as you are," Mirfar declared. "There are no wagons to carry you, and even if there were, the land is too rough and rocky. We don't have horses up this high. Only a mule to carry our supplies."

Brace looked around. "How'd I get here, then?"

"Bellock found you." Mirfar nodded at one of the other three. Bellock was the largest of them, with a large barrel chest, big arms, but a soft baby face. "He carried you up the mountain to our camp. He saved your life."

Brace looked at Bellock and said, "Thank you."

Bellock nodded and said something in Thellian.

Mirfar said, "The others do not speak your tongue. Only I do. Bellock says that he hopes he did not hurt you worse. But I fear that he might have. Your leg is damaged badly. I have wrapped it up with a splint."

"Splint?" Brace asked.

"I am a healer," Mirfar explained. "Broken bones heal better and faster if you can keep them from moving about. It may not heal right, but at least you are alive."

Brace reached down and touched the thick branch that was tied to his leg. It was tied tight, and Brace couldn't move it. A throbbing sensation pulsated from his legs. Mirfar shoved a bowl of thick liquid under his nose. Without much thought, Brace drank it. It had an odd fruity taste, which made the thick substance bearable.

"That will keep your leg from hurting so much," Mirfar said. "It will not make the pain go away, but it will make the pain not so bad."

"It is not so bad now," Brace said stoically.

Mirfar smiled and replied, "You are a strong man, and your courage is well known. But you must rest, now."

"My message, it must get through."

"If it is written, I can have it delivered."

Brace fell back slowly onto his back and let out a long sigh. "No, it must be delivered in person."

"Important, then?" Mirfar asked.

"Yes, very," Brace replied.

Mirfar cleared his throat and asked carefully, "It is not a declaration of war, is it?"

Brace smiled with his eyes closed. "No. Not war. Peace."

"Then I will help you with your message," Mirfar said. "Rest, and I will discuss this with the others."

***

Conner stank from head to toe. It had been probably the most miserable job that he could have ever imagined doing. Although he had grown up around animals and knew their stench, it was completely different when they were confined to small spaces. There was no wind to blow away the smell. The horrid reek of wet manure hung in the air, thick as his aunt's pea soup. He could have handled the horse barn where the stalls of the precious mares and geldings spent their nights. Those were changed on a daily basis, a ritual event for the younger squires. Fresh straw bedded the stalls after the horses were taken out for the day. It was an easy job that didn't take too long. But the pens of the pigs were a different story.

With the great festival of summer coming the following month, the cooks of the castle were to prepare a hundred hogs for roasting. They had to be large, fat hogs, full of juicy, tasty meat. They had been brought in from outside the city only two weeks ago, and the pens were already a disgusting mess. Conner figured that the pens had not been cleaned since they were brought it. So two weeks of urine and excretion had turned into a sloppy mess that caused Conner to continually gag. A towel had been tied around his mouth and nose, trying to keep most of the smell out, but it also made it hard to breathe. And it didn't work really well anyway.

He hadn't been alone, as three other squires serving the same punishment were relegated to this duty. But while they worked slowly to avoid having to return to the training grounds, Conner worked as fast as he could so that he could return to training. But it was to no avail, as he not only missed the morning training session with the other squires, he missed his afternoon training with Goshin. He had skipped lunch, hoping to finish that much quicker. But the only thing that did for him was to make him extremely hungry by the time dinner came around.

Eventually, he did finish, but he was covered in slop, and he feared that he would never be the same again. Every pore in his body seemed to absorb the smell of pig. Every crevice, every nick, every cranny, was filled with manure. He stank and stank badly.

It was dark as he walked through the city, back towards the castle. The pens were far away from the castle so that the king would never have to experience the putrid smell of pigs. His hands were sore, his back ached, and he wanted nothing to do with the squires who wouldn't work fast enough for him. He had left them some time ago, taking a left when they took a right. He thought briefly about muggers until he remembered how bad he stank. No one in their right mind would try and get within ten feet of him.

"Conner! Is that really you?"

He stopped in his tracks and looked up. His heart sank. Princess Elissa was standing in front of him, a thick wool cloak pulled tightly around her. He wanted to find a hole to crawl into, but there were none nearby. He could only nod in his filth.

"Uh, what…" her words got stuck as the scent of pig reached her nose.

"Pigs," was all that he could say. He was mortified. He would have rather come across the king himself than to have Elissa see him in his condition. He started to walk away.

"Wait!" she shouted, coming another step closer. "I haven't seen much of you lately."

"I've been a bit busy," Conner replied.

"I see," she said, laughing again, putting her hand to her face to cover her nose.

"What are you doing out here?" he asked.

She shrugged her shoulders. "Sometimes I walk the streets at night."

"It's not really safe, is it?" He looked around, expecting someone to be lurking in the shadows, ready to pounce on them. They were alone in the streets.

"Safe enough," She replied. "It's not like there are murderers and thieves around every corner." She gave him her wide, pretty smile.

There was an awkward silence as he hoped that she would move on and she hoped that he wouldn't.

"How goes your…" her question trailed off.

"Training?" Conner said. "It goes fine. Mostly. Except today, when I made Sir Plendoor angry, and he had me clean the pig pens."

She covered her mouth with a hand to stifle another laugh. "I hear he is a moody sort. But a fine knight."

"I guess so," Conner replied. "He does not like me very much."

"Are you getting good, yet?" She asked innocently.

Conner gave her an inquisitive look and asked, "Good? Good at what?"

"At being my champion, silly!" Elissa said with a giggle.

Conner was suddenly reminded that although she had grown into her woman's body, she was still a girl at heart. And she would be for some time. Standing there, in front of her, with his heart melting at the mere sight of her, Conner felt alone and overwhelmed. He was doing this for her, and he was failing. Every muscle in his body ached. Every pore was saturated with the smell of pig. He was not good, at least not yet. He wondered if he was ever going to be worthy of serving as her champion.

He missed his bed, even though it was really not much of a bed. It was just the corner of a small room in aunt's house. But it was his bed. It was hardly more than a pile of straw and the blankets that his aunt gave him were barely enough to keep him warm, but he still missed what he had called home.

But Princess Elissa stood in front of him, her long blonde hair framing her perfect face. She was as beautiful a woman as he had ever seen, and every time he laid eyes upon her, his heart leapt right out of his chest. He found it hard to think, much less breathe around her. He didn't know what to say. He stumbled over his words, trying to find just the perfect thing to say. But he knew he always sounded dumb.

The seed of something bigger had been planted in him from the beginning, and it was starting to take root. He wanted more than to just be her champion, he finally admitted to himself. He genuinely liked her and found her friendship something that he really desired. And if he were to leave now, he knew that he would never see her again. She might even forget about him. For certain, he would spend the rest of his life, thinking about her day and night. He couldn't leave. Despite the loneliness, the tired and sore muscles. Despite being nearly beaten into submission every day by his fellow squires, he knew that he had to stay. It was not for her, but because of her, he told himself.

He dropped his head partly because he was tired, partly because he was too ashamed to speak his mind. "It is late," he said and started to walk towards the castle.

Princess Elissa fell into step with him and said, "So, Conner. Tell me about your home."

Conner did not want to talk. His aching body was begging for sleep. His mind was numb, and his words were barely able to come out, but he told her.

"My parents died when I was young. My mother of some disease when I was real little. My father when I was a bit older. They say he went to bed one night and never woke up."

"Oh…" her voice cracked. "I had no idea. How awful!"

Conner smiled at her response. "I hardly have any memory of them, so I guess I don't miss them. Really, it's okay."

Tears formed at the corner of her eyes. She knew what it was like to be without one parent, but she could only image what it would be like to be without both parents. "You really don't miss them? Not at all?"

"I live … well, I slept at my aunt's place. My dad's sister. She took me in, but she was kind of a mean old lady. She was much older than my dad and pretty much raised him growing up. I guess she didn't really care to raise another one."

"I'm sorry."

"Don't be. I had a fine childhood. I spent much of it in the woods hunting. Sometimes I'd be gone for weeks, sleeping under the stars, living off the land."

His pace slowed as her jaw dropped. "Really?" she asked with a smirk.

"Seriously!" Conner replied with a laugh. "The first time I did it, I was really mad at her about something. A month later I came home carrying a big buck on my back. She didn't say a thing. We skinned and gutted the deer, cooked and cured it."

"How old were you?"

"Ten."

"Ten!" she exclaimed. "It wasn't until I was twelve before my father would let me even ride through the woods. And then I had to be escorted by a dozen Royal Guardsmen!"

"Sometimes I miss it. My aunt. My village. It was my home for so long. But I guess this is my home now." He glanced at her, and she smiled back at him. When he looked up, he realized that they were only a few feet from the castle gate.

Elissa stopped him with a soft hand on his shoulder. "Thank you for walking me home."

He smiled. "It was nice to talk to you."

"We should do it more often," she said, returning his smile.

"I would like that," Conner said.

Her hand moved out and touched his, giving it a gentle squeeze. "Tomorrow night, then. In the garden." She spun on her heels turning away from the gate, her blond hair whipping in the wind.

Conner gestured towards the castle gate. "Are you not coming?"

She smiled with a twinkle in her eye. "I come and go another way."

***

Conner didn't want to move. He could have if his life depended on it. But since it didn't, he didn't move. He sat with his back against the cool cavern wall, sweat pouring down his face, stinging his eyes. He was too tired to wipe his forehead, and if he had tried, his muscles would have rebelled, as they were too sore to move. He had let the sword drop carelessly at his side, landing blade-side down. If Goshin had seen the blade treated so casually, the old man would have had a fit. But at the moment, Conner didn't care. Nothing mattered at the moment, only that he was in perpetual pain.

Until recently he had been sleeping soundly at night. Between his morning sessions with Goshin and afternoon training with the squires, there was little else for him to do. He had the chores of a squire in waiting, which he was mostly able to do. Many times he hurried through them so quickly, they weren't good enough for his instructors, so he ended up with extra work, such as cleaning out pig stalls. But sleep was no longer coming easily to him at night. After he had started spending time with Princess Elissa at night, walking under the moonlight through the labyrinth, his mind was just too active to shut down and allow himself to sleep. She was beautiful, but everyone knew that. But there was so much more to her. In their time together, they talked about so many different things, and she taught him so much. He was also amazed at what she knew about the kingdom. They talked about the city and how the government worked. They talked about how goods from the Taran Empire made their way across the gulf to the docks of the city, through the kingdom, and even up north to Thell and the other eastern kingdoms. Sometimes Conner forgot how young she really was. She was barely a woman, just old enough to bare children, but certainly still young enough to play and joke around like a child. And she did plenty of that, but she still walked and talked like the princess she wanted to be.

She talked at length about wanting to follow her father and rule the kingdom. She shared what she had learned from her father, from him directly, or from just watching him. And then she would get quiet, as she would talk about how she knew her father did not think of her that way. He thought of her has his little daughter, almost as a favorite toy, something that he could take out and play with when he wanted to, and put her on a shelf when he became bored. He was a loving and doting father and would do all he could to protect her. But she knew he never thought of her as the next leader of the kingdom.

Conner was fascinated by her. She was so young but so smart. He had never really thought of her that way until she started to talk and share her feelings and her ideas. It also made him a bit insecure around her. She could read and write as well as anyone. He had learned to read a little bit, but he really had no reason to write. Maybe he would talk to Goshin about that. That would surely make him better in her eyes.

All thoughts of Princess Elissa faded when Goshin approached with a number of scrolls tucked underneath his arm. "Rest time almost over," Goshin declared.

Conner tried to smile as a bit of humor came over him. "Are you now to teach me from your mysterious scrolls?"

Ignoring the comment, Goshin started to carefully insert the scrolls into leather cases. "These are ancient writings from a people called the Ishralla. I have spent much of my life studying their works. While you rest, I do not. I study. But rest time is over."

"Ishralla?" Conner asked, trying to extend the conversation. "I have never heard of them."

Goshin turned his head and gave Conner a fatherly smile. "Of course not. Their kingdom no longer exists, and their peoples are scattered across the earth. They have no country or king, but they do have a history." He paused for a moment as he set the leather cases into a wood cabinet. "They are the favored people of God."

"This is the one God that you talk about?"

"Yes," Goshin replied softly. "The scrolls were written many thousands of years ago by people inspired by God. They have been passed down by the people of Ishralla, carefully preserved since they were originally written."

"Those scrolls are thousands of years old?" Conner asked. "What do they say?"

"No to first question. They were written twenty-five years ago by a monk, copied from one of the many other copies that exist. I do not know if the originals exist, but plenty of copies do. As to other question, they talk of many things. Some about the past, some of things to come."

"Things to come?" Conner asked, his curiosity more than piqued.

"Yes. Prophecy. The plans of God have been laid out since the beginning of time. The Word of God is written to help us know and understand Him and what is to come. Many of the prophecies seem to revolve around the fact that someday, God will return to His kingdom, back to earth. "

"Oh, like Mishan and Tishan, the gods of the sea and land are to come back to…"

"No!" Goshin retorted sharply. "The prophecies are not about your gods, but about the one God. He will come back to save the world. At least that is what the prophecy reads. But I do not understand much of it. It is written in a language that is not used anymore, by men and women that were much closer to God than I am. I do not understand all of the prophecies, but there are some events that are listed that proceed the coming of God. One such passage talks of a light growing in the west."

"A light?" Conner asked. "What kind of light?"

"It is not clear, but it could mean a star," Goshin replied. "The king has a looking glass that he uses to look at the moon and the stars. He has spied one star that suddenly appeared. It could be the light that the prophecy is talking about. Or it could be coincidence." He eyes strayed back to the cabinet that held the scrolls.

"What does it mean?" Conner asked.

"For you, it means it is time to train." His face was as stoic as it always was. But Conner could see that there was something different in his eyes. For the first time since Conner started training, Master Goshin was not totally focused. He was distracted.

"I need more rest," Conner said, closing his eyes and leaning his back against the cold cavern wall.

"No rest," Goshin declared. "We have much to do."

Conner shook his head. "I cannot. I want to, I really do, but I cannot do any more today."

Goshin's already narrow eyes narrowed. "You have much training. We cannot waste any more of the day. Enough has been wasted already. Now it is time to get to work."

Conner wanted to cry, but he forced his eyes to remain dry, and his voice strong. "You constantly tell me to listen to my body. And now my body is telling me to rest."

"Your body is telling you to be lazy, and you are listening," Goshin said between clenched teeth. He was clearly trying to hold in his anger. "I tell you to listen to how body works, so that your mind and body are one. I do not tell you to let your body rule you. Your mind rules your body. Your body can do anything your mind tells it to."

"My mind is as tired as my body. I cannot go on."

"You are weak," Goshin spat the words out. "I should never have started this. You cannot learn the ways of the Sak'hurai. We are done. You may return to your barracks and sleep there."

Goshin turned quickly and walked away.

Conner pushed himself up, every muscle screaming in pain. Without thought, his hand grabbed his sword. "I am not weak, and I will be Sak'hurai!"

Goshin stopped but did not turn around. "Your mind is far from Sak'hurai. A Sak'hurai thinks nothing of those around him, thinks nothing of anything around him. They train from the day they can walk until the day that they die. They live Sak'hurai. Every waking moment is Sak'hurai. For you, you spend some time here with me, learning the moves, but you do not learn Sak'hurai. You walk late nights with your princess when you should be letting your body rest. Your mind is not Sak'hurai."

"I have learned, and I am Sak'hurai!" Conner shouted back.

Goshin spun, a sword in his hand. Conner did not know where it had come from. But it was not a dull training sword. It shone brightly in the yellow torch light of the cavern. Conner moved, lowering his base as he was taught, letting his sword come up and absorb the force of the blow. Goshin's blade was deflected away from Conner's head just at the last moment. Conner stepped back, finding himself in the right stance, his sword up and ready. His heart pounded, but his breathing was calm. Just as he had been taught.

"A Sak'hurai does not stop. Such a blow by me should be met by attack, not defense. You should have pressed the attack."

"You are better than me, you would have..." Conner protested.

"A Sak'hurai does not know better," Goshin snapped back loudly. "A Sak'hurai is better. He is either the best, or he is dead. He does not back down from one better because he knows no better. He is best." Goshin lowered his sword. "You are not Sak'hurai."

"I can learn," Conner pleaded. "I can be Sak'hurai!"

Goshin watched his pupil for a moment, studying not his stance, but the focused look in his eyes. Finally, he said, "Truly, in a short time, you have learned much. In fact, more than I thought you might. But you cannot be Sak'hurai."

A look of astonishment flashed across his face. "But if I am to be the princess' champion…"

"You do not need to be Sak'hurai to be her champion. You are her champion by being."

Conner felt his remaining strength fall away. The adrenaline rush that had been fueled by Goshin's attack was gone. He let the point of his sword drop to the ground. It took all his effort to keep the sword in his grasp.

Goshin stepped forward and placed a hand on his shoulder. "You are her champion now," he said. "You do not need to be Sak'hurai to be her champion."

"I want to be," Conner protested.

"You cannot be both her champion and Sak'hurai. A Sak'hurai sacrifices all. I do not believe you are ready to let her go."

Conner let the sword fall to the ground. "It is over, then?" Conner asked.

Goshin stood silent for several long moments before finally speaking. "No. I shall continue to train you. But not as a Sak'hurai. You are not ready for that. I do not know if you will ever be ready for that."

Conner surprised himself by allowing a tear to streak down his cheek. He lowered his head in shame. What little strength he did have left was swept away like a beach in a storm.

"A Sak'hurai has no feelings. No emotion. But you do. Maybe that is why you cannot be Sak'hurai."

"Then I have failed," Conner said.

Master Goshin took a deep breath. "No, it is I that have failed you. As much as you cannot learn to be Sak'hurai, I cannot teach it to you. I can teach you the moves. I can teach you to dance with swords, but I cannot teach you to be Sak'hurai. And that is my failing."

"Then I have failed, "Conner said.

"What now," Conner asked.

"Kin San," Goshin replied. "I can teach you to be Kin San."

"What is that?"

"It is a word that means fighter or warrior. To a Sak'hurai, it is someone who can fight with a sword but is not really trained. It can also mean a soldier in an army. But I must call you something and Kin San is as good as anything." Goshin smiled at the worried look that came across Conner's face. "Do not worry. The moves and skills that I teach, you are that of a Sak'hurai. There are just some things that you will never be able to master until you can become Sak'hurai. Shall we begin?"

Conner could barely move. He could barely hold up his sword, but he nodded.

Goshin held out his sword for Conner to take. "You will need this."

Conner looked down at the sword that Goshin was handing him. It was the twin of his own, the one that Goshin had refused to let him use.

"It is time for you to learn to dance with your swords. You may never become Sak'hurai. But maybe, just maybe, you might be able to fight like one."

Chapter Twelve

Brace put a little weight on the leg, and it felt as if someone drove a knife deep into it, twisted, and then pulled it out. He used all his strength, power, and courage to keep from letting out a shout.

Mirfar leaned close and whispered into his ear. "It is still too early. Your leg has not healed."

"I am fine," Brace said between gritted teeth. "I have done nothing but sleep for days, and I will go crazy if I have to sit for one more!" Using a long limb freshly cut from a nearby tree to lean on, he hobbled his way towards the camp fire.

"You are a stubborn people, you Karmons," Mirfar said with a smile.

Brace stopped and turned back to the man who had saved his life. He could have left Brace to die, but he didn't. And not only had he kept him alive, but he had made sure that his leg was taken care of well enough that he would soon be able to walk on it. Brace simply smiled and let out a soft laugh, unable to come up with the words that would express his gratitude. He knew that he would not have done the same thing. His hatred of the Thellians had run deep. But now, he looked at the man who called himself Mirfar, and he looked no different than any typical Karmon. He smiled, he laughed. He was not an animal, but a man. It was a shame that he had spent so much of his life hating.

Bellock, the big man, had made a thick rabbit stew. He dished a scoop into a wooden bowl as Brace approached. The other two men were already eating and looked up from the bowls for just a moment before returning to their dinner. The other two never talked. They were old, but not quite as old as Mirfar, but much older than the youthful looking Bellock. Mirfar had explained that they were nomads, wandering across the mountains while the weather was still good. They would make their way west as it got closer to fall to avoid the harsh winters of the north.

The rabbit stew was good. Most anything that Bellock made was tasty. He had a fine hand with cooking and an ample supply of spices. Brace raised his bowl in appreciation to the big man, who smiled back in return.

"It has been decided," Mirfar said in between bites. "Kirwin and Lillimar will take your message to the king. They are trustworthy."

Brace shook his head. "The message will not be the same if it is not from me. I must go."

"You are unable to ride with that leg. If we had a cart, we'd throw you on the back and haul you there. But we are in the mountains, and we have no cart. If the message is as important as you say, then this is the only way." He patted Brace on his good leg. "If your message is well received, then maybe our countries are entering a new age of peace. I have known nothing but fear of you Karmons for as long as I have lived. It will be nice not to have to live with that fear."

"Fear?" Brace asked. "What do you fear from us? It has been your soldiers that have gone south into our lands, killed our villagers…"

"We fear the Knights of Karmon," Mirfar said, cutting him off. "If you wanted to, you could march through our cities, killing us all. We have an army, but it is made up of farmers and merchants. We have some soldiers, but I have met them, and I despise them. They are no more soldiers than the dogs that run with them. True soldiers are honorable. Like you!"

Brace blushed. "Not all of us are," he said softly. "We are still killers at heart. It is what we do."

"And why are you here? For peace? You are not all killers."

Brace reached into his tunic and pulled out the wax sealed message that the king had given him. He handed it to Mirfar, hoping that he was as truly honorable as he seemed. The old man wrapped it up in a piece of hide and handed it to Kirwin, who took it and stuffed it inside his own shirt.

"They will leave soon and will return in four days. Two days there, two back," Mirfar said. "We will remain here until they return. You will rest and heal some more."

Brace nodded his acknowledgment. He still did not buy into the fact that he had to give away the message. He had made a vow to the king that he would deliver it himself. But then again, Brace thought with great sorrow, he has broken many such vows.

***

Conner adjusted the shield, gripping the inside leader strap tightly with his right hand. His left hand lightly gripped his wooden practice sword, and he swung it several times, ensuring that he had a good feel for the sword's weight. He was getting better with fighting left-handed, but he was still slower than everyone else. There wasn't a time when he actually ever won a practice match. But he knew it was working. There was no doubt about that. The strength and skill of his left hand was slowly catching up to that of his right. Goshin promised that someday he would be able to fight with either hand as any Sak'Hurai could. But Goshin always stressed that someday was really some year, far into the future.

He was also getting less and less tired each day. He figured the more he trained, the more tired he would be. And at first, that's the way it was. But Conner had suddenly noticed that he didn't constantly feel like he wanted to take a nap all the time. Arms and legs didn't ache as much, or as long. The blisters on his hands had calloused. But most importantly, he knew he was getting stronger. He could see on the faces of the squires when he connected with a solid hit. It actually hurt them as much as he was hurt when they struck him.

Today ended the week's training, which meant that they would have tomorrow off. Well, everyone else would have tomorrow off. Conner would still work with Goshin. But at least he would only have one training session instead of two. The training session was also lighter today because they would end it with some one-on-one practice sessions. Each squire was matched up, and they would fight using tournament rules. But rather than the blunt steel that was used for tournaments, they would still use their wooden swords. They couldn't kill or even cause much damage, but it still hurt. Headshots were not allowed, as this was still training. A strike on a limb was one point, and strike to the body was two points. The first fighter to ten, as scored by their instructor, was declared the winner.

They trained in a yard behind the stables. There was some grass, but it was mostly dirt now from the squires' long hours of training. A large open window about halfway up the castle wall allowed spectators to look down upon the training in the comfort and protection from sun, wind, or rain. Occasionally a curious knight would settle down at the window and watch his future warriors battle it out. But every once in a while, when the castle was quiet, and there was little else to do, someone of a little higher stature would make an appearance.

***

"I am sure there are other ways to spend our time," the tall girl whined. Her long and curly brown hair flowed across her shoulders and halfway down her back. "We could ride through the country, or walk through the garden. Anything but this!"

Princess Elissa looked out the big open window. The skies were gray without a hint of blue. It even smelled like it was going to rain. She turned to her friend and said. "Melanie, it is going to rain. We just had our hair done and I will not have it ruined by a ride in the rain." She smiled a sweet smile while Melanie pouted. She could have just said that she was the princess and this is what they were doing. But it just didn't feel right. Melanie was her friend, and she genuinely liked her and liked spending time with her. "When the weather clears, and the sun comes out, then we shall ride."

Melanie plopped on one of the cushioned seats that an attendant had carried up three flights of stairs. "They are all dirty and sweaty," Melanie protested. "I bet they stink, too."

Princess Elissa sat down next to her friend and looked out the window upon the squire's training ground. Conner was there, as she was told he would be. She watched him closely as he swung the wooden sword, pretending to stab, then to slash. Then he suddenly stopped at looked up and their eyes locked.

And when their eyes locked, Conner lost all feeling in his limbs. She was there with her friend, a girl that he had seen before, but had never met. When she smiled at him, he lost his breath. He did not understand what this meant. Yes, she was beautiful, but the girl next to her was pretty, too. Yes, she was the princess, but was that it? Was this feeling that was so excruciatingly painful and joyful just because she was the princess? A bead of sweat started high on his back and made its way down to his waist. He let the itching sensation come and go while he held her smile with his eyes.

She gave him a little wave, and then he caught a flash of movement. At the very last moment, he lifted his shield across his body to protect his head. The sword struck hard, hard enough to send him to the ground. If he had been an instant slower, the sword would have caved in the side of his head. His heart exploded, he could feel blood pumping adrenaline through his body, driving his reserve energy stores to his limbs.

He had not heard the start of the match, and if he had a moment to think about it, he would have thought that the instructor had intentionally started it when he was distracted. But he didn't have time to think, he only had time to react.

With him fighting with his left hand, and his opponent fighting with his right hand, it meant that the traditional use of the shield as a defensive weapon was not very useful. But it also meant that it was useful as an offensive weapon. As soon as Conner found his feet, his opponent, a much older squire named Eyron, used his shield in just that manner. The shield struck Conner in the face sending him back onto the ground and stars flashing in his eyes. Conner rolled, avoiding a sword strike while he was down, and kept rolling until he was out of range and could collect himself and get back on his feet. Conner attacked with his sword, but his left hand was still much slower and weaker than the squire's right hand. Thrust, parry, slash, parry, thrust again, parry again. No matter what Conner tried, the squire easily countered him.

But what made Conner angrier than anything, was that Conner knew he could beat him. If he could ditch the shield, change from the heavy and thick longsword to a light Sak'turana, he would dance around this buffoon. But he used the traditional blunt force style of fighting that everyone was taught. Conner could predict the squire's movements, calling them out in his head. He even knew how he would counter and attack if he weren't forced to use these stupid wooden weapons.

It wasn't long before Conner lost his patience and pressed the attack, opening up his side for Eyron to smack him hard. Conner winced at the blow and his anger escalated. He stepped back to let his side recover from the blow. He knew there was going to be a big bruise there in the morning. It had been a solid hit from the flat of the wooden sword. He ignored the pain and sprung forward, ignoring everything that he had been taught. His only thought was on defeating the squire who had made him look bad in front of the princess. In quick succession, before Conner quite realized what had happened, he was slapped on the leg, then on the arm, and then finally on the side again. The last strike was in the same location as the first hit and it sent a shockwave through his body that caused him to fall to his knees. Gripping his side, he accepted his defeat and sulked off the field without a glance back up to the princess.

Princess Elissa watched with her mouth agape, too stunned to say anything.

Melanie, however, did not hold back. "That is your champion?" She let out a snort. "He was beaten to the ground!"

Melanie went on, but Princess Elissa did not hear. She watched him walk off the field, shoulders hunched, sword dragging on the ground. It was a mistake. This whole champion thing was a mistake. That wasn't the same young man who had saved her life in the woods. That was a little boy running away with his tail between his legs. She fumed with anger at her own stupidity. This boy could not protect her or save her from killers. He had killed to protect her, to save her life. But she had seen with her own eyes that he could not even stand up to a squire. How then could he stand up to a real threat? What had happened in the woods was just lucky, she realized. He really wasn't the man she thought he would be.

He was still walking away when she stood up, ignoring the prattle coming from Melanie. His shield was still strapped to his right hand and he dragging the ugly wooden sword with his left. She looked at the other squires, most of whom were cheering on two other combatants. Their swords were in their right hands. That made her think, and then she became even angrier. Why was he using his left hand? Why was he trying to lose the fight? She stomped off furiously, too angry to cry.

Chapter Thirteen

Conner looked into the closet and cringed. Partly because of what he saw and partly because he moved again. His side still hurt, and even Goshin realized that his wound was more than just sore. The purple bruise was as ugly as it was painful. With regret, Goshin let Conner have the day off to rest his side. However, instead of being sent to his barracks for resting, he was sent to the tailor.

"Oh, Conner," Filbert Crossin said with a heavy sigh. The finely dressed tailor had shown Conner the best of the best, and the response that he got was not one that he had expected. He had expected that Conner would drool with excitement at the intense colors of the fine silk clothes, expertly and painstakingly stitched by the finest clothiers of the Taran Empire. "These are the clothes that even the emperor would wear! They were delivered over land some years ago to avoid the harsh salt of the sea that would linger with the clothes forever. Yearly, these caravans would come with a handful of clothes, and invariably, the caravans would lose one or two with each crossing." He waved his hand at the closet full of clothes and continued talking. "At least a dozen good men have given their lives so that we can have the finest clothes the world could offer."

Conner walked into the closet, fingering the doublets, cloaks, hose, tunics, leggings, and other garments that he did not have a name for. They were full of colors, some that he had never even considered for clothes, and some he had only seen on the ladies of the castle. Dresses full of the bright reds and greens and blues on the young ladies was fine, but he could not picture himself in them.

"Other squires and knights wear these?" Conner asked.

"A young courtier, one who has the eyes and ears of the princess should be dressed as finely as he can," Filbert said with a nasally tone, his eyes narrow and thin lips stretched into a permanent grimace.

"I am just a peasant boy," Conner said softly.

"You walk straight and tall, with confidence and purpose," Filbert said. "You may pretend that you are a simple boy, but there is much more to you than what is on the surface. You are to mingle with royalty, so you should dress the part."

"Royalty…" Conner repeated.

"Here, this bright blue tunic will make you look the part. And looking the part is what counts." Filbert held up the tunic for Conner to see. It was thin silk that would easily tear if he were to wear it out in the woods, but it did look comfortable. "With this thick leather belt and a pair of dark blue hose, you will look as if you belong."

Conner took the clothes from Filbert, fingering them, and wondering how they would look on him. But more importantly, he wondered if he would indeed feel like he belonged. He knew he didn't. He knew where he stood in the scheme of things. He wasn't royalty and would never be. Only the gods could declare who was to be king. He could never be a knight for he had the wrong blood flowing through his veins. Only those with the right pedigree would ever take the training and kneel before the king and become one of the greatest warriors that had ever walked the earth. But he was taking the training. The same training that the other squires were getting. And then he smiled to himself. He really was not getting the same training. His arms were hard, and his body lean and toned. But it wasn't because of what he did with the squires. It was Goshin. His evil teacher who pushed and pushed, and then pushed some more. But the muscles were no longer sore. His chest no longer heaved with pain when he ran around the city. He would be better than a knight. Better than any knight.

He looked around for a private place to change, but there was none. Filbert stood a few steps away, looking bored as he always did. He turned his back to the tall and the thin man quickly switched out his dirty garments for the fine silk ones.

Clad in his fresh silk, he walked the halls with his head held high. He had no purpose, other than to show off his new clothes. He meandered from one corridor to another, taking a path that had the most voices. The finely dressed courtiers that walked the halls themselves all nodded their head to him, not caring who was in the clothes. He smiled back. Soon he was getting comfortable with the nods and the smiles. Faces that he recognized no longer looked down upon him, but acknowledged him as an equal. And that's how he felt. Finally, as an equal.

He ate lunch on the lawn behind the castle, overlooking the crashing waves of the ocean. It was a surprising invitation, and he still did not know who it was that invited him. But as he was striding purposefully, he came across a group of slightly older men and ladies, all finely dressed as he was. Two servants walked behind, caring large baskets full of food. He had long since stopped only nodding to those who passed him by but offered a word or two of greeting. After a short conversation later, he was given the invitation to join them on the cliffs.

The lunch was a good meal of dark bread, cheese, and fruit. He would have preferred something a bit meatier, but it was tasty none-the-less. With his belly full, and the conversation of the weather and late spring flowers grown dull, he leaned back on his elbows and looked out across the bay. Somewhere over there was a different land. The Empire of Taran. He had rarely thought about the empire, but now, as he looked across the wide expanse of water, he wondered what it was like. He had heard a little about it, mostly stories from the other villagers who had heard stories from travelers. Some of the tales, such as wizards walking the streets casting spells left and right seemed just a bit too fantastic. But others, of grand cities stretching for miles upon miles, boggled his mind.

"My young man," one of the courtiers said, interrupting his thoughts. Mayfair was the eldest son of one of the king's advisors. He had lived his entire life in the castle, only making his way into the city when absolutely necessary. He spoke with the same nasally tone as Filbert did. It was an odd tone, and it seemed entirely unnecessary. It was as if they wanted to speak differently than everyone else. "Your eyes look far and wide across the bay. What thoughts do you have this day?"

Mayfair sat down next to Conner, joining him in looking across the water. Conner wanted to laugh at the self-described poet, but he held it in. He was tall and thin and didn't seem to have an inch of muscle on his entire body. He probably had never lifted anything more than a hair brush his entire life.

"Taran," Conner said. "Just thinking about what it would be like to visit there."

A couple others joined them on the soft green grass. Robert was another son of some lord from the south part of the kingdom. Lauran and Gayle were both children of knights. Their brothers were squires in training, but they spent their days in the castle, waiting for a husband to take them out of the castle. They were both young and pretty, but could barely hold a conversation.

"Oh," Lauran said, fear spreading across her face. "That is an evil place. I hear they sacrifice their first born to their god, Wartell."

The others murmured agreement.

Mayfair laughed. "You are silly young children." He seemed to be the leader of the group of courtiers, possibly the eldest, but also clearly the smartest. "Taran is a grand empire of incredible culture. They have the greatest scientists, able to move water from the rivers around their great cities to the center of town without so much a bucket. They have medicines that can cure diseases that would fall the greatest knight. And their works of art are beyond belief. Paintings and sculptures. Poetry and works of literature that would make the strongest man cry like a baby."

"You have been there?" someone asked.

"Yes," Mayfair said softly to the astonishment of them all. His voice was low and soft. "When I was young, my father went on a diplomatic mission to Tara, their capital city. I was young, four I think. All their streets are cobblestone but smoothed from a thousand years of foot traffic. Their buildings, stone structures built to withstand eternity, stretched as far as one could see." He paused to look back over his shoulder. The city of South Karmon could be seen behind them, stretching quite a ways in the distance. But beyond, they could see the forests. "Our city would be but a small section of Tara. Of the memories that I have, I remember looking out from a small tower of the emperor's palace and seeing nothing but stone buildings and wood houses. We can see the trees of the forest from here, but from the center of Tara, the only thing you see is more city."

Conner listened intently and was enthralled. He had lived his life in the forests, hunting for his food, huddling close to the warmth of the fire during the cold winter months. And when he came to South Karmon, he was amazed. The castle was impressive, but the city was just as amazing. There were so many houses and buildings. More than he could have ever imagined in one place. But as Mayfair continued to describe the city of Tara, Conner became enchanted with his poetic descriptions. He described stone buildings that were bigger than their castle, taller than the tallest tower. Some were wider and bigger than the entire grounds of the castle, including the gardens. His mind wandered as he pictured himself walking the cobblestone streets, filled to the brim with people walking here and there. The tall buildings sending shadows across the streets. With Mayfair's poetic voice, he knew he was there, even if it was only in his mind.

"I will go there," Conner suddenly announced.

"But you are just a boy!" Gayle exclaimed, covering her mouth in astonishment. "It is not a place for you."

Conner laughed. Where he was now was not the place for him, but he did not share those thoughts. "I will ride my horse down the cobblestone streets, from the first city gate to the palace. And then I will make an audience with the Emperor, and I will meet him."

"The Emperor meets with no mere man," Mayfair said. "There are millions of people in the empire. All would want to see him, but hardly any will. Only the greatest of men will have an audience with him."

"Then I will be the greatest of men," Conner declared with a wide smile.

This caused an outburst of laughter from everyone around them. He sat up, laughing himself. But their laughter seemed just a bit too hard. And just when their laughter was about to subside, they would look at him, and their laughter would begin anew. It didn't take too long before he realized that they were doing more than just laughing with him, they were laughing at him.

"I'm serious," Conner said with some force. "I will be the greatest of men, and I will go before the emperor. In fact, he will ask to see me."

This caused more laughter. Lauran, between fits of laughter, said, "But you are just a peasant boy. You are nothing." And then the rest burst out into an even greater fit of laughter.

Conner stood and proclaimed, "I am the Princess' Champion!"

For a moment, the laughter ceased, as they observed his anger. But then one giggle led to another, and then their laughter continued. The anger didn't just come to a slow boil, like a pot of water, but it exploded from nowhere. He picked up Mayfair by the front of his tunic, grabbing more than a handful of silk. His fingers ripped right through the thin fabric, but he had grabbed enough to hold firm. He pulled the taller, but much lighter man to his feet and tossed him like a rag doll across the lawn. Mayfair went tumbling towards the cliff. Only a small hedge kept him from falling to his death.

Conner turned to the next man, another skinny courtier who tried to scurry away on his hands and knees. But Conner caught him, pulled him to his feet, and planted a closed first across the cheek. Screams followed. Lauran and Gayle had been closest to him, and they hiked up their dresses and ran crying towards the castle. Two want-to-be heroes stood up to Conner, but they had spent their lives being primped and cared for. They did not know how to fight. One push, one punch, and they both fell and crawled away.

The two servants had run away, calling for help. Almost immediately, two royal guards showed up, armed with short swords. The anger still burned inside of Conner and it did not abate even when he saw the armed guards running towards him. He did not think, he only acted at what he perceived to be the threat. He moved forward, unafraid that being unarmed and going into a fight with armed soldiers might not be a wise choice. Goshin had taught him well.

Conner moved left just as the two guards approached, ensuring that he would take on only one guardsman at a time. They tried to speak to him, to calm him down, but Conner was not listening, his newly found instincts had taken over, and his anger was strong. The first guard took a fist in the face, his nose exploding in blood and mucus. He fell to the ground, dropping his sword and holding this broken nose. The second guard, attacked with his sword, not stabbing as he would normally do with the short sword, but swinging with a wide blow, the flat of the sword aimed at his head. It was not meant to kill, but only to incapacitate him. Conner, recognizing the non-lethal strike, took the blow with his left forearm and drove his foot into the knee of the guard. The knee popped, and the guard fell.

"Hold fast!" the shout of a familiar voice broke Conner from his anger fueled outburst. Conner stood still, but Marik shouted again, "Hold fast!"

Then Conner turned and noticed two other royal guardsmen perched atop the castle walls, bows in hand, arrows aimed directly at him. Marik was not shouting at him, but at the guards who were about to plant arrows in his back.

"You have some explaining to do," Marik said angrily as he approached Conner. He looked back up at the guards, arrows still aimed at them. "Stand down, I said!" Marik shouted out at the guardsmen. Reluctantly, the guards stepped away.

To Conner, Marik said quietly, "They itch to be more than the simple guards that they are. You are lucky that I was nearby when I saw your little outburst or the princess would be without a champion."

Conner looked around at the mess that he had made. Mayfair was still on the ground, moaning. The man that he had punched was kneeling and crying with his head buried in hands. The two guards that Conner and taken out were being tended by three others that had run to their rescue. They all looked at him with a bit of anger and a much disgust. Conner moved towards the guards, to apologize, but Marik held him from moving.

"Now is not the time," Marik said. "You can make amends later when they are not as angry and less likely to lash out at you." He pulled Conner's face to look him in the eye. "You are the princess' champion, which means something. It is more than just an oath that you took to protect her. It is a duty to serve this kingdom. Your little temper tantrum is not acceptable. Not because of the result, but because you lost control. A warrior, a true warrior, knows when to fight. He knows how to control his emotions and not lose it. But also, because you have taken an oath to be the champion of Princess Elissa, you must comport yourself above and beyond who you were before. You are no longer a simple peasant hunter."

Conner shook his head. "They laughed at me. They made me mad and I...I will never be like them."

Marik took Conner by the shoulder, and they started walking away. Mayfair's friends had returned and were tending to him. "No one is asking you to be like them."

"But you said..."

"I said you are no longer a simple peasant hunter, I did not say that you are to be like them." He waved his hand back at the silk clad courtiers. "You are to be better than them. Especially if you are to serve Princess Elissa."

"I think I should get rid of these clothes," Conner said. Somehow in the melee, a rip had formed on his sleeve. "They do not seem to hold up in combat."

Marik laughed, and they walked in silence for some time. They walked around from the back of the castle towards the knight's barracks. The sound of training drifted towards them.

"How goes the training?" Marik asked.

"Okay," was all Conner would say. He was tired of the squire training. Goshin had allowed him to go so much further in his abilities, but he could never show off his new skills. The old sword master had made it perfectly clear that he was to never show off what he had learned. It didn't make much sense to Conner, and he reluctantly agreed. He didn't like it, but he went along with it.

"How will you do at the Summer Festival?"

"Probably not well," Conner said. He knew that if he were able to use everything that he had learned from Goshin, he would win many prizes. But with only being able to use his left hand to fight, the yearly squire competition would be an embarrassment for him.

"Goshin has not taught you anything?" Marik asked, a smirk spread across his fast.

Conner turned and shared his own smirk. "He has taught me much."

"Then you should do well," Marik pressed.

Conner lifted his left hand. "If I could use more than this, then maybe."

"There is much benefit to learning how a knight is supposed to fight," Marik said. They had reached the edge of the training grounds and were now watching a handful of knights, dressed in thick leather armor, training with one another.

"If you know what your enemy is going to do next, you can anticipate his moves."

Conner looked over at Marik with a raised eyebrow. "How is training to fight as a knight is going to make me fight my enemies better?"

"The fighting style used by Karmon Knights is not unique. Many warriors have imitated this style to some degree of success. Many warriors are trained this way, including Thellian warriors. To fight the Thellians would be like fighting your brother knights. The difference is that they are not taught quite as well, or train quite as hard."

"What about the Tarans? How do they fight?"

"Tarans?" Marik repeated thoughtfully. "I am not an expert, nor have I ever seen them fight, but I have heard many tales. They fight with numbers. In battle, they will always have more soldiers than their enemies, and that is why they rarely lose. They do not fight from horseback, but from the ground. They use archers by the thousands, sending waves upon waves of arrows upon their enemies. They are well-disciplined and efficient, but not necessarily highly skilled. One on one, a Karmon Knight would easily defeat a Taran Warrior. But they are also very inventive and have come up with some war machines that

I can barely describe. They can hurl burning rocks from a mile away, making it easy to knock down city walls from a distance, and then charge their warriors through the broken walls. It is rare for them to face defeat." And this caused Marik to smile.

The smile was contagious, and Conner could do nothing but smile back. "What?"

"Their biggest defeat came some several hundred years ago. It is not remembered because it happened so long ago, but it is something that all Karmon Knights learn about."

"What happened?"

"The emperor of that time wanted to stretch his realm as far as he could, and when he realized that our little kingdom was here, he decided it was ripe for the pickings. So he loaded up many ships full of his warriors and sent them across the bay. And we met them on the beaches and turned them back. They could not offload their warriors fast enough. As soon as they landed, our horses were upon them. Wave after wave they came until they finally gave up and went home. The next year they tried the mountains, but when they came out of the passes, only half of their soldiers had survived. Again, we slaughtered them. Our knights against their foot soldiers were too much for them. The following year, a single boat came to offer peace. Our isolation protects us some, but the skill and courage of our knights protect us even more. They are a force to be feared, and I would never want to take them on if they had the full might of their army. As much as we were successful in repelling them, we were lucky because of where our kingdom is. Mountains to the north and deep forest all around our shores make Karmon a tough place to conquer."

"I had no idea that the empire ever tried to invade us," Conner said. "I had always heard about the dangers of the Thellians to the north, but never about Taran."

"We are insignificant in the scheme of the world. We are a tiny kingdom compared to most others. Even Thell is larger than us."

"Larger?"

"There is a map on the back wall of one of the king's chambers. Thell's land goes far to the north and quite far to the east. Three, maybe four times our size. But much of their land is cold and desolate. Which, I think, makes them cranky and irritable, and why we have never been able to find peace with them. Taran stretches far, so far that it takes months on horseback to travel from one end to another. They are seemingly constantly at war with one nation or another.

Which is why it is easy for a small kingdom like ours to go unnoticed. We have little to offer them that they don't already have, and we have no interest in making trouble with them. So I guess, they just leave us alone."

They watched the knights for some time in silence. Only the sounds of the wooden practice swords and the grunts of the dueling knights filled the afternoon air. Conner watched them intently, knowing that he could beat them. They were powerful but slow. The skills that Goshin was teaching him would allow him to so easily defeat even the best knight, as long as he could stay away from their heavy blades. He was quick, too quick for them. He watched and studied their techniques, and it did not take long for him to understand how to easily beat them.

"You will do well at the Summer Festival," Marik said. "It is a time for squires to show their best. I hope you do that."

Conner nodded, but he knew that unless things changed, he wouldn't be able to.

"Being a fighter or warrior is one thing," Marik said. "A knight must learn more than how to swing a blade. He must control his emotions, control his anger, lest he will become impatient and he will lose."

Conner touched his sore side. "You saw?"

Marik smiled. "Of course. I saw you lose your composure. Even fighting with your weaker left hand, you could have defeated that squire. But you let your emotions get the better of you. You must learn to fight with a cold, methodical bearing. Once you start to let your emotions get involved, you will fail."

"But I will never be a knight, why should I learn to be one?"

"The moment you stop caring about being a knight will be the moment when you reach your potential."

"I have never wanted to be a knight," Conner said.

"Then why do you keep bringing up the fact that you will never be one."

"Sir Marik!" They turned to see Arpwin walking towards them. As he got closer, Arpwin asked, "A moment, if you please."

Conner stood, but movement at the stables distracted him. Four saddled horses were being led from the knight's stables. Two were large, dark brown war horses. The other two were smaller. One was a spotted gray mare and the other was bright white. The smaller riding horses were adorned with silk trimmings and soft blankets. Conner watched with anxiousness, suddenly feeling lonely in the cold confines of the stone castle. He had been able to explore around the perimeter of the city on occasion, but it had been some time since he had been able to ride out into the forest. And he missed it. He missed the great expanse and solitude. He was about turn towards Marik and Arpwin to learn what was being said when further movement caused his heart to stir.

Princess Elissa emerged from the stables, dressed simply in a long pink gown, her hair tied behind her head. She had a wide smile on her face as she chatted with her good friend Melanie. Two squires, dressed in thick leather riding clothes stood to the side, waiting for the girls to mount their horses. As soon as they approached their steeds, two attendants appeared with stools to assist them in climbing atop their horses. It was then that Elissa looked over and caught Conner's gaze.

Conner smiled and waved, but Elissa's smile turned to a frown. She tossed her hair back and settled herself atop her horse. Conner was too stunned to react. His confusion grew as he saw two large sacks strapped to the back of the large horses. They were going out for a ride out into the forests without him. What was going on? Elissa had promised him, not a week ago, that he would accompany her on their next ride out into the woods. He had shared with her his feelings of loneliness for the forest, and she talked of missing the woods herself.

Marik turned towards Conner as Arpwin left. "The king has requested my presence. Knight Captain Hawkden was expected back days ago and has not been heard from. I presume to think that the king will ask me to seek him out." Conner was still staring over at Elissa and Melanie, who were waiting for their escorts to secure the sacks and mount their own horses. "Oh, the Princess is going for a ride." He looked from Conner and back to the princess. She sat stiff and tall, her head held high, a serious look on her face. Conner did not hide his feelings well.

"And her champion is not escorting her?" Marik asked quietly. Then he added with a smirk, "That is odd."

"I would request a horse to take for the afternoon," Conner asked. His face contorted into anger as he watched the princess ride through the gate and into the city. His knuckles went white from squeezing his fingers into a fist.

"If you show the same anger you felt earlier towards the princess, you will only make things worse. I will give you permission to take a horse, but only if you can let your anger go."

Conner let out a long sigh and relaxed his hands and let his chin drop to his chest. "I do not know what is going on. The look she gave me…it was like she hated me."

Marik laughed and slapped Conner on his back. "Boy, you are one emotional wreck! One bad look and you think she hates you? Maybe she didn't even see you, maybe she was looking at someone else."

Conner shook his head, not getting Marik's light-heartedness. "No, she looked right at me, gave me a nasty look, and then looked away."

"Then go, my young friend, and see why the princess' heart is black to you." Conner turned to leave, but Marik had a firm hold on his shoulder. "She is royalty. You are not. Her fate is not with you, you must understand that."

"I do," Conner lied.

"Her love will only be for the man that will be the next king of this land. King Thorndale has but one child, and since it is not a male heir, when he passes, the kingdom will fall to the man chosen for the princess. I do wish it otherwise, but the laws of the land do not allow for the princess to gain the throne. Even a sitting queen cannot rule. Her firstborn son would rule. Or the god-chosen son of the firstborn female. King Thorndale is still healthy, despite his gray hair and wrinkled face. It would not be uncommon for him to rule for another twenty years. But nonetheless, a husband will soon be provided for her. The rule of the kingdom must be uninterrupted." Marik paused to consider the pained look on Conner's face. He continued, "You are still her champion. That duty cannot be undone. Not by anyone. You have declared it. That gives you certain rights. One of them is to be there for her. When she needs you. Physically, emotionally. There is no law that says you cannot be friends. So be gone! Go after your good friend!"

He gave Conner a slight push and Conner gave his friend one last smile before he raced towards the knight's barracks.

***

Marik approached the double oak doors that led to the king's private counsel chamber. One of the Royal Guard, dressed in shiny chain mail armor and a deep blue surcoat, snapped to attention. His eyes were cast forward, towards the back wall. In his right hand, he gripped a long halberd, ceremonial in most ways, but its tip still sharp and deadly. With two sharp raps with the blunted steel end of his halberd, the guard announced the arrival of someone seeking an audience with the king.

Marik waited. He stood still, eyes cast forward, unwilling to look at the guard who had one of the most prestigious posts in all the kingdom. It was an enormous honor to serve the king by standing outside his chambers, as still as the night air, for hours on end. As a Karmon Knight, he would never have the opportunity. Only the best of the king's royal guard ever got a chance to serve this post. And he would never even see the king unless he was in dire need of assistance. The king came and went through the back entrances of the apartments. Everyone else went through the two large oaken doors. But walls were not thick. He heard just about everything that went on inside the chambers, which was one reason why only the most honorable and deserving Guardsman ever manned the post. The guard at the door had the authority to deny anyone to the king's chamber if he felt that the man, or woman, would pose a threat to the king. But ultimately, it was the squirrelly, thin court attendant, Denlin, that controlled who actually saw the king.

Denlin appeared between the doors as he pushed them both open at the same time. He looked young, maybe a little older than Conner. But he was much older. The problem was his short stature and his baby face. There were remnants of peach fuzz on his face, certainly nothing beard-like. His deep blue eyes looked Marik over, up and down. His head swiveled slightly as if telling Marik that no, he could not enter.

Marik knew he was not presentable to the king. He was not in his best tunic, not by a long shot. The old, stained tunic he wore was something that he trained in. Normally he did not care that he could be smelled from several feet away, or that last week's soup was still stained on the front. His leggings were ripped, and where they were not ripped, they were patched. His hair was not combed, nor his face shaved clean. Several days' worth of stubble covered his dirty face.

"I have been summoned," Marik said firmly. His voice was strong, but it took much effort to keep his knees from shaking. From behind Denlin, Marik could see the king, standing over a table, reading a scroll. Marik had never been summoned to the king's personal chambers. He had met him several times in the main hall or in the dining hall. They even had shared a walk in the garden some time ago. Each time his palms sweated and he feared that whatever came out of his mouth would insult the king. But now, more than his palms sweated. A bead of sweat had pooled at his neck and was now trickling down his back. He wanted to itch, but he seemed frozen in time.

Denlin seemed to ponder Marik's words for a moment before he replied, "His Majesty would prefer you to dress more appropriately."

Out of the corner of his eye, Marik saw the royal guard smirk. He was a Karmon Knight, who feared nothing. Except for the king. Part of him wanted to turn and run, get away from the chamber as quickly as he could. But no man would stand in his way. The fear that had been there just a moment ago was gone. In its place was anger. As a Karmon Knight, he was bound by duty and honor to both king and kingdom. His loyalty would not be questioned, and if the king called, he came. If Marik had waited a moment longer, the guardsman might have regained his composure and would have been prepared. Ignoring all protocol and the domain of the royal guards, Marik pushed his way through the doorway. The young attendant took the brunt of Marik's forearm across the chin, and he fell flat on his back, eyes blinking away swirling stars.

The king looked up at the commotion, and a smile came across his face. The guardsman had entered the room, chasing after Marik, trying to put the pole of his weapon in front of the knight to impede his progress. Marik, walking faster than the armored guard could move, kept pushing the halberd away.

"Hail, Marik!" the king called out, stepping away from the table with a smile. "Be gone," the king said to the guardsman with a slight wave of his hand. "I have summoned Marik. He is welcome here."

The guardsman gave a stiff bow and retreated back to his post.

"Sire?" Denlin asked, brushing invisible dust off of his silk tunic.

"You, too," the king said. "This conversation is for Marik's ears alone."

Denlin's neck turned red as he bowed low. "As you wish." He spun on his heels and marched out of the room.

"They are devoted and loyal," the king said, watching the door close. "I shall never understand why the Knights of Karmon, so strong and powerful, cannot get along with my guards."

Marik had his opinion, but he kept it to himself. He had crossed one line already, a line that he probably should not have crossed, especially in the presence of the king. As he approached the king, he dropped to a knee, his eyes cast down. It seemed as if every pore in his body was leaking. He stank. He cursed himself for not bathing more frequently.

"Stand, Sir Marik," the king said. "You serve me well, and there are times that I feel that it should be I that is bowing to you."

Marik's face blushed as he stood. This king was easy to be loyal to. "I am yours, your majesty," Marik said, almost automatically. "I have come as you asked."

"Indeed," King Thorndale said, his eyes returning to a scroll. After a moment of reading, he continued, "I fear for your captain. He has been gone too long. I would like you to follow him, and see if something has happened to him."

"Where did he go?" Marik asked, his heart skipping a beat. He feared for Brace, too. His friend and captain had been acting so odd lately. Coming and going at strange times. Being gone for days at a time. He even missed the last formal squire introductions.

"He did not tell you?" the king asked. "You two are close. I thought that maybe he would have shared with you."

"He has been very secretive lately. In fact..," his words trailed off. Marik was afraid to speak further.

"Go on," the king demanded.

Marik didn't want to say more. He didn't want to implicate that he was beginning to have doubts about his friend's loyalty. After a long pause, he continued. "It seems that he has been gone on long trips lately. And he has not said much about them."

"Do you doubt his loyalty?" the king asked.

Marik shook his head, trying not to show his true feelings. "No, sire. I do not."

King Thorndale smiled while he studied Marik's face. Finally, he replied, "Good. Sir Brace is a good man. And I would like him found."

"I will do my best," Marik said with a slight bow. "Where has he gone, so that I can begin to try and track him?"

"North," the king replied. "Far to the north."

"North?" Marik repeated as if he hadn't heard the king correctly the first time.

The king nodded and said again, "North."

"How far north?"

The king took a deep breath and then let it out slowly. "He was to deliver a message. To Thell."

"Thell?" Marik practically spat out the word. "Why?"

"A message of peace," the king said softly. "Yes, peace. For many months now, I have been communicating with their king. We both have grown weary of the dispute between our kingdoms. The time has come for our peoples to come together and make peace. This last message was to seal a treaty that would allow our kingdoms to have that peace. But I have not heard from Sir Brace. Or even a response from Thell."

"You fear that something happened to Sir Brace?" Marik asked.

"There are those who would have nothing to do with the Thellians," the king said. "I have done my best to keep our communication in secret, and I am sure that Sir Brace would not have told anyone of his mission."

"They are barbarians and do not deserve our friendship!" Marik said sharply. Too sharply, Marik suddenly realized as soon as the words left his lips.

The king frowned behind his gray beard. "That is the attitude that we must change. They will be our friends. We will commence trade with them. They have much more to offer us as allies instead of enemies."

"I am sorry," Marik said, falling to a knee, and bowing his head. "I did not mean to raise my voice to you."

"In time we must all learn to change what we think of our neighbors. But I know it will take a while. Your reaction will be the most common. We have been at odds with them for as long as there has been a Kingdom of Karmon." The king paused to look over his knight, who still was on a knee. "I have had much time to think of this. To ponder the good and the bad of a treaty with Thell. You, like the rest of the kingdom, have only thought of them as our enemy, so I know it will take time. It will be a slow process, learning to first understand them, and then to befriend them. But I do believe it is in our best interest to have them as our friend, rather than our enemy."

Marik felt horrible. He wanted to turn his head and throw up. But that would not be a knightly thing to do. He took deep breaths, trying to control the emotions that were sweeping through him. The king had revealed too much. Marik desperately wanted to just return to his forest.

"I have told no one of my plans, other than Sir Brace and now you," King Thorndale said. "Even the messengers that I used did not know of the plan."

"They have hated us as much as we have hated them," Marik said. "Is it possible that their king had a change of heart? Or Sir Brace was captured?"

"That is what I must know," King Thorndale said. "I am hopeful for peace, but I am not naive to the world. But before I act, in whichever way is appropriate, I must know what happened to Sir Brace and that message. That is why I need you to find him."

"I will find him, your majesty," Marik said, rising from his knee. "I do not know if we can ever have peace with Thell, but if my king says they are to be our friends, then it will be my duty for them to be my friend as well."

The king gave him leave, and he raced out of the chambers as fast as he could, running straight to the first open window to discharge his lunch.

***

King Thorndale liked the ranger and knew that he was trustworthy. He trusted all his knights, for becoming a Karmon Knight was not only about skill in battle, but character and heart. But some knights rose to the top and were simply trusted more than others. He hadn't wanted to share with Marik about the pending peace treaty with Thell. He simply did not want to put that on the young ranger, but Brace needed to be found. The message needed to be delivered. The peace treaty was still not secure. Thell did not trust him, nor did he really trust them. And any one thing could send the treaty tumbling down a rocky cliff.

Once Marik had departed, and the apartment was empty, he fell into a plush, comfortable chair. It was as old chair, carved and put together by a long forgotten king. A thick, red pillow on the seat and a similar one attached to the back of the chair made it one of his more favored places to rest. And think.

He feared for his kingdom. Times were good, and that made him wary. It had been almost thirty years since the last open conflict with Thell. His father had led the Karmon Knights into battle, and a fierce battle it was. Many hundreds dead and dying, blood covering the long summer grass, cries piercing the warm summer breeze. He wasn't at the front of the battle, but he still fought. He killed and was almost killed himself. It was only after his father fell in battle that he was whisked away for his protection. But even without their liege lord to lead them, the tide of the battle never turned against Karmon. They were better warriors. They didn't have the numbers, but they had the strength. They turned away the Thellians, forcing them to retreat back to their own lands. The generals leading the war let the Thellians go, not pursuing them for fear of having too many more of their own dead.

To some degree, King Thorndale regretted that, as the unfinished war only made relations worse. The Thellians never admitted defeat, but they constantly raided the border villages and even attacked the castles of the lords in the north. Karmon always retaliated in kind. A little slap for a little slap. War was too costly. Too many fathers, brothers, and sons died. And even daughters, he thought to himself, looking at a large painting of his daughter hanging on the wall. Maybe they could have squashed the Thellians, taking their lands and their cities from them. But there was too much land and too many villages. Karmon could never take Thell by force. They had the best warriors in their knights, but there were too few of them to mount an invasion force to conquer all of Thell.

But there was always diplomacy. He just hoped that the message would get through.

Chapter Fourteen

Conner wasn't an expert horseman, but he knew how to ride fast. The city was the most treacherous part of his route, as he needed to avoid running over stray pedestrians. But the sound of the heavy hooves of the warhorse gave most everyone ample notice to get out of the way. He thought he could catch them before they reached the city gate, but they were nowhere to be found as he burst past the royal guard who manned the gates. He kicked his horse through the streets outside the gate, his eyes scanning side alleys and pathways. He could only guess where they went, so he turned his horse north, towards the most obvious place that they would ride.

The forest to the north wasn't quite as thick close to the city, which made it easier to ride quickly through the trees. There were many game trails and paths to follow. Streams were abundant to keep both horse and rider from getting thirsty. Game animals were plentiful for the hunters as the larger predatory animals such as wolves and bears tended to stay even farther to the north.

Conner had guessed correctly and picked up their trail quickly. They were riding four abreast and following a wide two-track path, making it easy to track them. Without having to worry about chasing someone who didn't want to be found, Conner gave his horse a kick to the belly and it surged forward. Its thick legs drove the animal and its rider quickly along the path. After several minutes of pushing his horse as fast as it could go, he pulled it to a stop, and he listened carefully. He heard laughter coming from the trees and new they must close. He spun in his saddle, peering closely through the trees. It was their bright clothes that gave them away. With a slight nudge of the reins, he started making his way towards them.

The girls were laughing in the saddle, sharing a joke or a funny story. Their two escorts rode a few paces behind, silently keeping watch on their charges. He didn't want to startle them, which is what would have happened if he just rode up on them. He knew the two squires by name but didn't know much about them. They were a couple years older than him and were both on the verge of taking the final tests to become knights. They sat stoically in their saddles, keeping watch to the left, right, and ahead, but they never looked back. It should have been the most obvious thing to do, to watch one's back. But they did not. Whether it was boredom or a false sense of security, they just kept their eyes ahead of them.

Conner directed his mount around them on a parallel track through the woods. He didn't try to move silently. In fact, he made some effort to make a sound. But the girls were too noisy and the squires not observant enough. It was only when he pulled even with them, but still, several horse-lengths away, that he was noticed.

"Hey there!" one of the squires, Hollin, called out. "Stand your ground!"

Conner turned his mount towards them. The other squire called for the girls to stop. They also turned to see who the intruder was. Conner kept coming forward, despite Hollin calling out again for him to stop.

Conner stopped his horse just shy of Hollin's.

"Are you as deaf and dumb as you are a swordsman?" Hollin growled when he realized who it was. "I called for you to stand your ground."

Conner ignored him. Elissa and Melanie had turned their horses towards him and shared a few whispered words between them. Conner didn't know what to expect from the princess, but the hard, cold look wasn't it. She looked straight at him, eyes sharp and full of anger.

"Elissa," Conner called out to her.

Hollin drew his sword and swung his horse around to get closer to Conner. His eyes blazed with fire, and his whole face had flushed red. "How dare you insult the princess!"

The other squire, Franken, had moved his horse towards the girls, putting himself directly in Conner's path. He didn't draw his sword, put kept his hand on the pommel of his sheathed weapon.

"I just want to talk to the princess," Conner said meekly. He had left without a sword. He had a dagger stuffed in his belt, but it would do no good against the long steel that Hollin held. A bow and quiver hung from the saddle, but the bow wasn't strung. By the time he could pull it out and ready it for use, Hollin would have cut him down. But he also knew that Hollin wouldn't strike him. The squire was acting tough, probably trying to play it up for the two pretty girls. But nonetheless, Hollin's sword wasn't a wooden practice sword. It was sharp steel, and if he had guessed wrong, it would be a short fight.

Hollin glanced back at the girls, who were watching them carefully. "I don't think she wants to talk to you," he said. "You are not welcome here, so be gone!"

Conner said nothing. He simply sat in his saddle, his mind spinning in place, trying to figure out what to do. In the ride from the castle, the words had flowed through his mind. But now they were gone. The great speech that he had prepared for the princess now seemed trite and silly. He had raced out here to prove that he should be her protector and champion, but in reality, it was a job any squire with a sword could do.

Hollin was almost a knight. It would only be weeks before he would don the white surcoat that signified his knighthood. He had trained for many years, since a boy, and the rippling muscles in his arms and shoulders showed it. He was strong, one of the strongest squires. He also knew how to use his sword as well as any other. On several occasions, they had been matched up in training, and Conner had always ended up on the ground, dirtied and bruised. He was just doing his job, Conner realized. Doing his duty in protecting the princess. Conner felt low, about as low as he could get.

There was nothing for him to say, so he just sat on his horse, unmoving. Hollin pulled his horse away and sheathed his sword, and gave Conner a sly grin. He joined up with Franken and urged the girls to continue with their ride. With a deep sense of despair wafting over him, he watched them take a wide game trail deeper into the forest. He sat there until he could not see them anymore.

He would leave. Return to the woods. He would go back to his aunt, who probably didn't realize that he had been gone. He would bring a doe or maybe a buck. They would gut and clean the deer and then maybe she would finally make those boots that she had been promising to make. He would be a hunter again, and he was okay with that. Or maybe he would settle down and find a young woman, marry her, and have a bunch of kids. He chuckled to himself at the thought. His mind flipped through the available girls in the nearby villages, and none of them really appealed to him. There were lots of other little villages throughout Karmon. There had to be at least one with a young woman that would appeal to him.

But his mind's eye couldn't shake the image of Elissa. He knew that they were meant for each other, and he hated how he had failed her. He had tried so hard to be there for her, but he just didn't fit. He could never be a knight because he didn't have the pedigree. Maybe he could join the royal guard, but those were mostly seasoned soldiers, who had cut their teeth on border conflicts with Thell. He didn't have that kind of experience, and he really didn't have the kind of skills that a royal guard needed. He couldn't fight with a halberd or longsword. Sure, he was good with the Sak'turana, but royal guards didn't carry the light sword that he was learning. He was just a farm boy. A peasant from a village far from the hustle and bustle of the city. He was a hunter who needed to live and breathe amongst the trees.

He would say his good-byes to Goshin as soon as he returned, and then he would be gone. Hopefully, it would be before the princess returned to the castle. He turned his horse back towards the way he had come and kicked into a light trot. With each passing heartbeat, he felt his heart break apart. He was turning his back on Elissa, but it was a silly promise that he had made. He was not a champion of anything. He was just Conner, the simple boy from the forest. She would understand and eventually, she would forget him.

***

"You have said nothing since he left," Melanie said, glancing back at the hulk of a squire who was following him. Hollin did not bat an eye or appear interested in any way. It made Melanie smile.

Princess Elissa followed her friend's gaze back to the squire and rolled her eyes. "You need to stop flirting with our escorts."

A wry smile appeared on Melanie's smooth, round face. "Soon he will be a knight, and having a knight for a husband will suit me just fine. Especially one as strong as Hollin."

"His father is lord of the whole eastern forests. He owns much land and is very, very wealthy. I think that appeals to you more than his looks."

"And if you had your way, you would be married to a farmer living your life smelling like pigs," Melanie retorted.

"You make presumptions," Princess Elissa said, nose high in the air.

"You cannot hide it. The way you look at him, even when you don't want to."

"He is a pig," Princess Elissa said sharply. "I do not like him."

Melanie laughed and said, "The look on your face when he showed up here in the forest was precious. Your face blushed, and I could see your heart beating right through that dress of yours."

"He made a promise that he never intended to keep," Elissa said. "I do not care for him at all."

"My ladies," Hollin interrupted from a discrete distance away. "Nightfall will be upon us before too long. It is time to return to the castle."

Melanie turned toward the squire and batted her eyes. "Why, we just started our ride."

Hollin averted his eyes from hers, and a slight hint of red appeared on his neck and slowly spread up to his cheeks.

"I think we should ride a bit longer, don't you agree, Princess?" Melanie flashed a smile at their escorts and continued to bat her long, dark eyelashes.

The blush on Hollin's face grew, and his voice changed to a slightly higher pitch. "Yes, milady. As you wish."

Melanie kicked her horse into a trot, giving Princess Elissa an evil smile. Elissa smiled back, shaking her head. She followed her friend along the trail, with their two squires in tow.

***

Conner arrived at the castle gates as the sun was making its way down towards the Gulf of Taran to the west. It was a horrible ride back. With each passing moment, he regretted leaving the princess. He knew that she was in good hands. Hollin was a capable squire, and as long as they weren't attacked by a squad of Thellian soldiers, he would be able to handle anything. But he at least thought that Elissa was his friend. They had spent much time together, talked quite a bit. At least until lately. She had her own things, whatever they were. And he had his training. Between the sessions with Goshin, and the squire training, he had little time to eat or sleep. He should have stayed there, ignoring

Hollin. But he could not forget the look that Elissa had given him. It was not the look that friends gave one another.

By the time he left his horse at the stables, he had finally convinced himself that he did the right thing. He had left her to more capable hands, and that was all that mattered. She was protected, and he didn't need to be that protector. As he walked down the last hallway towards the squire's living chambers, he was feeling pretty good about himself. He actually felt relieved at no longer having the pressure of the duty of being Princess Elissa's champion. No more training. The farm life and the forest were looking pretty good. He strode through the doorway of his chamber thinking only about packing up and leaving the castle for good.

At one time the chambers that the squires slept in served as prison cells. Gone were the bars, but they were still cold and damp. There was little more than a bed in them, but in reality, only his sleeping hours were spent there. Every other waking moment was doing something else. It was too early for other squires to be around, so he was a bit surprised when there was a light tapping on the wall.

Conner's heart skipped a beat when he saw who was standing there. It was the last person he wanted to see right now.

Master Goshin stepped into the room and said, "You were missed today." The anger was clear in his voice and on his face.

"I went..." Conner started to say.

"I know where you went," Goshin snapped back. "Your duties are here. And you have failed today. It can never...never happen again."

Conner thought he would be angry at the way his teacher was talking to him, but he wasn't. The decisions had already been made, and he really didn't care what the old, short man thought. He wanted to say that, but he still held much respect for him, so he kept his mouth closed.

"We will train," Goshen said, his voice calmer, but still firm. "Now. Gather your swords."

Conner shook his head.

Goshin took a deep breath and let it out quickly. "I have spent much time teaching you the ways of the Sak'hurai. It will not be wasted. You cannot miss one day."

"I am done," Conner said softly.

"No," Goshin said. "You will train now. Sleep comes later."

"No," Conner said, raising his voice slightly. "I am done. For good. I am going home."

Goshin slapped the wall sharply with his palm, startling Conner enough that he flinched. "This is your home."

"My home is my village," Conner said. "In the forest. It has been and always will be. This place here is not for me. I don't belong here."

Goshen let out a grunt and was silent for several moments. Then he asked, "You did not find your princess in the forest?"

"Uh, no," Conner replied with a puzzled look. "I found her."

"You found Princess Elissa in the forest, but you did not find your princess," Goshin said. The blank look on Conner's face put a smile on the old sword master's face. "She is growing up and will have less and less time for her friends. Even those that she likes."

"She did not even act like she liked me," Conner said. "I thought we were friends."

"You must understand that she is a princess which is much more than a name. She has duties to perform, and she must uphold her status to the kingdom."

"But I am also her champion," Conner argued.

"She has no need of a champion," Goshin declared as softly as he could. "Every knight in the kingdom would give their life for her. The royal guard as well. There are more than enough swords in this castle to protect her. And soon, a husband will be found for her, and he will become her true champion."

Anger began to grow from deep inside. "But I am her champion!" Conner exclaimed loudly. "We made a promise and the king even declared me her champion!"

Goshin stepped forward and gripped Conner by the shoulders. "Then be one!"

Conner shrugged the hands away. "I cannot be her champion when I cannot fight! You make me use my left hand, and I cannot fight that way. I have trained and trained with my swords, and you will not let me use them!"

Goshin took a step back and looked over his pupil thoughtfully. He saw the anger that was still inside. He saw a young man desperately trying to break out of the shell that he was in. He trained him as he knew how. As he knew best. As a Sak'hurai. But Conner was not Sak'hurai, nor would he ever be. He could be better, though. But only if he was allowed to be.

"You are right," Goshin said. He bowed his head in shame. "I was wrong."

Conner, sensing that maybe he had come on too strong and was too harsh with his master, said. "No, you were right to teach me to use my left hand. It is just time to show everyone. To show Princess Elissa that I can be her champion. That I am worthy."

"You do not need to prove your worth. Your worth is from who you are and what you do. The moment you try and prove your worth to someone is the moment that you tell them that you are better than them. Do not do that. Do not be arrogant in your worth."

Conner smiled a wry smile. "Are you still trying to teach me ways of the Sak'hurai?"

Goshin's face was hard as a stone. "No. That is more than Sak'hurai. That is the way of being a man. You must choose now. Go now or stay. But if you stay, then you cannot choose to go again when things don't go your way. That is also the way of being a man. You must be committed regardless of what happens."

Conner nodded. "I will stay."

Goshin gave Conner a quick bow. "Yes. Of course. But you must still train."

Conner let out a moan. He was beaten. He could barely stand. Longingly, he looked at his bed.

"Very well," Goshin said. "You may rest. But tomorrow, you work twice as hard."

Conner gave a slight nod of thanks before dropping onto his bed and falling into a deep sleep.

Chapter Fifteen

Marik gently touched the rocky path, his hands scanning the stones and rocks scattered about. There were a couple deep gouges, which could have been anything. But his trained eyes told him that they were caused by the struggle of a horse trying to keep from falling into the deep chasm. A stream had cut itself a path deep into the mountain, creating the deep chasm that seemed to be bottomless. But Marik knew better. He had spent many long months in the mountains scouting and doing…other things. Right here, next to the trail, the drop-off was steep and deadly. If anything fell here, it was a long way down with seemingly no way out.

Although it was steep, if one knew how to maneuver down the side of the cliff, it was not difficult. Marik had done this before, many times. Keeping his feet in front of him, and his weight as far back towards the cliff face as he could, he started sliding down. It was mostly loose gravel, making the going fast, but not too dangerous. He used his hands to control his descent, digging into the cliff face when he felt himself going too fast. Before he expected it, his feet struck the ground, catching himself off balance. He tumbled forward, face first into the slow running stream that had spent an eon cutting into the mountain.

The smell hit him first, and he had to force himself to keep from throwing up his lunch. Covering his face with the crook of his elbow, he looked over the dead horse. It had certainly once been a knight's mount. But now the poor beast was half devoured, its entrails strewn across the ground. The saddle was still in place, but there was nothing else. No body, no sword, no armor. Starting at the carcass, Marik scouted the area in an expanding circle, looking for any sign of Brace. He finally found one on the other side of the bank. A small tree had been cut down, its branches cut off from the main trunk and left on the ground. There were some dark stains on some of the larger rocks that could have been blood. After another hour of searching, he finally picked up the trail. It led upstream, deeper into the mountains, and towards the northern border of the kingdom.

He touched a partial boot print and said softly into the wind, "I am on your trail, my friend, and you are alive. I will catch up to you. I promise you that."

***

Brace jumped down from the embankment. He had been slipping and sliding most of the last ten feet and rather than fall on his face, he jumped. Although he tried to land only on his good leg, he still came down on his bad leg. He let out a sharp shout as the pain shot up from his foot and through his spine. He hopped for two steps, trying to maintain his balance. But the pain was too much, and he collapsed to the ground. Brace wanted to cry. It was a pain that he had never experienced before, far beyond any of the slices and stabs that he had endured during his tenure as a knight. He tried to let the pain go away through willpower. With eyes closed, he slowed his breathing, trying to calm it away. But it would not go away.

Finally, he slammed his fists on the ground and let out a loud shout.

Mirfar had been leading the way, and at the sound of Brace's outburst, he turned. "We will rest here," the Thellian nomad declared.

Bellock was still at the top of the last hill, trailing them with the pack of food and supplies on his back. He easily slid down the embankment into what had once been a stream that ran at the base of the mountain. He dropped his packs onto the ground and started to unpack some of the supplies to prepare their lunch.

Mirfar leaned down and studied the leg. "It is not swollen," he said with an encouraging smile.

"What does that mean?" Brace asked.

"If it were swollen and red, hot to the touch, then infection would have set in, and death would soon follow. The wound is healing, but the leg, the bones, I am afraid, are not healing well."

"I can stand the pain," Brace said. "Until it is fully healed."

"You are a brave man, Brace Hawkden," Mirfar said. "But I wonder if some of the bravery is really stubbornness. We have been traveling for two days when you should have been resting."

"I will rest when I am dead," Brace retorted sharply.

Bellock said a few words and handed Brace a chunk of bread and piece of dried meat.

Mirfar smiled and said, "Our big friend says that if you don't slow down, then you will indeed be dead."

"The leg will be fine," Brace said. "I can handle the pain. It is only temporary."

"The good news is that our path will be much easier. We have climbed out of the mountains, and now the land slopes down towards the northern steppes of Thell. If Kirwin and Lillimar were able to find horses for the return trip, we should be meeting up with them sometime today."

Brace looked back at the mountains. It was hard for him to imagine that they had made it as far as they did. His leg was in constant pain, and he couldn't walk very fast. Mirfar had cut a thick walking stick to help him walk. It had taken some getting used to, but as long as they were on flat ground, he could make decent time. But most of the past two days hadn't been flat ground. It had been uneven, rocky terrain. There had been no path to follow. The footing was treacherous with two good legs. With only one, Brace was simply thankful to the gods that they had seen him through.

He then looked out away from the mountains. It was different on this side. Trees were not as abundant. Unlike the grand forests that were pervasive throughout Karmon, Thell was mostly flat with smaller clumps of woodsy areas. They were still up in the mountains, but they were well below the steep, rocky parts. It looked like the entire kingdom of Thell was laid out in front of them. They were high enough still to see for miles and miles.

Brace squinted his eyes, trying to find a break in the flat land where a city might exist. "Where is Thellia?" he asked.

Mirfar raised an eyebrow at the question. "You do not know? You were to deliver a message to the king, and you do know where the city is?"

"I know where it is, just not from where we are now. I had directions through the White Mountain Pass. Directly north, follow the first river that I came across, and that would lead me directly to the city gates." Then he added with a slightly irritated tone, "I do not normally spend much time north of the mountains."

Mirfar seemed to ignore the tone and answered, "We are some miles to the west of the pass. The river that you were to follow, the Jorgan River, as we call it, meanders quite a bit. Following the river would take you an extra day to get there. Now, since I know exactly where the city is, I have taken us in a direction directly towards there." Mirfar finished by pointing directly towards their destination, a spot on the horizon a bit west of north. His eyes following his hand, but the surprise at what he saw kept his arm suspended in air.

Brace stiffened at the same sight. If Mirfar had not pointed it out directly, neither of them would have seen the glint of steel and the shadow of a mass of men moving in their direction.

"It is the army on the move," Brace said softly. If they had arrived at this spot an hour sooner, the mass of moving soldiers would have been too far away to see. "Five miles. Maybe a bit more," Brace added after a moment of reflection.

"We are still quite a bit higher up than them," Mirfar said. He looked around. They sky was perfectly clear. The sun was still crawling its way up towards its noon height. Just about perfect conditions for seeing long distances. He had spent much of his life in the mountains and had a good handle on how far he could see. "I believe they are much farther. Ten miles, I'd say."

Brace wasn't going to argue. The army was far enough away that he could not really see individual soldiers. It was just a moving mass of bodies with the occasional glint of steel reflecting up to them. "We should avoid them."

"They may offer a quicker way back to the king so you can deliver your message," Mirfar said.

Brace shook his head. "I am a military man. Have been most of my life. They will not look kindly upon me this far north. I fear they would treat me more as a spy than a messenger. We better get moving before they see us."

Mirfar picked up a sack of supplies and slung it over his shoulder. "I agree we should get moving, but it will be another day before they would be close enough to see us. We are but specks in the haze of the mountain to them. Likewise, we only see them as a mass of men."

After their short break, they moved slowly down the mountain. The rocky terrain that had slowed them to nearly a crawl had been replaced by a rolling landscape of hills and crevices. Brace moved as fast as the pain would allow, but still much slower than he wanted. They had many days travel in front of them unless they were able to find a stray horse. Or borrow one.

Brace felt naked being so out in the open. Trees were sparsely scattered about, offering little protection if they were to need it. With one eye on his path, he kept his other eye on the army mass that looked like it had yet to move. Indeed, the army was still many miles away. But after a couple of hours of descending down the mountain, they could no longer see it. At one point, Brace turned around to see how far they had traveled and was surprised at how tall the mountains were. Despite his slow gait, they were making decent time.

Just as he was getting used to traveling peacefully through enemy territory, Brace thought he heard the snort of horse and froze in his tracks. Mirfar, who had been walking slightly ahead of Brace kept walking. Almost a full minute later, Mirfar finally realized that he was walking alone and stopped to turn around. Brace silenced the forthcoming question with a raised finger. He tilted his head, trying to listen for more sounds. His eyes scanned the area. A stream ran nearby, marked by trees along its banks. Their water skins were still mostly full with water, so they weren't planning on stopping to fill them, although they had discussed it some time ago. There were other patches of trees, but none packed so tightly that a horse could hide. His hand unconsciously fell to his empty hip.

After what seemed an eternity to Mirfar, Brace finally started walking forward, although his eyes still scanned the trees that ran along the creek. When he reached Mirfar, he said softly. "I think we are being watched. I heard a horse."

Mirfar raised an eyebrow. "I did not hear…"

The old man's words were cut off by the crash of horses through the underbrush by the creek. Brace spun around, falling into a defensive position with Mirfar behind him. Five soldiers, astride dark black mounts, surrounded them. Four were clad identically in chainmail armor underneath a plain red surcoat. Their heads were topped with simple conical helms. All four had swords drawn and ready to use. The fifth soldier was helmetless but had the same plain red surcoat over his chainmail. His hair was long and curly, unkempt and windblown from riding. He stayed behind the other riders, keeping his distance. He was clearly the leader.

"Hail, strangers," the leader said with a thick accent in Brace's native tongue.

Brace looked him up and down, and then at each of the soldiers. They carried themselves as professionals with hands and eyes firm.

"Hello and well met!" Mirfar said as cheerfully as he could.

The lead soldier ignored the greeting and kept his attention on Brace. "Who are you?"

"Travelers."

"From?"

Brace nodded to the south. "From over the mountains."

The soldier smiled and said matter-of-factly, "Then you admit to being spies."

"No!" Brace protested, stepping forward. "We are travelers!"

"Seize them."

The four helmed soldiers quickly dismounted.

"I have a message for the king!" Brace shouted. He reached into the folds of his tunic and brought out the message with the seal of King Thorndale on it.

The five soldiers all shared a glance. Finally, the lead soldier dismounted and strode to Brace where he grabbed the message and tore it open.

"That is for the king," Brace protested.

"I am sure my father won't mind me reading it." He flashed a wide smile. "I am Prince Toknon. I have, in fact, been looking for you for some time. It seems two of your friends stumbled upon my army just the other day." He looked into Brace's eyes and his smile grew. "I know all about you, Sir Brace Hawkden. Or should I call you spy Brace Hawkden?"

"Read it," Brace replied firmly. "I am no spy."

Prince Toknon read through the message, and his eyes grew wider at each line that he read. "Well, this is most interesting. My father and your king have been very busy the past few months."

"The message is delivered. If you will, please let us return," Mirfar said meekly. He finished with a tip of his head.

Prince Toknon dropped to a knee and ripped the paper up into small pieces. He pulled out a flint stone and struck it several times with his dagger before he was able to get a spark. The spark took quickly to the dry parchment that the message was written on. In only moments, the message was gone. He stood, watching the remnants of the message scatter in the wind.

"I am unaware of any message," the prince said. "It seems that this little game that my father and your king have been playing is over. My army marches south. We will conquer your fabled knights and then we will march upon your grand city. And then, Karmon will be no more. It will only be Thell."

Brace burned deeply with anger. He looked around, searching for anything that could be used as a weapon. But there was nothing to be found, other than a few blades of grass. The soldiers were young and fit, imposing figures. One on one, he would easily kill them. Even two on one he would have a good chance. But five on one, he would be cut down before the first parry. "Your army is no match for the might of the Knights of Karmon!" Brace shouted in defiance.

"You are right, I am afraid. And that is why you have survived as long as you have. My father soils his robes when he thinks about your fabled knights. But there are other ways to fight a war." He mounted his horse and grabbed the reigns. "Your king and my father have been conspiring for some time. But I dare say they have not been conspiring as long as I have." He turned to one of his men. "Palin, Gar, you both will stay with the spy and escort him to tonight's camp. Be sure that you bind his arms tightly."

"What about them?" the soldier named Palin asked. He nodded at Mirfar and Bellock.

Prince Toknon looked down at the old man from atop his horse and declared, "There is only one way to deal with a traitor of the realm." He spurred his horse forward and in one motion unsheathed his sword and swung it down at Mirfar's head. The old man, too surprised to react, did not move as the sword cleaved his head from his body.

Brace jumped after the Prince, letting a scream of rage escape his lips. But before he could take two steps he was felled by a sharp blow to the back of his head.

Chapter Sixteen

Lord Neffenmark and his escort plowed through the city, heading straight for the castle gates. The four riders, his four best swordsmen, formed a wedge ahead of the horse-drawn carriage that pulled the lord. Already hot and tired from the long ride, his irritation grew with each passing moment. What should have been a quick trip straight through the center of the city up to the castle was a slow crawl through peasant infested streets.

He poked his head out through the curtains and shouted at his nearest escort. "Move these people out of the way!"

The man turned to Lord Neffenmark and shook his head ever so slightly. "There are so many. They fill the streets, and they are heading away from the castle while we are trying to go there."

"Run them over if they are in your way!" Neffenmark shouted before shutting the curtain in anger. He let his enormous girth fall back onto the pillows, rocking the carriage back and forth for several moments.

It was not too much longer before the sounds of the crowds dissipated and the speed of the clop of the horse's hooves increased. The lord eased the curtain open slightly and peered ahead, seeing the castle gates only a couple of blocks away. He closed his eyes and let his anger subside. He needed to be angry when confronting the king, but not a real anger. It needed to be the false anger that he so easily displayed and allowed him to think clearly and rationally. If he let his real anger show, he knew that his mouth would get him in trouble, as it had many times before. If he were to follow through with the lie, then he needed to be in complete control. The last thing that he needed was to let slip any detail or deviate in any way from his well-conceived deception.

The carriage stopped, and he could hear his men dismounting from their horses. His curtain was pulled back, and he found himself facing a closed portcullis, blocking their entrance to the castle. A young boy was standing behind it. He was dressed in a simple red tunic and white hose. His hands were at his side, and he stood stiffly, staring back at them.

"I am to see the king," Neffenmark announced from his carriage.

"Um," the boy muttered. "He is not here."

Lord Neffenmark waited for further explanation, but the boy just stood, staring back at him. As one second became ten, and the silence still hanging over them, Lord Neffenmark was surprisingly not angered. He was just simply surprised.

"Well?" Neffenmark asked.

The boy shrugged his shoulders. "Sire?" the boy asked.

"Where is the king?" Lord Neffenmark's words exploded from his mouth, spittle flying out of the carriage and all the way to the portcullis. His face went instantly red, and his heart started beating strong and hard. If he had the ability to get up, he would have done so and charged the thick metal gate, grabbing it and shaking it until it fell down. But his enormous size kept him planted firmly on his pillows.

The boy took a step back, his calmness washed away. His face was ashen, his eyes wide with fear. "He is at the fields, sire," the boy said softly. "It is the time of the great Summer Festival. Today is the squire tournament."

Neffenmark's anger subsided enough to allow him to smile at the boy. "Thank you, my young boy. And..." the lord was about to chastise the boy, but before Neffenmark could say another word, the boy turned and ran out of sight. Lord Neffenmark spat on the ground, cursing the king, his castle, and this wretched city.

"Karl," Neffenmark shouted. "To this festival of theirs. And quickly!"

***

Melanie took her seat next to Princess Elissa. Their tent was atop the hill that overlooked the training grounds just outside of the city walls. In times of war, the training ground was used to teach swordsmanship and pike handling to the peasants called to battle. In times of peace, it was used by the knights in their horsemanship drills, and just as the first warm days of summer arrived, for the Summer Festival.

"A fine day," Melanie said. A smile was plastered on her face, and she was doing all that she could to cheer up her friend. At first, the princess was not going to attend, but her father had insisted. And when she still refused, he demanded. Although the princess was attending, she did not like it, and she was doing everything that she could to not enjoy it.

"It's too hot," Princess Elissa replied. With no wind to cool them off, it was hot even in the shade of their tent. Her tone was harsh. More so than she expected, or wanted, but she was in too much of a mood to apologize to her good friend. She stayed in her own world, her eyes watching the knights help set up the arena for the squires, but her mind wandered. She tried not to think about Conner, but she couldn't really help it. It was really the only reason that she was here, to watch her champion humiliate himself. And the more she thought about it, the angrier she was. Not so much at Conner, but at herself. He was a handsome boy with a pleasant personality. They seemed very much alike in many ways, even though she was a princess and he was…not. When they were still friends, they had spent many hours just talking. Sometimes serious, sometimes not. But mostly she just enjoyed being with him. He had saved her life in the woods, but that was all he ever really did. She could see that he would never be more than the hunter that he was. He could never be a knight and to think about him actually donning plate armor and really being her champion made her laugh out loud.

But then she caught herself. Her eyes found him, standing with the other squires, far in the distance. He wasn't like the rest. He was a little taller and ganglier. He would never be the thick muscular knight. He would just be a skinny peasant boy. But she caught herself not breathing when she saw him. A flutter went through her stomach, and a tear touched the corner of her eye. He stood there, out of place. Wide-eyed like a lost rabbit among a pack of wolves. The anger faded and in its place came pity. He did try. He tried to be her champion, but it was just not to be.

She had seen many of these tournaments before and even though they were supposed to be friendly matches, they were usually anything but. Every couple of years, a squire would take a wooden sword the wrong way and would not make it out of the tournament alive. Many squires came out with broken bones. Hardly any were left unbruised or unbloodied. It was the nature of the contest which Princess Elissa really didn't care for. She knew it would be a while before Conner would enter the contest. He was probably the worst of the bunch and would be chosen as a fighting partner last. The squires with the first choice were the ones ready to take the next step into knighthood, and they would choose the strongest opponent and not the weakest. In the end, it was all about honor. There was no honor in defeating the weak.

She settled back into her cushioned seat, wishing she were anywhere else.

***

Conner looked around, eyes wide in awe at the site of the festival. Most of the city gathered outside of the walls to watch the various events of skill that the knights and squires put on. The training area was in a deep, natural bowl. This allowed the crowd to sit as if they were in one of the fabled Taran arenas. But instead of sitting on hard stone, they sat on soft grass. The tents of the important nobles, including the king and the princess, were stacked on one end of the arena. As the sun began to rise above the horizon, the first of the day's crowd appeared. By the time the sun was high in the sky, and the festivities were about to begin, the arena was lined with thousands of cheering spectators.

The squires were the first event of the day. While the lords and nobles fed upon their lunch, the knights-to-be showed off their skills with the sword. To the oldest, it was the first step in their rite of knighthood. The best of the best would fight, with the winners getting a leg up on being chosen for knighthood. For the rest, it was a time to make a name for themselves. The winners would be remembered for the valiant skill, while the losers would simply be forgotten, hoping to make a better show at the next festival.

But they were simply the warm-up to the main show. The crowd was really waiting for the knights to make their appearance in their finely polished plate armor to show off their skill with lance, sword, and bow. Although they all wanted to win the competitions, it was more about showing their skill and bravery to the people of the kingdom. The Karmon Knights were the best of the best, and the show gave the people something to remember them by. They competed hard, but in the end, they had fun with the competitions. They were brothers-in-arms and winning was never more important than honor. But for the squires, knighthood could be won or lost at the day's competition. It was their one time, outside of battle, to show the knights who had what it took to attain knighthood. Although honor and courage were synonymous with knighthood, if a knight couldn't fight, he was no good to the kingdom.

Conner found himself gawking at the crowd, trying to see each and every face cheering them on. Their faces blended together, though. It was too much. The loudness was crushing, fraying every last nerve. His palms sweated and his heart raced. A push on his back sent him stumbling forward, and he almost lost his balance.

Conner spun around, suddenly oblivious to all that was around him. It was Hollin, the best of the squires.

"Move along, little boy," Hollin said. He stood with feet wide, hands on his hips. He wore a leather vest over a tunic that had the arms ripped off. His bulging biceps were exposed, and he flexed them more. Hollin would be a knight before the end of the year. He had it all, size, strength, stamina, intelligence, and bravery. The problem, Conner knew, was that he was more jerk than anything else.

"Watch yourself," Conner growled back, standing his ground.

"Stand aside and get back to the end of the line, where you belong," Hollin said, a slight smirk spreading across his face. The squires were to march out onto the field and be presented to the king in an order determined by their skill in training. The best of the squires would be first, and he would be presented personally to the king, while the rest of the squires would simply be announced by name. Then the first squire would choose his opponent, calling him out to the center of the ring where they would do battle with wooden practice swords. The winner would then call upon another squire, who would then, in turn, call out his opponent. Although a squire could call out any remaining squire, it was prescribed practice to call out an opponent who was equal or even better. A win over a lesser opponent was not treated as well as a loss to a superior opponent. A brave knight would stand and face the greatest of opponents without fear. By sending him to the back of the line, Hollin was putting Conner in his place.

Conner said nothing, letting Hollin and the rest of the squires pass. He looked back at the large tent where the squires had prepared themselves. Goshin was there, arms crossed, a blank look on his face. In each hand, he held half a broomstick, each half about three feet long. Conner gripped the wooden broadsword strapped to his side, a weapon that he knew he would never use. It was not his, nor would it ever be. He let the words of Hollin just fall away. He was a bully. Always had been, and would always be. He was strong and courageous but lacked something that he saw in other knights, like his new friend Marik. He had to let the words go; he knew he could not let them bother him. Goshin had taught him well, and now it was up to him to take those lessons to practice. He could not fight with anger, or the anger would blind him. He needed to fight without emotion, with his eyes and hands, brain and heart. He gave the nod to his teacher and turned back towards the other squires and followed them out onto the field.

**

King Thorndale looked down upon the festival and was saddened. The crowd was as large and boisterous as ever. This was a great day for the kingdom, as food and wine flowed as swiftly as the great Tyre River. The city shut down for the day as food was prepared and everyone enjoyed a day of celebration. He was as proud as ever to have a large group of squires competing to see who would earn the honor of knighthood. He loved to see his regal knights in their full dress armor, surcoats draped across their shoulders, their swords hanging at their sides. But there were two knights missing. Brace was a good friend, and although he didn't know Marik all that well, he trusted him. Two of his best were gone, and he couldn't show his fear. Normally it was the honor of the Knight Captain to introduce the games. It weighed heavily upon the king's heart that his best knight was not here. And he even might be dead. He was anxious to hear from Marik, to hear about his good friend. But he knew the kingdom must go on. The festival must go on. He could not show his fear, for the kingdom relied upon him for its strength.

He glanced to his right to see his most trusted servant, Arpwin, standing his post, ensuring that the king's cup was filled. Two royal guard, familiar faces, but names unknown, stood behind and on either side of the king's plush chair. His ears perked at a commotion, and Arpwin's eyebrows raised. The slight movement of his guards to grip their swords caused him to look back towards the entrance to the tent. An enormous man filled the entire opening, his face red from exertion.

The two guards pulled their swords partially out of their sheaths, but the king lifted a hand.

Huffing and puffing, the fat lord of the north entered the king's tent. "Your majesty," the man said with a feeble attempt at a deep bow.

"Lord Neffenmark?" The king asked, surprised to see the fat lord so far from his home.

"Your majesty," Neffenmark said between gasps for air. "I have urgent news."

The king stood, straightening his loosely fitting tunic. He had little time for this beast that he could barely call a man. "I have a duty to attend." His voice was firm, and he tried to keep emotion out of it.

"It cannot wait," Neffenmark barked.

The king had started to turn, but then turned back his face reddening. "Right now, unless the Thellians are marching on the gates of the city, there is nothing more important than the Summer Festival. These young men will be the next knights of the realm. They will be our protectors and saviors. It is our day to honor them."

"Sire, forgive me," Neffenmark said, bowing as low as his large frame allowed. "It is just…"

The king lifted a hand and cocked his head as if listening for something. "I do not hear the battle calls of the gate guards, so I must assume there is not an army banging on our front gate. You may stay in the royal tent as my guest, but there will be nothing said until the festival is over."

Lord Neffenmark let out a long, slow sigh. "Yes, your majesty." The king turned and walked away. The lord's eyes narrowed and glared daggers at the back of the man whom he desired to conquer.

"Young squires!" the king shouted. He had made his way out of the tent to the edge of the arena where all could see and hear him. "Today is your greatest day. Today you fight for your kingdom. The winners shall revel in their glory. But even the losers will be praised for their effort and honor in defeat."

Cheers erupted from the crowd. With a hand, the king silenced them. He continued, "Today we begin the Summer Festival where the warriors of the kingdom prove their honor and worth. The greatest warriors in all the earth, the Knights of Karmon will show their skills in jousting and with the sword." He paused again, to let the crowd raise up and cheer. After a moment, he lifted his hand, and the crowd settled down. "But first, those who would be knights, the squires who struggle and strive to knighthood will show their skills in battle."

He turned to look over the gathered squires, dressed in old, used leather armor. His eyes scanned the group until they fell upon Conner. Conner caught the gaze, and his heart sank. The king, like the others, was disappointed in him. Conner had one shot, though, to prove that he had not failed them at all. He took the long, deep breaths that Goshin had taught him. He needed to be calm and be prepared. The edges of the king's mouth seemed to curl up into what might have been a smile. Then the head nodded down. Just slightly. Maybe it was his imagination or maybe it wasn't. Conner looked back towards where he had last seen Goshin. The two broomstick handles were there, waiting for him. The king's gazed had moved away, as he scanned all the squires. Conner casually moved to gather the broomsticks.

"You will not be judged by your victory alone," the king said to the squires. "Some of you will choose your opponent and some of you will be chosen. Your choice will show your character. Your bravery will be revealed." He gave one last long look to the squires while the crowd cheered once more. "I call upon the squire who has earned the first choice. Hollin Bronnblade. Step forward young squire."

Hollin took a step forward from the rest of the squires and bowed low, bending at the knee, so his forehead was just inches from the ground.

"Hollin Bronnblade," the king continued. "You have earned the honor of first choice. Choose your opponent."

Hollin rose and turned back to his fellow squires. What they had gone through was just a formality, a show for the crowd. Most of the opponents were already known. Hollin had already told Squire Morgan that he would be chosen as his opponent, as Morgan was considered the second best squire. Morgan would lose no honor by losing, and by making a good showing, he would gain even more honor.

"I choose my friend, Squire Morgan," Hollin announced. Morgan was taller than Hollin but leaner and not quite as agile. He had a longer arm reach, which made him dangerous. But Hollin was still the superior swordsman.

Trying to hide both a wide grin and his excitement, Morgan stepped forward from the front ranks of the squires and drew his sword. Likewise, Hollin drew his sword. The rest of the squires retreated away from the center of the ring, and the king started to back away. But he stopped when he saw Conner moving forward.

Conner had wanted to try and bait Hollin into choosing him, but Goshin knew that Hollin would never fall to being intimated by someone he did not find intimidating. So instead, Goshin had come up with a better idea. Conner marched to the center of the field and stood his ground in between the two squires. His eyes were on Hollin when he addressed the king.

"Your majesty," Conner said with a deep bow. "As the Princess' Champion, I insist that I be given the first battle. I have earned that right!"

Princess Elissa, completely unaware of the events that were unfolding was munching on an apple when she heard his voice. Her heart jumped at the sound of it, and she dropped the apple when she saw him standing between the two squires. But then she almost laughed along with the rest of the crowd, as he stood there not with swords, but with two broomsticks. Anger and humiliation quickly followed. She covered her eyes in shame.

Hollin was too stunned to speak at first, but he saw the broomsticks in Conner's hands, he let out a loud whooping laugh, joining in with the rest of the crowd. Morgan, unsure of what to take of the situation, simply stood to the side.

"Go away," Hollin finally said after his laughter subsided. But the crowd continued to laugh, hoot, and holler.

Ignoring everything around him, Conner spun the broomsticks in his hands, as if they were swords. They were slightly lighter than the swords that he normally used, but the weight was close enough. He would actually be a little faster with them. Cut to the exact the same length, the ends that he held with his hands were wrapped with leather strips, ensuring he had a strong grip. He crouched into an offensive stance.

"If you want a fight, then a fight you shall have," Hollin said, lifting his sword in a two-handed grip.

Conner looked at Morgan and smiled. "You better get ready, because you are next."

Conner had argued with Goshin about fighting them both at the same time, but Goshin insisted that surprise and speed will be on his side. If he were quick enough, he would only really face one at a time. Conner drew on Goshin's confidence and attacked.

The king said nothing, only backing away from the fight. But he did not need to take too many steps before it was over.

Conner was quick. Too quick. Everything that Goshin had taught him worked. He trusted the instincts that he built up from his many training sessions. Conner only had to dodge the first attack, which was clumsy and too powerful. Easily stepping aside from the blow because he had only the lightest of leather armor on, Conner moved into Hollin, his elbow striking the squire in the gut, knocking the wind out of him. A quick slash on the knee and Hollin was on the ground, howling in pain and agony.

Conner moved to Morgan, who actually offered more of a challenge than Hollin. Conner had to avoid the long reach of the taller squire. The broomsticks held up enough to parry the first strike, and then Conner spun and danced, raining quick blows down upon Morgan, who could not defend himself. The final blow was Morgan's own fault, as he ducked into a quick strike, taking the full force of a broomstick across the side of his face. He crumpled into a heap.

Conner stood in the center of the ring in silence. Thousands of spectators had just witnessed a fight that their brains could still not process. The king could only stare. He had witnessed hundreds of battles and tournaments and had never seen such a demonstration. King Thorndale looked from the two fallen squires to Conner, and back again. Hollin was on his back, still gripping his knee, which had suddenly swollen up to twice its size. Morgan was laid out flat on his back, his eyes closed, but his chest still moving up and down. The king had seen broken bones, blood, and every few years a squire took one blow too many and did not survive the competition. Many times they were accidents or just unfortunate circumstances. Sometimes a squire was so outmatched that he just couldn't protect himself. But never had the best two squires in a given year been so badly beaten.

The crowd was still, but murmurs ran through it. They didn't know if they should cheer or boo. The king didn't know if he should be happy that his daughter's champion was that good, or angry that two of his up and coming knights were humiliated. After only the slightest of hesitations, he stepped forward and gripped Conner's wrist, as was custom when announcing the winner of a competition. With a wide smile on his face, he lifted the hand of the princess' champion into the air, and the crowd erupted in shouts and cheers.

With the crowd suddenly going crazy around her, Princess Elissa sat still, her mouth open wide, unable to say a word. It had happened so fast, she could not be sure that what she really saw was what had happened. But the two best squires were on the ground, defeated.

And Conner was standing there, her father lifting his arm into the air, announcing his victory.

Conner let the ruckus of the crowd lift him up. No longer was he the peasant boy, he was Conner, the Princess' Champion. The king turned him towards the entire crowd, and then finally to the knights and squires who were lined up along the castle wall. The knights were clapping their hands, following the lead of their liege. Whether they were truly happy or not, no one could tell. But they all put on a good show in support of Conner. But the squires showed their opinions clearly on their faces and with their body language. They stood still, uncomfortable in their displeasure at what they had just witnessed. Two of their own were felled, and everyone was cheering it. Their angry looks were directed right at Conner. At least the knights had the maturity to keep their emotions to themselves.

Conner knew he would never be one of them. His blood was not noble blood. His father was not some wealthy landowner who had come about his money because his father's grandfather's grandfather was given a tract of land by a king whose name no one could remember. But now he knew for certain that it didn't matter. He didn't need to be one of them as long as he was who he was. But he also didn't want to be against them, either. That would have to be his next task, to win them over.

The king turned him around so that all could see the victor. The last turn had him facing the pavilion of the king and his court. Princess Elissa was there, her hands covering her mouth, her eyes wide with surprise. But his eyes didn't fall upon her. They fell upon the largest, fattest man he had ever seen. His body swallowed up the chair he was sitting in. His long, flabby jowls hung low and seemed to be permanently molded into a sneer. He was also another of the crowd that was not cheering or clapping.

Chapter Seventeen

The king walked into his chamber tired. He poured himself a tall goblet of sweet wine and drank deeply, soothing the ache in his throat. A feeling of relaxation swept through his body, and he let out a long sigh. It had been a long day, but it was a time he thoroughly enjoyed. Sitting next to his people made him feel close to them. He could see their faces, hear the shouts, and share in the same fun. They cheered when he cheered, and he cheered when they cheered. For a short time, he was able to step away from the business of running his kingdom and be entertained. A sharp knock on his door brought him back to reality. Lord Neffenmark had insisted on meeting with him, and the king knew he couldn't put it off any longer. He wanted it done and over with before he was expected at the ball.

"Come!" the king shouted.

The door opened, and Lord Neffenmark burst through, huffing and puffing from the exertion of walking up the stairs to the king's apartment. "Your Majesty," Lord Neffenmark said between gasps for air.

The king gave his lord a stern look and drank deeply from the goblet of wine. "You have my ear," the king said after setting his goblet back down on a nearby table. "But only for a few moments. The feast is in full swing, and I will not miss the dancing."

"I am sure they will wait for your return," Lord Neffenmark said, still trying to catch his breath.

"And that would be rude of me," the king replied angrily. "I have many duties and obligations that go beyond telling everyone what to do. The people of this city expect me to be out there, to join in the celebration. So make this quick."

"Very well, my king," Neffenmark said as honestly as he could muster. He looked around for a place to sit down, but the only chair was on the far side of the room, and the king was standing directly in front of him. He cleared his throat and said, "Quite a show, huh?"

"Yes," the king said with clear impatience.

"That young squire. That was quite a sight to see," Neffenmark added.

"Yes, it was," the king agreed, crossing his arms in front of him.

"I didn't think your knights were being taught such a..." Lord Neffenmark paused to thoughtfully think of a word. "…an elegant fighting style."

King Thorndale was still a bit in awe of what he saw. Conner had surprised him as much as everyone else who saw his display. But, as many knights had reminded him, he was not fighting a knight. He was fighting an inexperienced squire who was clearly taken aback at a strange fighting style. His best knights insisted that there was truly nothing special about the display and it would not be a style that would hold up in true combat. Despite what he was told, his eyes told him a different story. It happened so fast that he could hardly remember the whole fight. Maybe there was something to this Conner boy after all.

Turning back to Neffenmark, the king asked, "What is it that you want?"

Lord Neffenmark put on his best sour face and lowered his eyes to the ground. "It is news that I could not entrust with a messenger. It is the gravest of news."

The king waited patiently while Lord Neffenmark unwrapped a sword that had been tightly bound in a leather wrapping. He approached the king and handed it to him.

"A sword?" the king asked.

Lord Neffenmark nodded and asked, "Do you not recognize it?"

"It is finely crafted, likely by Master Goshin himself," the king observed, casually turning it over several times to try and recognize its owner.

"It is the sword of a messenger that was traveling north," Lord Neffenmark finally said.

The king's heart stopped. He looked at it more closely. It could have been Sir Brace Hawkden's sword. It was finely made with an intricate design on the hilt. The leather wrapping around the grip was worn from use, but the blade was sharp and flawless. "How did you come by this sword?" the king demanded with a loud, booming voice. Any fatigue that he had felt was now gone.

"I have patrols throughout the forest," Neffenmark answered. "They ride in groups of four as there have been more and more Thellians coming across the mountains looking to scout or spy, or to just cause havoc. As the story was told to me, one of my patrols came upon a man fighting a group of Thellians. One on five. Before they could arrive to help, the man was felled and his body thrown into a deep gorge. The patrol drove off the Thellians, and when they scouted the area, they found the swordsman's weapon. It is the weapon you know hold."

King Thorndale held the sword in front of him, gripping it tightly as if he were about to use it. Death was not unknown to him. He had fought in many battles and had seen good men, close friends, fall in battle. But they've had some semblance of peace for so many years, he forgot the pain of a friend's death.

"The swordsman was described in detail," Lord Neffenmark said softly. "The description reminded me of someone." He paused, allowing the king to gather his thoughts for the lie that he knew would come. "Was it really your Knight Captain, Sir Brace Hawkden?"

The king would not lie, but he also knew that there was a limit to the information that he was going to reveal to Lord Neffenmark. He was in pain, but his wise mind still spun quickly and sharply. "Yes, it was," the king replied.

"I do not wish to pry at such a moment, but I have to ask why he was in the mountains, heading north towards Thell." Neffenmark tried hard to keep a smile from spreading across his face. He knew he had trapped the king and he was about ready to pounce on any lie or deceit that was spoken.

"He was carrying a message for me," the king said. He surprised himself for being so forthright. "Lord Neffenmark, I have been communicating with the Thellian king for some time. I have been trying to arrange a peace agreement with them."

"Sire!" Lord Neffenmark exclaimed with a loud, surprised shout. He knew why Brace was there. He just had not expected the king to admit it, so his surprised response seemed genuine. "They are our sworn enemy, how could you! And behind our back! Who else is in this with you?"

King Thorndale tried to keep himself from getting angry. He tried not to let his past experience with Lord Neffenmark affect him. Calmly, he answered, "I am the king. I do not need to ask permission for anything I do."

"But I am on the front lines. If there were to be an invasion, it would be my land, my men, my villages who would be attacked first. Do you not think that I should be kept abreast of what is going on? Especially when it directly affects me?"

The king stood up, standing as tall as his aging body allowed. With as firm a tone as he could muster, and without showing anger, he replied, "Peace affects all of us, Neffenmark. It is this response of yours that demonstrates why I kept this a secret. Our kingdoms have been at war for as long as there has been a history. But for the past few years, conflict has settled down. It is time for us to meet together and try and at least be civil. I am not asking for us to be friends, but for us to at least exist together without fighting."

"It seems your message is falling on deaf ears," Lord Neffenmark replied dryly. "The Thellians who attacked your man, they were not just mountain raiders trying to make trouble. They were described to me as soldiers, clad in armor and bearing the crest of the king himself. Maybe your message was not to their liking. They have never liked us. They are jealous of us. We have fertile land, while they can barely harvest enough food for themselves. We have grand castles and gardens, while their cities are dirty and smell of garbage. They have led you to your demise. I can only guess that they are gathering their army and getting ready to invade as we speak."

"I have brokered peace," King Thorndale said firmly.

"You have brokered nothing!" Lord Neffenmark shouted back, sensing a chink in the king's kingly armor. "They slaughter your emissary, the one who delivered your message of peace. And you can still not see through it all?"

The king was speechless. For a moment, his anger was about to boil over at the tone that Lord Neffenmark was using with. But the words somehow sunk in. They actually made sense. There could be no other explanation for Brace's demise. It had to be deceit. Their king had promised him peace, while he was preparing his own kingdom for war. After a long silence of contemplating Lord Neffenmark's words, the king said, "We must gather the council of the lords."

"And then it will be too late," Neffenmark replied calmly. "With your knights and my army, we can field enough men on the battlefield to deliver a severe blow to them. But only if we act now and attack before they march through the mountains. And while we march, the other lords can build up the army so that we can finally drive a stake through their heart! We must attack now!"

The king was silent as he gathered his robes and sat back down upon his plush chair. He looked around him, at all that he had. There was not a luxury or a desire that he could not obtain. His walls were draped with tapestries purchased from merchants that had traveled thousands of miles to deliver them. He drank from finely wrought goblets, filled with the finest of wines. There was not a day that went by that he was hungry or even thought of eating. His attendants were constantly putting food in front of him. He did not have the unlimited wealth of the emperor, but it felt like it.

And yet, for all that he had, he could only focus on the one thing that had eluded him and those that had come before him. True lasting peace. It was true that they were not currently actively at war, but there was always the threat of it. Until recently, not a season went by without a messenger from the mountains describing a Thellian raiding party sweeping through one village or another, terrorizing the villagers, stealing whatever they could carry. Rarely were the raids truly violent, but on occasion, innocent lives were lost.

But he had done it. He had brokered peace. It had been almost six months since he had last heard of a raid. The Thellian king was doing his part. The words of their communication had always been sincere. He had to believe it. But now, there was this. His messenger. One of the greatest knights who had ever lived killed by treachery. His confusion and shock slowly morphed into anger. He became hot under the collar as he thought more and more about the Thellians and their lies and deceit.

Lord Neffenmark did all he could to not smile. He could see the change in the king. It was time for him to add fuel to the fire. "Sire, I acknowledge that we have not always been in agreement."

The king looked up, wanting to respond, but he could not find the words. Not being in agreement was a true understatement. But he let Lord Neffenmark speak.

"We have had our differences, but I have always been loyal to the kingdom and to your rule," Lord Neffenmark said slowly as if he were choosing his words carefully. But in reality, they were words that he had spoken in his head many times over the past few days. "But regardless of those differences, we must work together. You as the leader of the kingdom, and me as your humble servant." He lowered his eyes, and then his head in dramatic fashion. "I have not always treated you as such, and for that, I beg your forgiveness. But the past few days, with the threat of the Thellians upon us, I have come to realize the need for your strong rule and leadership. We are a small kingdom, but we have great men all around us. The Knights of Karmon could stand against any army. We have wealth greater than nations many times our size. This city is the grandest that I have ever seen. We live and thrive as a kingdom because of strong rulers like yourself. But that means that others will be jealous of us, and we must be willing to fight for what we have rightfully earned."

The king, still seething with anger from the thought of the treachery of the Thellians, did not realize how powerful his emotions were, and how dangerous they were. Riding the wave of those emotions, he said, "I accept your apology, and hope that we can finally work together to rid the world of the Thellians. At first light, I will send messengers throughout the kingdom to call the men of the kingdom to arms. But in the meantime, the festivities are making their way to the great hall where the dancing and merrymaking is going on without me. We will have one last night of celebration before I shall call the knights together and we march northward."

The king straightened his robes, puffing out his chest, and let out a long, slow sigh. "Lord Neffenmark, we will prevail once and for all. Shall we proceed to the great hall?"

"Your Majesty," Lord Neffenmark said with one last bow. "You must excuse me as I need to get back to my castle as soon as possible. If my men are to join yours on the battlefield, I do not have a moment to spare. Plus," Lord Neffenmark added with a smile. "Dancing really is not my thing."

***

Conner walked through the shadows of the courtyard. The sounds of the celebration echoed all around him. It was a mumbled mess of sound from the laughter and shouting of merrymaking to the stringed instruments playing their music. He wasn't interested in joining in the fun. Dancing certainly wasn't something that he wanted to attempt. Watching through the open doors of the great hall, he could see the nobles and knights and squires spinning and moving about the floor. He tried to follow the moves, but they did not make any sense to him.

But it was clear that they had all worked hard on it, as they all moved in unison.

The Princess was in the middle of the dance floor, her long blonde hair tied up in a bun, tight against the back of her head. A wide smile was on her face as she danced arm in arm with the skinny Mayfair. He too had a smile on his face. They spun and turned to the music, following the dance steps that they had been taught since they were barely able to walk. It was the perfect place for her, Conner thought. She was in her element, with her people.

He stood in the darkness, in the shadow of a tall hedge where the light of the nearby torches couldn't reach. While the music continued to play, he watched her and smiled. She was who she was, and he was who he was. There was nothing that was going to change that. He felt happy for her that she was able to enjoy the festival and have fun with her friends. He finally felt okay with it. He would be her champion, and he would protect her. He hoped that he had proved that he could be there for her if she needed him.

After some time, the musicians took a break and the dancing stopped. The Princess got lost in a crowd of people, so Conner decided it was time to move on and find Master Goshin. Conner found him in his chambers carefully placing his delicate scrolls into leather cases. But that was clearly not the only thing that he had been doing. His chamber was as neat and tidy as it had ever been. All the weapon making tools were neatly put away. Even the floor was swept.

Goshin looked up as Conner approached. "Conner, it is good to see you."

"And you, Master Goshin," Conner replied wearily. He suddenly realized what Goshin was doing and asked, "You're packing them up?"

"Yes, I am." Goshin lowered his eyes. "I was hoping that you would spend more time at the festival. There is not a ball for the squires and knights and the ladies of the castle?"

"Dancing is not my thing," Conner said coolly.

"You are the Princess' Champion. It would be good for you to be at her side. Or is it that you don't know how to dance?"

"I…"

Goshin stood up and grabbed Conner by the hands. "I shall teach you, then!"

Conner pulled away, slightly irritated at first, then when he realized that Goshin was not serious, he laughed with the old man. "I think I would do better on my own."

"That is wise. I do not know how to dance, either."

Conner looked closely at the leather cases and then realized there were also two saddle bags stuffed full sitting on the floor. "You're not just packing up, you're packing to leave?"

Goshin let out a long sigh. "It is true." He waved his hands at the scrolls. "These are just the start. I must find a library to complete my research."

"Research?"

Goshin nodded. "There is an ancient prophecy of my people that foretells our future. King Thorndale has discovered what could be one part of that prophecy. If true, then the world as we know it could end. Or change in a way that will not be good for us. If this is the case, and if indeed the prophecy is about to come about, then King Thorndale would like to prepare his kingdom. And if this discovery means nothing...Well, King Thorndale would like to know that as well. But I need to find more information on the prophecy, and I need to go to the Great Library in Taran to continue my research."

"Why you? Why now? My training…"

"Your training is complete," Goshin declared. "Well, at least as much as I can teach you."

Conner shook his head. "No! You have so much more to teach me. I only know a little of being Sak'hurai or even Kin Shan! Who is teach me everything that I need to know!"

Goshin stepped to Conner and put both hands on his shoulders. "Sak'hurai is more than being skilled. It is here." He tapped Conner on the center of his chest. "It starts here, and it ends with the sword. You have it. And you proved it on the field today. I have given you what you need. Now you need to hone it. To forge it on your own. Sak'hurai have learned the same skills for centuries. The moves have not changed. The fighting stances. Even the weapons have not changed."

"And you haven't taught me all of it yet, there is so much more to learn!"

"You will take what I have taught you. What you learned as a squire. And what you will learn from the other knights. And you will be more than Sak'hurai. You can become a swordsman of such skill that no one can stop you."

"But not without you."

"I will only hold you back. I have taught you what I know, but it will be not enough." Goshin squeezed Conner's shoulders and stepped back. "I was to leave in the morning after I talked to you. But since you are here, I will take my leave now."

"Will I see you again?"

Goshin nodded his head. "I do have more to teach you." He tapped Conner on the side of his head. "Next time for head to learn, not muscles. I only wish there was more time. But time is gone."

He tucked his scrolls under his arms and picked up his bags. "Goodbye, Conner. You are a great young man. Do not let the world change you. Ever. Be who are. Be who you are supposed to be."

"I don't..."

Master Goshin smiled. "Do not worry that you don't understand now. You will. I do not know how long I will be, but I will try and return by next spring. Until then, take care of the princess, and take care of yourself." Then he turned and walked away.

Conner watched him leave in silence, confused at the suddenness. The day had started exactly as he had planned, with him able to finally show the king, and the princess, the skills that he had been learning. But when he had hoped that the squires and knights would treat him better, they had not. They weren't mean to him, they simply ignored him. Not even those who had been friendly to him before acknowledged him. And now, his master, the man who had made him who he had become, was gone. He felt as alone as he ever had. He sat on a stool and buried his head in his hands and wept.

"Conner?" the soft voice broke him from his trance.

He had no idea how long he had been sitting on the stool with his head in his hands. He lifted his head with what little strength he had left. The voice came from the darkness and Conner could only make out a shadowed form standing in the doorway to the barely lit chamber.

"Elissa?" Conner asked.

"I have been looking for you," Princess Elissa said softly. "We missed you at the ball. And...I wanted to talk to you."

"I didn't think you want to talk to me anymore," Conner replied sharply. The humiliation that he had felt out in the woods when she and her friend and treated him like he did not exist had morphed into anger. The tone was really harsher than he had intended, but he felt relieved when he let it out. They had been friends, talking and sharing their thoughts and feelings. But something had changed.

She had dropped her head at his words and looked down at her feet. "I did not think that you wanted to be my champion anymore."

Conner was even more surprised. "What? What are you talking about? Being your champion is the only way that I can even be near you!" His emotions and thoughts suddenly became perfectly clear to him. The moment the words came out of his mouth, it all made sense. "We spent so much time together, running for our lives, and I liked being with you. But I'm a peasant boy. You're the princess of a kingdom! How can I compare to that! How can I compare to the other suitors? The other lord's sons that hang out at the castle spending their entire day doing nothing but eating and merrymaking. And me, I clean pig pens, horse stalls, and let myself be pummeled by arrogant little kids that I could whip in a second. If it weren't for being your champion, then I would have been sent back to my village, to live out the rest of my life hunting and fishing and just being. But being your champion, I can be with you. Be with someone I really care about."

"Conner…" tears had welled up in her eyes. "I like you, too, but…But you are…"

"I look at you and my heart stops. I see you laugh and have fun with someone like that skinny jerk Mayfair and I burn with jealousy."

"I cannot…" Her words got lost in her sobs.

"You cannot what?"

"I am a princess. I have duties, responsibilities."

Conner let out a forced laugh. "Really? Responsibilities? You play dress up in your fancy gowns. You parade around the gardens. What responsibilities do you really have?"

"Someday I will rule the realm." Princess Elissa declared.

"Rule? As queen? And who will be your king?" Conner countered with a sneer.

"I don't need a king," she replied, lifting her chin.

"The gods gave your family this kingdom, but only a man can rule it."

"Well, maybe the gods are wrong!" she shouted back. "I do not need you or anyone else to tell me what I can and cannot do!"

"Know your place in this world!" Conner knew he had gone too far as soon as the words came out. He regretted the tone as much as words, but he kept his lips tight because there was a small part of him that believed what he had said.

Her face turned a deep red, and she replied with a lowered voice, "I could have you flogged for speaking to me this way."

He looked at her for a long moment and then asked, "Why?"

"Why, what?!" she asked confused.

"Why could you have me flogged?" Conner asked.

"Because I am the princess," she snapped back. "Is that what you wanted to hear? I can't change that. I can't change who I am any more than you can. I will always be a princess."

"And I will always be a peasant boy," Conner said. The anger that had filled him was leaving just as fast as it had risen up inside of him. "So I can never measure up to you."

Conner looked around at the empty chamber and wondered how long it would take him to catch up with Master Goshin. He could join him in his studies. And then he would be able to see Taran.

"It is time for me to leave," Conner said softly.

Princess Elissa shook her head. "I do not want you to go," she said.

"I'm done with what you want," Conner said. He turned and marched out of the chamber.

He did not see Elissa crumple to the ground, sobbing uncontrollably.

Chapter Eighteen

Marik bent down to look closely at the head. Small animals had nibbled at it, and there was already a small swarm of bugs flying around the severed body part. He held his breath, trying to avoid taking in the horrible stench that emanated from it. The head was from an old man with a shaggy gray beard. The dress of the nearby body indicated that he was likely a mountain nomad, most likely Thellian. The cut was clean, either from a very sharp blade or very strong man.

The grass of the field at the base of the mountain was still covered in morning dew, making his leather boots wet and his feet cold. But it also helped him see the way the grass blades had been bent by the events that had transpired the day before. The old man had died here. A younger man, much larger, was slain about a hundred feet away, possibly as he was trying to run away. Three had arrived on foot. Someone who limped and two others. He was fortunate that one of them limped as it made for better tracks to follow. It could have been the old man, but it didn't appear that the old man had any sort of leg injury. His only other conclusion was that it was Brace who had been the limper.

The horses had come from the trees that lined the small creek, so he followed the tracks to a spot that was well matted and torn up. The horses had been there for some time, presumably waiting for Brace and his companions. He spent a few minutes searching, but there were not any signs of who the attackers might have been. Only torn up dirt clumps and matted grass could be found.

He took the opportunity to fill up his water skin from the creek and splash some water on his face. The winter snows from the White

Mountains fed the creek, making the creek free flowing and fast. It was very cold but refreshing. While kneeling at the bank of the creek, he looked over at the other side of the creek. The ground was flat and appeared torn up as well. With a running start, he was able to leap across the expanse of water, thankful that it was but a small creek and not a wide river.

There were clear prints that lead out of a thicker grove of trees. After pushing his way through some unusually thick underbrush, he found the abandoned camp. There was only the remnants of a campfire and matted grasses to show that anything had been there. He scouted the perimeter quickly but found nothing of interest. Whoever had here arrived from this side of the creek came from the north, and then crossed the creek to kill the old man and take Brace. Either the horseman had happened upon Brace and the two dead men by chance, or they were lying in wait for them.

Marik returned to the clearing and the two dead bodies. He thought briefly about burying them, but he didn't have any time to waste. And even if he did have the time, he didn't know if he would have. They were Thellians, the enemy. For his entire life, he had hated them. He had fought them and killed them. It didn't make him feel proud, but he didn't really feel sad about it, either. But now that the king was trying to make peace, and Brace had risked his life for peace, maybe he needed to rethink what he thought of the Thellians. For a moment, he looked at the two bodies and didn't think them as Thellians, but as people. Men with fathers and mothers. Maybe children. The old man likely had grandchildren. He turned away from the bodies and towards tracks that led north, towards the army encampment. Right now, he needed to focus his energy and finding Brace. After that, he would have a lot of thinking to do.

***

"Father?" Princess Elissa said from the doorway.

King Thorndale turned at the sound of his daughter's voice. The smile on his face faded at the sight he saw. "Elissa?"

She stepped into his chamber, and the royal guard attending the doorway pulled the double doors shut behind him. She tried to smooth out the wrinkles of her gown, but it was to no avail. There was also nothing to do about the dirt stains. If she had looked in a mirror, she would have been horrified at her presentation.

Arpwin, who had been helping the king put on his armor quickly crossed the room and took the princess by the hand and led her to a couch. "Are you okay, your highness?"

She ignored his question, for her eyes were focused on her father. "Why are you wearing your armor?"

"Elissa, what is wrong?" the king asked. "You looked like you slept with the horses."

"I am fine," she said sharply and asked again, "Father, why are you in your armor?"

The king was silent for a moment as he pondered his answer. He glanced at Arpwin, who remained silent. He was on his own on this one. "It fits a bit tighter than the last time I wore it. I did not know that metal shrinks over time." He smiled, but Elissa did not share in his humor.

The king did not wear the same suit of full plate armor that his knights did. His was a finely crafted breastplate that not only protected his chest and back, but had plates that covered his shoulders. It was as functional as it was ceremonial. It was highly polished and nearly flawless in its smoothness. The last time he had worn it was from the back of the army, and he never had to test its effectiveness. The chain mail shirt that he wore underneath covered him from head down past his thighs. The helm was fashioned similar to his chest plate. It was carefully wrought and polished to the same shimmer. Unlike the breastplate that fit almost too snuggly, the helm fit perfectly atop his head.

He pulled off the helm and set it carefully on a nearby table. "The men of the realm have been called to arms. The army will be raised, and as soon they have gathered here at the castle, they will follow the knights northward."

"War?" Elissa whispered.

"Yes," the king said. "I will be leading our soldiers into battle."

"War?" she repeated. The announcement had taken her by surprise, and she was not sure how she should react.

"Yes, war, I am afraid. The king of Thell has refused my offers of peace and has committed an act of war. I cannot sit idly by while he executes my emissaries. He will pay for this transgression through his own blood." He turned to his faithful attendant. "Arpwin, please help me out of this."

Arpwin left Elissa's side to help the king get out of the armor. After several minutes of struggle, the king pulled a thick robe on and settled himself in a plush chair with a goblet of sweet wine. "Lord Arrin, Lord Kor, and Lord Martin have been summed to the castle. They will govern the city while I am away."

Elissa was still in a daze. The words were hard for her to comprehend. She had never known war or even a major conflict in her lifetime. She looked at her father and could only see the worst. "Father, you cannot go."

"I must," the king replied. "It is my duty as king and leader of the realm. I cannot ask my knights and the men that I rule to take up arms if I am not willing myself."

"But you might die," she said, her lower lip trembling.

"I am old, my dear. I might die any day. If the gods will…"

"Damn the gods!" she said fear suddenly being replaced by anger. "You cannot go to war. I cannot lose you, too!"

The king quickly jumped from his seat and took his daughter in a firm hug. "My dear," he said, his eyes watering. "You will not lose me like you lost your mother. I will always be here for you."

She responded by holding her father tightly, her anger going away just as quickly as it came. In its place were uncontrollable sobs.

King Thorndale held her close until her sobs became soft whimpers. He released the hug and held her at arm's length so he could look into her eyes. "And I have nothing to worry about, for I know that you have a courageous champion who will always be at your side."

"I need you, father," she said, pushing herself back into his arms. "Not some silly boy."

"I will always be here for you, but I also have a duty to the kingdom, to ensure its safety. Your champion proved himself yesterday." He pushed Elissa away again to look back into her eyes. "Did you not see how he embarrassed those squires? It was amazing how quick he was. I never could have imagined that Master Goshin would do so much, so quickly. He is an amazing warrior."

"Master Goshin?" she asked.

"Yes. He has been training with Master Goshin from the time he arrived at the castle. You did not know?"

She shook her head.

"That Conner is an incredible young man. Training with the squires during the day and with Master Goshin pretty much every other waking moment." He smiled at his daughter with a twinkle in his eye. "And he seemed to spend whatever time remained with you."

"He is a peasant," she said harshly. "And just a boy."

"Oh my young princess, he is a boy no more. He may yet fill out into his body. But he is strong and will do well as your protector. He is smart, too, from what Master Goshin has told me about him. He knows how to read and write, you know."

"I did not know," Elissa said, her eyes dropping to the floor.

"Master Goshin is teaching him. He may be no scholar, but reading and writing will do well for him in the castle."

"He seems to no longer like the castle," Elissa said. "Or to be my champion."

"Unfortunately, that is no longer a choice of his," the king said firmly. "He is duty bound to you and to me. He will give his life for you, if necessary. He will protect you to the end. That is his duty and the promise he made. And you will abide by that promise, as well. While I am on the field of battle, he will be by your side. Day and night."

His voice softened as he continued, "You and I are all that remain of the royal family. My brothers died so long ago. And you mother. Well, she died so soon after you were born…"

"Why did you not remarry?" Elissa suddenly asked. It had been a question that she had thought to ask many times, but really never had a chance, or the guts, to ask. "I mean…if you wanted another child, a male heir…"

This time, it was the king's eyes that watered. "Your mother was a special woman. One of a kind. Irreplaceable." His voice cracked and faltered. He turned his head so that his daughter could not see the tears streaming down his cheeks. At times he hated himself for this, for feeling the way he did about his wife. It would have been easier if he didn't love her so much if he hadn't missed her so much. If he had been willing to remarry, to have another queen, to have his heirs, then maybe he would have gotten over his grief.

The king took a deep breath to collect himself and turned back to his daughter. He looked at her, sitting in what was once the prettiest dress in the realm, but was now not much more than a tattered rag. Her hair was messy and tangled. She looked more waif than princess.

"I wish I knew her," Elissa said.

"She was just like you," the king said, desperately trying to hold back tears. "Beautiful, loving, and kind. And strong. I was not ready to be king when your grandfather passed on. But she was there for me and helped me become who I am today. I owe everything to her. She would not have liked me going to war, either. But because the gods have put me in charge of the realm, I have to make the hard decisions. I just hope it is the right one."

"If you have doubts, then why go to war? Have you not tried talking to the Thellian king?"

The king straightened. His initial reaction was defensive, how dare this little girl question his authority! But the thought quickly passed as he realized his daughter was no longer the little girl that he wanted her to be. She was grown up. Almost the same age that her mother was when they first met. "I have been talking to their king. King Lorraine and I have been in communication for almost a year." He dropped his eyes to the ground because he could not bear to look into her eyes at the moment. "We had settled upon a peace treaty of sorts, and the final details were being hammered out. However, he decided to go back on the deal by killing my messenger."

"He killed one man, and you go to war?" the princess asked. "Isn't that a bit silly?"

It was, the king agreed to himself. "Wars have been started for less," the king said aloud. "Wars start more from personal insults that anything else. It's not just this. This is just the last in a series of events. Lord Neffenmark has been suffering from their assaults on his land for years. He bears the brunt of their actions as he holds the northern lands."

Elissa wrinkled her nose. "I do not like that man. He looks at me funny."

"His family is one of the oldest in the kingdom. At one time, his family ruled most of this land that is our kingdom. That was when we were just a bunch of tribes struggling to survive. One of your ancestors, about five hundred years ago, was able to align the tribes into a cohesive government. He built the first city of Karmon and turned the wilderness into a kingdom. Neffenmark's ancestors were vital to keeping the kingdom together, but it was our own ancestor, Raven Thorndale that was given the blessing of the gods and became king. A descendant of that first Thorndale king has held the crown ever since."

"I have not heard this history before, how come?" Princess Elissa asked.

"I did not know that history interested you," the king responded. "It's well known. I guess I kind of assumed that you already knew it."

"Can you tell me more?"

"Of course," the king said with a wide smile. "What do you wish to know?"

Princess Elissa returned a smile to her father and said, "Everything. Start from the beginning."

Chapter Nineteen

Conner woke with numbness in his arm. He rolled over and his arm flopped along a moment later. He shook it and a warm pain flooded through it. The tingling went all the way to his fingertips. He kept shaking his arm, waiting for the feeling to get back. The light that trickled through the window at the end of the hall where his chamber was located told him that he had slept in late. He jumped up in a panic and started to quickly dress. As a squire in training, he was always supposed to be up before the sun, fed and dressed and ready for the day's work.

With his shirt pulled up over his head, he suddenly realized that he was no longer a squire in training. He did not need to get up early. The second wave of panic came over him as he realized that Master Goshin would now be long gone. He finished dressing while yelling at himself for falling sleep. Maybe with a fast enough horse, he might catch him before night fell, assuming he could find his trail. He rummaged through his belongings and collected a thick wool cloak, his bow, quiver, and a handful of arrows. He had a few coins stashed away and stuffed them into a small leather purse. His next stop would be the kitchens where he would try and steal away with a loaf of bread and maybe some cheese. He would need enough to get through the day without having to stop and forage for his own food. Once he caught up with Master Goshin, they would be able to survive off the land.

With sack in hand, he ran through the halls of the squire barracks. It didn't surprise him that they were empty, as they should all be out training. What did surprise him was the hustle and bustle of the rest of the castle. The halls were filled with people moving quickly from one place to another. There was electricity to their actions. They all looked excited at doing their jobs, which seemed as mundane as hauling sacks and crates of this and that from one part of the castle to another. He found the kitchen to be packed full of cooks and servants busy cooking like there was to be a grand feast in the evening, but he could not remember what it could be. Fortunately for him, the busyness of the kitchens made it easy for him to grab two large loaves of bread and a handful of dried and cured meat.

What piqued his curiosity, though, was when he passed by the training field. He wanted to avoid it all together, but it would have required him to backtrack through the entire castle. Rather than spend one more minute longer in the castle, he decided to just walk past as quickly as he could and hope that no one bothered or cared to notice him. He noticed the lack of sound even before he arrived. The field was empty. Even the day after the festival, the squires were still supposed to be training. Every day. Rain or shine. They always trained. But now they weren't.

The stables were next, and they were nearly as empty as the squire practice field. All of the knight's horses were gone. Only a handful of the smaller horses used for messengers were left. That was okay with him, as he wanted a faster, lighter one anyway. But it concerned him that all of the war horses were gone. He was about to claim one of the smaller riding horses when he noticed the stable warden carrying an armful of hay.

"Sir Kal!" Conner called out.

The aged master of the stables had long since passed the days of swordplay and jousting. Bent from age and misuse of his body, he was one of the oldest living knights and spent his days managing the stables. It was an easy job because he had a team of servants and squires to do his bidding. He simply needed to walk around the stables telling everyone what to do. It was actually odd for the old knight to be carrying anything.

The old knight turned to look at Conner. He squinted, trying to figure out who was calling his name. Conner walked forward until he was just a few feet away. "Squire Conner? Is that you?"

"Yes, Sir Kal, it is," Conner replied.

"Looking for a horse for another ride through the forest?" Sir Kal asked with a toothless smile.

"As a matter of fact, I am," Conner said.

Sir Kal shook his head. "Sorry, young man. But there are none that are left. They are all gone."

Conner looked around. He counted five that he could see. "But there are still some left. Over there are two of them. And three against that far wall."

Sir Kal cleared his throat. "Those are for the royal messengers. They are not to be used but by the messenger who must travel to the field of battle."

The words caught Conner off guard. "Field of battle? What are you talking about?"

"The battlefield," Sir Kal replied. "The war."

Conner stood with his mouth agape. "War? What war? And where are all the other horses? The knight's war horses?"

"They have all mustered for battle," Sir Kal replied. His words were so matter-of-fact it was as if going to war was a daily occurrence.

"Sir Kal, you are not making any sense. What battle are you talking about?"

"Were you not called to arms this morning?" Sir Kal asked. "All the squires and knights were called. They are being fitted with weapons and armor. Many are leaving this afternoon to scout the way north. Those who are left are to scour the city to gather all the men and prepare them for war." He shook his head, as if he were talking to a crazy man, and walked off with his armful of hay.

Conner's head spun. War? And against whom? Were they finally going to invade Thell? Or did Thell decide to invade us? The thought of war was both exciting and horrible at the same time. Everything he did for the past few months had really been about this moment. They didn't train for peace, they trained for war. A strange feeling of dread started in the pit of his stomach. He really couldn't comprehend what war meant. He had heard about it. There were stories of glory and honor about it. But the last real war that Karmon was in happened way before he was born. He really had no idea what going to war truly went.

Conner looked at the closest riding horse. It was in a stall about fifteen feet from where he stood. It was a light tan color with a black mane and tail. It was currently rummaging through the hay at its feet, being picky about what it decided to eat. Conner could have it saddled and ready to ride in two minutes. No one would know. No one would catch him. And certainly now, with the squires and knights called to battle, no one would surely chase after him. But the thought of war really scared him. Not because he was afraid of combat, but because he was afraid of what it meant for the kingdom and for Princess Elissa. His hesitation told him what he should do. Now was not the time to run away.

He returned to the squire barracks to put back his bags and supplies. Oddly, he found Arpwin, the king's personal assistant wandering the halls of the barracks. Conner was about to walk right past him, but Arpwin raised a hand and smiled at him.

"Ah!" Arpwin said in greeting. "It seems that your services are being requested by the king himself." He motioned down the hall towards the castle. "Shall we?"

"What is going on," Conner asked without moving.

"It is war," Arpwin replied. "Have you not heard?"

"Yes, but who? Why?"

"The knights are marching to the north to battle Thell," Arpwin said. "As to why King Thorndale believes that peace can never happen through diplomacy. He believes it is now time for a military solution."

"Then I should prepare as well. Where are the knights meeting?" Conner turned to leave, but Arpwin put a gentle hand on his arm.

"It is not the battlefield where you are needed," Arpwin said softly. "The king wishes you to attend to your duty."

"I am not going to sit back and babysit some snot nosed princess!" Conner shouted. "I am a soldier, and I am going to battle."

Arpwin lifted his hand off Conner' arm. "I am but the messenger, but I think your promise to the king and to the princess should not be overlooked."

"The princess has plenty of guards," Conner said. "The king's guard are not going to war, are they? They will still need to be around to guard the city gates and the castle."

"That is true," Arpwin replied. He started to say more, but then stopped himself. He scratched his beard and looked from Conner to the ground, and then back to Conner. "Conner," he finally said. "I have been the king's attendant for many years. So many years I have lost count. I am no soldier or trained in any way to fight in a battle. I serve the king and do what he asks. We talk some, but mostly he talks, and I listen. I am not one to give advice. I do not have the blessing of the gods like the king does. But I have seen and heard much in my many years. It has been a very long time since we have been at war. There have been battles and skirmishes here and there. But not a war. Not like what is happening now. The line of King Thorndale is long and historic. He is a direct ancestor of the first king of Karmon. That needs to stay in place for the kingdom to survive. I hope you understand that. That means the princess must survive. In whatever way is necessary. You did it once, and you may have to do it again. I don't think that the king really trusts anyone else other than you right now."

"Really?" Conner asked.

Arpwin nodded his head and put a hand on Conner's shoulder and squeezed gently. "Come with me. For the princess and for the king. It is true that there are still a number of royal guard in the city and in the castle to protect the princess, but it would mean more to both of them if you would stay and fulfill your promise. Whether you like it or not, you are Princess Elissa's Champion. There are plenty of knights to fight on the battlefield, but there is only you to stand at her side and protect her."

Conner dropped his head, resigned to a fate that he did not want. Now that the knights and army have been called to arms, he knew that his duty should be to the kingdom. He should be taking up arms and fighting for his kingdom. And once the fighting is over, he would go find Master Goshin and continue his training. But he had made the vow. And as much as he didn't want to stay back, he knew now it was the right choice. With a slight nod of his head, he let Arpwin lead him back up from the dark halls of the barracks to the waiting king.

***

King Thorndale was dressed in a simple gray nightshirt when Conner was let in. There were dark stains under the armpits and down the front of the shirt. The king's hair was matted and unkempt, but he wore a wide smile.

"Conner!" the king shouted. "You must excuse my appearance. I have been spending some time reacquainting myself with my sword. It seems that at some point the past few years, the swords have gotten heavier!" He laughed at his own joke, but his laughter faded when Conner didn't join in.

Conner stood stiffly, still quite uncomfortable in the presence of the king.

An attendant handed the king a goblet of wine, and he gulped it down. "Wine?" the king asked.

"No, your majesty," Conner replied.

"You do not seem quite yourself," the king asked.

Conner didn't know how much he should really say, so he paused a moment to consider his words carefully. "Your majesty. I know I have made a vow to be Princess Elissa's champion. But I have trained very hard, and I feel..."

"Enough," the king said softly. "I know you have trained hard. I know that Master Goshin has taught you well, trained you well. But you are not trained for battle. You have not trained atop a horse. Fighting from a horse is more than just being able to swing a blade. You have to know your horse, know how it moves and reacts to both swordsmen and pikemen. Defeating a pikeman with a ten-foot pole is not an easy task. Trust me, I know. In my youth, I did fight in battles against ranks of pikemen. Man on man, a knight is dominant, but a good pikeman balances out the battle. Unless of course, you have trained to defeat them. Your training has been to defend the princess, not the kingdom."

"I know, but..."

The king approached and put an arm around Conner. "I know how you feel. The men and boys you have been training with are going to war and you are not. When I was young, the same thing happened to me. My father took arms against a rogue Lord, and I had to stay at the castle. Being the next in line for the throne, my life was even more important than my father's. I had trained even more than you. I had trained as a knight, trained to fight from a horse. And I was left with the women in the castle. It is a humbling thing. But we all have our roles to play. Mine is to lead this war to finally rid us of the threat of Thell. Yours is to stay and protect my daughter. She is the last link to the next generation of Thorndale's, and the lineage must not be broken."

Conner nodded his head. He still did not like having to stay back, but it was the right thing to do.

"Now that we have that settled," the king said with a hearty slap on Conner's back. "There is a lovely young woman wandering the battlements atop the castle alone. I think she could use some company."

***

Conner found her standing in the space between two sections of the battlements that lined the top of the castle. Down below them the knights and squires were preparing for war. Armor needed to be tended to. Swords needed to be sharpened. Tents, blankets, and all sorts of supplies needed to supply a force of knights marching to war needed to be loaded onto wagons. It was a business that seemed chaotic, but a careful eye revealed that that everyone was doing something with purpose.

The sun had climbed high above, casting the full heat of the summer upon them. There would be no more cool days for several months. The nights would still be pleasant, but the mid-day heat would get even more oppressive. Princess Elissa was dressed for the warm weather in a light and thin gown. Her hair was tied behind her head, which she rarely did. It hung in one thick strand down the middle of her back.

Conner stepped forward from the shade of the stairwell, and she turned to him. No smile, but no angered look, either.

"Princess," Conner said with a slight bow.

"You look well," she said approvingly.

He had finally found some clothes that fit him. They weren't the silky bright colors that the other courtiers like to wear, but they also weren't the rough, scratchy wool tunics and leggings that the squires were provided. His tunic was soft and comfortable, loose fitting, but not baggy. It made him feel... normal.

"What are you doing?" He wasn't sure how to start the conversation. He was nervous, and his palms were sweaty.

"Are we really going to war?" she asked.

"Yes," he answered. "Well, not everyone. But most."

"The Guard, too?"

"Some. Most of the Royal Guard will stay here. And some of the older knights as well to help train the army. And then they will march north with them. But the rest of the knights, they will be riding out in a few days."

After a moment, she asked, "You?"

Conner turned away from her and leaned over the chest-high battlements so he could avoid looking at her. "No. Not me."

"You sound sad," Elissa said. "As if you want to go war."

"Those that I have trained with over the past few months are going to war," Conner replied with an irritated tone. "And I am staying back. I should be with them."

"I'm glad you're staying," she said. She turned to him, and he turned to look at her. She smiled at him, and he gave her a weak smile back. "Walk with me," she said.

He did as he was asked. She led him down the steep stairs within the tower, across the courtyard that was filled with wagons, and through the castle gates. Conner had not spent much time in the city. With training both as a squire and with Master Goshin, there was little time for sightseeing. Stopping just past the gate, he looked out at the city and for the first time took in what he saw. From atop the tallest tower, the entire city could be seen. But even though the castle was on the highest ground above the city, from where they stood, they still could only see a smart part of the city. They city had evolved over time. The buildings and houses closest to the castle were the oldest. They were smaller and tended to continually be on the verge of falling down. The stone that made the walls were crumbling and always in a constant state of repair. As one walked away from the castle, and towards the city walls, the buildings became taller and more elaborate. Many of the larger buildings were constructed from stone blocks carved from a quarry upstream of the Tyre River. The stone masons had taken their time with those buildings, adding art to the architecture. But like all cities, there were good parts and bad parts. Even some of the newer parts of the city were not good places to walk after dark.

Elissa started to walk away, but Conner was not following. He seemed to be frozen, stuck in a place that he was not familiar with. Finally, she grabbed his hand and pulled him along. He didn't bother trying to release his hand from hers, nor did she try and let go. They walked for some time through the streets of South Karmon, hand in hand.

Their first stop was one of the many open-air markets. It seemed to be filled with as many vendors as there were patrons. Conner felt a bit claustrophobic in the crush of people, but Princess Elissa kept his hand in hers with a tight grip. She led him straight to an old woman selling fruit. They chatted briefly about the weather, then about the woman's sick husband. The princess ended up buying a small sack of apples.

"Do you not fear being here, alone?" Conner asked.

"But I am not alone," the princess said. She nodded in greeting to several passers-by. "I am here with you. And what would I have to be afraid of?"

"Well, it was just a few months ago that you were kidnapped, almost killed…"

She squeezed his hand and let out a childish giggle. "My silly champion. The festival is fresh in the minds of these people. They saw you. They saw what you did. They should be afraid of you."

"I am nothing," Conner said. "A peasant boy."

Elissa playfully squeezed his upper arm and then patted him on the chest. "You are hard, full of muscle. You are no boy."

Conner let her lead them through the city. At first, he thought she was giving him a tour of the city. Partly because her path seemed to have no reason to it and partly because she spent most of the time talking about the city. They passed several more markets, one with fresh fish that seemed to have been sitting out in the sun a bit too long. They quickly moved past and tried to stay as up-wind from the fish market as they could. But their seemingly random path suddenly came to a stop near the northwestern wall. The homes of this part of the city could hardly be called houses. They were built from scraps and leftovers. Many did not have any doors, and some were lacking a solid roof. He had never realized that there were homes like this in the city. He had always thought everyone in the city was wealthy and had a good home to live in. Some of the homes around his village fell apart after time. Sometimes it was after a big storm. Sometimes just because the house was old and the wood rotted. But when that happened, there was always a neighbor or someone to help rebuild the house. Conner realized it was probably easier to rebuild a house in the woods than in the middle of a city.

"Come," Elissa said, standing in the doorway of a nearby shack. There was no door, only a tattered blanket to act like one.

The house had a single room and smelled of sweaty and dirty bodies. There was little in the room other than a table with two chairs, one of them had only three legs. A pile of blankets was tossed into a corner of the room. She moved towards the blankets, and as she neared, the blankets started to move. A small ashen-white face appeared from underneath the blankets.

Elissa leaned down and whispered to the small girl. "Mary? How are you feeling?"

The young girl's eyes lit up when she recognized who was talking to her. "Elissa!" the young girl said excitedly.

Elissa rubbed the girl's face, pushing the matted hair off her forehead. "You look tired."

"I was outside yesterday," the little girl replied.

"Mary!" Elissa said in a sweet, but scolding tone.

"It was the festival. I had to see," Mary explained.

"See? See what?" Elissa asked.

"I wanted to see you in your dress that you were telling me about. The one that you had made for the ball. Did you dance with him? Is that him?" The girl looked up at Conner and smiled.

"Hello," Conner said.

"Did she dance with you? Are you Conner? You look like him. Big and strong. Just like she described."

Elissa's face turned red. Conner gave her a wide smile. "Princess Elissa talked about me?" he asked.

"She says I can call her Elissa because we are friends. Are you really Conner?" the little girl asked.

"Yes I am," Conner replied.

"She talks about you all the time," Mary said with a giggle.

Conner glanced at Elissa with a raised eyebrow. Then he asked the little girl, "What does she say about me?"

"Okay," Elissa said, interrupted. "That's about enough! Mary, you ask too many questions! Are you hungry?"

The girl shook her head. "Momma made me porridge for lunch. It was good."

Elissa rubbed the side of the girls face again. "You are tired. You should rest."

Mary rolled over onto her side and pulled the blankets up tight. "Okay," she said in a near whisper. "Will you sing to me?"

"Of course," Elissa said. She closed her eyes and began to sing. Conner sat on the ground and watched Elissa. Her eyes were closed, and her soft, red lips brought magic to their ears. For several minutes the princess went through the song until the breathing of the little girl settled down, and she was fast asleep. Letting the song fade, Elissa carefully bent over Mary and touched her lips to the little girl's forehead. With a last glance, she backed out of the house.

Conner stopped Elissa just outside the door. "Who is that?"

Elissa looked around at the houses. "She is just one of the sick. My father is a good man, but he never leaves his castle. He rules from the hill and never sees what I see." Tears had filled her eyes. "There are so many like Mary. She will likely never see ten years old. The sickness can spread so quickly."

"So do something," Conner said.

Elissa shook her head. "There is not much to do. I come here…"

"But you are the princess, surely there is something you can do," Conner said.

"There are too many of them." She waved her hands and turned around. "I can't help them all."

"There has to be something. Have you talked to your father?"

"He does not understand. He barely listens to me when I talk to him about it." She brushed off her dress. "Come there are others."

"Others? Like Mary."

Elissa stopped and looked at the ground. She squeezed her eyes shut, trying to hold back the tears. "No. They are worse."

***

Conner sat outside on the stump of a tree. He wished that the tree was still there as it would have given him shade. But he had to settle with just not being on his feet anymore. It wasn't long before Elissa came out, gave the mother a hug, a peck on the cheek, and sat on the stump next to him.

"I'm sorry," Conner said softly, wishing he could have stomached just one more visit. But he couldn't. The little boy in the broken down house was too young, too sick, and too close to dying.

"No, I should have told you what I was doing today. I was feeling lonely and just wanted to have some company."

"How often do you do this?" Conner asked.

"I try to do it every day."

Conner was amazed. "Really? Every day?"

"It's not like I have a whole lot of other stuff to do. But, it makes me feel...close to everyone. To walk among them. To talk to them. I like them, and I hope they like me, too," Elissa said.

"They do," Conner replied. "I can tell. They don't treat you like a princess. They treat you better."

Elissa looked at him with a confused look. "What does that mean?"

"When I was growing up, the king, his knights. You. Everyone in royalty was something that I could never be close to. The king is so powerful and so...full of awe that I could hardly realize what it meant. I could never image actually meeting the king, or talking to him. And you, the princess, the same way. These people, they don't treat you like far off royalty, they treat you like their friend. You have their respect because of what you do and because you care."

"I'm just trying to do what is right."

Conner put an arm around her shoulders. "And that is why you will be an excellent queen."

She leaned into him and his arm pulled her tightly into him. Her head fell on his shoulder, and she let out a long sigh. "I may be queen someday, but I will still be only queen to my king."

"I was so wrong about you," Conner said. "When the time comes, you will make a great leader of this kingdom."

"You are a silly boy, Conner," she said. "I am but a girl. I could never lead this kingdom."

He let her last statement go. There was no point in arguing it with her. Indeed their culture did not allow for a queen to lead the kingdom, but Conner knew in his heart that she had what it took. For a long time, they sat upon the stump, watching the city.

And the city watched back, seeing their beloved princess being comforted by a young man. A young man who was just like them. Not a knight. Or a noble. He did not come from a royal bloodline. He came from the same stock that everyone else came from.

They watched back with hope.

Chapter Twenty

Marik had killed before. He was trained on how to do it in many ways. He just didn't like doing it. It helped that the man was a Thellian soldier, but it still didn't make it any better. The soldier was walking the outermost perimeter of the camp. They were still several miles from the mountains, well inside their own territory. There was no reason to think that the enemy was nearby. So the soldier walked with his head down, his mind thinking about the warm summer evening. Marik snuck up on the soldier from behind, using the stealthy walk that he had perfected. When he was just behind the doomed man, he leaped forward, his left hand gripping tightly around the man's face, covering his mouth and nose while his right hand drove the dagger deep into the man's back. The soldier screamed, but the sound was muffled. Marik knocked the soldier's legs out and rode him to the ground, continuing to hold the dagger in the man's back and held his hand tightly on his face. It wasn't long before the soldier stopped fighting. He switched cloaks with the dead man and quickly moved away, towards the Thellian army camp.

Marik was thankful for the moonless night. If it was a full moon, one of the nearby sentries might have seen what had just happened. But the darkness of the night covered Marik's deathly deed. He sprinted from the dead soldier towards the rows upon rows of sleeping bodies. Most of the soldiers were sleeping out in the open. It was cool but not cold, so with a light blanket, there was no reason to pitch a tent. It would just have to be taken down and packed up in the morning. There were fires burning low throughout the camp, so Marik made sure to give those a wide berth. They didn't really give off enough light to see by, but they indicated where there would be clusters of soldiers.

From a distance, Marik hoped he looked like any other Thellian soldier wrapped tightly in a cloak. He kept his head straight forward, but his eyes moved left and right, searching for anyone who might notice that he was not who he pretended to be. He had reached the army as they were finishing their march for the day. He had sat high in a tree, watching them set up their camp from a distance. The cooks made a dinner, and the soldiers ate. When darkness came, the soldiers quickly fell asleep, as they were all tired from the long march. Marik cared little for anything other than a small group of soldiers at the center of camp. They had chained a man to a tree and were standing around, poking and prodding him. Marik could not see him clearly but was convinced it was his Knight Captain.

With delicate precision, he guided himself around sleeping soldiers, walking carefully and purposefully, trying to blend in and not call attention to himself. The closer he got to the center of camp, the more nervous he became. He knew that if he were to be caught, his life would be done. There would be no sense in trying to give himself up. He would fight to the end, killing as many of the enemies as he could.

As he neared the center of the camp, he spotted three soldiers that were casually guarding the prisoner. They were huddled together, talking and playing a game of chance with a pair of dice. Every so often, one of them would take a peek over at the prisoner. But it wasn't a long look. The closer he got to the group of three guards, the worse he felt about his chances of ever succeeding. Although he could only see the three that were awake, any sort of commotion would certainly send dozens of sword-wielding Thellians running directly for him. He wouldn't have a chance.

If that were the case, he just hoped that the end would come quickly.

At the center of the camp was a very large tent. Marik presumed it held the leaders of the army and hoped they were sound asleep or otherwise preoccupied. Its size provided plenty of cover for him, so he took the risk and angled his path towards it. The end of the tent also contained a makeshift stable that contained five horses. They were quietly munching on piles of long grass that had been placed at their feet. It was not far from the horses to where Brace was tied up.

Out of the blue, the plan quickly fell into place. What had at first been a simple plan of sneak in, sneak out, was not possible. He had been overly naïve to think that it could have been accomplished. But the new plan that was swimming in his mind could work. If only God would look down at him and smile. He closed his eyes and said a quick prayer, just as Master Goshin had taught him. It felt odd and refreshing at the same time. But it seemed to clear his head and focused him on what he was supposed to do.

Brace was snoring softly when Marik dropped to the ground behind him. Marik whispered in his ear, but the Knight Captain only let out a soft grunt. Only after a sharp punch to the shoulder did Brace stir and look around. His eyes widened at who was standing behind him.

"Marik!" Brace said between clenched teeth. "Go! I am done for. You must get a message back to the king."

Marik ignored the order and pulled at the chains, looking to see how he could release Brace.

"Listen to me!" Brace said, maybe a bit too loud. Both of them glanced at the three guards who were still busy with whatever game they were playing. Marik was behind Brace, hoping that a casual glance in their direction would not see him. "Go. I will only slow you down. You must get word to the king that Thell is marching on us."

"I think I can break the chain where it is attached at the base of the tree," Marik said, still ignoring Brace.

Then they both froze. One of the soldiers had stepped away from the other two and looked in their direction. He did not move for a moment as he looked more closely at Brace. Marik thought he was hidden well enough, but he was not going to let it go to chance. He grabbed his bow, nocked and drew an arrow in one easy motion and let the arrow fly. The doomed Thellian did not have a moment to let out a cry. The arrow buried deep into the soldier's chest, and he toppled over, dead before he hit the ground. He quickly nocked another arrow and sent it flying at one of the other two soldiers, striking him in the back and sending him tumbling on top of the third man. Unaware of what was happening, the last soldier pushed his companion off him and stood up, right into the sights of Marik's arrow. If he had stayed on the ground and crawled to safety, he would have survived and likely would have been able to sound an alarm. But instead, he took an arrow to the heart, killing him instantly.

Marik looked around. No one else was stirring or noticed what had just happened. He thought for sure there had been enough noise to bring attention to them, but so far, it appeared that they had not been discovered. He returned to the chain and tried to figure out how to break it away from the tree.

"My wrist," Brace said weakly. "Bound with leather, not shackles."

Marik pulled at Brace's hand, and sure enough, rather than iron shackles, his wrists were bound to the chain by several thick leather straps. It only took a moment for him to slice through the bindings. Brace, finally free, rubbed his wrists and looked up at his friend. "Thanks."

Marik smiled and put a hand on his shoulder. "We must leave. Quickly. How is your leg?"

"My leg? How did you…?"

"I am a ranger. I have been tracking you for days. The limping gave you away."

With the help of Marik, Brace stood and said, "I will do what it takes. Just can't run fast. Or maybe at all."

"Come, quickly. There are horses."

Marik would say it was divine providence, even though he really didn't fully know what that meant. Brace would say it was over-confidence of still being in one's own country. But regardless of the reason, the escape attempt so far went unnoticed as they reached the makeshift stable that contained the horses.

"Fortunate that there are only two," Brace observed.

Marik let a smile out. "There were five, but I sent the other three away. There must be others around, though."

"Not many," Brace countered. "Thellians fight from the ground, not from the horse. They don't use horses in battle. Only their commanders ride."

Just as Marik boosted Brace up into the saddle of his horse, a shout broke through the darkness. Marik leaped into his saddle, and the two spurred their horses away from the tent. The shouting caused everyone to come awake. Some more quickly than others. Marik led the way through the soldiers, winding and turning to avoid running over many of them. It wasn't that he didn't want to hurt them, he didn't want his horse to stumble and fall. That would mean certain death for them.

More shouting rose from behind, but Marik simply kicked his horse to run as fast as it could. The groggy soldiers, still worn out from their long march, dove out of the way of the rushing horses. Several tried to stand in their way but were run over by the charging mounts. Because they did not sleep with their long pole arms, the only weapons that most of the soldiers had were daggers or small swords. None were willing to stand up to a horse running full speed, although there were some feeble attempts to swing a sword as they passed. Marik used his own sword to parry anyone that tried. Given more time, if the soldiers were able to realize that only the lead horseman was armed, they might have directed their attack to the second rider. But everything was happening so fast, there was no time to think. There were no leaders on the field, either. They were not supposed to think, only to do what they were told. Since there was no one around to tell them what to do, they could only do what they had been trained. As foot soldiers who knew little else than to thrust their halberds and pikes at on rushing knights, they could do little else than watch the two riders plow through their camp.

As soon as they cleared the camp, Marik looked back for any pursuers, but there were none. He let Brace's horse catch his, and they continued in tandem. Brace kept his eyes forward, leaning his body forward into the neck of the horse. Pain was evident on his face.

"Should we slow?" Marik shouted.

Brace shook his head and shouted back. "We will have to push the horses all the way to South Karmon."

"Neffenmark's castle is closer!"

Brace pulled his horse to a stop. Marik, a bit slower, had to slow down and then turn around and come back to the Knight Captain who was stopped in the middle of the open field.

"Neffenmark is a traitor," Brace said. "We will not be safe there. We must get to the king as quickly as we can and let him know that the Thellians are marching."

"Neffenmark? How do you know?" Marik asked.

Brace dropped his eyes. Eventually, he would have to face the king and whatever punishment was given. It wouldn't be as bad as having to tell his friend. "He and I were in on a plan."

"The princess?" Marik asked, even though he knew the answer.

Brace nodded, more ashamed knowing how he hurt his friend with his deceit. "The plan was supposed to force King Thorndale to march upon Thell. The princess was to be taken, not harmed. We have gotten soft enough that Neffenmark...and myself...feared that Thell would see our weakness and exploit it."

"And it was the king that sent you to Thell with a message for peace," Marik said, his tone showing his anger. "What did you do with the message? Lose it? What happened?"

Brace glanced behind them. They were far enough away from that camp that it was unlikely that they could be seen. And it was dark enough that it would be impossible for them to be tracked. But they couldn't linger too long. Soon, their pursuers would mount up and chase after them.

"I realized some time ago that I was a fool and should not have gotten in league with Neffenmark," Brace said. "I tried...I tried to deliver the message. A message that would bring peace. But it seems that the son of the king of Thell has other ideas. It was he that captured and bound me." Then he added, "You should not have rescued you me."

"They would not have marched to war with you as a prisoner," Marik observed with a biting anger. "Maybe I should have left you to them."

Brace nodded. "I do not blame you for being angry with me. I would have gotten my just punishment." He touched his heels to get his horse moving forward at a slow walk. "I have failed the kingdom. But worse, I have failed the king."

Marik matched pace with the Knight Captain. "Enough of this!" Marik exclaimed, his anger still burning. "I cannot express how...very mad I am right now. And I am even more disappointed. I cannot imagine what led you to believe that you could make these sorts of decisions that affect the kingdom. Yes, you are a knight. You are the Knight Captain. Yes, you have a responsibility to the kingdom, but you also have a responsibility to the king as well. You must honor him as your ruler and let him make those decisions that affect the kingdom. It is not your place to step in his stead."

Brace's head hung low. He could not muster the nerve to say anything else, so he kept silent.

Marik kicked his horse suddenly forward to block Brace's horse. "Sir Brace. You are the Knight Captain, and despite your decisions of the past, you are still the Knight Captain, and you have a realm to protect. You can deal with your sullenness on your own time. Now it is time to correct the things you have done and right the wrongs. I will not listen to your self-deprecating words anymore. You have led men into battle. You have made countless decisions that are honorable and worthy of your stature. Yes, one bad decision can ruin everything. But that doesn't mean that you can just find some hole in the ground and crawl into it and let the kingdom fall apart. You started this mess, now finish it. But the right way."

Marik turned his horse towards the darkness that was the mountain peaks to the south. "Now we must ride. Are you strong enough?"

Brace nodded. "It does not matter. We will ride."

With much of the night still ahead of them, they rode towards the looming White Mountains and the wide gap between two of the tallest peaks.

***

The king sat upon his great white horse at the head of the column of knights. The knights had mustered outside the main city gate, allowing thousands of the city's citizens to see them off. Their armor was buffed, polished, and shimmered brightly in the bright morning sun. Squires had worked diligently to prepare their knights for the ride, most of them getting nothing more than a wink of sleep before they were woken to help with the morning preparations. Most of the older squires were on horses themselves, clad in a variety of chain and leather armor. They would be all ready to fight if called upon. But they would hang back at the supply wagons, guarding against attacks from behind. It would only be if things went bad that they would see any action.

King Thorndale turned towards the city and the men, women, and children who were cheering on their beloved leader. He lifted the face guard of his helmet to show his wide smile. His mouth moved, saying some great words of wisdom and encouragement, but only those nearby could hear him. The cheering erupted into an explosion as he waved his hand and pointed forward, directing his knights to proceed towards the battle. The knights, their own face guards lifted, did not smile like their king. Their serious, somber expressions reflected their duty towards their kingdom. Next came the squires, who could not hold back their excitement. None of them had ever been in battle before, so they did not comprehend the death and destruction that was yet to come. They waved at their family, at their friends, or at anyone who would wave back, smiles plastered on their faces. In their minds, they could only see themselves as heroes going off to protect the kingdom. They did not, nor could they, think about the true cruelty of war. Following them were the farmers and merchants who had answered the call to war. Some carried swords. Some carried axes. Many carried nothing, waiting for someone else to fall so they could grab a weapon to fight. They marched grimly, unlike the squires. They knew about life and death and knew that death was always just around the corner. But they didn't fight for honor or glory, they fought to defend their kingdom from the evil to the north. And so they marched, many believing that they would never see home again.

Princess Elissa watched from the top of one of the tall watchtowers that guarded the northeast corner of the city. Tears streamed down her face. She had no idea about battle or the devastation that truly came from it, but she knew about death. She knew that some if not many, of the knights would not come back. The tears fell for her father, whom she loved. In the pit of her stomach, she had a bad feeling that the vision that she saw now of her father would be the last one that she would see. But as much as she was sad and distressed, she was proud of him. He was a good king and the rousing sendoff reminded her that the kingdom loved him, too.

Melanie was there, standing next to her, holding her hand firmly. Percy, head of the Royal Guard was there as well. Conner stood behind them, still not comfortable in his place. He watched the Royal Guard carefully and could see the obvious look of envy on the man's face. He was as capable as any other soldier in the kingdom, but his duty was not to fight the battles in the field but to defend the castle and the royal family. Maybe it was a relief, Conner wondered, that he didn't have to go to war. It was beyond anyone's memory since the last time that fighting had come to the city and the Royal Guard had taken up arms in the kingdom's defense. There were four other Royal Guard that stood back behind them all, their swords at their sides, ready to jump to the defense of the princess. Conner then realized that he did not have his sword on. He was wearing his comfortable white tunic cinched at his waist by a thick leather belt. A belt that should be holding a sword. He vowed that this would be the last time that he would be seen unarmed. He had a duty to be prepared for anything.

Despite the tears that flowed down her cheeks, the princess stood stoically. She watched the procession, listening to the cheers. She did not move until the last of the wagons had departed, following the well-worn two-track path towards Lord Neffenmark's castle.

"Your highness," Percy said softly. "We should return to the castle. Lord Martin has already arrived and is requesting that you stay on the castle grounds. For your safety, of course."

Elissa did not respond. She continued to look out the open window, continuing to watch the procession. The mounted knights led by the king were now out of view, having followed the path into the woods. Only the trailing line of supply wagons and peasant fighters were still in sight. She watched as one-by-one, first the wagons, and then the everyday citizens of the kingdom, disappeared into the coverage of the woods.

When the wagons were no longer in view and the din of the city hand begun to settle down, Melanie released Elissa's hand and said to her, "Princess, it is time to go."

But she did not move. Her eyes were dry, but her cheeks were stained with her tears.

Conner let a few more moments passed before he stepped forward and laid a hand on her shoulder. Instantly, Elissa burst out into more tears, spun, and buried her head into Conner's shoulder. He held her tight, holding her close, his own eyes closed.

The sight of Conner and the princess in such an embrace was disconcerting to Percy on many levels. Not only did he not like the idea of a member of the royal family being so close to someone not of highborn birth, he simply did not like Conner personally. He cleared his throat, but to no avail. A few seconds became a few uncomfortable minutes before Elissa gently released herself from the embrace.

Percy motioned towards the ladder that led down to the lower level of the tower. "Princess, shall we?"

Two of the royal guard started down the ladder, followed by Princess Elissa, then Melanie. When Conner tried to follow, Percy put a hand on Conner's shoulder and gave him a slow shake of his head. He held his hand on the shoulder until the other two guardsmen were down the ladder and the princess was clearly out of earshot.

"Now that the king is gone, it is time for you to leave and return to your place," Percy whispered to Conner.

Conner pushed Percy's hand off his shoulder. He knew his place and knew it to be next to the princess. He was not going to let anyone get in his way anymore. Percy put his hand directly on Conner's chest. The Royal Guard was older and bigger and in a closed quarter fist fight, would probably turn Conner into a pile of broken bones. Knowing that it was not the time or place, Conner let the head of the Royal Guard descend the ladder first.

By the time Conner got down the ladder and jogged down the winding stairs to the ground level, the princess' carriage had already left, escorted by the Royal Guard. Percy was on his horse, trotting to catch up to the carriage. Since he had left the castle in the carriage, Conner's only recourse was to walk back to the castle. The walk did little to soothe his bruised ego and simply made him angrier with each step.

It was because he was seething in anger and was not paying attention to his surroundings that he stumbled over an old man. The man fell to his knees, spilling an armful of bread. Conner stumbled himself, and it was all he could do to not fall onto the top of the old man.

Instantly all anger left him when he realized his clumsiness. "I am so sorry!" Conner repeated several times, helping the old man back to his feet.

The old man grumbled some words to himself while he brushed dirt off his clothes. But then he looked up and saw who was helping him back to his feet. "It is you!" the old man said. He held onto Conner's hand and gripped it tightly.

"Huh?" was all Conner could say.

A small crowd had gathered around them to help pick up the spilled bread.

"It is you, is it not?" the old man asked. "At the Summer Festival, the one who beat up on the squire? With broomsticks!"

Conner's face turned beet red. Although he had felt so good about what he had done to Hollin, the more time that passed, the more he regretted it. In the beginning, the recognition of what he had done was wonderful. He liked the attention. But now, it was embarrassing. His goal was not to impress anyone other than Princess Elissa, but it seems that everyone else was impressed with him.

"It is Conner, the Princess' Champion!" someone shouted from behind him. Cheers erupted from the small crowd. In moments, the small crowd became large.

Conner looked around, unable to move, unable to think of what to say.

"You inspire us all!" the old man said. "With our brothers and sons going to war, knowing that you are here to protect the princess..." He could not finish his sentence as the crush of people had pushed him away.

Everyone had a question for him, but he could not answer even one of them. There was pushing and shoving as everyone wanted to touch him. He looked around for an escape, but he was surrounded. There was no getting away. He did not even know what they wanted. They asked questions, but they did not wait to listen for an answer. Many seemed like all they wanted to do was to touch him, and as soon as they got close enough, they just stood there, unable to speak.

Finally, he put up his hands and yelled, "Stop!"

But they did not listen. They kept pushing on him, and he had to scream at the top of his lungs, "Stop!"

This time they did. They backed away at his anger. "Listen, I am just like you." He looked around, making eye contact with those closest to him. "I am nothing special."

The old man, the one he had run over, pushed his way back to Conner, side. "No," he said. "You are special. We saw what you did. We've all seen knights fight and joust. None of us has seen that before. You are better than any knight!"

The crowd let out a roar of approval.

"Hold on," Conner said. "I am not better than a knight. The one I defeated, he was just a squire."

The old man shook his head. "You did something great. Something that every one of us has dreamed of doing. But none of us could ever do. You showed us that you don't have to have noble blood to do great things!"

The crowd rose up again in cheers and shouting.

As Conner was enjoying the attention and cheering, more shouts came from the back of the crowd. Conner could see the crowd start to part as the shouting got louder. He could see the helmed heads of Royal Guardsmen as they pushed their way through the crowd with Percy in the lead.

"What is all this commotion?" Percy shouted. "Break this up at once! Go on with your business!"

The crowd noise died down, but no one moved. In fact, most of the crowd turned to Conner, as if he could, or would, do something. There were only five guardsmen and maybe a hundred in the crowd. Even though they had weapons, they were heavily outnumbered. But they were not an angry crowd, just excited at seeing Conner walking among them.

Percy approached Conner and held out an arm that pointed back through the crowd where the carriage was now standing. "Let's go," he commanded.

Conner followed, to the dismay of the crowd. As he reached the carriage, he looked back at the crowd, and they were all watching him.

Princess Elissa, from behind the curtained door said, "I made them come back for you."

Percy gave Conner nudge, but Conner didn't move.   Instead, Conner said, "I'll walk back."

"Move!" Percy demanded, putting a hand on Conner's back and gave a harder push.

Conner shoved his hand off his back and gave the royal guardsman a stern look. "No," Conner said.

Princess Elissa pushed her head through the curtains that covered the opening and the murmuring of the crowd grew. She looked around for only the briefest of moments before she climbed out of the carriage. Percy started to protest, but she raised a hand to him and gave her own look back to him.

"I will walk back, too," she said.

"Your highness," Percy protested. "It is my duty to protect you and escort you safely throughout the city."

Conner, a wide smile on his face, turned to the crowd, which now was in the many hundreds and shouted as loud as he could, "Princess Elissa is in need of an escort back to the castle! Who shall join me!"

The crowd responded with a resounding cheer.

Percy stepped forward and grabbed the princess by the arm. "Princess Elissa. This is not wise. We are at war."

Elissa pulled her arm out of Percy's grip and replied back with a scowl, "These are my people. I will walk with them."

Leaving Percy and his guard behind, the Princess and Conner were escorted back to the castle by a crowd that only continued to grow.

Chapter Twenty-One

Conner stood atop the castle's highest tower. The sun had long since fallen below the western horizon behind him, casting darkness across the kingdom. The moon was nowhere to be seen, nor were there any signs of stars. The clouds had moved in soon after the king led his army northward, and they had yet to leave, making the days dreary, and the nights dark. Lights from lamps, torches, and outdoor fires dotted the darkness. There were many of these pinpoints of light, but not enough to make a dent in the night. He felt exposed atop the tower, but he knew that no one could see him. In the light of the day, unless the sun were directly behind him, his dark outline against the blue sky would be visible. But in the dark of night, he knew that he was unseen.

He shivered in a sudden cool breeze. It had been three days since the king had left to lead the army north. He knew that messengers had come and gone, but there was no news. It was a fairly easy march, but it was a slow one. The knights could have ridden ahead, but then they would have outridden their support. The city had been subdued for a day, but then it slowly crept back into its daily routine. But the castle was empty. There were servants to keep the castle running, but the halls eerily silent. He spent his days training with the Royal Guard. He would have like to have spent some time alone with Elissa, but Percy's men took their role seriously and stayed close to her. Elissa was sound asleep three floors below his feet. He knew he could be there in only ten heartbeats. He knew because he counted. But he needed this time alone, to feel the cool summer breeze on his face. He had forgotten how wonderful it felt. He had spent too many days and nights in the castle.

The creak of a door and the flash of light caused Conner to break from his stare upon the city. A shadowed figure appeared in the doorway that led to the stairwell.

"It is chilly up here," the man said.

Conner recognized the voice and cringed. It was Percy. "It is," Conner replied, not sure how to take the intrusion.

Percy leaned against a chest high battlement, looking upon the city himself. "Standing watch over the city?"

Conner wasn't sure if the question was genuine, or if Percy was trying to make fun of him. After a moment, Conner answered, "No."

"I come up here on occasion to clear the head," Percy said. "I like to look upon the city and watch it move."

"Move?" Connect asked.

Percy smiled. Conner could barely see the man's face in the darkness, but he could see just enough to catch a glint of white teeth. And it was the first time he had ever seen him smile. "The city moves. It lives and breathes. You really can't see it at night, but during the day, you really can see it. The people move. They move from one part of the city to the next, doing their jobs, or whatever errands they have for the day. Sometimes I recognize someone, but usually, it is just faceless bodies, moving around. They live. They work. They die."

Conner waited for more, but Percy seemed to have run out of words. He turned back to the city, to see if he could see it move. But he could only see darkness and small specks of light here and there.

"I saw you come up," Percy confessed after some time.

Conner again waited for the head guardsman to continue, but he stayed silent, his eyes cast out upon the city.

"You've been training with my guard," Percy said after a few more minutes passed. "At least those that are left."

"Yes," Conner said cautiously. He prepared his defenses, as he felt an offensive attack coming.

"It is good," Percy replied, eyes still focused straight out towards the city. "You push them."

"Master Goshin taught me," Conner said.

"He taught you well. Even the guardsmen who don't train with you see you. They see how you train and push yourself. They see the results." He finally turned to Conner and locked eyes. "They saw the results. They all saw what you did to Hollin and saw what it would be like to be you. They want to be able to stand up to the knights."

"Stand up to the knights? Aren't we all Karmons? Aren't we all fighting the Thellians?"

Percy broke eye contact and looked back towards the city. "We are, I guess. But it is the knights that lead the army. My Royal Guard who remain here feels left out. They feel some shame in being left here."

"Some must stay and defend the city," Conner replied. "The city and the castle cannot be left unprotected."

"I know that, and you know that. But where would you rather be? Here? Or marching north with the king?"

Conner knew he did not need to answer, but he did anyway. "We all have our duty. We cannot be ashamed in that."

"No, but how will you feel when the army comes back victorious, and you know that you had nothing to do with it, other than babysitting the city."

"I would be out there, you know," Conner said. "If I hadn't come across the Princess in the woods. I would have answered the call to arms. I would be marching north right now, following the king. But instead, I am stuck here, as you are. But we still have our duties."

"I have duties," Percy countered. "I have men to manage. Patrols to coordinate. Posts to man. Training to schedule. What precisely are your duties? Protect the princess? It is my men who stand guard outside her apartment. When was the last time you stood the night watch at her door?"

Conner opened his mouth to angrily respond, but Percy lifted a hand and shook his head. "No, I should not have said those things. I am sorry. It is not fair of me to say those things. It is not you who is at fault. I am a soldier. A guard. I trained for my job, and I earned it through my training. When I was seven, my father brought me to the castle, and for the next ten years of my life, I trained to be who I am now. Every day I work, and I train, living in a small room with ten other men just like me. I put on my leather armor, pull my surcoat about me, and walk the halls of the castle, protecting the king and his family from the Thellians and whoever else decides to declare war upon us. I am not a knight. I was not born to the right family. Knights train hard. But so do we. They are given their station because of their birth, not because they earned it. And that is what makes me angry."

"That is why you hate knights?" Conner asked.

"I do not hate them!" Percy retorted.

"It sounds like you do," Conner said. And then he added, "And me, too."

More silence, followed by a short sigh. Percy said, "It is not your fault. You saved the princess, and you deserve to be rewarded."

"But not like this," Conner observed.

"I did not say that," Percy replied defensively.

"But you thought it," Conner said.

"I have devoted my life to serving the king. The knights protect the realm, but it is the guard who protects the king within these walls. It is my men who stand guard outside the royal apartments day and night. We walk the halls, man the gates. And then when it is time to defend the realm, we are left here to sit idly by while the knights lead the army into battle."

"Many will not return, though," Conner said.

"It is better to die upon the field of battle than of old age," Percy said.

"I would agree with you if you have nothing else to live for."

Percy turned to look over Conner closely. "You really don't talk like a farm boy."

Conner grinned and replied, "Master Goshin taught me more than just how to swing a sword."

"So where is the old man? I heard he left a while back with a fully packed mule in tow."

Conner scanned the sky, looking for the star, but the clouds were too thick to see it. He ended up pointing in the general direction. "Out there is a star. It grows brighter by the day."

"I have seen it," Percy said. "On some nights, it seems brighter than the moon."

"Master Goshin believes it foretells some great event. He had a bunch of scrolls from some far away land that spoke of this event. He left to try and figure it out."

"What does it mean for Karmon?" Percy asked.

"I do not know," Conner replied. "Master Goshin did not know. But I think the king is worried about it."

"The king has more things to be worried about now. The threat from Thell is real. This shining star, how much of a threat can it really be?"

They stood in silence for some time. They watched the darkness, the dance of the lights of the city. Conner realized that maybe Percy wasn't so bad after all. At least now he understood where he was coming from. And in some ways, the guardsman was no different than himself – an outcast from the aristocracy establishment. They weren't better men than him or even Percy. They weren't necessarily better fighters. He had seen Percy train, and he was equal to just about every knight he had gone up against. But he felt inferior. Sometimes it was because of what others did to him, but in reality, it was more than that. He felt inferior because, in the eyes of most, he was. Because of his bloodline. He didn't have a mother or a father of noble blood. He was born and raised on a farm, a peasant in servitude to his liege, the king. He was on the lowest rung of the ladder. The most important rung, because without the farms and the peasants to work the land, there would be no food to feed the residents of the city. But no one ever seemed to recognize that fact.

He had heard that Percy's father was a merchant. And that would make Percy one rung up from him. Far from being a noble, but still far above the lowly peasant that Conner was. He thought it ironic that Percy would treat him with disdain because of who he was, and yet, hated the way the knights treated him, because of his blood. It confused Conner. Even after long nights of talking with Master Goshin about it, it still confused him. He lived among them, and he could not see them any differently than him. At first, many of those he came across could read and write, while he could not. But Master Goshin had taught him well, and although he couldn't read as fast as others, or write as well as others, he could read from nearly any one of the books that filled the king's library. Many times others talked differently than him. Used words that he had never heard of, but words that were just more fancy versions of words that he used. When he was cleaned up and dressed in his fancy silk tunic, he looked no different than they did. And yet, they treated him differently because of his blood. He had seen his blood, and he had seen the blood of knights. Both were red.

Percy stiffened. The sudden movement caught Conner's eye and broke him from his thoughts. "The gates have opened."

Conner squinted into the darkness, searching for the gates, much less the city wall. "I do not see…"

"There are lights outside the gates to light the way up to the wall. We have doubled the fires to ensure that no one could sneak upon the walls without being seen." He pointed towards where the gate was. "There is a large light there now, one that was not there a moment ago. I believe it is because the gates were opened."

Conner looked harder, but he could still not see what Percy was talking about. A moment later, a trumpet blared twice.

"Someone of importance has arrived at the gate," Percy declared. "It is very unusual that the gates would be allowed to be open at this time of night. It better be someone important, or I will be looking for new gate guards. Come. We will meet them at the castle gate. I want to personally see who it is before we open the castle to them."

"Me?" Conner was surprised at the offer.

Percy gave the young man a long look. "You are not a knight. You are not a guardsman. I can say you are a soldier, though. You handle a sword better than I've seen in my lifetime. At worst, you can take the first charge." With a flash of a smile, Percy turned and strode quickly towards the door that led to the stairs.

They heard the thunder of the horses long before they saw them. There were four of them. Two were clearly guards, their surcoats billowing in the wind as they drove their horses to the gate. The identity of the two others were hidden in the darkness. Conner stood, a single sword strapped to his side, but his hand resting on the end of the handle. Percy had called other guards; he stood in front of three others. His sword was drawn, but tip pointed down into the ground in as unthreatening manner as he could muster. If it were someone of political importance, he didn't want to insult them. But he also wanted to be prudent.

Three of the riders dismounted. Sensing no danger, Percy gave the signal to raise the portcullis. With the castle now open, the three who were walking led their horses through the gate, while one remained atop his horse.

"Captain," one of Percy's gate guards said in greeting.

"Varen," Percy replied with a nod. He wished others would address him with his title rather than his name like his men did. It was minor in the scheme of things, but he always felt that the knights slighted him and the concept of the Royal Guard by not addressing him and lieutenants by rank.

Varen turned to the cloaked figure to allow him to address Percy himself. With a quick flash, he pulled his hood off.

"Marik!" Conner shouted, stepping forward.

Marik gave Conner a quick smile in greeting, but he addressed Percy. "Sir Brace is injured and will need to be attended to."

"Nonsense!" Brace called out, sliding out of his saddle. He limped towards the rest of the group. "I am fine." He turned to his escorts and growled, "Be gone!"

Varen and his companion took their leave to return to the gate. Percy dismissed the rest of his men with a wave and sheathed his sword.

"Your men said the king and the army left days ago," Brace snapped. "We will take fresh horses in pursuit. And supplies. And as quick as you can!"

Despite his shouting, no one moved.

"You are hurt?" Percy asked. "Should you not rest and recover, so that you are able to fight?"

Brace stepped forward, right into Percy's face. "I am ready to fight. I could split you in two before you could blink. Now. Get out of my way. Get my horses. And get my supplies!"

Percy winced. He was nearly Brace's rank in the eyes of the kingdom, but he was still not a knight. The anger burned, but he knew now was not the time to let it loose. With as much calm as he could manage, he said, "Although you would offer much to the battle, the army that the king has raised is strong, and will easily defeat the Thellians."

Marik put a hand on his captain's shoulder before another outburst exploded. "The king marches toward an ambush," the ranger said. "The Thellians are waiting for us. They know our every move."

"Neffenmark," Brace added, his face red from anger.

Percy opened his mouth to say something, but no words came. No thoughts came. He was utterly stunned.

"But the knights are there to fight," Conner said.

"It will be a messy, bloody fight," Marik said. "But there are many Thellian soldiers, and they know that we are coming, they know the path that the army is taking. It would not take a very smart general to figure out how to attack such an army in surprise. I do not doubt that our army will come out victorious, but there will be loss of life like no one has seen for a very long time."

"Lord Martin should be awoken," Percy said softly.

"As long as you do it after you have gotten my horses and supplies," Brace said, his tone still full of anger.

"I will get your horses," Conner said. He started walking towards the stables before anyone decided to try and change his mind. The sound of footsteps caused him to turn. Marik had trotted to catch up to him.

"The fireworks between Brace and Percy will go on for some time, I fear," Marik said with a smile. "I will help you with the horses."

"Percy is not so bad," Conner said.

"No. No, he's not," Marik agreed. "But what makes Brace a great knight sometimes makes him difficult to deal with. Percy can be territorial sometimes, too. Makes him difficult to work with as well."

"He's just doing his job, protecting the king," Conner countered.

They passed through the doors of the stable and Marik gave Conner a slight push. "Just get the horses. Those two over there. The smaller riding horses."

"And the white mare," Conner said. "I'll take her."

"No," Marik said while gathering saddles.

"You can't stop me," Conner said. "I need to do this. I need to help. I am tired of sitting around this castle doing nothing." He let out a grunt and continued, "Princess' Champion. What does that mean? No really, what does that mean? Does it mean that I get a better seat at the dinner table? That I get a comfortable bed at night? Based on what's happened recently, that's about all that there seems to be to this champion thing."

"You do have a duty to the princess," Marik said while tossing the saddles from the tack room to the center of the stables.

"Duty? To protect her? Isn't that why there are three Royal Guard always hanging around her, following her where ever she goes? I'm not around to protect her. I'm doing nothing. So now, I'm coming with you, to fight like everyone else."

"I don't disagree," Marik said.

"Then why did you say no?"

"Because the white mare is Lilly. It is the princess' horse. You should choose another."

Ignoring the ranger, Conner continued putting her bridle on and pulled her out of the stable and came to a dead stop.

Marik smiled and said, "I told you that you should pick another."

Princess Elissa stood in the doorway of the stables. She had a blanket pulled around herself, keeping her warm. "What are you doing?" she asked.

"What are you doing awake, Princess?" Marik asked.

"Your bellowing awoke the whole castle," she replied. And then she asked again when they continued walking the horses out of the stables. "What are you doing?"

"We need horses," Conner said, stopping in front of here. "There are few to choose from, and yours is the best of them."

"No, I mean, where are you going?" She asked.

"To fight," Conner replied.

"Conner..."

"I am not going to argue. I can fight," Conner said.

"Conner," Marik interrupted. "Don't do this to prove yourself to anyone, including yourself."

"But you said I could come with you," Conner said.

"Well, not in so many words, but yes, you are welcome to ride with us," Marik said.

"Sir Marik!" The princess exclaimed. "You are not helping me!"

Marik turned and gave a slight bow to the princess. "Your highness, Conner is a fine warrior. I have seen him train with Master Goshin. The army will need good swordsmen."

"He is my champion. He has promised to protect me." All could see the tears that were filling her eyes. "You promised."

Conner looked from the princess to Marik, and then back again. He spoke while walking towards her. "I promised to protect and serve you as your champion. And I will."

"You cannot be my champion if you are dead!" Elissa shouted back, trying to hold back the tears.

He reached her and took both of her hands. "I do not want to be your champion." He continued through her sobs. "I want to be your friend. I love being with you, talking with you. I love walking the gardens with you. I want to..." He took a deep breath and plunged into the depths of his heart. "I want to be someone to you that I know I cannot be. So, to be close to you, to be friends with you, I will settle for being your champion. But I can't just sit around this castle, wearing these silk clothes, pretending that I don't have any feelings for you."

He gripped her hand firmly and continued. "I promise I will be here for you when you need me. When you really need me to be your champion and not just some trophy that you can pull down off the shelf when you have no other toys to play with."

"I do not...!"

Conner cut her short by placing a finger on her lips. "I know you don't mean to. But you are a princess, and you will marry someone of your station. This kingdom has lots of great men who would do well to be your husband. But I can't be Conner the Princess' Champion anymore. I can never be Sir Conner. I need to be Conner, whoever that is. And that person right now needs to serve the kingdom. I may not be a knight, or a guardsman, or of noble blood, but I can still serve this kingdom. And right now, that means to help Sir Marik and Sir Brace find your father and warn him about the Thellian army."

Tears were fully streaming down her cheeks. "I don't want to be a princess anymore." She fell into Conner's arms, sobbing.

"I don't want you to be either," Conner said softly. "But you are. We just need to be who we are."

He leaned over and touched his lips to her forehead. He wanted to tell her that he loved her, but the words would not come out. The words would have to wait for another time, another place. Movement caught his eye and he looked up to see Brace standing in the doorway.

"I must go," Conner said. "Sir Brace is waiting for us. We cannot lose any more time if we are to catch the king."

Conner tried to pull away, but instead, Elissa pulled him to her. She kissed him firmly on the cheek and embraced him tightly. After what seemed but an instant to Conner, but was an uncomfortably long time to the two knights watching, Elissa pulled away. The tears were gone. "Please do not ever stop being my best friend."

With regret, Conner stepped away and took the reins of Lilly. As he walked through the stable doors, he turned and gave Princess Elissa one last look. She smiled through fresh tears at him. Conner wanted to rush back and hold her one more time, but he knew that it was time to move on.

Marik led the other two horses through the stable doors and gave the young man a shoulder squeeze as he passed by. Outside the stable, Marik handed the reins of one of the horses to Brace.

"Ready to ride?" Brace asked Conner.

Conner nodded, unwilling to say anything for fear of breaking down into tears. The feelings that he was having for Elissa were so overwhelming and so confusing, they were nearly incapacitating.

"And you're wrong, by the way," Brace added. "The kingdom does have a lot of great men, but none more worthy to be her husband. I envy your love. It is a rare thing."

***

Hibold, the thin Taran emissary, picked up his robes as he walked from his covered and enclosed wagon through the mud. A handful of torches were set around the camp, casting enough light to see by, but leaving enough shadows to make Hibold think about what could be lurking just outside of his sight. An armed sentry manned the tent flap and pulled it open as he approached.

Inside was nothing less than what he expected. Lord Neffenmark moved around in comfort and ease, something Hibold appreciated, even though the barbarian was almost too much to stomach. The floor was covered with carpets, keeping the mud from spoiling the mountain of pillows that Neffenmark lay upon. Hibold gave a slight bow, giving the enormously fat man the respect he did not deserve.

"I am returning to Taran," Hibold said.

"Oh?" Neffenmark said, mouth overflowing with food. He quickly washed it down with several gulps of wine. "You are not staying to see the result of our work?"

"Battles are quite...messy."

Neffenmark smiled. "That is the best part. Heads and limbs slicing. Insides spewing out of bodies." He grabbed a slab of meat with his hands and pulled out a chunk and stuffed it in his mouth. "Blood everywhere. It is really a sight to see."

The Taran emissary closed his eyes to not only help himself from thinking about what Neffenmark was talking about but also to keep from seeing meat juice flowing down the fat chins. "That is for generals and others. Not civilized men," Hibold said.

Neffenmark let out a full belly laugh. "Have you ever stayed to watch one?"

"Once my part is done, the generals and kings take over," Hibold said.

"And you run away, hiding from a little blood and gore," Neffenmark said with a leer.

"Lord Neffenmark, we all have our place in this world. You have yours. I have mine. I am not here to be insulted by you. I am here to complete our deal."

"Very well," Neffenmark said. He held up a goblet. "Care for some wine?"

"No thank you."

"Oh?" Neffenmark asked. "Now you insult me by refusing my hospitality?"

Hibold rubbed his feet on the carpet, trying to get as much mud off as he could. "You insult me by trying to offer me a poisoned cup of wine. Do not be surprised. I know you too well. You may not know it, but most of the barbarians that I deal with try and think that they can kill me at the conclusion of the deal."

Neffenmark took another bite of meat and chewed it angrily. "We are not barbarians," he said with his mouth stuffed with food.

"In your eyes, no you are not," Hibold said. "But you have to remember who and what I serve. I serve an empire that is the greatest that this world has ever known. Our history predates yours by thousands of years. Our culture is refined and civilized."

"So civilized that you must start wars between nations?" Neffenmark retorted.

"Would you rather us march our armies through your kingdom and wipe out every man, woman, or child who calls himself a Karmon?" He held up a hand as soon as Neffenmark opened his mouth to protest. "Yes, you have your knights, but we have mounted soldiers as well. And foot soldiers. And soldiers that fight from chariots. And a navy. Do you have a navy? If we really wanted to, we could field an army of a million soldiers. What would your little kingdom and all its knights do against a million foot soldiers? Even if each of your knights killed ten of ours, we would still have more soldiers than your kingdom has people."

Seeing the fat man silenced made the Taran emissary smile. "But we have been through this before. Many times. We are not barbarians. We are civilized. We do not wish to destroy your kingdom, we just wish to have its resources for our empire. You will have your rule of this land as I have promised. Just remember who your allegiance is to."

"You, or your emperor?" Neffenmark shot back.

"As far as you are concerned, they are one and the same. You can rule your land as you see fit. As long as we get what we want."

"Speaking of getting what we want, do you have the last payment?" Neffenmark asked.

"Of course," Hibold replied. "And as before, it must be melted down. It would not go well to have the emperor's coins circulating through kingdoms, not in the empire."

"Shall I have my men retrieve the chests from your wagon?" Neffenmark asked.

"Oh, I do not have the last payment with me," Hibold said. "I would never release my leverage before it is time."

Neffenmark's eyes burned. "I am the one at risk here! And you dare insult me with your talk of leverage?"

"I trust no one, regardless of what leverage I hold. It is the nature of my business. It is how I stay alive." A wide smile fell across Hibold's face. "My wife would be very upset if I did not make it home after one of my jobs."

"I cannot believe a devil such as you even has a wife," Neffenmark said with a growl.

Hibold burst out into laughter. "And the barbarian continues with the insults. Your gold is in a wagon just outside of your camp."

The anger faded from Neffenmark's face quickly. "Then our business is concluded."

"Indeed it is. I would say it was a pleasure, but that would be a lie." He gave Neffenmark one last look before stepping backward through the tent flap. "Good night. And enjoy your rule. May it be long and prosperous."

***

Hibold had lied to Lord Neffenmark. He always stayed to watch. It was the biggest joy of his job. He just liked to do it from a distance.

It had taken him the rest of the night and nearly the entire next day to get to this very spot. It was at the highest peak of the mountain overlooking the battlefield, or what will soon be the battlefield. There was a thick outcropping of trees that concealed his camp. Two Taran centurions were sitting by a small fire that was burning in a pit deep enough that it could not be seen from a distance. A small rabbit was spitted across the fire, fat dripping into the fire with a sizzle.

"It smells good," Hibold said.

"It is just about ready," one of the centurions said. He turned the rabbit, checking to see that it was getting evenly cooked.

"Is the army is in place?" Hibold asked.

"The Thellians have been in place since yesterday. The Karmon army is camped about a half days march to the south. They should be coming through the valley mid-afternoon."

The Taran emissary pulled out a thick wool blanket and spread it on the ground. "Then tomorrow night, we shall head home."

***

Conner slipped off Lilly, his back aching and his legs so sore he could barely walk. Brace and Marik had already dismounted and were tending to their horse's needs. As best he could, he followed suit. Once they were fed and watered, Marik started a fire and began eating the last of their salted meat.

"We will catch them tomorrow late morning," Brace announced. He was looking around at the mountains and then up at the stars, getting his bearings. "Maybe early afternoon at the latest."

"Will it be too late?" Conner asked.

"The king will plan his march to be near the battlefield just as the sun falls below the horizon," Brace replied. "We came across their last camp late afternoon. They should be making camp tonight at the foot of the mountains. Tomorrow they are to march through the valley and then make camp on their other side, and that is where they plan to meet the Thellians."

"But they are not there," Marik said.

"No," Brace replied. "They will be waiting in the valley to ambush the army. But we will get there in plenty of time to warn them."

"Are you sure?" Conner asked.

Brace let out a long sigh. "I am sure of nothing but that the horses are as exhausted as we are. Probably more so. But there is little for us to do right now other than to rest a bit and hope that we are not too late."

"Should we not ride through the night, then?" Conner asked.

"It would do no good for us to arrive early on dead horses," Marik replied.

"We will rest for a few hours and leave before the sun rises," Brace said.

***

The king let his body fall onto the pillows. He felt a little guilty for having a soft bed to lie upon, while his army slept on the cold ground. But he was the king. He had earned the right. He had tried to push the army fast, but it could only move as fast as the slowest villager. If only everyone had a horse to ride, then they would already be through the valley.

Their scouts reported no activity, and he hoped that was good news. There were no Thellian spies tailing him or watching for them. At least not yet. He didn't dare send his scouts through the valley until morning. He knew the valley would be watched and once the first Karmon soldier or scout marched through, the Thellian army would know they were coming. He needed enough time to get through the valley so that when he met the Thellians on the battlefield, he would have his back to the mountains. They would not be able to flank him. He would have the high ground and the advantage. He predicted a slaughter.

With the thought of victory on his mind, he fell into a deep, comfortable sleep.

Chapter Twenty-Two

The wagons, horses, and foot soldiers that preceded them had made an easy path to follow. The army had no reason to hide their movements, so they left a wide swath of wagon tracks and hoof prints. But because the army was so big, they couldn't always follow the quickest path. Marik followed his ranger instincts and led them off the path many times, hopefully cutting hours off their travel. The army had to follow easy terrain, especially because of the wagons. The three riders on horseback had no such restriction.

They spoke little. Conner followed Marik. Brace kept to the rear, his eyes constantly on alert for anyone following them. Conner quickly realized how little he really knew about riding a horse. Sure, it was easy enough to climb on its back. To have the horse move with just the touch of knees, or to stop and start with just a soft word was something that he had never experienced. But they were constantly moving at such a fast pace, that it took nearly his full concentration to keep up with the ranger and not to fall off the horse. The foothills that led up to the mountains were woodsy, but hardly as dense as the forests to the south, so it made traveling on horseback fairly easy. Conner had no idea if they were making good time, or if they were falling behind. Marik said little. Brace said nothing. He just kept his eyes on the trail.

Without warning, Marik pulled his horse to a stop and turned to face his companions. "The horses have about had it," Marik said. "There is a river just ahead through the trees. We will stop to water them."

Brace and Conner dismounted, both grateful for the break. Conner watched the Knight Captain move slowly, trying not to wince with each step. Clearly, his leg was bothering him. He acted as if were as healthy as a young squire, taking both his horse and Lilly to the edge of the river to drink. Conner thought that Brace would be making him water the horses and do all the little menial tasks, but the Knight Captain seemed to want to do everything on his own. For a while, Conner thought it might be because they are on the field and everyone pulls their own fair share. But Brace seemed to want to do everything.

While Brace took the horses, Conner stretched his back and rubbed his muscles. Every part of his body was sore. He had never ridden this long in a saddle, or ridden as fast as they rode. He had no idea how knights could handle it.

"You get used to it," Marik said as if he were reading Conner's mind.

"Huh?"

"Rubbing the back, stretching the legs. You're sore from riding and you are staring at Sir Brace, wondering how he can be walking as well as he can, even with a bad leg. Well, after ten years of riding many hours every day, you get used to. Your back. Your backside. Legs. Everything. Your body does get used to it, and it isn't as painful."

"He's in pain," Conner said. "He can barely walk."

"Yes, but he does. He has a heavy burden to carry. And carry it he must."

Conner gave the ranger a curious look, but Marik only shook his head. "It is not for me to tell."

From the river, Brace shouted "We are behind. We should have gotten to the valley by now."

"We're pushing them as hard as we can," Marik shouted back.

Conner could sense the tension in both their voices. He had the feeling that it was taking too long. A feeling of gloom swept over him. The bulk of the armed forces that Karmon could muster was heading to a trap. If they didn't reach them in time, it would be a disaster.

"This will be our last stop," Brace said, leading the horses from the river bank.

It took a moment for Conner to realize that the Knight Captain was talking to him.

"The river here, it's called the Razor. It makes its way from the mountains. We are just a bit west of the valley. If you look closely, you can see where the mountain is split. When we get closer, you will see. The river is small compared to what it was many, many years ago. It cut right through the mountain, creating a valley. When we get to the valley, the battle will be engaged."

"Brace, we can still beat them," Marik said.

The Knight Captain turned on the ranger and replied with a sharp tone. "It is too late! We are too late! The battle likely has already started. It is a battle that has already been lost because of me. I have done this. From my own actions, I caused this war. The knights may be no more. They will be slaughtered in the valley."

Conner was stunned at the admission of Brace. "What have you done?"

Brace turned to Conner as if he were about to strike him down. Instead, he quickly turned away and took the reins of his horse. Ignoring the pain that was shooting through his leg, the Knight Captain mounted his horse and declared, "We ride. Now."

Marik brought Lilly to Conner and said softly, "Do not mention it again. Sir Brace feels enough guilt about the things that he did. Just know that whatever he did, he did for the kingdom. Not for himself, not for anyone else. But for the kingdom. And that's what a knight's oath is. To the kingdom. Now, get on Lilly before he rides too far ahead."

They followed the river, staying on a small game trail most of the way. Marik kept them at a steady trot. Not too fast to wear the horses down, but much faster than the walking pace at which the army moved. It wasn't long before they picked up the path that the army had taken. The tracks were fairly fresh, meaning they were gaining on them. Marik increased their pace to almost a run. They left the river and followed the path that the army had taken, which was a straight shot towards the valley.

They broke from the trees at the very foot of the mountains and continued running with the mountains on their left and the river on the right. They could see the opening to the valley, but the valley itself was hidden from them. The river made a sharp left turn to the north, where it had cut out the valley.

Their worst fears came to light. They had hoped to come upon the army before it entered the valley, but there was no army to see. The entire army had already entered the valley, straight into the ambush.

Lilly was the fastest horse, bred for speed and grace. As soon as she saw the open clearing ahead, it only took a nudge from Conner's heel to get her into a full run. She quickly passed Marik, leaving his two companions well behind. Brace and Marik both shouted at him, but he did not want to hear their words. The sound of battle spurred him faster.

And then Conner pulled Lilly up short, pulling hard on her reins. Brace and Marik darted past, their swords drawn and ready for battle. But it was the sight of the battlefield that stunned Conner. There were bodies everywhere. Clanging of metal on metal and the shouts of the living and the screaming of the dying filled his ears. The sight overwhelmed him so that he couldn't move. Even Lilly did not like what she saw and smelled, prancing impatiently in place, waiting for Conner to do something.

Bodies were strewn as far as Conner could see. Knights still in their shiny, well-polished armor lay dead next to peasants. For many, shields and armor did no good. There were hundreds of dead bodies, each felled with multiple arrows. Lilly started to move forward, and Conner let her. Slowly moving between the bodies, he realized that not all of them were dead. Some lay on the ground crying or moaning from their injuries. Most would end up dying. Maybe some would survive. A young man with matted blond hair sat up as Conner passed, an arrow embedded deep into his leg. He had clearly been crying, but he did not call out to Conner as he passed, he only held out a hand, as if somehow Conner could help him. There was nothing that he could do, so he kept moving forward.

He didn't know what to do. The thought of actually being in battle really hadn't sunk in. Up to this point, it had just been the idea of a battle. But now that he saw the dead bodies, could hear the ring of metal on metal, it suddenly became real, and he was afraid. He knew that Master Goshin had trained him, and had trained him well. He had proved himself that he could swing a blade with quick precision. He had killed, but it had been from afar. He had thought about what it would be to strike someone down with a blade. He had imaged it countless times while training with Master Goshin or with the squires. But it had never been real like it is now.

His kingdom was at war. Men and boys that had been on the streets of South Karmon just days ago were fighting to the death. Men and boys from his village and every other village throughout the kingdom were out on the battlefield. His king was out there somewhere. It was clear, even to Conner, what had happened. The army had moved into the valley, stretched as a marching army tended to do. The knights were up front, leading the way. Once the entire army was in the valley, the arrows had come down from the mountain. Many men had lost their lives in only the first few minutes of the battle. The ambush had caused chaos, sending the untrained peasants into a panicked fear. Instead of charging forward to meet the enemy, many ran only to have an arrow find them and knock them to the ground. The knights, however, stood their ground to meet the Thellian army. They came from the north, all on foot. Pikemen with their long spears. Foot soldiers with sword and shield. Arrows continued to rain upon the knights until the Karmon soldiers were able to engage the main Thellian force. Forced into a charge to meet the new threat, the main army was left unprotected. The archers, trained soldiers, came down from their perches to meet the untrained peasants.

Conner was afraid, but he drew one of his light swords and held tightly to Lilly's reins as he kicked her into a sprint, heading towards the center of the battle. Lilly was not a war horse, but she did not fear the smell of death. Maybe it was because she was stabled with true warhorses. Whatever it was, she raced with the wind, directly towards the fighting.

As Lilly ran forward, Conner looked for Marik and Brace. He had lost sight of them, and he knew he needed to stay close to them if he were to survive. Off to his left, up from the valley floor, Conner noticed a small skirmish. A handful of knights had found themselves unhorsed and surrounded. Without a thought, Conner touched his right knee to the side of Lilly, and he turned towards them. Lilly aimed directly for the fighting. It was as if she were a trained war horse and had been bred for carrying knights into battle.

Just as Lilly approached the fighting, Conner pulled back on the reins, and she slowed from her sprint and came to a sliding stop. Conner drew his other sword and slid off Lilly's back. His approach had not gone unnoticed. Three Thellian soldiers approached him, their clothes and faces smeared with blood and other bodily fluids. Their eyes were ablaze with a frenzy that made them seem inhuman. It made it easier to dispatch them. Conner was quick about it, just as Master Goshin had taught him. The longer a fight lasted, the better chance there was of losing it, the old man had always said. He thought that maybe the soldiers were stuck in the mud because they seemed to move so slowly. He could see their blows even before they delivered them. He easily countered, and then struck one with a slash from neck to belly. Another slash cleaved a head clean off another soldier. The last fell from a stab straight through the heart. With swords swinging in a controlled fury, Conner cut a path to the unhorsed knights. Conner recognized them. He didn't know their names, but he knew their faces. He knew some of them had jeered him and probably even hated him. But right now, he was covered with the same blood they were. The blood of their enemy and that was all that mattered.

The hole Conner had cut through the Thellians had caused a short reprieve for the handful of knights that had once been surrounded and faced certain death. They took a moment to catch their breath while the Thellians regrouped. One knight fell to a knee, a bloody hand trying to hold in whatever was coming out of his belly. Conner stepped in front of the knight and took on the resurgent charge of Thellians. With a fresh body and a sword faster than anyone could follow, the knights felt a renewed energy. Once again, they beat back the Thellians. This time, the Thellians retreated and left the small group of knights alone.

Conner turned to the knight that he had protected. He had fallen over and was not moving. His eyes remained open, and a trail of blood dripped from his mouth. The moment finally caught up with him. The death and destruction around him was pressing down on him, and he suddenly couldn't breathe. He felt bile coming up and then he fell to his knees and everything that was in his stomach was suddenly on the ground. With deep gasps, he sucked in as much air as he could, trying to keep himself from throwing up again. A hand gripped him under the armpits and pulled him to his feet.

Conner looked into the eyes of Sir Brace Hawkden. They blazed with a fury that he had never seen. The Knight Captain shook Conner harshly.

"The battle is yet to be won. Get your swords."

Conner looked around him. He was sure there were twice as many dead as living. But knights were still fighting. Peasants armed with swords and spears were still fighting. His arms fell limp at his sides. He had no strength.

"The king is trapped," Brace said. "We need to move now, or he will be cut down."

"I…" Conner started to speak, but no more words came out.

Brace moved closer so he could speak without shouting. "You have already proven yourself worthy. You have spilled blood with your sword, and you hate it. I know. I know exactly how you feel. Each time I strike down a man, even if it is the enemy, I feel sick. Because it is not just the enemy that I am killing, it is a man. A man with a family.

But if I don't kill him first, he will kill me. That is how this works. Your king needs you. You made a vow to Princess Elissa to be her champion, and now you must follow through with that. You must help protect your king. It is your duty. Your obligation. And not just because of your vow, but also because of who you are." He paused to look deep into Conner's eyes and knew the answer before he asked it, but he asked it anyway. "Are you ready?"

Conner answered by picking up his swords from the ground.

There were only ten of them. Conner on Lilly and nine knights atop large warhorses itching to get back into the battle. They smelled blood, and it brought them into a wild, snorting frenzy. Even Lilly was caught up in the berserker rage. It took all of Conner's strength to keep her in place. As soon as they were all mounted, Brace led the charge. The fighting had split into smaller pockets of skirmishes, and the Knight Captain led them towards one such group atop a small hill.

Without speaking, each knight knew what to do. They had practiced this maneuver countless times, and now it was time to see if they could succeed. The king and a handful of knights were surrounded by a larger group of Thellians. As they approached, even Conner could see that it would be only a matter of time before each knight, and then the king would be killed. They kicked their horses from a gallop to a sprint just before they crashed into the Thellians. Brace was the point of their diamond formation and didn't even bother to swing his sword. He simply held his horse firmly and guided it as it crashed into Thellians soldiers, crushing them underfoot. The trailing knights had their swords drawn and swung them at anything that moved.

Once they crashed through the line to the remaining knights, they dismounted and began slaughtering the Thellians. Conner did not hesitate to join in the fray. As soon as it was clear enough to get off his horse, he did so with swords in hand. He swung them fast and furiously, pushing the Thellians back. Between the initial crush of their charge, and the ten extra swords, they were able to turn the Thellians away. Once their numbers were cut in half, the Thellians turned and ran. Most of the remaining knights found their horses and began pursuit. Conner and Brace turned to the king. King Thorndale was on the ground, the remnants of an arrow in his shoulder. His hands clutched his side, trying to hold back the blood that was pouring out.

"My king," Brace said as he fell to the king's side.

The king gripped Brace's shoulder, but King Thorndale's strength was failing fast. His lips trembled. "My son," the king said.

Tears streamed down Brace's face. "Do not call me that, my king. I am not so. I have failed you."

"You have failed nothing," the king said. "My daughter…" His eyes drifted off of Brace and landed on Conner. The king reached his hand out to him.

Conner dropped to his knees and let the king put a hand on his shoulder. "My daughter. You are all she has left. You will no longer be just a champion. You will be the Queen's Champion. You will be the only one that can keep this kingdom together."

"Sire," Conner said. "I…"

The grip became stronger as a surge of strength and energy suddenly flowed through the king. "Promise me!" the king shouted. When Conner paused, the king said it again, "Promise me you will be there for Elissa!"

Conner nodded his head. "Yes. I promise."

King Thorndale closed his eyes and took one last breath.

Brace let out a blood-curdling cry, throwing his sword as far as he could throw it. He then pulled off his helm and threw it as far as he could. He dropped to his knees and buried his face in the bloody, muddy ground, his sobs drowned out by the screams and cries of the dying.

***

The Thellians, having lost the surprise of the ambush, had retreated completely out of the valley. The knights pursued to ensure that they stayed away, but there were not enough of them and other soldiers to mount an offensive strike. To make sure the Thellian army didn't try a second strike, many of the surviving mounted knights pursued them for some miles, catching stragglers and inflicting their vengeance upon them. But for everyone else, the bloody work of cleaning up the battlefield began in earnest. Knights and the commoner army worked side-by-side to pile the dead into burning pyres. Their deaths would be honored at sundown. The king was ceremoniously wrapped in a thick wool cloak and placed atop one of the few wagons that had survived the assault. He would make the long trip back to the city to be buried with his ancestors in the caves below the high cliffs of South Karmon.

It would also give the citizens of the city a chance to say goodbye to their king.

Marik walked among the dead, looking for any survivors. A few were found, but most that were still breathing were put out of their misery. A quick death was always preferable to a slow one. As he walked among the fallen, he began to see something odd with the arrows. Not all of them were the same. There were many poorly made arrows, as he would expect from the Thellians. They were not archers. Soldiers from Thell had bows and used them, but they did not have the skill and knowledge to be experts.

He kneeled down next to a dead peasant, an arrow stuck deep into his chest. With a sickening slurp, Marik pulled it out and looked at it carefully. He had never seen an arrow like it before, but he had heard about it.

He jumped up and began running towards where he had left Brace and Conner.

Conner, was in the middle of tossing a dead soldier onto the pile of dead bodies when Marik came running up, out of breath.

"Brace," he said between gasps. "Where is Sir Brace?"

Conner pointed to a nearby wagon where the Knight Captain was sitting, his back against one of its wheels. With Conner in tow, Marik approached his Knight Captain.

"Sir," Marik said softly. In his hands, he held the arrow that he had pulled out of the dead man and another arrow that he had picked up off the ground.

Brace took a long, deep breath before he looked up. His eyes were red and lifeless. "What?" he snapped.

Marik held the arrows out for Brace to inspect.

Brace glanced at them for a moment before looking up. "Arrows?"

Marik shook his head. "Look closer. This arrow," he held up the arrow he had found on the ground. "It is long and thin, the fletching is at the end of the arrow." Then he held up the arrow that he had pulled out of the dead man. "This arrow is thicker. Heavier. The fletching goes from the end all the way down to the middle of the arrow. And it is about half the length."

Brace took the smaller arrow, ignoring the blood on the shaft and tip. He turned it over, looking at it carefully. "I have heard of something like this…"

"Crossbows," Marik said. "Thellians don't use crossbows."

"Centurions," Brace growled. He jumped up, throwing the crossbow bolt to the ground. "Taran is behind this."

"The Taran Empire?" Conner asked.

"It all makes sense now," Brace said softly. "Neffenmark is in league with the Empire. It must be."

"Lord Neffenmark?" Conner asked. "What does he have to do with all of this?"

"The princess was only part of the plan," Brace said.

"Princess? Princess Elissa? What plan?" Conner exclaimed, but neither Marik nor Brace were paying attention.

"I should have known that the fool was not the one pulling strings." The Knight Captain turned and punched the side of the wagon. "I should have known. What a fool I have been!"

"What is going on?" Conner asked. He pushed his way in front of Marik. "Sir Marik? What is going on?"

Marik looked over at the Knight Captain, who was spitting curses and was clearly not in any mood for explanations. "Neffenmark was behind the princess' kidnapping."

"What!" Conner exclaimed. "Lord Neffenmark?"

Brace turned and said, "He was not alone. We worked together."

"You?" Confusion was causing his head to spin.

"I was a fool," Brace said. "And I know I can never have the trust of the kingdom again."

"I don't understand," Conner said.

"I didn't either. I thought I was helping the kingdom. But I was misled by Neffenmark. He convinced me that to start a war with Thell would keep the kingdom pure. He was afraid that peace between our kingdoms would make us weak."

"And while he worked your plan, he worked with the Empire behind your back?" Conner asked.

Brace nodded his head. "Yes. Neffenmark is a traitor, but he is no fool. The plan was with the empire the whole time. I was just a puppet. He fooled me twice."

"What do we do?" Conner asked.

"You and Marik must get back to South Karmon as fast as you can. Warn the guard. They must be ready for anything. Get as many knights as you can to go with you. Send a messenger to Tyre to have them march whoever they can to South Karmon." Brace picked up his sword and sheathed it. "And find me a horse."

"Where are you going?" Marik asked.

"Neffenmark."

"Alone? He has mercenaries guarding his castle. He will kill you. I will go with you," Marik declared.

Brace shook his head. "Your duty is to the kingdom. You must get back to the city and defend it. This…" He waved his hands around the battlefield. "Must have been just a diversion. The real battle will be at South Karmon."

"Real battle?" Marik asked. "What are you saying? The Empire is marching upon our city? That this battle was only to pull us away for our city?"

Brace looked back across the field of battle. Many of the dead had been piled high, ready for burning. Many still lay dead. Or dying. The screams had stopped, but the cries had not. "I hope I am wrong," Brace said. "For if I am not, and the Empire is marching upon our city, then there is little left to stop them. Now get me a horse."

"I'll get it," Conner said and moved off quickly to find a horse.

With Conner gone, Marik moved closer to the Knight Captain and said, "You don't have to do this. We need you. With the king gone, there will be no one left to lead our army,"

"I have done enough. I cannot fight on the battlefield with the way my leg is. I am slow and weak."

"Neffenmark will have his men ready for you."

"I have enough left in me to kill him. That is the difference between them and me. I do not care if I die."

"We have already lost the king, we cannot afford to lose you, too. You hold the knights together!"

"No," Brace countered. "You do not need me. I am a failure to the king and kingdom. This I must do, and I must do it alone. I must atone for my treachery."

Conner returned with not one, but two horses. "I am coming with."

Brace took the reins of one of the horses and replied simply, "No."

"I vowed to protect the princess, and Lord Neffenmark must be stopped."

"I said no. This is something that I must do myself. I will have no more blood on my hands. The only blood left to spill will be Neffenmark's and my own."

"You can barely ride. Barely fight. You will be cut down by the first soldier you come across. I am coming."

Brace looked deep into Conner's eyes for a long time and then finally said, "This will be a one-way trip."

"Not for me," Conner replied. Then he mounted his horse. "Let's ride."

Chapter Twenty-Three

Goshin walked through the main gate of Tara as the morning sun was marching up the eastern sky. Looking up at the massive stone columns that lined the cobblestone streets, he had forgotten how much he loved the capital city of the Taran Empire. It was more than just the culture that permeated through the city and the citizens, it was the history. The gates, for example, had not been closed in almost a thousand years. They stood open to let anyone and everyone come and go from the city. The empire did not fear anyone. There was no army that was large enough to march upon the gates. Therefore, there was no reason to close them.

He followed the crowd because he had to. He could have pushed his way through, but there were so many people coming into the city, he just went with the flow. He knew where he was going, but he also knew he had plenty of time to get there. So instead of taking the direct route, he let himself wander through the streets.

Massive structures dotted the city, and he made a point of trying to pass by them. There were many small amphitheaters scattered throughout the city. Most days they held plays or concerts. But they were also home to gladiatorial games where soldiers and citizens alike took up sword and shield to see who was the strongest. As Goshin passed by one such amphitheater, he cringed at the sounds of the crowd raising their voices and shouting at the battle taking place. He found it both ironic and sad that the most cultural city in the world was also the most barbaric. Mostly, though, it did not surprise him. He knew the heart of man, and it was not cultured and refined. It was barbaric.

The farther away from the business district, he walked the fewer people that he saw. If it were the middle of the night, he would be wary, maybe even a bit frightened. It was generally a safe place to live and work, especially if you had the few extra coins to bribe the centurions to watch your back. There was plenty of crime, like in any large city, but it didn't define the city. Centurions patrolled the city streets from the wide tree-lined boulevard that cut down the middle of the city to the darkest of alleys. But they couldn't be everywhere all the time. Goshin wasn't a fool. He knew that he was safe walking the streets of the city, but only while the sun was up. He knew that once the sun fell and the lamps were lit, the denizens of the bad side of the city would awaken. With an increased pace, he headed for the Great Library.

Goshin stepped tentatively through the wide archway that marked the entrance to the Great Library. Giant pillars filled the cavernous hall, spaced equally apart, and carved with intricate designs. Each one was designed from a scene of Taran's history. Most involved battles scenes wrapped around the circular columns, but a handful were carved in the shape of a man or a woman, presumably someone important to the history of the empire. Goshin recognized the one closest to him. The column was carved in the shape of the upper torso of a man, head bowed, and arms spread wide, the ceiling resting on the man's shoulder.

He stared at the carving for quite some time. Others watching him made the mistake that he was studying the incredible detail in the carving. But Goshin saw not the stone, but what the stone represented. The culture of the Empire had long since moved away from believing in the old gods. No one really believed in Jaka, the god of war, Harra, the god of fertility, Osillia, the god of peace, or any of the hundred other gods that once were a part of their culture. Although you might hear their names in conversation, no one prayed to them anymore.

The people of Taran followed their emperor, who believed in little but himself and the power of steel. Temples that had once dominated the city had been torn down and the stone used for building amphitheaters. It made Goshin sad, as the people of the city had no place for a belief in a divine god. Their souls were lost, and they didn't know it. To them, their emperor was as close to a god as they would accept. They bowed down and worshiped him as if he were something greater than just a man. But they were thoughts he knew he had to keep to himself. Others like him had tried to spread the word of the One God, but their words were not received kindly. Those that gave up quickly moved on to outlying cities. Those that didn't end up with their heads on the end of spikes. Goshin knew that to die a martyr was not a horrible way to go. He knew there was an afterlife and it was waiting for him. But he also knew that he had much to accomplish. Or at least that's what he believed.

Finally, he let out a long sigh and started walking through the hall towards the main library chamber. A short man in a shabby gray tunic was standing in his way. He was old and wrinkly with a long, curly beard. His eyes twinkled in the harsh light of the torches hanging from the walls.

"Sire, may I assist you?" the man said pleasantly.

"Yes," Goshin said carefully, responding to the Taran in his native language. He could understand the old Taran well enough, but he had a hard time speaking the language. He held up the scrolls that he had tucked under his arms. "I have studying to do. I am looking for the room of Urganna."

"Ugranna?" the man said, surprised. "We do not get many requests for that period. There are not many works from that long ago. Most of the scrolls of that time that survived are here, but many of those are damaged and incomplete." He turned to walk away, and when Goshin did not follow, he gave a little wave. "Come. Follow. I will take you there."

"I am Rardus," the man said as they walked. "I am a resident scholar here at the library."

"Goshin."

"Well met, Goshin," Rardus said.

Rardus led him out of the hall and into a dark corridor in the far corner of the library. This part of the library was so rarely used, the wall torches were not burning. Rardus took a burning torch with them, lighting the unlit torches as they passed by. When they reached their destination, the man had to push his way into the room, stirring up inches of dust.

"I am afraid that this room has not seen the light of day in many years. No one cares about the time before the Empire."

"There is much to learn about our history," Goshin countered as politely as he could.

Rardus gave Goshin a friendly smile. "Even the days of our uncultured ancestors provide some teaching moments for us."

Goshin did not like the man. Like most scholars Goshin had met in his travels, this man was at the same time arrogant and ignorant. He was very intelligent, which was one reason why he was a scholar and not a soldier. And with that intelligence came a sense of superiority over everyone else. He knew things that no one else would ever know. And from that knowledge would come his haughtiness. Rather than using his knowledge to better himself and the world around him, he would hoard it and protect it, keeping himself above everyone else. For the briefest of moments, Goshin considered a retort. A long time ago, when he was much younger, he would have. He would have put Rardus in his place, and it would have made himself feel better. But it certainly would have made the scholar angry, and he would no longer be of any help. Goshin still might have need of the scholar's assistance in finding the documents that he was looking for. So he kept his mouth shut and simply nodded his head.

"Do you need any assistance?" the Rardus asked.

Goshin did not want the scholar around any more than necessary, but he would need some help. He might be arrogant, but he wasn't a scholar by lacking intelligence. "Yes," Goshin replied, forcing himself to be polite. "I could use some help with these scrolls."

Goshin spread one of his scrolls across a table. Rardus was intrigued and approached to look at it more closely.

"It is J'kartin," Rardus said emphatically.

"Hurai," Goshin corrected.

The scholar looked closer and let his hands traverse the fading ink that marked up the scroll. "The parchment is old. Crispy old. The J'kartin were one of the first to write on parchment. Their histories were recorded with exacting detail. I do not know much of the language, but I do know some words. There are others in the library that could verify it."

"It is Hurai," Goshin repeated.

The scholar looked closer and the scroll, and then up at Goshin. It was as if Rardus had seen Goshin for the first time. Up until this moment, he had seen a lesser man, one whose details were not worthy of his time. But now, as the scholar opened his eyes, and his mind, he finally saw Goshin for who he was.

"You are from the western provinces. You are Hurai, are you not?"

A smile crept across Goshin's face. Take the arrogance out of the man, and he might be tolerable. "I am."

"You can read this?" the scholar asked softly as if his words might hurt the document spread out in front of him.

"Of course," Goshin replied with a nod.

"How old is it?" Rardus asked.

"The scroll itself is about three hundred years old."

"Oh…" The scholar's word trailed off into a silent disappointment.

But then Goshin added, "But it is copied from text that is five thousand years old."

Rardus lightly touched the lettering and asked, "What does it say?"

"It is actually poem. A beautiful poem in Hurai. But not in Taran. Some Hurai words have no meaning in Taran." Goshin adjusted the scroll so that he could read it. "The poem was written by a young king who conquered a civilization called Mizerites. They are people that no longer exist. Do not think they have descendants. The poem says each last Mizerite was killed. God told them to do this. The Creator God. One who gives life."

"Each culture has their own god or set of gods," the scholar said in an almost practiced way. "Taran herself has many gods that people pray to. But I do not believe they exist. There is no evidence of them. They do not walk among us. They do not perform magical miracles. If there were gods, we would see them."

"The Hurai have but one God. The God. He walked among us thousands of years ago. He chose us to be his people."

"And where is he now?" Rardus asked. "Why would a God abandon his people?"

"He did not abandon us. We abandoned him. It is why he left. But he did not abandon us. He's still around, for he is Creator."

Rardus shook his head. "Well, he chose his people poorly, I am afraid. The Hurai have no land of their own. No country. Their land is now in the western provinces of the empire. Maybe you should ask him to come back."

"The Hurai are not a land. Or an island. We are a people. We do not need a king or a castle, for we have our God." Goshin suddenly realized that his voice had risen to almost a shout. He quickly lowered his head and continued in a softer voice. "We have asked for thousands of years for him to come back to us. Some say he has already answered us and that this poem holds his answer. It foretells four events. Three of which have already come to pass. The fall of the Hurai nation is the first. Taran invaded our island about two thousand years after the original poem was written."

Rardus chuckled. "That could have been a coincidence. Your island might have been small, but its people were a military threat to Taran. They had to be conquered. Any reasonable man would have figured that one out."

"Even so, it was still foretold," Goshin countered. "The second event was the rise of a man he named Sh'dan. He was to destroy the earth unless one worthy man would step forward."

The mirth that had been showing on Rardus' face faded. "Emperor Shardan rose to power fifteen hundred years ago. He was a barbaric, evil man. He caused a civil war and nearly broke Taran apart. Almost half of our people died of a plague that swept through the cities. Barbarians from the north even marched all the way to the gates of our city. He refused to close them because he thought our empire was infallible."

"Yes," Goshin said. "I know the story. Well, I have studied your history carefully. Emperor Shardan was killed by one of his servants who rallied soldiers to defeat the barbarians."

"It is a story our children are told," Rardus said proudly. "It was our greatest moment. Our empire rose to even greater heights after that. What is the third event?"

"A star will appear in the heavens, and it will light day and night without moving."

"The star to the north," Rardus said quickly.

"You have seen it?" Goshin asked.

"Of course. We have all seen it, though there are many reasonable explanations."

Goshin lifted an eyebrow. "And those are?"

"It was always there. We just never saw it before." The answer caused a chuckle to escape from Goshin's lips. Rardus quickly asked, "What does the scroll say about the star?"

"Only that is a precursor to a fourth event."

"And that is?"

"I do not know, but I have my suspicions," Goshin replied.

"The poem does not say?" Rardus asked.

"No," Goshin replied. "It does not. It makes reference to other works. Scrolls written by other Hurai. Scrolls long since lost. But it does not say what the fourth event is, only that there is one and that it comes after the third event."

"And that is why you are here?" Rardus asked. "To find those scrolls?"

"Yes," Goshin said. "But, but there is more. The poem not only refers to a fourth event but also foretells of two paths that the world could follow. One of darkness and one of light. I fear we are at crossroads. We must solve the riddle of the poem to save the world."

The scholar let a smile escape his lips. "Although I have no doubt about the validity of your poem, I think it is hard for a man of intellect such as myself to believe that they truly foretell the future."

"You may believe as you wish," Goshin replied. "I too, have my doubts. But it is my duty as a Hurai to search the truth. So I shall."

The scholar gave a slight nod and said, "Then I shall leave you to your search." He turned to leave, but at the last moment, asked, "What do you think that the fourth event is?"

Goshin looked down at the poem and took a moment to give his answer. "I think God intends to return to reclaim this world as his kingdom."

Rardus froze, wanting to race through the door as fast as he could. But his heart was beating so hard, he thought he was going to die. The rumors were true, then. He had tried not to believe them, had hoped they were not true. He looked at the door, and then back at the old Hurai. He felt a kinship with the strange man from the west. They were both scholars in pursuit of knowledge. But Goshin was not Taran. First and foremost he owed his loyalty to the empire.

"Good day, my friend," Rardus said as calmly as he could. His voice shook, and he hoped it was not noticed.

Goshin had already turned back to his research, looking over an ancient scroll that needed more translation. He did not notice the cracked voice, or the white ashen face. "And good day to you," Goshin said.

***

Rardus wiped his forehead. His heart raced, and his clothes were soaked with sweat. It certainly wasn't because he was hot. The chamber that he stood in was almost cold, even though it was the middle of summer. He wasn't sure exactly where he was, but he knew that he was led deep underground. That would explain why it was so cool. But the cool temperature of the chamber didn't help his sweating problem.

Two centurions dressed in their leather armor and red surcoats had escorted him through long corridors. Neither had said a word to him other than the occasional one-word command. They were as imposing figures as any soldier would be. They were tall and muscular and carried sharp swords. But it was not them that caused fear to fill the scholar's every being. It was the man who now stood in front of him.

He had come from a dark, unlit corner of the chamber. He had not heard a door open. He just appeared from the shadows. He was taller than the centurions. The top of the Rardus' head just reached the man's chin. He was dressed in a long black robe that was cinched around his waist by a jewel encrusted belt. Atop his head was a thin gold crown. It was not the ornate crown that the emperor wore. It was just a simple circlet of gold. There was not a weapon on him, but Rardus knew he was the most dangerous man in the empire.

"Your highness," Rardus said, dropping to a knee and bowing his head.

Prince Tarcious, the brother of the emperor of Taran, did not have any patience for this man. But the old scholar had the information that he needed, so he had to be tolerant. At least long enough to get the information.

"A Hurai came to your library," the prince said.

"Yes," Rardus responded. "The curator of the library had said that you were to be informed immediately."

"And yet," the Prince said with a sneer. "It has taken you several hours to contact me. Immediately means immediately."

A look of horror spread across the scholar's face. "I...I wanted to be sure and to know what he was researching. I didn't want to come to you without knowing that he really was Hurai. I needed to ask questions. To be sure."

Prince Tarcious closed his eyes and took a long, deep breath. His lips moved, reciting words from an ancient language. The moment the first sound left his lips, an electricity filled the chamber. The centurions had felt it before and had witnessed what was about to come next. They each leaned away from the poor scholar. The prince lifted his right hand and thrust it out directly at Rardus. A small ball of fire exploded from his palm and struck the scholar in the chest, sending him flat on his back.

The prince stepped forward and looked down at the old man, who was gasping for breath. His eyes were wide in fear and sobs came from his lips.

"My instructions were clear," the prince said. "It is fortunate for you that my abilities with managing the web of magic is limited right now. In time, though, such a demonstration would leave you a charred chunk of flesh and bone. When I command you to do something, I expect it to be done. Exactly as I have commanded. Am I making myself clear?"

Rardus nodded.

"Get him up," the prince demanded.

Quickly, for fear of their own lives, the two centurions pulled the scholar up to his feet. The old man could barely stand on his own, so the two centurions had to hold him up. The center of the scholar's chest was charred where the fireball had struck. The skin would eventually heal, but the fear that was put in him would last forever.

"I will give you one chance to tell me what you know. If you leave out any detail, I will know, and then I will kill you. If you lie or try and deceive me, I will know. And then I will kill you. Now speak!"

The faint scent of charred cloth was replaced by the pungent scent of urine.

Rardus' face went ashen and then he grabbed at his chest. He fell to his knees, gasping for air. The centurions tried to keep him up, but the old scholar slipped through their hands. A moment after he fell to his knees, he collapsed to the floor, his eyes wide with fear, for he knew he was dying. He looked up at the Prince with the last breath of life in his lungs and prayed to a god that he knew would not listen. And then blackness enveloped him.

Between clenched teeth, the prince growled, "Find the Hurai. Bring him to me. I don't care how. Just make sure he can talk."

The two centurions bowed in unison before hurrying as fast as they could out of the chamber. They had seen enough to scare them into obedience. They did not want to disappoint.

***

The emperor sat in the darkness of his chamber, as he often did. From the height of the tallest tower of his palace, he looked upon his city. Fires and lamps lit roadways and buildings, bringing a nearly never-ending brightness to his city. For hours on end, he could just sit and watch his people, enthralled by the greatness of his own making.

He turned his head slightly at the change in the air caused by the slight parting of a curtain. The stillness of his chamber was nearly absolute, so it was easy to know when something disturbed it. He could see movement in the shadows and kept his eye on whoever it was that approached.

"My brother." The words shattered the peace as harshly as a hammer breaking glass.

Prince Tarcious had stopped a respectable twenty feet away and dropped to a knee.

"Tarcious," Emperor Hargon said. "Come."

The emperor's younger brother approached with what had become a daily liquid treat. He handed the tall, bronze goblet to the most powerful man in the world and watched in silence as the emperor gulped the drink down.

"A most intoxicating drink," the Emperor said with a smile. He could feel the warmth spread through his limbs and his head was emptied of all worries and cares. "Now, you have news for me."

"Your spies are thorough, brother. Do I really need to repeat what you already know?"

Emperor Hargon turned to his brother and said, "Of course you do. It helps me to figure out who is lying to me, and who is telling the truth."

"Have I ever lied to you?" Prince Tarcious asked.

The Emperor let out a burst of laughter. "I do not know if you have ever spoken a word of truth to me! Now lay your lies and deceiving words upon my ears!"

"Of course, my brother. The news is from the east."

"The east? Who cares of the East," the emperor blurted out with a slurring of his words. "The east is of little care to me. To the north, the barbarians are massing again. A quarter of my legions must be committed to keeping the gold flowing from the mountain mines. And the southern provinces have always been salt in my wounds. They keep more than their fair share of taxes and refuse my demands for more fealty. The West is just too big to govern properly. We have expanded too far. I fear that we may lose half the continent if we can't keep those darn barbarians at bay."

"But brother, the East holds..."

"The east!" the emperor shouted, jumping to his feet. "Enough of the east! Are there mines of gems and jewels to the east?"

"No, but..."

"Are there rivers of gold to the east?" the emperor yelled at his brother. "Are there legions of men ready to declare their loyalty to me?

To lay down their lives by marching to the north to slaughter barbarians?"

"No," Prince Tarcious said with as much patience as you could muster. "But there is open land. And forests. We do much trade with them and the resources of the land could be ours for the taking, instead of having to trade for it."

The Emperor shook his head. "Trade? We steal from them as it is. Spices from the west. Tapestries and sculptures from our own artisans. And in return, we get leather from their livestock. Wagons of grain. Large timbers of wood from their forests. Horses for our chariots. We give them nothing for much in return."

"But it could be ours. Yours, I mean. Rather than trading with them, it could just be all ours."

The emperor sat back down and said with a more subdued tone, "And then we would have to govern them. And garrison their cities. And keep the peace. And they would rebel, and we would have to squash them. No. It is better for us like it is. We steal from them, and they can govern themselves. I care not for them. Now, I want to know how we are going to wipe the barbarians off the face of the earth! They are a threat to this empire. They breed like rabbits, and they fight like rabid dogs."

Prince Tarcious let out a long sigh. This process was taking too long, and the emperor was not cooperating. He glanced at the goblet that the emperor was still holding, wondering if he could increase the dosage without it becoming fatal. He did not want death, he just needed the emperor to cooperate. It would just have to take more time. But time was running out and soon he would have to act out of desperation instead of through thoughtful planning.

"General Urgal's legions are on their way to join the battle. If all goes well, we will push them back to their homes."

"Yes," the emperor said. "That is the news I was looking for. He will be ordered to continue the fight back to their villages. Slaughtering and burning the whole way. We must wipe their existence from the face of the earth."

"Of course, my brother," Prince Tarcious said. "Your will shall be done."

"Now be gone! I have many more things to ponder before the night is through."

Prince Tarcious gave his brother a deep bow and left as silently as he had arrived.

Chapter Twenty-Four

The morning sun was about to make its appearance. The eastern sky was a slightly lighter shade of dark than the rest of the clear night sky. The stars were especially clear, especially the very bright northern star that Goshin had been so concerned about. Conner hadn't thought about the old man in quite some time. He had been too busy with trying to stay alive. A sudden feeling of loneliness swept through him. He had been racing around the countryside for so many days, he couldn't even remember how long it had been since he left South Karmon. But even through Brace was sleeping soundly just five feet away, the loneliness was overpowering. He missed the old man and his quirky ways. He missed the warmth of his own bed and the friendly faces of the castle staff.

And of course, he missed Elissa. He could not image the grief that she would feel when the news of her father's death reached her. His heart ached for her and the pain that she would go through. There was nothing that he could do, especially being so far away. But even if he were there, he could at least provide a shoulder for her to cry on. He wanted to be there for her, to comfort her. It was a selfish thought, he knew, because he just wanted to be with her.

He shook his head at his silliness. Trying to keep the thoughts from creeping into his mind, he tried to distract himself by stirring the fire. He moved the burning logs around, allowing the flames to grow when a sudden pop came from the fire. It wasn't real loud, but loud enough to stir his companion.

Brace Hawkden sat up from what had been a deep sleep and looked around, bleary-eyed. As his mind processed his surroundings, Brace jumped for his sword, landed awkwardly and stayed on the ground, writhing in pain.

Conner held his laughter inside and called out, "Are you all right?"

Brace sat up holding his head. "I don't know what hurts more, my head or my leg. What happened?"

"You were exhausted. About five miles from the valley, you simply fell off your horse and hit your head pretty hard on the ground. You didn't move for some time, but you were still breathing. So I dragged you into the woods where our fire wouldn't be seen and made camp."

The Knight Captain touched the wound on his head, and his hand came away sticky with blood. "Ow. How long was I out?"

"It was midday when you fell," Conner said. "And now it is nearing morning. So half a day and a night."

Brace jumped up, ignoring the pain in his head and leg and grabbed his sword. "Get the horses. We must ride."

"Are you okay?" Conner asked.

"No, but I don't need to be," Brace replied. "We lost much time. Too much."

"You needed rest," Conner said apologetically.

Brace stopped in mid-step and let his chin fall to his chest. "You were right to let me rest. I have been on the go for so many days. I have no idea when I last slept."

"I have food," Conner added.

"And I am starved. But we must eat on the go."

It took only minutes to break camp. Generally, Brace tried to clean up his camps to prevent the untrained eye from recognizing that there had been a camp. But Brace was in too big of a hurry. He knew they were way late and likely had already missed Neffenmark. If the fat lord was going to make a play for the crown, then he would likely have already started for South Karmon to stake his claim to the throne. If that was the case, then they still might be able to chase him down. Lord Neffenmark's wagon train didn't move fast, barely at the pace of a walk.

The horses were more than ready to go after getting plenty of rest. The moment Conner touched his heels to the side of Lilly, she shot forward at a canter. He had to pull her back and keep her from running too fast. Brace kept them at a pace that pushed the horses hard, but not hard enough to hurt them.

***

Brace Hawkden squatted behind thick foliage at the edge of the woods. In front of them was Neffenmark's village. It had a name, but Brace had no idea what it was called. He had never been in it; he had always bypassed it and the front entrance to the castle. Even though the secret entrance up through the cliffs of the mountain was not widely known, it was still watched closely. He knew most of the lookout points, and they were inaccessible from the outside, and even a well-placed arrow would not reach the lookout guards. Since they had arrived some time ago, they had not seen one villager or even evidence that anyone was there. Even as twilight was descending, there were no lights or lamps lit in any of the homes or shops.

"Let's go," Brace said. He stood and checked that his sword was secured in his scabbard. Conner followed, next to, but a step behind the larger man.

Cautiously they approached the village. They avoided the main road, coming up through a trampled field instead. They scanned the nearby houses looking for any movement, especially the tip of an arrow sticking out. Brace tried to walk in an unthreatening manner to avoid being noticed, but he was still clad in his chain armor. The only unthreatening part of his approach was his obvious limp.

The village was spread out across a large area. The uneven terrain of the mountains kept the inhabitants from building close to one another. Here and there three or four buildings were clumped together, but mostly the buildings of the village were spread out. They passed the first building without incident. It was a small thatch-roofed house with its door cracked open. Brace kept his eye on the door as they passed, but there were no signs of its occupants.

The crunch of their boots on the ground seemed to echo loudly. There was not even the sound of birds chirruping or dogs barking.

"Where are they?" Conner asked as quietly as he could.

Brace shook his head slowly, his hand gripping the pommel of his sword even more tightly. They continued walking in silence, straight down the center of the village towards the castle.

Neffenmark castle was built out from the lower slopes of the mountain. Half of the castle was actually in the mountain, having been dug out during the original construction. The rest of the castle was not as elaborate as the multi-spired stone building that perched atop the cliffs in South Karmon. But it was serviceable when it came to defense. The castle was but a single square structure with a tower at both corners. Battlements lined the top of the walls. A single gate at the center of the outermost wall blocked their way.

The two doors that comprised the gate were each twice as tall as Brace, easily allowing a rider on a warhorse to enter the castle without having to duck. The doors were half as wide as they were tall. Maybe two riders could ride abreast, but it would have been a tight squeeze.

"Should we knock?" Conner asked.

Brace looked up. There was a wide gap in the battlements atop the wall just above them. It was wide enough for a barrel or two of hot oil to be pushed on top of unsuspecting assaulters.

"Should we not have been challenged? Where is everyone?" Conner asked again.

"I do not know," Brace replied. "Nothing about this village makes sense." He looked more closely at the doors and realized there was an odd gap between them. He drew his sword and took a step back.

"Push it," Brace ordered.

It took Conner a moment to realize what Brace was asking and then he walked up to one of the doors and gave it a hearty push. It moved easily, to his surprise. He jumped back and drew his swords.

The doors opened up to a long corridor. At the far end was another gate, but it was open. In between was thirty feet of open space. Arrow slits were cut into the wall about ten feet above the ground. There was a reason the gates were so narrow. If the castle was assaulted, it was a real bottleneck for the assaulters. Many, many men would die in the assault. Brace and Conner moved slowly, their eyes on the arrow slits. With each step, their eyes were stuck on the arrow slits expecting a razor sharp arrow to suddenly appear and shoot them down.

"Is this wise?" Conner asked. "We can easily be killed."

"It is likely a trap, but that is why we are here. To spring it and kill Neffenmark before he can do any more damage."

As they reached the inner gate, Brace gave Conner a quick push, and they jumped through the doorway, expecting the portcullis to drop on them. But it didn't. Brace quickly scanned the inner courtyard, but it was as deserted as the city. There were patches of grass in the courtyard, but mostly it was dirt covered. Directly in front of them, about a hundred feet away was the face of the mountain. A set of closed double doors faced them, cut directly into the stone of the mountain. The courtyard stretched about a hundred feet both to their left and right. A large wood structure was to their left with the smell indicating that horses were stabled inside. Or used to be stabled inside.

To their right was a square stone building with several doors leading into it.

Spinning slowly while walking through the courtyard, Brace scanned the castle walls for signs of an ambush. He only relaxed after he had crossed the courtyard and stood at the doors directly across from the castle gate.

"Should I check the stables?" Conner asked. "Look to see if there are any horses?"

Brace nodded. "There is an entrance from the back of the stables into a hallway that leads to the room behind this door. Move slowly and silently."

"You don't want to wait for me?" Conner asked with a whisper.

"I'll be okay."

Conner nodded, unsure that Brace would really be okay. He moved as quickly as he could without making noise. Just as he reached the open archway that led to the stables, Conner glanced back to see Brace step through the double doors.

Like the village and presumably the rest of the castle, the stables were deserted. There was still the strong scent of manure, so he knew that the horses had only recently left. He glanced in each stall, just to be sure. There were a few saddles and miscellaneous tack on the ground as if the riders had left in a hurry. There were two torches still burning, but they were almost burned out. Soon there would be no light left as the sun no longer offered light to the enclosed stables. He sheathed one of his swords and took the longer of the two torches and headed towards the far end to find the hallway that Brace had mentioned.

***

Brace stepped through the door and heard the whiz and knew what hit him before the pain exploded through his shoulder. He spun around partially because of the force of the crossbow bolt and partially because his fighting instincts kicked in. His spin caused him to land on the ground, and he rolled once more away from the doorway. A second bolt whizzed past his head and buried deep into the wall.

Brace lifted himself to a knee, raised his sword and scanned the room. He didn't care who was firing the crossbow, he just needed to find a way to get out of the shooters line of sight. In less than a second, he took in the room. He had been here before, so he already knew its layout. The room was Neffenmark's audience chamber. Along the far wall were stacks of pillows where the fat lord held court. Curtains were draped along both walls covering doors from adjoining hallways. Various tables and chairs were to his left where he knew Neffenmark's favorites were allowed to feast on the lord's exquisite food. With his bearings set, Brace dove for the table and chairs hoping one of them could provide him enough cover until Conner could come.

Another crossbow bolt struck the wall where Brace had just been.

"You are quick for being lame," a voice shouted from the far end of the room.

Brace peeked around a table and noticed movement from behind the curtains on the far wall. He hoped that the shooter was reloading the crossbow, so he exposed himself momentarily to pick up the table and push it over. Once settled behind his thick oaken shield, he looked around the corner of the table just as he saw the crossbow between the folds of the curtain. Before he could react, the crossbow was shot, and the bolt buried itself into the table, inches from his face. Fortunately, Neffenmark had his tables constructed from thick and hard oak. A lighter wood might have allowed the bolt to fly through. With a grunt, Brace pushed the table forward about ten feet.

"Where is Neffenmark?" Brace shouted out.

"Lord Neffenmark has left his castle," the shooter called out. "He has other business to attend to."

Brace's heart sank. He was too late. The pain that he had been able to ignore until now overwhelmed him. The bolt was sunk deep into his shoulder, possibly all the way through. His right arm felt useless. Each time he squeezed his right hand, pain shot through his entire body. He had felt worse pain, but not by much.

"Where is he?" Brace shouted back.

"Does it matter?" the shooter said. "You will be dead soon enough."

Brace caught a slightly odd accent to the man's words. He realized the shooter was likely a mercenary from Taran. Neffenmark liked to bring in disposable soldiers. Pushing aside the pain for a moment, he put his back against the table and pushed it another five feet forward. Another bolt was shot, sticking into the table, but not through it. Brace peeked around. The shooter was still behind the curtains, hidden from view. If he got close enough, he knew the shooter would get only one shot. It would take the shooter too long to reload. There was no pain in the world that could stop him from killing the shooter if it came to that.

Brace took a long, deep breath and winced at the pain. He was going to have to rest a minute to gather the energy for his next push. "Who are you?" Brace asked.

"The man who is going to kill you."

"I'm already dead," Brace shouted back. "The arrow hurt me bad. At least give me the courtesy of knowing who killed me."

"You seem to be moving pretty good for a dead man," the shooter said. "I will, unfortunately, let you die not knowing. I know it is a cruel thing to do. But I am a cruel person."

"You are not Karmon. And likely not Thellian. That would make you Taran," Brace said. "How much did Neffenmark pay you?"

The shooter let out a chuckle. "To kill you? Nothing. I paid him for that honor."

Brace gave the table another push and another bolt followed into the table. This time a sliver of the tip punched through.

"We could make this easier," Brace shouted.

"This seems pretty easy as it is," the shooter called back.

"I will give you one free shot. If I survive, I get a free shot on you."

The shooter laughed. "That would be unfair to you. I would put the bolt between your eyes, and your death would be too quick. I would prefer you to have a death that will take some more time. Time for you to reflect upon your treacherous acts."

"I don't know what you are talking about!" Brace shouted back. He leaned over to peek around the table. As the curtain shifted, he pulled his head back and a bolt whizzed through the space where his head just occupied.

He was still about twenty or so feet away. A feeling of dread came over him. There was no way that he could charge and survive. His breathing was shallow, and the pain that was spreading through his body made it difficult to even blink. His only hope would be to force the shooter to fire a bolt and then he could charge before the shooter was able to reload.

Just as he was about to peak around the table to see where the shooter was, he noticed the curtain billow out on the other side of the room from the shooter.

***

Conner pulled the door open and stepped aside, half expecting a flurry of arrows to cut him down. But only darkness greeted him. He stuck the torch through the doorway. The hallway went about ten feet before making a sharp turn to the right. Cautiously, he stepped into the darkness.

The torch had nearly expended its fuel, so Conner moved more quickly than he wanted to. Because he was in near total darkness, the little light the torch did give off gave him enough to see by. At the corner, Conner reached the torch out to see what was there. The hallway around the corner was wide enough for three people to easily walk side-by-side. And there was a door on the left wall.

At the door, he turned the doorknob slowly and gave it a little push. He stuck the torch in the room. What little he could see told him that it was likely just a storage room. There were shelves full of bags, boxes, and jars. He closed the door and moved on. Ten feet later, there was another door. Again, he carefully opened the door and was greeted by starlight coming in from windows high up on the wall. This was clearly a kitchen. Another set of doors were on the wall directly across from him. He thought for a moment about going through the kitchen and checking on what was behind those doors, but his instincts told him to move on. So he did. He closed the door and continued down the hallway.

After about twenty feet, the hallway ended at a door. With a little less caution than before, he pushed the door open and found himself looking down a very short hallway, only about five feet long. It was not as wide as the hallway he was just in, maybe half the width. At the end of the hall was a red curtain that was moving, probably from when he had opened the door.

"Your treachery will be well known through the land," a voice said from the room beyond. Conner tilted his head, trying to recognize the voice. The words were also spoken in an odd manner as if he didn't know how to speak the common language of the Karmon people.

Conner tossed the torch back into the hallway that he had just come from and closed the door. As quietly as he could, he drew his swords and inched towards the curtain.

***

Sir Brace Hawkden shouted back, "You may call me what you will, but I am a servant of the kingdom of Karmon!"

Laughter erupted from the shooter. "Servant? You are but a common soldier. A peon who serves a dead king!"

Anger burned deep within Brace, but he knew that he couldn't let it control him. He was a Karmon Knight, the best warrior the world had ever known. And it wasn't only because he was a skilled swordsman, but because he was more than just a fighter. He had to control his anger, or it would control him. He had to keep his mind clear, despite the pain that throbbed in his shoulder. Brace took one last glance at the curtain and thought for sure he saw someone behind it. It had to be Conner for he was about to bet his life on it.

"Conner!" Brace suddenly called out. "Far wall! Charge now!"

The command of the Knight Captain startled Conner into action without thought. The part in the curtain was right in front of him, so he pushed through with swords drawn. Brace had been behind a table, but now he was charging out from behind it, screaming at the top of his lungs. The movement at the far end of the room caught his attention, so he started running towards it. A thin man clad in a silky black cloak stepped from behind a curtain, leveled a crossbow at him and fired.

Conner's sword flashed up, striking the bolt just as it was about to get to him. The remnants of the bolt scattered to the floor. He did not think about what he did, he just kept charging at a full sprint.

The shooter, his eyes wide with surprise, pulled another fully loaded crossbow from the floor and aimed it Brace, who was just feet away. The bolt didn't have far to go and embedded deep into Brace's stomach. The Knight Captain fell to his knees, but he kept his legs moving, trying to get to the shooter. But the pain and shock to his system was making him unable to take another step. He simply fell to the ground.

Conner drove his sword deep into the right shoulder of the shooter who was trying to load another bolt. The shooter had tried at the last instant to parry the blow with the crossbow, but he was too slow. The sword was buried to its hilt. The crossbow fell to the floor. As he was taught many times by Master Goshin, Conner expected the desperate dagger attack. The shooter, using his left hand, struck out with a small dagger. Because he knew it was coming, Conner easily stepped aside from the attack. He released his right hand from the sword that was buried in the shooter's shoulder, switched his other sword from left to right hand and slashed down on the left arm of his opponent. The hand fell to the floor, still grasping the dagger.

The shooter was in shock. His eyes were wide, and his mouth hung open. All color drained from his face as quickly as the blood was pouring from his stump. Desperately, the shooter tried to pull the sword from his shoulder, but he couldn't get his remaining hand to work right. Conner plunged his sword deep into his chest. A look of desperation crossed the shooter as he realized he was taking his last breaths. Conner pulled the sword out slowly and then the shooter slumped to the floor and did not move anymore. He then turned to Brace, who was trying to sit up on his own. Conner dropped to his knees and helped the Knight Captain to sit up.

Brace smiled. "I am dying." His hands touched the end of the bolt that was buried deep into his gut. Only a small part of it was sticking out from his front, the rest was pushing his chainmail away from his back.

"You are the Knight Captain, you cannot die!" Conner said, continuing to hold the Knight Captain up.

Brace shook his head. "No, that is all that is left for me. Help me to the wall."

Conner pulled the much heavier man up to his feet and used himself as a crutch to guide Brace to a nearby wall. As gently as he could, Conner let Brace slide down into a sitting position.

"It is almost all the way through," Conner said, looking underneath his chainmail shirt. "I think I can pull it out."

Brace closed his eyes and shook his head. "No. Leave it. I am ready."

Not knowing what to do, Conner slumped down next to the Knight Captain. In front of him lay the crossbow shooter, his bloody stump lying in a widening pool of blood. The man died with his eyes open, and they were staring off into nothingness. Conner looked down at himself, and he was a bloody mess. He wasn't sure if the blood was his, the shooters, or Brace's. His twin swords lay near his feet, covered in blood.

And then it finally hit him.

He had been on the move for so long that he really hadn't had time to think. Even when he was alone in the woods waiting for Brace to recover from the fall of his horse, he didn't think. He had spent most of that time hunting, keeping his mind occupied with trying to find dinner. But now, with nothing but death around him, he had little else to do but think. He had killed a man. But he had done more than that, he had slaughtered him. And the same with the many other men back on the battlefield. He justified his actions back there because he was in battle. They were trying to kill him, and he had to defend himself. But so did this man – this crossbow shooter. He had fired a crossbow bolt at him, and he had miraculously deflected it. If he hadn't killed the shooter, he would have done the same to him.

"You think he has any family?" Conner asked quietly.

"They all do," Brace replied. "Someone will miss him. Someone always does. But he would have killed you. Without worrying about whether or not you had a family."

"I know," Conner replied. "It doesn't make it any better."

Brace reached a hand out and put it on Conner's shoulder and squeezed with what strength he had remaining. It wasn't much.

"I think I'm going to throw up," Conner said.

Brace chuckled. "He wasn't your first, and he won't be your last. You are an incredible warrior." He squeezed Conner's shoulder harder. With a demanding voice, Brace said, "Look at me, Conner."

Conner did. He could see death in the Knight Captain's eyes. He didn't have long to live.

"I have never, ever seen fighting like what I saw from you. Ever. Whatever Master Goshin taught you, it is incredible. You are too fast. Too fast for me. There is not a Knight or soldier anywhere in the world that could stand up to you in a one-on-one fight. Even the Taran with a crossbow couldn't stand up to you! That was pretty incredible to see you knock that bolt out of the air. But listen closely." Brace paused to catch his breath, squeezing his eyes shut to try and ignore the pain that was shooting through his body. "Listen. What makes you great will not be how you fight or your skill with a sword. It is who you are here." He tapped Conner on the chest. "And here." Then he tapped Conner on the forehead. "Whatever you do, don't become numb to killing. Killing is not your job. It is not the job of a knight. Anyone can kill. But not anyone can be a knight."

A wry smile crept across Conner's face. "I can't be a knight, you know."

Brace laughed and then winced at the pain. "You are right. But my point is, don't be afraid of your distaste for death. Hate it. Don't embrace it. Honor the man you just killed, even if he is your worst enemy. Fight only when you have to. When there is nothing else left. Listen carefully. I have failed as a knight. As a man. I let my own ego get in the way of my honor. I let Neffenmark convince me that I myself could preserve the kingdom. And I believed him because I felt

I was a great knight. I ended up being a failure of a knight. I caused this war with Thell. I caused the death of the king, and now I accept my punishment."

"Sir Brace, you have done so many great things, do not let this one thing destroy who you are!"

"When you are in my position, the leader of many men, many knights, anything you do means everything. And yes, this one thing has ruined it all. That is my shame, and I must live with it for eternity."

"I will get Neffenmark for you," Conner declared proudly.

Brace reached back and grabbed Conner on the arm and shouted, "No! Do not be a killer. Do not kill for pleasure or revenge. Only do it because you must. Neffenmark must be dealt with. But you are not an assassin. You are not a murderer. He must be brought to justice."

"You are so much like Master Goshin," Conner said.

"He and I are so different," Brace replied, releasing his grip on Conner. "Very different."

"No. He says the same things. I guess I never realized you would say those things as well."

"When you're on your deathbed, the strangest thoughts come to mind," Brace said. "He is a good man. I hoped you listened to him."

"What do I do, now?" Conner asked.

"You must go back to South Karmon. There will be a play for the throne, and the princess will be caught in the middle."

"Who will be king?" Conner asked. "There is no heir."

"I do not know. Neffenmark has his mercenaries. He just might be able to convince enough of the lords that he is strong enough to take it. He may try and claim the princess as his bride, and then it will be his son that will take the throne."

Conner wrinkled his face at that thought. "Could he?"

"Take the throne or have a child?" Brace said with a prolonged smile. "I am not sure if he is physically able to procreate, but the laws of the land are clear. Only the first male heir may claim the throne. Princess Elissa's first male child will be heir."

"And if she doesn't have a male child?" Conner asked.

"War. And unless she takes a husband soon, I fear there will be war anyway. Civil war. Someone will claim the throne, but the kingdom will never be the same. Neffenmark pulled in Taran soldiers to help fight us in the valley. I would not put it past Neffenmark to march on the castle with a full complement of Taran centurions."

"Then we must go." Conner stood up and took his swords.

Brace shook his head. "I will be dead soon. I cannot move. I am done." He closed his eyes. His breathing became very shallow.

Conner knelt back down next to the Knight Captain and asked, "Do you have any family?"

"My father lords over his land on the east coast. He is old and senile. The last time I visited, he did not recognize me. Mother. Dead. Long time ago," Brace's voice trailed off to a whisper.

"No wife?"

"No time," Brace answered. "If I said no regrets, it would be a lie." He closed his eyes one last time, and he said, "Her name was Ilasha. Daughter of a merchant. Long time ago…wish I could see her one last time."

He let out one last long sigh, and then he was still.

Chapter Twenty-Five

Princess Elissa lay in her bed, her eyes closed, but her mind already awake. She was comfortable under her warm blankets and did not want to get up. She had not slept well. In fact, it had been many days since she had a good night's sleep. If not for Melanie coming in with breakfast, she probably would not have gotten up today.

"I know you're awake," Melanie said. She set a tray of sweet rolls on a nearby table. "The sun has been up for hours. You must get up."

"I know," Elissa said. She sat up, hugging her blankets close to her. "It has been days without hearing anything."

"Percy said that it takes several days for the army to march to Thell. He does not expect any word for a day, maybe two."

"Percy? As in Royal Guard Percy?"

A slight redness touched Melanie's cheeks. "He is not so bad."

"If you like creepy old men!" Elissa said with a chuckle.

"He is not that old. Only ten years older than you and me!" Melanie took a small pillow and tossed it lightly at Elissa.

The princess continued to laugh, and soon Melanie joined in. They laughed hard for several minutes. And then suddenly the laughter turned into tears. And sobs. Elissa buried her head in her hands. "I cannot take this anymore. I do not know if they are dead or alive. And I fear the worst!"

Melanie sat on the bed next to her friend. "Do not be afraid, I am sure they are all safe." She took Elissa into a warm hug.

After a few minutes, Elissa let Melanie go and asked, "Are the rolls still warm?"

Melanie grabbed the tray and handed it to Elissa. With her mouth full of sweet, frosting covered rolls, she was about to ask her friend if she would go for a ride in the woods when a bell rang from a distance. Elissa snapped her head to the window and listed. A second bell rang. It was clearly coming from a distance, which meant from the main gate. A third bell rang. Elissa's heart began to beat fast as she waited and hoped for the last bell. Four bells meant the arrival of the king. Just as she was about to give up, the fourth bell rang. Still in her white sleeping gown, she jumped from her bed and sprinted to the door. She opened it just as Arpwin, her father's attendant appeared.

A smile was on his face. "It appears that your father has returned!"

She let out a squeal and raced through the castle to the stables. She would ride to the gates and greet her father in person. She took the first horse in the stall, a small roan mare that she didn't bother to saddle. The gate attendant got the castle's portcullis up just as Elissa reached it. Ducking under the thick metal bars as she passed through, she kicked her horse into as fast a run as she dared. She had to maintain some control, allowing innocent bystanders the chance to jump out of the way as she darted for the main gate.

A crowd had gathered there, but she didn't take much notice. Only at the last minute did she pull back hard on the reins and her mount came to a skidding stop. She slid off the horse's back, and she ran through the crowd, pushing her way through. At first, some protested until they realized who she was. Word was passed that the princess was coming and a path opened up for her. Her walk turned into a jog and then a run as she approached the gate.

She expected her father to be sitting atop his mount, his knights at his side. Likely it would be his Knight Captain there, Sir Brace Hawkden. And hopefully, Conner would be there, too. But as she passed under the gate, she realized there was no cheering or shouting. In fact, there was barely a sound at all. The realization was slow, but when it hit, it hit her hard. Everyone was looking at one wagon, and everyone had tears in their eyes. As she stepped forward, the whole crowd looked at her, and she froze.

Elissa had always seen her father as a physically powerful man. He was big and strong. In his younger years, he trained with the Knights and was as strong as any of them. Even though he trained less and less as he aged, he still had a powerful presence. But what she now looked upon frightened her. It looked like her father. The same hair. The same beard. But his face was an ashen white, frozen in a grim look of pain. It looked like him, but it couldn't be him. Whoever it was, they stretched out on the back of the wagon, the king's surcoat stretched across his lower body.

She could not believe that someone would use her father's surcoat to cover a dead man. Anger began to burn inside of her. She looked for someone to yell at. A bloodied knight, using his sword as a crutch to help him walk ambled over to her. His eyes were full of tears.

"I am sorry, my Princess." He dropped to a knee.

She looked past him, looking for her father. He had to be around someplace. She spun around, looking for him and then she realized that the entire crowd had dropped to a knee. Even the wounded, barely able to walk, fell to a knee. She remaining standing, still looking for her father. He would never kneel. He was the king. He could not kneel. He could not fall. He could not die.

Blackness surrounded her as her knees gave out and she fell to the ground.

***

Lord Martin was not the imposing man that King Thorndale had been. He was short, shorter than most men. He liked to keep himself clean shaven because when he let his beard grow, it only grew out in patches. Even his voice was high-pitched, almost squeaky. His hands were soft as a woman's, having never lifted a sword in battle. At first glance, he was hardly the kind of man that other men would follow. But he was well liked and respected as a man of integrity. He was one of the late king's most trusted advisors. They had grown up together when King Thorndale's father had ruled. That friendship had lasted through the years. It was a friendship that everyone respected and honored. Even the knights, who had little respect for anyone who didn't know how to swing a sword or shoot a bow, respected Lord Martin because of his relationship with the king.

Now he sat on the throne. Not because he wanted to, but because there wasn't anyone else. The late King Thorndale had put him in charge while he was gone and in those few days, there was little to do but to decide on the evening meal. But now, the weight of a kingdom was suddenly on his shoulders. He sat on the throne, trying to hold back tears. They weren't tears of sadness, they were tears of despair. The king was gone. The beloved king. There were few in the kingdom that did not love the king, and that made his dilemma worse.

Under typical circumstances, the eldest male child of the king, regardless of age, would be called to the throne room where the lords of the realm would declare their fealty to him, and the prince would take the crown, and he would be king. But there was no eldest male. The queen had passed away before she could bear another child. And the king, adamant in his love to his wife, refused to take another as his queen. There was some hope, with the king still being relatively young, that he would have survived to see his grandchildren live. And then the eldest male grandchild would take the throne.

There was also the option of someone claiming the throne as his own. Lord Martin, as the current caretaker of the throne, would be the most likely to make that claim, but he knew he was not king material. And he loved his king too much to do that. If that option was taken, and there was not unanimous support from the lords, civil war would likely ensue. To Lord Martin, it seemed like all paths led to war.

The double doors at the far end of the room opened and Arpwin, the king's personal attendant entered. For a brief moment, the loud commotion outside the throne room overshadowed the quiet peace that Lord Martin was trying to maintain. Lord Martin was relieved at the site of the elder servant. He knew the castle, knew how it was run and was helping him to keep it running the way it should. With a slight smile, Lord Martin had a sudden thought that the one person most suited for the job was Arpwin.

The old servant approached and nodded his head in greeting. "It is becoming boisterous, my lord. Lords are clamoring to hear news and find out who will take the throne."

"I fear the worst," Lord Martin said.

"Oh?" Arpwin replied with a raised eyebrow.

"The king has no heir, and I fear that there will be a fight over who will be given the throne," Lord Martin replied.

"Be given the throne?" Arpwin asked.

"Yes," Lord Martin explained. "With no male heir, the throne must be given to someone."

"The bloodline of the king goes back many hundreds of years," Arpwin replied incredulously. "The gods who created the earth bestowed upon King Thorndale's ancestors the throne of the Karmon! That cannot be broken."

"There is no choice," Lord Martin said. "With no male heir…"

"Again, you bring up the male heir," Arpwin interrupted. "Where is it written…?"

"It does not need to be written!" Lord Martin shouted back in his high pitched voice. Instantly regretting the tone, he let out a sigh and continued. They already had this argument. Many times. He was tiring of it, even though in his heart, he knew Arpwin's argument did have some merit. "What you imply cannot happen. The lords will not accept the rule of a woman."

"And why not?" Arpwin asked.

"There would be a civil war," Lord Martin replied.

"There will be civil war anyway," Arpwin countered. "If any lord lays stake to the throne, the other lords will rebel. They don't mind giving our undying fealty to the crown, but they will surely not give it to one of their peers."

"She is but a girl!" Lord Martin cried out, trying in vain to find any argument against what he knew was really the right choice.

"She is a young woman," Arpwin replied calmly. "Older than many kings when they took the throne. King Thorndale was only two years older than Princess Elissa when he took the throne. He had help. He didn't make all his decisions himself. The lords helped him when he needed it. I know because I was there. From the moment he put the crown on his head, I was there. He was an impetuous child. Prone to temper tantrums and he drank too much sweet wine. But we survived. The kingdom survived."

"But will she accept it?" Lord Martin asked with a heavy sigh.

"If she were the eldest boy, she wouldn't have a choice," Arpwin said. "It should be hers." And then he added after a moment, "Whether she likes it or not."

Lord Martin slowly shook his head. "I cannot see us surviving. We will be weak with a young girl – woman – on the throne. Thell will see it as a sign of weakness, and they might just march on us. We lost so many men and boys up north. I cannot see us surviving a long campaign with them."

Lord Martin buried his hands in his face. "We are beaten and bloodied. We must regroup and heal our wounds. And we must begin preparations for defending our kingdom."

A crashing of the doors behind him caused Lord Martin to jump up off the throne.

Three chainmail clad soldiers, each holding long hauberks, escorted the very large form of Lord Neffenmark into the chamber. A number of similarly clad soldiers followed the lord into the chamber, pushing aside the Royal Guard who were trying to keep them out.

"What is this?!" Lord Martin shouted in as strong of a voice as he could muster. "This is a private meeting, and you are not welcome, Lord Neffenmark."

Neffenmark continued to march forward, his jowls jiggling with each step. Three paces from the throne, the lead three soldiers stopped and struck the floor with the base of their weapons. Neffenmark smiled and said, "I have come to pay our fallen king my respects."

"You insult the King by marching in here with your mercenaries," Lord Martin said.

"My guardsmen are ceremonial, I assure you," Neffenmark said. His face twitched as if he wanted to smile.

"You need twenty guardsmen?" Lord Martin asked.

"There are eighteen of them," Neffenmark corrected. "But like I said, they are ceremonial."

The room started to fill up. Curious onlookers filtered into the room to see what was about to happen. A low, excited buzz permeated the room. More Royal Guard inched into the room as well, their hands resting near their swords.

"What are your intentions, Lord Neffenmark?" Lord Martin asked sharply.

Spreading his hands wide, Neffenmark replied, "Why, like I said, I am here to pay my respects." This time he let his face twist into a toothy smile.

Lord Martin sat back down on the soft, cushioned throne and said, "Neffenmark, your actions are as transparent as you are fat!"

A light laughter circled through the room. Neffenmark's smile faded while he glanced around him. "Very well, then. As there is no proper male heir to the throne and with the king having left the defenses of the realm in shambles, it is only proper that someone with the resources to restore Karmon to its greatness take the throne."

"And who would that be?" Lord Martin asked.

"Tyre is beset by political infighting," Neffenmark said. "There is no one strong lord who commands a large enough presence to lead the kingdom. We must look elsewhere. For someone who has the power and resources to lead this kingdom back to greatness. Is there such a man in the kingdom? Do you know of one?"

Lord Martin kept silent, is mind churning. He had never liked Neffenmark. The man was a pompous and arrogant bully. His army of mercenaries was drawn not only from the dredges of Karmon but Taran as well. There were even rumors of Thellian men serving in arms for the fat lord. But he was also one of the largest landowners. His castle and village were virtually self-sustaining. If he grew his army large enough, he could probably be his own kingdom. But Lord Martin knew he wanted more. The prize of the throne of Karmon was too great of a prize. He also knew how he ruled. He ruled with an iron fist. Punishments were severe and rarely just. His peasants were kept in line through fear and intimidation. He could not let that kind of leader ascend to the throne.

"No?" Neffenmark asked after watching Lord Martin squirm for some time. "We all know that you will not take the throne." Neffenmark had called Lord Martin out as a coward many times and unfortunately, Lord Martin had yet to prove Neffenmark wrong.

Weakly, Lord Martin replied, "Yes."

"Yes? Yes as in, you will make a claim for the throne?" Neffenmark asked with a raised brows and a wide smile.

Lord Martin stood and straightened his tunic. He looked down at the fat man. There was no way that he could let Neffenmark sit upon the throne. There was only one way out of this.

In a voice as loud as he could muster, Lord Martin said, "The reign of King Thorndale has come to a close." He looked out across the men and women who had gathered in the chamber. The murmuring and whispering stopped quickly. Everyone wanted to hear what was to be said.

"Go on," Neffenmark prodded, a smirk on his face. It was clear to him that Lord Martin was going to attempt to place himself on the throne. Neffenmark knew that Lord Martin did not have the support of the rest of the kingdom, so it would be a failed gamble to prevent himself from being given the crown.

"The line of King Thorndale has been unbroken for hundreds of years. Generations upon generations of Karmon men and woman have prospered under the rule that the gods of our ancestors set in motion. The Knights of Karmon are the greatest warriors the world has ever seen!" Boisterous shouting and whooping followed for several minutes before it became quiet enough for Lord Martin to continue.

Once the cheering subsided, Lord Martin continued. "It is for that reason that the line of King Thorndale must continue. Our noses have been bloodied, but we are not broken. We will heal. As a kingdom we will heal as well. And the only way to do that is to keep the line unbroken. Therefore, as the blood heir of our late King Thorndale,

Princess Elissa will be given the crown of Karmon and rule as Queen Elissa Thorndale."

Lord Martin's voice rose in volume as he finished his speech. But silence greeted him as his words came to an end. The men and women, soldiers and servants, guardsmen and mercenaries were too stunned to speak. Even Neffenmark was caught off guard. His joyous, smiling face drained of all color.

***

Princess Elissa was still in bed, legs pulled up to her chin, wool blanket pulled tight around her. Tear stains streaked her cheeks. She sat quietly, staring at nothing. Arpwin and Lord Martin stood at the foot of the bed, trying to be patient.

Marta, Princess Elissa's personal attendant, sat next to her, stroking her long hair. "She must be allowed to rest." Marta was an older woman, not quite as old as Arpwin. But not many in the kingdom were as old as Arpwin.

"Marta," Lord Martin said softly. "You may go now."

"The princess has been through a lot," Marta said with a soft voice. Then she turned to the men and snapped, "Her father is dead! She must be allowed to grieve and mourn. You must leave her be."

Lord Martin, feeling rejuvenated by his speech in the throne room, responded in anger. "A lot of fathers are dead! The time for mourning is over. The kingdom will fall apart if we don't keep together. Neffenmark wants the throne. Is that what you want? You want that conniving bastard leading this kingdom? We will have both Thell and Taran on our doorstep ready to attack us."

"She is but a child," Marta pleaded.

"Where is Conner?" the princess suddenly asked.

As it was her first words since collapsing at the gate, all three turned their attention back to the princess.

"He has not returned from battle," Lord Martin said.

"He is dead, then," Elissa said in a soft monotone. It was not a question, but a statement.

"We do not have any word of him," Lord Martin said.

A fresh tear appeared at the corner of her eyes. She let the tear drip down her cheek without bothering to wipe it away. It dropped off her chin and onto her blanket.

"Your highness," Lord Martin pleaded once again. "You must listen to me. Your kingdom needs you. They need you take up the crown."

"My father is king," she replied softly.

Lord Martin turned away, exasperated. To Arpwin he said sharply, "There must be another answer. There must be someone else."

Arpwin just shook his head. "It is her or Neffenmark. No others would dare go against Lord Neffenmark. He has too many spies, too many mercenaries. Too many stories and rumors of what he has done to those who dare oppose him. The other lords are truly afraid of him." For the first time, he allowed private conversations that he had with the king to leave his lips. "The king did not trust Neffenmark. Nor do I. And nor should you."

"Princes are raised knowing that someday they may take the crown," Lord Martin said. "It is a part of their life. They are tutored in etiquette and procedures. They learn how to lead in battle. And how to lead a kingdom. Girls, however, are not raised thinking they will ever wear the crown unless it is as the wife of the king. She has never been trained or taught any skill that a ruler needs."

"But she can be taught," Arpwin countered. "And if we keep good advisors around her, she can rule effectively. But we must keep the line of Thorndale intact."

There was a knock on the door. Glaring at the arguing men who didn't budge to answer the door, Marta stood and walked quickly to open it. Words were quietly exchanged and then she finally pulled the door open to reveal the large form of Lord Neffenmark.

A deep anger burned within Lord Martin, but he did his best to hide it. Neffenmark ambled in dressed in a freshly clean purple silk tunic. He tipped his head in greeting.

"Lord Neffenmark," Lord Martin said coldly.

"I believe we are at an impasse, are we not?" Neffenmark asked, ignoring any pleasantries. "The kingdom is up in arms at the thought of the princess taking the crown on her own."

"Getting right to the point, huh, Neffenmark?" Lord Martin growled. "The princess taking the crown is the only option."

Neffenmark smiled and said, "It seems that you have grown a sharp tongue and some courage, Lord Martin."

"From the fear of you wearing the crown," Lord Martin replied. "You are not fit to rule. You are an embarrassment to good men everywhere."

"You know," Neffenmark warned with a sharp look. "I have plenty of friends around. Killing you would be an easy chore. I would suggest that you keep your bitter tongue to yourself from now on."

"Are you threatening me?" Lord Martin asked.

"Why, yes, yes I am," Neffenmark replied. "But I did not come here to trade barbs with you. There will be plenty of time to deal with the likes of you in the coming months. I have come to offer the solution."

"As long as it doesn't involve you wearing the crown," Lord Martin said.

"Your attempt at circumventing the laws of our kingdom by putting a girl on the throne is an insult to every king who ever placed a crown upon his head," Neffenmark said.

"There is no law preventing Princess Elissa from taking the crown," Arpwin interrupted.

Neffenmark turned to Arpwin and glared at him for a long moment as if he were taking in his presence for the first time. "And who are you? The king's handmaiden? The one who wipes his behind when he is too old to do it himself?"

The insult angered Arpwin into silence. He knew his place, and it was not in arguing with the potential ruler of the kingdom. He held his anger in check, accepting the fact that he was beneath both the lords. That was one reason why he had loved the king so much. The king always spoke to him as an equal. He knew his place, but when they were alone, it didn't matter.

Neffenmark turned back to Lord Martin and said, "The law may not be written anywhere, but it is what the people think it is. And what the lords of the realm believe it is. I do not care about laws, but I do care about this kingdom."

Lord Martin laughed. "Other than yourself, there is nothing about this kingdom that you care about. You care about yourself and power. That is it. And it is the law of the land that has kept this kingdom together while the empire stretches its boundaries each year. We are safe from them because of our strength and part of that strength comes from adherence to the laws of the kingdom, not in ignoring them for your own personal gain."

Neffenmark chuckled. "That hurts me. Deeply. I care very much about this kingdom! And because I care so much about this kingdom, I offer a plan that will prevent civil war. And I do believe my answer will fit into your so called law." He took a moment to make sure that he had everyone's full attention. "I shall offer myself as the husband of the princess. This will allow us to follow your law. The princess will be queen. I shall be king only and until our firstborn male is of age. And then I will cede my power to him. And the line shall continue."

"And so for the next fifteen, twenty years, you are the ruler of our realm," Lord Martin. "Thinking about that just makes me ill."

Neffenmark's smile grew. "Your words continue to hurt me so deeply. I see no other way."

From behind them all, a new voice shouted, "And how about if I just kill you where you stand!"

They all turned to see Marik, sword in hand, standing in the doorway. Dried blood still stained his face and clothes. His eyes glistened with anger. "This traitor has been plotting for this moment for years! He will not cede his kingship. He craves power too much. His only goal was to gain the throne. And once he has it, he will never let it go."

"I hope you have some solid evidence for your accusations, or you may just find yourself headless," Neffenmark said with a deep growl.

Marik did not move, but he kept his sword up and ready. Neffenmark spread his hands wide and waddled to the window. He pushed open the shutter to let in the cool morning air. The strong scent of the ocean filled the room. The crashing of waves hit their ears.

"Look beyond the cliffs and to the horizon," Neffenmark said. He stepped aside so that Lord Martin and Arpwin could see. Marik did not move, for he had already seen them. Lord Martin walked slowly to the window, his mouth open in disbelief. Sure enough, on the far horizon, he could clearly see the sails of vessels heading their way.

"Now more than ever we need someone who can lead us," Marik said. "We cannot stand against the might of Taran without the kingdom being together."

Neffenmark smiled and said, "I couldn't have said it better myself, Sir Marik."

"I was not talking about you," Marik growled.

"As you can see, coming across the ocean are vessels from Taran. They will make landfall later today. There also a contingent of centurions coming down from the north. They will arrive in the morning, I fear."

Marik took a threatening step forward, but he did not advance. "Our eyes were to Thell while Taran slipped around our flank."

"You knew about this?" Lord Martin asked Neffenmark.

"They have come for peace," Neffenmark replied without directly answering the question. "But with me. And only with me. If I do not hold the crown, then there will be war. The reach of the empire will touch us and swat us off the world." He turned to Marik and said, "So, Sir Marik. I shall ask you, which would you rather have? Me upon the throne, or shall you strike me down, and we will have a war like you have never seen before?"

Marik turned his eyes from Neffenmark and looked at the princess, still huddled on the bed, her eyes wide with fear. He could not imagine what it must be like for her, to have her entire world come crashing around her. He had trained for this. He was a warrior. He knew that his sole purpose in life was to die for his kingdom. To serve it for as long and as well as he could, but ultimately, he knew he had to be willing to give his life so that future generations of Karmon's could survive in peace. But for Princess Elissa, all she knew was living a comfortable life in the castle. And now she was thrust in the middle of a war not only between nations but between men. He had no qualms with rushing forward and driving his sword into the fat man's chest. Even if he were killed in the process, it would be worth it because he would rid the kingdom of its worst evil. But a pact had been made with the devil and he could not risk the kingdom for his own personal hatred.

He lowered his sword and bowed his head in defeat.

Chapter Twenty-Six

Conner walked Lilly along the cliff's edge. To his right, the waters of the Gulf of Taran pounded rocks, the spray of the water rising nearly halfway up the sheer cliff. The smell of the salt water was strong, almost pungent. He had forgotten the smell, even though it had not been too many days since he was gone. He had lost count. Maybe it was ten. Maybe twenty. They all blended into one another. Amongst the days were battles. Battles and much blood. Too much of it spilled by friends. His body was sore from riding. His mind was sore from thinking and contemplating on all that had happened. He wanted to get back quickly, but he was not ready for it, yet. He missed Elissa, but his heart was heavy from the loss of the king, and he could not bear the thought of seeing her in pain.

The mountains were far behind him. On a clear day, their outline could be discerned against a deep blue sky. But gray clouds covered the entire sky, threatening a rain that he knew would only make the end of his journey that much more miserable. Ahead of him, he knew the city of South Karmon was near. But the terrain between here and there was hilly enough and filled with enough trees that it was still hidden. He trudged on, following the path. It was a two-track path that wagon trains of merchants followed when trading with the far cities of the empire. It was well worn from the dozen or so treks that the merchants made each year. Lilly walked behind him, her head low. She was as worn out as he was and would be glad to be back in her stall where the princess could spoil her once again.

The tall spires of the towers of the castle were suddenly in view. The path bent around a large outcropping of trees and the open plain that city sat upon opened up in front of him. The castle was in clear view of the city laid out around it. Between him and the great walls of the city were scattered thatch-roofed houses of the farms that tended the fields. The two-track took a nearly direct route straight for the main gate, which was just out of view. He stopped, and Lilly stopped, too. She let out a little whinny as if she knew home was nearby. Taking the opportunity, the horse started pulling on grass that grew next to the path.

His eyes scanned the city, looking for signs of war or battle. There were none. He was afraid that Lord Neffenmark would lead an army to take over the city. It was a silly thought, he knew, for even though the knights were beaten pretty badly, there were still many of them and would prove to be a formidable force. His eyes caught movement in the water, and that was when he noticed the tall sailing ships that were anchored in safe water, just off the coast, away from the rocks and crashing waves. There were too many to easily count. He squinted his eyes to try and see more clearly, but the ships were too far away to make out if they were occupied or not. The looked big enough to carry troops. His heart began pounding in fear.

He mounted Lilly and tired or not, she would have to carry him quickly to the city. He had never seen Taran warships before, but he had heard them described enough to know what they were. Without any signs of fatigue, Lilly brought him quickly to the city gates.

The main city gates were open, but there were clear signs that something was wrong. The Royal Guard, who manned the gates were too preoccupied to care who came and went through the gate. Even the people of the city seemed subdued. They walked about doing their business, but it seemed at a sluggish pace. In the center of the market, which should be the loudest and busiest part of the city, was nearly empty. No one looked at one another, but occasionally he caught someone looking at him. But as soon as he tried to make eye contact, they would look away and walk away as quickly as possible.

Conner kept moving through the city, not stopping, but eyes wide open looking for something to happen.

The portcullis that led into the castle courtyard was down. Two Royal Guard, dressed in their ceremonial dark blue surcoats stood guard. They each held long pikes and stood at attention.

Conner dismounted and approached. Their eyes looked past him.

"Hello?" Conner asked.

One of them glanced at him, but otherwise did not move.

"I need to speak with Lord Martin and Princess Elissa," Conner said.

The guardsmen on Conner's left snapped to attention and said, "The gates are closed until the wedding ceremonies have been concluded."

"Wedding? What wedding?" Conner asked.

"Princess Elissa and Lord Neffenmark are getting married," the guardsman said.

Conner was speechless. He tried to speak, but his mind was so confused and shocked that words would not come out. The guardsman who spoke returned to his stance. Conner took a deep breath and stepped back into Lilly, who bucked her head at him. He could not believe what was happening. There was no possibility that the princess would marry anyone like Neffenmark. He knew there was no chance that this was done voluntarily. She had to be doing this under duress. And he was her champion. Her protector. His anger was at himself more than anything. He had left her alone, and now she was in trouble. It was time for him to save her.

"Do you not recognize me?" Conner suddenly blurted out. "I am the princess' champion. Conner. You will let me pass."

The guardsmen glanced at one another. The one who had spoken earlier snapped to attention and said, "There is a large iron gate between you and us. It will not be lifted until the morning after the marriage has been consummated."

The thought of them consummating their marriage left a sickly feeling in his mouth. He looked around, wondering how he could climb the wall.

"The entire contingent of guardsmen are upon the wall," the guardsman said. "I would not recommend trying to climb the walls. You will not get far."

Conner stepped away, his mind spinning for any way to get into the castle. He looked up and indeed, every fifteen or twenty feet, a Royal Guard in their ceremonial surcoat stood at attention. Several of them were looking down at him, fingering their longbows. He took Lilly and started following the wall through the city. He knew of one possibility that might get him into the castle.

The northern wall of the castle went all the way to the edge of the cliff, but the city stopped about a few hundred feet before the cliff wall. Mostly used for ceremonies or fairs, the land was barren and unkempt. He walked all the way to the edge of the cliff. A small stone wall, about waist high, had been built from the castle wall all the way to the northern city wall. It wouldn't do much to hold someone from falling over the cliff, but it did mark where the cliff was.

He glanced up at the top of the castle wall to see if any of the guardsmen were watching him. Maybe they were, but he couldn't tell. He would have to hope that they did not know about the cave entrance. After checking the guardsman, he peeked over the cliff, searching for where the cave entrance was. It was hard to see, nearly impossible unless you knew exactly where it was. It took a few moments, but he finally spotted where it was. The entrance was not visible, but he recognized the rock formation that indicated where it was.

He climbed up onto the small wall as he heard shouts from the top of the castle wall. He took in a deep breath and jumped as far out as he could. As he fell, he could see arrows flying above his head. He closed his eyes and tensed up just as he was about the hit the water. His only thought was of hitting a rock and dying instantly or even breaking his neck, but somehow surviving. Then he would die a painful and slow death from drowning.

The force of the water striking him was sudden and shocking. It hurt a lot more than he thought it would. Holding his breath, he tried not to panic as he sank towards the bottom of the gulf. All he could think about was that he was still alive. But now, he needed air, and he had to get up to the surface soon. Just as he was about to panic because he wasn't sure what to do, his feet hit the rocky bottom. Pushing off as hard as he could, he turned himself into an arrow by clasping his hands above his head. He flailed his legs, trying to propel him faster and just as he was about to give in and breath the water, his head broke through the surface. He took a deep breath and then a wave crashed over his head, knocking him back under. He kicked and paddled, trying to get his head back above the waves. The moment he did, he sucked in as much air as he could before he was knocked back under. Kicking his legs as hard as he could, he found that he could keep himself afloat just enough to keep from sinking.

Then an arrow struck the water near him. Conner looked up to see a guardsman knocking another arrow and aiming it right at him. Doing his best to swim, he kicked and paddled to the rocky shore as arrows began raining down on him. As soon as his feet touched the bottom, he started running through the water as fast as he could. Breathing heavily from the exertion of swimming, he jumped out of the last few feet of water and sprinted for the small cave opening. A few more arrows rattled on the rocks behind him, but he was safe. And alive. He actually smiled as his chest heaved, trying to take in as much air as he could.

He splashed through a small pool of water at the cave entrance and up a small embankment to the flat area where he had spent so much time training. He paused for a moment as he took in the memory of his time with Master Goshin. He missed the old man and hoped that he was finding what he was looking for. After a sentimental moment, he remembered what he was doing and why he was doing it. He raced through the cave and up to the lower level of the castle. He had spent so much time in these levels that he didn't need to even think about getting lost. The only problem was that he had no idea where he was going.

The most likely place was the princess' apartment. The royal chambers were set in a wing separate from the rest of the castle's rooms. It was also only reached through a single hallway. One that could be easily defended in case of attack. Or easily blocked to keep a crazed and wet man away. He didn't care. He will fight his way into her room if need be. He adjusted his path to head directly for the hall that led to her room.

The castle was busy with activity. There was much to do and very few servants around to do it. Many of them had taken up arms with the king, and quite a few had not returned. This meant that everyone was too busy to take note of Conner running through the castle halls. His face was known to everyone, so his appearance was not unusual. No one would dare raise the alarm with the princess' champion in the castle. It was only when he turned into the hall that led to the royal chambers that he came upon his first problem.

There were four of them. They weren't in chainmail and weren't wearing the deep blue surcoats of the Royal Guard. They were wearing the plain white tunics that knights wore. As soon as he stepped into the hallway, he came to a sliding stop and all four drew their swords at once. Conner followed suit and reached for his swords. But they weren't there. They were still strapped to Lilly. He crouched into a defensive stance, hands up and ready. Maybe he wouldn't need the swords if he were fast enough.

The largest of them stepped forward with a wide grin on his face. "Hello, Conner," Hollin said. The other three knights, all recently promoted to knighthood fell in behind their leader. Swords raised and ready.

"Hollin," Conner said. "I need to see the princess."

"That is a problem because I am between you and her. And there are four of us in the small hallway. And we have swords."

"He was in the valley," one of the knight's behind Hollin said.

"Sure he was," Hollin growled. "I was there, in front, about ready to march into Thell when we were attacked from behind."

The knight who had spoken lowered his sword. "And I was in the middle. With the king. I was there when Conner came. He saved our lives."

"Sir Jardonne!" Hollin called out. "You will raise your sword and defend your princess."

"I am here to save her," Conner said.

"There is nothing to save," Hollin countered. "She has committed herself to preserving the kingdom. This wedding will do that."

"And you believe that?"

"I am a Knight of Karmon," Hollin cried out. "My duty is to the kingdom first and foremost. This wedding will preserve the kingdom for years to come."

"Neffenmark is a liar and a traitor. His only goal in life is to gain power at the expense of anyone and everyone else. He does not care about the kingdom or the princess."

A door opened behind the four knights. All eyes turned on the man who walked through.

"Sir Marik!" Conner shouted out.

Face grim and dark, he commanded his knights with a sharp voice, "Sir Hollin. Let Conner pass. And sheath your swords. All of you!"

The four knights sheathed their swords at once.

"Conner," Marik said with a softer tone. "You will come with me."

Hollin let out a low growl and stepped aside to allow Conner to pass.

Warily passing the four knights, Conner followed Marik through the doors at the end of the hallway. Marik closed the doors behind them.

They were in an antechamber that had two sets of doors leading out of the room. Conner knew that one of the doors led to the princess' chamber up a flight of stairs. The other door led to the royal apartments reserved for the king and queen. The antechamber was warm and friendly with bright tapestries hanging from the walls and a shaggy rug covering the center of the room. But Marik's demeanor brought the brightness of the room down.

"You should not have come," Marik said.

"The Princess needs me," Conner said.

"She is to be married. Once married, there will be no use for a champion. The reason that you were around was to serve as her protector when she needed. To stand in for her when attacked. But with a husband, you won't be needed."

The realization stunned Conner. "What will I do?"

Marik put a hand on his shoulder, and the friendly smile came back. "I can get you assigned to the Royal Guard. Or you can return to your home."

Conner shook his head. "I don't want to go back home." He looked at the closed doors that lead to her chamber. "There is nothing for me there. Only here."

"Conner," Marik said with a sigh. "I know how you feel about her, but you need to understand that she must move on. The kingdom needs this. Without it, the alliance with Taran will fall apart."

"Alliance?"

"It seems that among the things that Neffenmark did, he brokered an alliance with Taran. And it is only in place if Neffenmark has the crown."

"What are we going to do?" Conner asked.

"We are going to do nothing," Marik said. "There isn't anything we can do. Until Sir Brace can return to bring the knights together…" Conner's eyes dropped, and Marik picked up the meaning and simply nodded his head. "He won't be coming back."

"No."

"Okay," Marik said. "But we will figure something out. But not today. Not tomorrow. Soon. We need to gather our strength before we can figure out how to get Neffenmark off the throne."

"Can I see her?" Conner asked.

Marik looked at the doors and let a long sigh out. "If anyone finds out, it could be my head. You were supposed to be detained on sight. If Neffenmark gets word…I could be in serious trouble."

Conner smiled. "I'll be quiet."

Marik nodded to the doors. "Her chamber. Her attendants are there. They won't tell anyone. Just be quick about it."

Conner sprinted through the doors and took the stairs three at a time. It was farther up than he thought imaginable. By the time he reached the top landing, he was out of breath. Without thinking, he burst into the room.

Everyone stopped what they were doing and looked at him in shock and fear. Princess Elissa, surrounded by a number of attendants, was in the process of having her dress fastened. Her face, framed by her golden hair was all he could see. To him, there was nothing else in the room. Her eyes, frozen open, went from surprise to fear, to joy, to tears. The attendants, used to surprises happening around the royal family, quickly went back to work trying to finish getting the princess' dress on. Instead, she shooed them away. She stepped forward in her dress, only partially fastened.

Conner was speechless. In all the time that he had running up the stairs, he did not think about this moment. He did not think about what he might say. He was only focused on seeing the princess. And now that he was here, he did not know what to do.

The princess took another step forward, tears forming in the corner of her eyes. "Conner. You are alive. I feared…" Her voice cracked, and she could say no more.

"I don't know what to say," Conner said.

She took a deep breath and said, "You do not need to say anything. I am to be queen. The kingdom will be safe." She said the words as if she were trying to convince herself of their truth.

"I am sorry," Conner said, trying to stifle his emotions.

"For what?" she asked.

"I could not save your father," He answered. "I am sorry."

The tears began to flow, but her voice did not waver this time. "I know. I heard. Sir Marik told me all about it. You are my hero, Conner. I don't know how to thank you. But it is me that is sorry. I am sorry because I cannot be there for you. You have always been there for me, but I cannot be there for you. I have a duty to this kingdom. To my people. I have to make sure they not only survive this but thrive. My father started a legacy of peace and prosperity. I have to continue to do that. And it can't be done if Lord Neffenmark is alone in charge. Or if the Tarans invade us. I have to be ready to do anything for this kingdom, and this … this wedding is it."

Conner shook his head. "I cannot let this happen. Neffenmark is evil. He is a traitor."

"I know," Elissa said, her eyes dropping to the floor. "Sir Marik has told me everything. About Sir Brace. About my father. About you."

"I will kill him," Conner said, anger starting to boil inside of him.

"No!" she replied sharply. "You cannot! We must play this out. We must keep peace with Taran. Whatever arrangement he has, it will be bad for us if he is killed. They will attack us. Not just attack us, invade us. We will no longer be Karmon. We will just be a part of Taran."

She moved closer until they were inches apart. She rested a hand on his chest and looked directly into his eyes. She took his right hand and set it right over her heart. Her skin was incredibly soft and warm. Tingling rocketed through his entire body. "I want you to understand very clearly what I have to say." She took a deep breath. "I love you. I love you with everything that I have. You and you alone have my heart. I will never, ever give it to anyone else. No matter what happens. No matter what you see, what you hear."

Conner dropped his chin and closed his eyes, pressing the tears away.

She grabbed his chin and pushed it up and looked into his eyes. "Hear me. No matter what I say. No matter the words that come out of my mouth, you and you alone have my heart. I need you to understand that. Forever and always, my heart is yours. No one else's." And then the tears flowed, and the sobs started.

He pulled her close and wrapped his arms around her, letting her cry and sob as long as she wanted.

Chapter Twenty-Seven

Goshin rubbed his eyes. It took all his concentration and a tremendous amount of effort to read the language of his ancestors. Not only were the words different, but the letters were different as well. He had to translate each word individually, and then reread each phrase and sentence to understand its meaning. Many times he only guessed at the translation, so the meaning that he derived did not make sense. That would then force him to spend as much as another whole day to retranslate the text. It was a frustratingly slow process, but one that held so much importance, he did not care how long it took.

There was a knock on the door just before it swung open. He had expected the scholar Rardus, but instead, it was a younger man.

"Are you Goshin?" the man asked softly, but with a shaky voice.

"Yes," Goshin replied. The hairs on the back of his neck stood up. The sense of danger that had always kept him alive was screaming at him. He looked around at the scrolls and ancient papers scattered about on the table in front of him. He wished he could cover it all up, to hide what he was researching, but there would be no time.

The man pulled his head back from the doorway, and a moment later, someone else stood there. He was a tall man in a black cloak pulled tightly around his body.

"Yes?" Goshin asked after waiting for the man to say something.

The man's eyes narrowed. "Is that how you address one such as me?"

"I do not know who you are," Goshin said. His eyes now glanced around the room for something to use as a weapon.

"Of course," the man said with a chuckle. "You are a foreigner. How would you know that I am the second most powerful man in the world?"

"You are the son of God?" Goshin asked. Prince Tarcious' lips turned into a sneer. "You mock me when you should be bowing to your knees?"

"I am Hurai. I do not mock. I speak only truth."

"The truth may get you killed."

"Then it shall. I am not afraid of death."

"You may not be afraid of death, but you should be afraid of how you die."

"I fear only my God," Goshin said. "Not you, Prince Tarcious."

"Then you know who I am."

"Yes, I do now."

"And yet, you do not bow. I could have you flogged. Or even executed."

"Like I said, I am unafraid of death."

"Of course not," Prince Tarcious said. "Why would anyone such as you fear death? For what comes after death is so much better than what you have here on earth. I just wonder why you don't take your own life to experience the afterlife."

Goshin raised an eyebrow. "My God has provided a plan for me. When the plan has reached its course, then I shall see him in heaven. Until then, it is for me to live my life in a way that serves him."

Prince Tarcious stepped into the room and closed the door. "Of course. I would not expect any different answer."

"Why are you here?" Goshin asked sharply.

Prince Tarcious replied, "You are direct. No fear. Direct. I like that in a man."

"I am old," Goshin said. "I do not have time to wait for chit-chat."

"You are busy here. Researching, I presume. Manuscripts and documents from the past, I see. They are old and frail. From a time long since passed." Prince Tarcious walked forward to look more closely at the documents scattered about the table. "I had no idea our library contained such blasphemous works."

"They are historical," Goshin retorted. "You cannot hide from history."

"Yes I can," Prince Tarcious said. "The documents that you are researching are from an age that no longer exists. The documents should no longer exist. If I had known, they would have been destroyed a long time ago."

"They hold something that you are afraid of?" Goshin asked.

Prince Tarcious slammed his fists on the table and leaned towards Goshin. His eyes grew wide, and the pupils appeared to flash a bright orange. "It is you who will be afraid before this conversation is done."

"As I said, I am not afraid of you," Goshin said. "You are here to find out what I am doing and to stop me. You can stop me. That is fine. But what you cannot stop is what God has planned. And that is why you are here because you do not know what God has planned. And you expect me to tell you."

"Of course," Prince Tarcious said.

"And I will," Goshin said. "My research is not fully complete, but I have a pretty good understanding of what the plans of God are. He had placed clues throughout the ages. Prophets who carried his message kept those clues alive. Just the fact that you did not know about this room, about these documents, proves that God is certainly more powerful than your little empire. He hid all this from you. He left it for me to find."

"It will do you no good, however," Prince Tarcious said. "What you learned, what you have read. These documents will not last the day. They will be burned out of existence. And so will you. You will not survive the day. How does that sound?"

"I have served my God faithfully," Goshin said. "I will happily return to his kingdom and serve him in the afterlife."

Prince Tarcious looked over the old man carefully. After a few silent moments, he said, "So you come here, learn what you learn, and you do not care that it was all in vain? That no one will ever hear of what you have learned."

"If it is God's will," Goshin. "Or do you not believe in God?"

The smile crept back onto Prince Tarcious face. "Of course I believe in God. How could I not? Oh, does that surprise you? That I believe in God? In your God and not the gods of my people? The gods of my people are stories to tell little boys and girls to frighten them into behaving. It keeps them believing in something, gives them a false hope that I can easily pull away from them when it no longer suits me. Even my brother, great Emperor Hargon believes in all those gods. But like you, I know the truth."

"Your truth and my truth do not seem to be the same."

Prince Tarcious pointed a finger at Goshin. "They are. Well, they are almost the same."

"You believe in God, but you do not serve Him. You serve the Deceiver."

Laughter burst from the prince. "Deceiver! That is what I could call your God, for he deceives you into thinking that he is the ultimate being, the creator of all the universe, the savior of humanity. I serve the Adversary. The one who opposes your God. Your God, who treats his people as slaves and commands that you do his bidding. The Adversary demands fealty, as a king or emperor demands it of his people, but the Adversary does not command his people to be slaves."

"I willingly serve my God," Goshin said. "He does not ask me to be his slave. The Deceiver has tricked you into following him. The only truth is from God. And only he can save your soul."

"And that is where you are so wrong, and that is why I am here. For the Adversary has put it upon me to bring his message to the people of earth. He will come here to serve as lord and master to the people of earth, and I will be there to administer his justice."

"He will only bring death and destruction," Goshin said. He looked at the documents on the table and on the dusty shelves. With a wave of his hand, he continued, "As it is written throughout history and in the documents here, the Deceiver has only one desire, and that is the death of anything good and just. He wishes to conquer and destroy. Despite what you say, it is the Deceiver who desires slaves. He will not have any followers, for no one would ever follow him. Humanity will reject him and defeat him. It would only be through the destruction of Earth and the enslavement of humanity that he will reign. But that will not happen. As the prophecies clearly state, he will oppose two forces that will join to defeat him. The sign has already been given, and it is only time before the prophecy is carried out."

"The star in the sky is the sign."

"Of course it is," Goshin said. "You did not know?"

"Just confirming."

"Your Deceiver did not reveal this to you?" Goshin asked dryly.

"The Adversary," Prince Tarcious said sharply. "Only reveals that which he wishes for me to know. Just like your God. He does not tell you everything, does he? Or why would you be spending day upon day here in the library reading texts that are thousands of years old? And like your God, who uses different people for different things, has used you to reveal to me their plans."

"I have told you nothing, other than to confirm that the star in the sky, the one that never moves, and burns brightly through the night, is a sign from God."

"You have told me about the two forces that will attempt to oppose the Adversary," Prince Tarcious said. "Now you will tell me details about them."

"I know no details," Goshin replied. "Only that there will be two forces."

"Then you will die a horrible death," Prince Tarcious said.

"Like I said before, I am prepared for death."

"You are not prepared for the death that I will give you. It will not be quick or painless. It will last for days. Maybe weeks. You will be begging me to end it quickly. And I will only do so when you have provided me the information I desire."

Prince Tarcious backed away from the table and opened the door to the small chamber. "Centurions. Come. Escort this old man to the dungeons."

Goshin stood, allowing himself to be shackled with heavy irons. He closed his eyes and reminded himself that God indeed had a plan for him and that he would have to trust Him. With a slight tug, the centurions escorted him from the room. As he passed by Prince Tarcious, Goshin picked up the slight scent of burnt skin. The prince flashed Goshin a quick smile before his hands lit up in a ball of fire. With a thrust of his hands, the prince cast the fireballs into the small room where all the paper lit up instantly. The fireball exploded out of the room, sucking air from the corridor. Prince Tarcious was in the center of the ball of fire, but he was not singed or felt any heat.

Prince Tarcious locked eyes with Goshin and said, "The Adversary protects me. Will your God protect you?"

Chapter Twenty-Eight

Conner looked down at the waves that crashed upon the rocks far below. Over and over, the water broke upon the large boulders in a rhythmic dance of sheer force. Eventually, in thousands of years, those large boulders would be worn down to nothing. But he would not be witness to it. He would be long gone. The world would be changed, too. He wondered if the castle walls would still be standing. Would the empire finally notice the little kingdom to the east and bring its full might and power upon them? Would there just be a pile of rubble leftover where the walls were? Would the houses last? Would the people?

He looked out into the gulf to see the sailing ships of the empire still moored out in full sight of the castle. It was an impractical place for them to anchor as there was no place nearby to land even their small tenders. The Tyre River dumped into the Gulf of Taran more than a mile to the south. That was the closest place to land. Keeping the naval vessels in full sight of the castle was all for show. It might have been for Lord Martin and the other lords who held some sway over Elissa, or for Lord Neffenmark to remind him how he attained his throne. Maybe it was for the people of Karmon to see that the Empire still existed and could be a threat.

Conner wondered how long it would take to swim to one of them. He knew he could jump from the cliff and survive, but would he still have the energy to swim that far? And would they even take him aboard? He glanced to the north at the distant peaks of the White Mountains. He would likely have to take the long way if he ever wanted to see Taran.

The sound of trumpets startled him. There were five long blasts from twenty trumpeters that lined the topmost battlements. He turned back towards the castle and noticed Marik walking towards him. The knight was walking slowly, his shoulders hunched.

Conner turned back to the crashing waves of the gulf.

A moment later, Marik slid in next to him and said with a heavy sigh, "The trumpeting declared the sharing of vows. It is done."

"I still do not believe it," Conner said. "I don't know how this could have happened, and so quickly."

"It is not over, either," Marik said. "Neffenmark..." He shook his head and smiled at Conner. "I don't think I can stomach calling him King. Neffenmark is just getting started. He has always been power hungry, and I fear for this kingdom. He will tear it apart. The lords from Tyre are already talking amongst themselves. If it were not for fear of the Tarans, I do not think Tyre would stand for Neffenmark being king. But they fear the empire more. So they will talk among themselves and gripe and grumble, but they will not do anything."

"What about the knights?" Conner asked.

"Those of us that are left will have to swear our fealty to him. We have no choice."

"Do you really not have a choice?"

Marik opened his mouth to reply, but new thoughts were in his head. After a moment of reflection, he said, "What you ask is treason. Punishable by death. We are Knights of Karmon, and we took an oath to protect the kingdom. The moment we stood up to the king, he would send every soldier at us. We would be arrested, tried, and executed before the sun rose. The kingdom is bigger than any one king. Our honor needs to outlast any man. We have to stay firm to those beliefs, even if we don't believe in the man who wears the crown. So tomorrow, in a ceremony of honor and respect, the Knights of Karmon will dress up in our polished armor and kneel before the king and swear our loyalty to him."

"I will do no such thing," Conner said.

"And I do not blame you," Marik said. "You have been relieved of your duty."

Conner looked away and shook his head. "No. I will always be her champion."

"She has a husband, now. She has no need of a champion."

"No," Conner said. "I think she needs me more now more than ever. She was forced into this marriage under the pretense of protecting the kingdom."

Marik put a firm hand on his shoulder. "Conner, you must release yourself from her. It will not go well for you. Neffenmark is evil. As pure as it comes."

"Then we must fight him!" Conner said loudly.

Marik glanced around and up to the battlements were Royal Guard were patrolling. He was sure they heard Conner, but they kept their eyes averted from them. Softly, the ranger whispered, "You cannot say such stuff. Not now. Even if you believe it, you cannot let anyone overhear you. If word got back to Neffenmark, he could have you imprisoned. You cannot do any good shackled to a dungeon wall."

"They will not take me without a fight!" Conner said.

"And you cannot do the Princess...I mean Queen Elissa, any good dead, either," Marik said with a firm, but quiet voice.

"But I have to do something. I cannot just sit around and do nothing. Watch them be married, watch him be on the throne." He turned to the White Mountains and continue. "I think it is time for me to go. Master Goshin could probably use some help with whatever it is that he is looking for. I can go find him."

"I know it would be tough for you to hear, but I think it would be good for you to be here. And I think it would be good for Queen Elissa, too. She will need as many friends around her as she can have. As difficult as it is for you, just imagine what it must be like to be her. She is the one who is really stuck in the middle of this. She is the one who lost her father, and her life turned upside down. She went from a princess with no responsibilities to the queen of the kingdom. Plus, a marriage to a man that she surely does not, and probably could never, love. She may not need a champion, but she does need good friends."

Marik waited for a reply. After a few moments, he added, "At least give it some time. Just don't abandon her right now."

Conner gave a slight nod and said. "Very well. What about you? What are you going to do?"

"The battle with Thell hurt us badly. But it was the loss of squires and young knights that hurt the worst. It will take some time for us to get our numbers back up to where we can protect the kingdom fully. And when I say some time, I mean years, not months. We could have easily absorbed some loss. But we lost about a quarter of the knights in service and almost half of the squires. And since it takes a good ten years to train a young boy up to be a knight, it could be a long time before we have the numbers again. So I, and all the other knights will be spending our days training young boys to become knights. "

"You know," Conner said. "It only took me a few months."

"Master Goshin did a fine job training you to fight with a sword," Marik said. "But he did not teach you to ride a horse, or to take care of a horse, or to fight from a horse. He did not teach you how to forge a blade or how to fight with other weapons. Or to make a weapon foraged from the forests. He did not teach you how to lead an army or other men. He did not teach you how to act in court, or to dance."

"Well, no…"

"There is more to being a knight than being able to swing a sword. That is what makes a Knight of Karmon so great, so powerful. We are not just soldiers, we are trained in many ways. If the kingdom just needs soldiers, we can do that. We can teach anyone to swing a blade or to use a pike or halberd in a couple of weeks. Knights are smart and disciplined. And that's what makes us great. We just also happen to be pretty good with a blade, and that makes us dangerous."

Marik squeezed Conner's shoulder. "And that's what makes you most dangerous of all. Because I have never seen anyone else better with the blade. Now, it is time to stop sulking and come back to the castle. We're going to have to figure out something for you to do."

***

"This will be your post," the guardsman told Conner. He pointed to the wall next to a flight of stairs that went up.

"Here?" Conner asked. He looked around at the empty corridor and then up the flight of stairs that took a turn to the right after five steps. "Where are we?"

"The back entrance to the royal apartments is up those stairs. Or at least they will be their apartments for a while," the guardsman said. "King Thorndale's chambers are being redone to meet the needs of King Neffenmark. Until the construction is done, they will be sharing the apartments up there."

"This isn't really what I expected when I offered my services," Conner said. He put a foot on the first step, but the guardsman placed a hand on his shoulder.

"No," the man said. "We are only to enter the apartments if the king and queen are in dire need of our help. Until then, we are to stand watch."

"I just wanted to see if they are okay," Conner explained.

The guardsman shook his head. "Only if they need us."

"So, we just stand here?"

"Yes."

"All night?"

"Yes."

"And we do nothing else?"

"No."

Conner let out a long sigh. "Definitely not what I meant when I said I would help in any way."

"This is the most important job in all the kingdom," the guardsman said proudly. "It is our duty to put life and limb on the line for the preservation of the king and queen. We are the last line of defense."

Conner turned away and glanced up the stairs. He had hoped that at least he would be able to see Queen Elissa. She was just up those stairs. Close, but so far away. And he would never know if she came or went. His only duty was to keep anyone from sneaking into the apartments through the back entrance. It was going to be a long and boring night.

"What's your name?" Conner asked.

The guardsman was standing at stiff attention and only moved his eyes to look at Conner. He kept his head still. "Shh," the guardsman said softly. "We are on duty."

Conner wasn't going to stand for an entire night. He put his back against the far wall and slid down until he was sitting on the cold stone floor. He looked up at the guardsman, who glanced back down at him. The idea of helping out Queen Elissa by serving as a guard to her chambers had initially been an appealing one. He had thought that he would have an opportunity to interact with her, or at the very least, to see her. It was not his intentions to be stuck down a back hall, waiting for something to happen. The castle grounds were secure. No one was going to sneak in and assault the king or the queen in their own chambers. Their only job would be to direct a lost servant away from the doors.

Several silent minutes had passed when the guardsman said, "Narimar."

Conner's mind had drifted, and the man's voice caught him by surprise. He looked up at the guardsman, who was looking down at him. "Huh?" Conner asked.

"Narimar," the guardsman repeated. "My name is Narimar."

Conner stood up. "I'm Conner."

"I know who you are," Narimar said. "Everyone knows who you are. Or who you were. You were the Princess' Champion."

"I was," Conner said softly.

"What was it like?" Narimar asked. "To train with the knights. To be with them?"

Conner looked up at the guardsman. He wasn't sure how old Narimar was. Maybe five or at most ten years older than him. He had a worn and tired look about him, as if he had lived a harsh life. There were dark circles under his eyes and his skin sagged on his thin face. But his eyes were wide and bright, full of anticipation.

"It was nothing special," Conner said. "They were just like you and me."

"No really," Narimar asked. "What were they like? To be next to such great men day after day?"

"They weren't any greater than you or me," Conner said. "They might have had noble blood in their bodies, but it did not make them special. It did not make them stronger, or faster, or braver. I fought next to them, and they died just like everyone else dies. They were just men."

"Just men!" Narimar burst out. "They were the Knights of Karmon! The greatest warriors that have ever walked the earth! Couldn't you just feel their great presence? Weren't you awed by them?"

Conner shook his head. "No. They were just men." He could not get the thought of Sir Brace Hawkden out of his mind. To hold him while he died had really touched him. There was a sadness to how he died. It was an honorable death, but only after so many bad decisions. He had been a good man, but his own ego and pride had done him in. Conner was glad that Brace had figured out in the end and made some amends for what he had done. It was a shame that his legacy will be that of a fallen knight. He just hoped that history would be kind to him.

The sound of something falling from the king and queen's chamber caused Conner to stand up. Instinctively, he placed a hand on the pommel of his sword.

"What was that?" Conner asked.

"You never know, and it's none of our business," Narimar said. Then his eyes twinkled, and he added, "It could be just a little foreplay."

"What?" Conner snapped angrily.

"You know, what comes right before they consummate their marriage."

Conner opened his mouth to spit back an angry retort, but the innocent look on Narimar's face held his tongue. There was no way that he could know about his feelings for Elissa. And they weren't really his feelings to have, anyway. He was a nothing peasant, and she was now queen. She had every right to consummate her marriage. Even though just the thought of it made his stomach turn.

Another crash from upstairs caused both of them to take a step towards the stairwell. It sounded like wood splintering.

Conner glanced at the Narimar, who said, "No. We cannot. Only if they call for us."

"Something is going on," Conner said. "We need to check it out."

The guardsman shook his head. "It is not our duty. Only if they call for us."

A muffled cry that was clearly from Elissa caused Conner to move into action. He turned and took the steps two at a time, with Narimar racing up the stairs right behind him. At the top of the stairs was a small landing. He ran to the door that led to the king and queen's chamber and gave it a firm push, but it was locked from the inside. There was another crash, followed by what sounded like the thump of a body hitting the ground, and then a scream.

"Elissa!" Conner yelled.

"Conner!" Elissa shouted back.

Narimar grabbed Conner from behind and ran them into the door. Conner bounced off the door and turned into the guardsman and drove his fist as hard as he could into Narimar's unprotected face. His nose exploded in blood and mucus, and Narimar fell back onto the stairs.

Conner took two steps back and ran hard into the door, driving his shoulder into the thick wood. He bounced off in pain, but he had felt the door give. Ignoring the throbbing in his shoulder, he ran at the door again, this time, the lock on the door gave, and he tumbled into the room. Using his momentum to his advantage, he did a forward summersault onto his back and then to his feet. Neffenmark was in front of him, a long tunic draped to his knees. His face was flush, and his chest was heaving from exertion. His eyes were wide and full of anger.

"How dare you!" Neffenmark shouted. "I am the king of this land! I will have your head for this intrusion!"

"Stand down, Conner!" Narimar called out. The guardsman had recovered his senses and stood in the doorway, his sword drawn.

Elissa was on the floor at the side of the bed, blood flowing down the side of her head. Her eyes were red, and a large bruise was visible on her cheek.

Conner felt an anger that he had never felt before. His heart pounded in his chest, and his muscles tingled with adrenaline. He drew his sword and stepped towards Neffenmark. He did not have his normal set of light swords, but it was the double-edged longsword that was given to Royal Guards. He had never fought with one before. It was much lighter than the broadswords that the knights used and a bit heavier than his own swords. But it was still a sharp blade, and without even having to think about how to use it, he knew how to use it.

Narimar rushed around him and put himself between Conner and the king. "No! Do not do this! Think about what you are doing! He is the king!"

"Move away," Conner said. He could not tear his eyes away from Elissa and the wounds on her face. The sight of her kept feeding his anger until it boiled over. With cool precisions, Conner moved towards Narimar, swinging his sword across his body. The slash was easily parried. But Conner was not looking to kill Narimar or even fight with him. As soon as their swords touched, Conner sidestepped up to the guardsman and sent an elbow across his chin. The man dropped, out cold.

"Stay back!" Neffenmark shouted. He held a long dagger in both hands. His eyes blazed with anger, his teeth pulled back into an evil snarl.

"Conner!" Elissa shouted.

But Conner did not hear either one of them. He heard nothing. He felt only anger. In two steps he was at Neffenmark and knocked aside the fat king's feeble attempt at attacking him with the dagger. Conner took advantage of the longsword's thrusting capabilities and thrust the sword directly into Neffenmark's chest, killing him instantly. Neffenmark fell to his knees and then onto his back, eyes still open, mouth agape in a silent death scream.

Conner did not see him fall. As soon as he dealt the fatal blow, he let go of the sword and rushed to Elissa's side. She was on her knees, head buried in her hands, crying. Conner dropped to her side and put his hands on her, but she pushed him away.

"What did you do!" she screamed.

"He hurt you," Conner said softly.

His words touched her, and her own anger dissipated. She reached to him and pulled him into a tight hug. She buried her head into his shoulder, letting her tears stain his tunic. He held her close. After only a moment, she pushed him away, holding him at arms-length.

"They will kill you if they catch you," Elissa said.

"I was protecting you," Conner said. "He was hurting you. He beat you bad."

She shook her head. "It does not matter! You do not understand!"

Conner pushed a few strands of hair away from the bruise on her cheek and held the side of her head in her hand. "He hurt you," Conner repeated.

"I know," Elissa said. Tears began to well up in her eyes. "It didn't hurt badly enough, though. It will only get worse, though."

"No," Conner said. "It will be better. Now that you are Queen, you can finally rule the way you should have."

"I do not want the throne! Not this way!" The tears stopped, and the anger came out. "You do not understand. Neffenmark was keeping the Tarans at bay. Now with him gone, who knows what will happen?" Elissa pulled herself away from Conner and stood up. She stumbled slightly while she tried to regain her balance. Conner tried to help her, but she pushed him away. "You must go. Now. Before they come."

"Elissa…"

"Listen to me, Conner. They will not care who you are, who you were. They will only see you as the one who killed the king. You must go. Run. Hide."

"Where…?"

Elissa pulled him to the far side of the room where a long fireplace filled the entire wall. She gave a push on a brick and a hidden door popped open.

"There," Elissa said. "This will take you through the walls and into the city. You must go, now. I can hear them coming! If they catch you, they will kill you!"

"Where will I go?" Conner asked.

There was a pounding on the main doors and shouts for the king to answer. Elissa pulled and pushed Conner into the hidden door. "The forest. Back home. Anywhere but here. If they ever find you, they will kill you. No, go!" She gave him one final push and the pounding on the doors became more incessant.

Conner crouched through the short doorway and found himself in a dark and damp corridor. He turned as Elissa gave him one last long look before she pushed the doorway shut. The darkness was complete. He could not even see his hand in front of his face. Even though he heard the shouting from inside the room, Conner tried to push on the door to open it again. He did not want to run. She was beaten, and Neffenmark deserved to die. But the door would not open. He pushed hard, even kicked at it, but it would not open.

Conner sat back, resting against the far wall, listening to the guardsmen as they rushed into the room. He heard them shouting and cursing his name. He heard the orders to find him and bring him back dead or alive. To a man, the guardsmen vowed to bring in the king's killer. He sat with his hands up and ready to swing at the first man who came through the door, but the door never opened. It seems that maybe only Elissa knew about the door.

After quite some time, after the shouting had settled down, Conner began crawling through the dark tunnel, wondering what he would find at the end.

Chapter Twenty-Nine

The tunnel ran for what seemed an eternity. Conner just kept putting one hand in front of the other, pulling his body along. His one regret was that he had left his sword buried in the chest of Neffenmark. If he did come across anyone, he would have no way to defend himself. Even if he came across a first-year squire, he wouldn't last very long. And he had no idea how his captors would handle him. Would they capture him alive, torture him, or just slay him on the spot. The people of Karmon had lost two kings in such a short amount of time. There was no telling how they would react.

Everyone had loved King Thorndale. They had loved his father and his father's father. The line of Thorndale had gone back to the first days of the kingdom. And while there might have been some who did not like a particular king, they were always respected and revered. There had never been an active revolt or resistance to the king's rule. Peace, at least inside the borders of the kingdom, had always existed. Partly because of the steady rule of the Thorndale family. Partly because of the strong military might that this tiny kingdom could muster. But now, both of those reasons no longer existed. The reign of the Thorndale's was over. The might of the Karmon Knights was at its lowest. The kingdom was reeling from too many deaths. No one cared that they had won the battle with their northern neighbor. They only cared that too many fathers, sons, and brothers failed to make it home from battle.

And now, they had to deal with the death of another king. He knew that Neffenmark was evil. He knew that Brace Hawkden was dead because of Neffenmark, and it was Neffenmark that started everything in the first place. If it weren't for Neffenmark, Elissa would still be a princess, he would still be hunting and living in the forest, and many men and boys would still be alive. But the rest of the kingdom didn't know that. Many had seen Neffenmark as a savior – a man who stepped up to fill the void of the fallen king. But he knew better. Many others knew better. Marik knew. Elissa knew.

At the thought of the princess, Conner came to a stop and bowed his head in the darkness. He would have to get back to the castle to see her. Even if it was just for a minute, he needed to see her one last time. He looked back, thinking that maybe he could return and figure out how to open the door. And then he turned forward, looking into the darkness ahead of him. It was just as dark in front of him as it was behind him. He knew that Elissa was back there. But so was every armed man in the castle. He was sure that they were turning over every loose brick looking for him. Going back would be certain capture and likely death. Going forward might not be that much better, either. But he knew he would at least have a chance to escape if he kept moving. He picked up his head and began shuffling forward.

He continued crawling for a long time. He had no real concept of how much time had passed, or how long he had been crawling. For a while, he counted each time he put his right hand forward. When he reached five hundred, his mind was too numb to keep counting. He took a long break to stretch his legs and back. He knees were tender from the constant crawling on the hard tunnel floor, and he realized that at some point, he would be unable to keep moving. Conner's worst fear was that he was in a circular maze with no exit. He would be lost forever, and no one would ever find his bones. With his mind wandering too much, Conner decided he just needed to keep putting one hand in front of the other.

Conner tried to imagine where the tunnel was leading him. At first, it had made several left turns that made him think that he was indeed in a circular maze. But eventually, the tunnel made a right turn followed by a very long straightaway. There were more turns. Lefts and rights in no pattern that he could discern. At each one, he had the thought that maybe he was at the end, so he would take some time to search for a door or a latch. All he found was the same smooth wall.

After another long straightaway, his hands touched a wall in front of him, so he searched for a door. When none was found, he turned to the left and found a wall. Then he turned to the right and started to shuffle forward, but he ran into another wall. He let out a loud grunt and rubbed his head where he had hit the smooth stone. He was at an end. Finally.

Conner turned back to the end wall, and he pushed hard on it, hoping there was a door behind the wall. But it did not move. He moved his hands along the wall, searching for anything that would open a door. He found nothing. Clearly, he missed a turn or a door that would get him out. He sat back, suddenly feeling despair. He was not yet thirsty or hungry, but soon he would need food. And water. He looked back into the darkness, feeling a knot of despair in his stomach. He would have to backtrack through the entire tunnel searching for the door that he missed.

He let out a loud shout of frustration and the sounds echoed back to him from above. His heart skipped a beat as he looked up and saw a grayness far above him. He did not directly see a light, but he could see a ceiling lit by some light source. He stood tall and stretched. The ceiling was far above him, but he was sure the tunnel continued up there. He would just have to figure out a way to scale the wall. He moved his hands along the smooth stone wall and discovered that it was missing bricks spaced just far enough apart that he should be able to climb the wall.

Inch by inch, he climbed up the wall, moving his feet slowly from one hole to the next. About ten feet from the top, he could see that the vertical tunnel ended at the ceiling, but another one continued to the right. With increasing speed, he climbed until he reached the top and pulled himself into the next tunnel.

The brightness of the light hurt his eyes, and he had to blink several times before his eyes adjusted. The final tunnel ended about fifty feet away from him. The only problem was that iron bars blocked the opening.

Conner crawled slowly, wondering what was on the other side of the opening. He heard noises, but could not quite figure out what they were. But as he neared the end of the tunnel, he realized that there were street sounds, something that he would hear from outside the castle, not inside. He carefully approached the opening and looked around cautiously. Another wall was directly across from him, and it appeared that the tunnel opened out into an alleyway. With a firm grip, Conner grasped the iron bars, hoping that they were rusty or broken and would just give way. He shook them and the ease at which they moved surprised him. They were hinged on top and unattached on the bottom. Quickly, he pushed on the bars and slid out of the tunnel.

He stood up and looked around. He was in an alley, outside of the castle walls. At first, he was confused because he had started on the second level of the interior of the castle and had ended up climbing up some distance just to get back to the ground level. Then he realized that the tunnel must have sloped slowly down, making multiple turns back upon itself. He looked back at the grate that covered the opening. It appeared that there should have been a lock to keep it closed, but there was none. A slight smile kept across his face. So this is how she came and went without her father knowing.

Loud voices and shouting startled him into movement. He had no idea who the voices were or where they were coming from, but he had to assume that they were guardsmen looking for him. Conner turned away from the sounds and started walking quickly out of the alley.

The city was abuzz with activity even though the sun about to set. People were walking and talking as if nothing disastrous had happened. There was the casual laughter and casual conversations that would happen on any given day at any given time. The lamplighters had made their rounds through the market, lighting the lamps that would allow merchants to continue selling their wares after the sun had fallen below the horizon. Conner walked among them, his eyes scanning down alleyways and cross streets for any signs of Guardsmen marching through the streets. He kept getting sideways glances that caused him to be nervous until he realized he was still wearing the Royal Guard tunic. But he had no sword, nor did he wear any chainmail. It was standard practice that whenever Royal Guard were on patrol in the city, they wore their armor and had a sword at their side.

A trumpet from far away blared three long blasts followed by three short blasts. Conner, along with everyone else stopped what they were doing and looked around. It was a signal that wasn't used very often. The trumpet signaled for all the gates to be closed, something that only happened in times of war or for other extreme reasons. Like the Royal Guard looking for the king's murderer.

Conner kept moving through the market square while everyone else stood still, looking towards the gates that were hidden behind a row of tall stone buildings. The silence in the market area was disconcerting. No one wanted to move or to break the silence. Stunned faces just looked from one person to another. Conner wanted to stop, to act like everyone else, but he knew he needed to keep moving or the Royal Guard would catch up to him. He forced himself to walk slower and hoped that he didn't stick out as much as he felt like he did.

Just as he was about to reach the edge of the market area and disappear into a dark alley, he spotted a company of Royal Guard marching together, heading down the street towards him. They were still far away, and there were many people between them and him. Conner hoped that he was not spotted, but he wasn't going to take any chances, so he ducked quickly into the first building that he found. It was a small tavern that was empty except for a single elderly man sitting at a table along a wall at the back of the main room. Conner looked around, hoping for a place to hide.

"Good evening, sir!" the old man said, standing up. He walked over, and Conner realized that he wasn't really as old as he had thought. His hair was gray, and he had a scraggly beard, which made him look old. But he didn't walk like an old man, nor did he talk like one. He wiped his hands on his thick leather apron. "Fresh out of dinner," the man said. "But the keg of ale is still good."

Conner moved farther into the tavern, away from the doors. He continued to scan the room, looking for a place to hide or a back way out.

"Ale, I guess," Conner said. He didn't care for its bitter taste, but it only made sense to try and blend in.

"Right at it," the barkeep said. He moved behind the bar, which filled the center of the room. He poured a frothy mug of ale in a tall earthen mug and set it on the bar.

Conner, eyes still watching the door, walked up to the bar and took the mug. He took a sip and forced the strong liquid down his throat.

"Strange happenings," the man said, watching Conner's eyes flash from the mug of ale to the door ever few seconds. "Gates haven't been closed in years."

"It is strange," Conner replied, hoping that no one would come through the doors. If someone did, he wasn't sure what he would do. Maybe he should go looking for a back entrance, just in case. Or maybe the guardsmen knew about it and were going to come through both the front and the back doors at the same time. He really wished he had his swords. Without them, it felt as if he weren't wearing any clothes. Then he had the sinking realization that he would never see his swords again. There was no chance that he would ever make it back to his barracks to get them. Somehow, he would have to find something. Even if it was a long dagger.

"You keep eyeing that door like you know someone is coming through," the man said.

"No," Conner replied quickly. He took another long drink from the mug.

Suddenly the door burst open, and Conner dropped his mug and jumped back from the bar. He turned, ready to greet his attackers with his fists before they could attack him.

But it was only one man who came through the door. He was not dressed as a guardsman, nor was he carrying any swords or any other visible weapons. He was dressed simply, as a commoner might.

"Paul!" the man called out excitedly, ignoring Conner and the spilled ale on the floor.

"What is it, Havid?" Paul the barkeep asked.

"The king!" the man, Havid, said. His voice dropped to an excited whisper. "They say he has been killed!"

Paul's face turned white, and his eyes got large. He glanced at Conner. The other man then noticed Conner for the first time and became stiff. Both their eyes were looking closely at Conner's garb. There was silence in the bar for several seconds while the noise from outside escalated.

Finally, Havid broke the silence. "Who are you?" he asked.

Conner looked from one to the other and didn't think that either one was a threat. But that didn't mean that they wouldn't shout an alarm if they told him who he was or what he had done.

"Are you Royal Guard?" Havid asked.

Conner shook his head.

"You wear one of their tunics. They are looking for someone."

"Who is?" Paul asked.

"All of them," Havid replied.

"All of who?" Paul asked.

"All the Royal Guard," Havid replied. "They came running out of the castle gates and are tearing through the city. Searching every dark corner. Every building."

"I don't want any trouble in here," Paul said, moving out from behind the bar.

Conner could hear the shouting from the streets getting louder. It would not be long before they would come into the tavern. He had to leave. His head swiveled, looking for the back door. He took a step towards the back of the building, but Paul stood in his way. Havid was closing in as well.

"Why are you in one of their tunics?" Paul asked. "What are you running from?"

"Did you really kill the king?" Havid asked.

Paul shot the man a harsh look.

"I would not be sad if you did," Havid added.

"Havid!" Paul shouted at the man. "You cannot say such things!"

Havid let out a low growl. "I never cared for that fat lord. He was a cheat and a scoundrel. He never should have been king. Princess Elissa would have made a fine queen without some fat lord at her side. Anyone would have been better than him."

"What you said is treachery," Paul whispered. "You cannot say such things. You are the head of the Merchant's Guild! In your position, you must respect and honor your king. Saying such things is as if you did it yourself!"

"I do not care!" Havid shouted. He stepped forward and extended a hand to Conner. "Did you do it? If you did, I would shake your hand. The world is a better place without that fat lord."

Conner gripped the hand, and Havid pulled him close and patted him on the back.

"What is your name, my young, brave, man?" Havid asked.

"Conner."

Havid, still gripping Conner's hand stepped back and looked closely.

"As in the Princess' Champion, Conner?" Paul asked.

A wide smile grew on Havid's face. "How fitting that her champion would step in and do what's right. You are now the Queen's Champion!"

Conner shook his head, feelings of guilt swarming through his body. "I killed him. I was angry at what he had done, and I just killed him. I should not have. It was murder."

"What did he do?" Paul asked.

"He beat her," Conner replied, tears filling his eyes. "He hit her. I know it was not my place to step in, but I could not bear to hear what was happening to her."

Havid guided Conner to a chair. "You must not feel guilty about what you have done. It was the right thing to do."

Conner shook his head. "I killed him. Out of anger."

"But you have killed before," Havid said.

"Yes, but not like this. That was war. This wasn't. This was murder."

"I think they are coming close," Paul said, glancing at the door.

"Conner, you must understand it was the right thing to do. You said he was beating her. You were defending her. You are her Champion. It was your duty."

Conner shook his head. "No. Once she married, I was no longer her Champion."

"Were you not her friend?" Paul interjected. "I had seen you before. Several times in the city. You walked with her to the outer streets. Places that decent folk stay away from. But she went there, and you went there with her."

"Yes," Havid said. "We have all heard stories. The servants come to the taverns to fill their bellies, and they talk. They come to the markets, and they talk. They talk about the friendship of Queen Elissa and her Champion. They do not do it to spread gossip, but they did it because it was something that surprised them. A commoner like you and the Princess – the Queen – were friends. Good friends. And you were just defending your friend."

Crashing and shouting caused them to jump to their feet.

"They are next door," Paul said frantically. "They will be here next. You must go."

"Where do I go?" Conner asked.

"With me," Havid said. "I know ways in and out of the city that are not through the main gates. As the head of the Merchant Guild, there are certain secrets that I must keep. Now move. And quickly."

***

Elissa sat against the wall behind the bed, her knees pulled tight to her chest, her head buried in her hands. The sobbing had stopped some time ago, but the tear streaks remained. Occasionally she would let a whimper escape from her lips. She ignored the activity around her. She ignored anyone who tried to talk to her or comfort her. She wanted none of it.

Someone sat down next her, but she did not move to see who it was. After some time, she finally picked up her head to see Sir Marik sitting next to her.

"Have they found him?" she asked.

"No," Marik replied. "They have looked through the night, and there is no sign of him. No one knows how he escaped or where he went."

"What will happen?"

"If they find him? If he makes it back to the castle alive, he will be executed in public."

Her head dropped back into her hands. But there were no more tears left.

"Are you okay?" Marik asked.

With her head still buried in her hands, she shook her head. Gently, Marik lifted her head so that he could look at her face. The blood had been cleaned up as soon as she was found, but there was no hiding the bruising. It covered the entire left side of her face. Her lower lip was split and swollen, and her left eye was puffy not from crying, but from a punch.

"He deserved it," Marik said softly. "No man should ever be allowed to do what he did. Conner should be commended, not condemned."

"Then you must find him first," Elissa said.

"My queen," Marik said softly. "I cannot get involved. The Royal Guards are on a rampage. Twice their king has fallen on their watch. One in battle and now under their roof. They will not want me, or any knight, getting in their way. And after the battle with Thell, I think there are more of them than us that can wield a sword."

"I do not understand," Elissa said with a soft anger, "why you cannot work together."

Marik chuckled. "That is a good question. For too long the Royal Guard and the Knights of Karmon have been at odds. We each do our own thing. I would say it is probably more of a habit than anything."

"Maybe it is time to change that," Elissa said. She wiped the tears from her eyes, carefully avoiding the bruise that covered half her face.

"You cannot change generations of men who only know one way."

A wry smile crept across Elissa's face. "Maybe it'll take a woman to change them."

Marik's eyes narrowed. "What are you talking about?"

The smile disappeared from her face. She took a deep breath and stood up. As soon as she did, several attendants flocked towards her, offering words of comfort and support. She harshly shooed them away. She stepped to the center of the room and all activity stopped.

Percy, who had been angrily arguing with Lord Martin cleared his throat and stepped forward. "Your Majesty," he said with a low bow. "Your guardsmen are scouring the city for the king's murderer. We will find him and bring him to justice."

"You will recall your men," Elissa said.

Percy's eyes went wide. "Your Majesty, the king must have justice! You cannot just let it go!"

"I can," Elissa said. "And you will."

A new voice interrupted them. "Just because he is your…was your champion does not give him a reprieve of his crime."

Everyone turned to look at the speaker, a tall man with dark hair and graying temples. He stepped forward.

"Who are you?" Elissa asked.

"Admiral Hester, Your Majesty. Commander of the fleet of Taran ships anchored just off your coast." He spoke the Karmon language flawlessly without the hint of the typical Taran accent. "I admire your devotion towards your friends, but a crime is a crime, and it cannot go unpunished. To do so would be to invite anarchy and chaos. We must have order."

"Yes!" Percy said. "We must have order and civility if we are to survive this atrocity!"

"Do you not see her face?" Marik shouted out. "Neffenmark beat her."

"King Neffenmark," Percy corrected. "You will offer our fallen liege the honor he deserves."

"He deserved what he got," Marik replied angrily.

Swords suddenly became unsheathed. Marik left his in his scabbard, but he did not retreat or back down. He glared back at Percy.

"Enough of this!" Elissa shouted. "Put away your swords! We are no longer fighting among ourselves."

"Your Majesty," Admiral Hester said. "If I may…"

"No, you may not," Elissa snapped back. "And why are you here? Someone get him out of here!"

No one moved.

Admiral Hester smiled and said, "Your Majesty. King Neffenmark had an agreement between Taran and Karmon. I am here to ensure that the treaty is carried out to the letter."

"There is no king," Elissa said firmly. "I am queen! I will sit upon the throne. It was my father's, and now it is mine."

"My Queen," Percy said softly. "You cannot. There must be a king…"

"There shall not be a king!" Elissa shouted. "I am the ruler of this land, now and for as long as I live." She looked around the room from the guardsmen who had rushed to her side as soon as her screaming began, to the man her father trusted most, Arpwin. He stood at the back of the room, as he always did, waiting to serve. He had much wisdom to offer, but he rarely let it out. Just seeing him in the room comforted her. She would spend much time talking with him in the coming days and months. Her eyes drifted across Lord Martin, who lorded over most of the farmable land outside of the city. Their eyes locked, and he showed a hint of a smile. Two other lords who had remained from Neffenmark's coronation stood nearby. Lord Arrin and Lord Kor had large tracts of land on the far eastern edge of the kingdom. They were so far away they had little to say about the politics of the kingdom, but they still held power. The only other lord of consequence, Lord Kirwal, governor of Tyre, was not in the room. She was not sure if his absence was a good or a bad thing. If he wanted to, he could band all the lords against her, and she would have to fight for her kingdom. But if he were on her side, all the lords would fall in step.

Marik pushed his way forward and drew his sword and fell to a knee. "Your Majesty," the Knight Ranger said with bowed head. "You have my sword and the sword of every knight."

Admiral Hester's smile faded away and drew into a sneer.

Percy, not to be outdone stepped forward and drew his own sword to present it to the queen. "Your Majesty. You have my sword and the sword of every Royal Guard. Your life…"

"No!" Elissa shouted, her eyes filling with tears. "There will be no more knights. No more Royal Guards. There will be only Karmons. We will stand together. As one."

Percy's face went ashen while Marik's lit up. This was who she was meant to be, Marik thought.

"Percy!" Elissa said, adrenaline still burning through her system, so her voice was filled with more anger than she really wanted. "You will disband the search for Conner. You and your men will escort every Taran out of the city."

"Queen Elissa," the Admiral said. "We have a treaty…"

"Start with this fool," Elissa said. When Percy did not move, she said sharply, "Now! Get him out of here! I never want to see another Taran centurion in this city again!"

Percy quickly escorted the Admiral out of the room. Everyone else was silent and still. Elissa looked around at those that were there. Marik still was kneeling in front of her. Lord Martin was in the back of the room, sweat dripping from his face. He was also unsure what to do. If he were to support the queen and no other lords did, he could lose his lands and possibly his life. Lord Kirwal, his cloak dusty and muddy from the road, stepped forward. He was an elderly man, around the age of Elissa's father and had always treated Elissa as one of his own. He had also been a staunch defender of the male leadership of the kingdom. He looked around the room and knew what he had to do. He approached Elissa and gently held her face in his large, thick hands.

"My sweet Elissa," he said. He was an opposing figure, the tallest in the room. His hands fully engulfed her face. "I remember the day you were born. What a sweet treasure you were. You have grown into a beautiful young woman."

Everyone in the room held their breath because they knew he was the only other person in the kingdom that could lay a stake to the throne. The people would follow him because they would have no other choice. He swept his cloak from behind him and dropped to a knee, holding her hand.

"My Queen," he said softly. "You have my support. May you govern wisely and honorably."

One by one, the other Lords of the realm came forward to offer their fealty to Queen Elissa.

Chapter Thirty

Conner followed Havid and Paul through the city streets. They walked purposefully, but not too fast. They kept to the shadows of alleys and side streets and avoided the main lamp-lit thoroughfares. The dark blue Royal Guard tunic that Conner had worn was traded for a simple woolen one that would help him blend in with everyone else. Several times they had come within sight of a group of guardsmen marching through the streets. They stopped everyone they saw and rummaged through every building they passed. But darkness was their friend, and the guardsmen were not being covert by any means.

Their closest call came when a rider suddenly appeared behind them and nearly ran them over. They ducked into an alleyway only to see a company of ten guardsmen just around the corner. The horseman pulled his horse into a swift stop and leaped off in one smooth motion. He shouted orders to the guardsman, but none of the three could hear what was being said. They could only see the strange reactions. Swords were sheathed, and the guardsman fell into formation and began marching back towards the castle. They passed right by them without looking at them or at anyone else they saw.

"What was that all about?" Conner asked.

Neither Havid nor Paul said anything. They watched the horseman mount his ride and race off in another direction. A moment later, three short trumpet blasts rang out from the direction of the castle, followed by three long blasts.

Havid and Paul shared a look.

"What is it?" Conner asked.

"The gates are opening," Havid said. "If I were to guess, I'd say they are calling off the hunt."

"That doesn't make sense," Conner said. "They haven't found me."

"Let's keep moving," Havid said. "Stay to the shadows, and we act like they are still chasing us. At least until we know what is going on."

Havid took the lead again, and they wound their way through alleyways and side streets until they reached the main city gate. The entire area around the gate was lined with large lamps, illuminating a wide area that gave those who came and went plenty of light to see. It also gave the gate guards plenty of time to see anyone trying to assault the gates. Or if they were looking for someone, plenty of light to see the faces of those who came and went.

"No extra guards," Paul said. They stood casually in a dark corner of a building well away from the light.

"We only need one to recognize him," Havid said.

A handful of people moved through the gate. Some were pulling or pushing wagons of merchandise. Others were just casually strolling through, minding their own business. Late at night maybe only one or two would be passing through in an hour's time. But with even a small handful going through the gate, it would not take the guardsmen much effort to take their time studying each and every person who walked through.

"Smuggler's Tunnel?" Paul asked.

Havid nodded. "Let's move."

"What is smuggler's tunnel?" Conner asked.

Paul patted him on the back. "I hope you like cold dark places."

Until today, he didn't mind them. Now he despised them.

Conner was led through another winding path that led them away from the gate and the walls and towards the slums of the city. There were no more street lamps to light their way. Occasionally a house had a window open that gave them some light to see by, but mostly it was through the light of the stars that they walked. Conner feared that at any time a desperate mugger or even a company of guardsmen would jump from the shadows of an alley. But no one bothered them. Every once in a while, they passed by someone walking the streets, but they were ignored. Not even a glance or a nod for a greeting. They all kept to themselves.

Suddenly, Havid gave a quick look around and then ducked into a house that was more shack than home. Paul pulled Conner through the doorway quickly.

There was an elderly couple that had been sleeping on a blanket-covered pile of straw. They jumped up as soon as the three entered.

"The robin is red," Havid said quietly.

The elderly man nodded and pulled two shovels from under the straw. His wife rolled over, pulling the blanket over her head while Havid and the old man began shoveling the dirt in the middle of their house. It didn't take them long to dig through six inches of soft packed dirt. But even after the trap door was exposed, they kept digging until the entire door was visible.

The old man then pulled out a small iron stick with a notch at the end and tucked it into a particular spot on the door. The iron stick caught, and the door came up.

Havid dropped a few coins into the old man's palm and then turned to Conner. "Down you go," Havid said softly.

Conner looked down into the darkness and hesitated. The old man handed a lamp to Havid, who handed it to Conner. "We'll light it once we are in the tunnel. If we light it too soon, the light will be seen from all around us."

Paul stepped forward and extended his hand. "This is where I leave. Take care Conner. I am not a person who likes to see people get killed, but as Havid can attest, Neffenmark is well known to the Merchant's Guild. He is no friend of ours. His trade practices are criminal, and he uses thugs to get his way. We will not be sorry to see him out of our hair. He might have been king in name, but he was no king of ours. As far as we are concerned, you did us all a favor."

Conner nodded, but he could not say anything. Although the words helped his conscience, he still felt horribly guilty about the way he had killed Neffenmark. He just hoped that someday he would be able to stop feeling guilty about it.

Without another word, Conner stepped through the doorway onto the ladder that led into the darkness. As soon as his feet touched the ground, Havid followed. A moment later, the door was closed. Paul and the old man began shoveling dirt onto the trap door. With a quick flick of his wrist, Havid struck a flint to stone, and a spark started the small oil lamp. The light of the lamp extended a dozen feet down the tunnel.

Conner looked up and around. Unlike the smooth stone of the tunnel within the castle walls, the smuggler's tunnel was rough. But at least he could stand. The tunnel sloped downward at a steep angle, but always the tunnel was tall enough that he could walk upright.

"Let's move on," Havid said. "The tunnel was dug out many hundreds of years ago. Grank Thorndale was king then."

"Don't you ever worry about it collapsing?" Conner asked.

Havid slapped a thick cross timber just above his head. It was supported vertically by two thick timbers along the tunnel's side walls. "Every ten feet. These keep the tunnel from collapsing."

Conner paused to touch it. The timbers were hard and solid, despite being underground for hundreds of years.

"Thellian miners helped construct this."

"Thellian?"

Havid smiled. "King Grank Thorndale had stopped all trade with our northern neighbors during another of our kingdoms' little spats. However, there were a few special Thellian items that some of our nobles could not do without. One of them was Queen Pollip, who could not go without Harmmis on her eggs."

"Harmmis the spice?" Conner asked.

"Eventually we figured out how to grow it down here where it is warmer, but back then, you could only get Harmmis from Thell. And boy did the Queen get mad when she was told she could not get it on her eggs. It made her nuts, too. She eventually went so crazy that she leaped into the oceans and cracked her skull on the rocks below. Or at least that's the way the story goes."

"So the tunnel was built so the queen could get her illegal spice?"

Havid chuckled. "Yes. But it has come in handy quite a few times over the years. And as far as I know, no guardsmen or knight has ever discovered it. Only a handful of us in the guild know about it. Mostly, it really isn't necessary anymore, either. Trade is free flowing, and as long as the king's tax is paid, no one cares where it comes from, or where it is going. I don't think I've had a need to use it five years."

They stopped at a stone wall. The stones had been chiseled out to make a hole to pass through.

"Is this the wall?" Conner asked.

Havid touched the stone as they passed through. "Little known fact that the walls were not only built up but also down. The ground was soft enough that they could not just build right on top of it. They had to dig down. About forty feet, here."

Conner let out a soft whistle.

"And thanks again to the Thellians," Havid added. "Yes, the Thellians helped us build the walls. Master miners and stonemasons they are. We owe a lot to them. It's a shame that they are our enemy."

"They shouldn't be," Conner said.

"Agreed! If we could have open trade with them, I'd be wealthy beyond compare!"

"King Thorndale tried to, you know."

Havid stopped and gave Conner a look. "The same King Thorndale that led our knights and soldiers into an ambush?"

"It's a long story," Conner said. "And we won that battle, you know!"

"Not without much cost, my young boy," Havid said. He continued walking. "Maybe Queen Elissa can figure it out."

"Figure what out?"

"How to have peace with Thell. It really can't be that hard."

"If it can't be so hard, how come it's never happened?" Conner asked.

Havid let out loud laugh. "You may look like a man, but in some ways, you are still a boy. We can't have peace because people have to get involved."

"I don't get it."

"People with pride and ego."

Conner shook his head. "I don't understand."

Havid slapped Conner on the back. "When you do, then you'll know. But by then, you'll be old like me!"

They continued to walk in silence until the ground started to slope up. The tunnel ended at a ladder. A rope hung from the ceiling and Havid gave it two sharp pulls and then sat down.

"It could be a while," Havid said. "First they have to hear the bell, and then they have to dig out the trap door."

Conner sat down and said, "Seems like a lot of work.

"It's kept it a secret for hundreds of years. If it were easy, it would have been discovered."

After some time had passed, Havid stood and gave the rope two more quick pulls and sat down again. This time, they heard digging above their heads. They waited patiently until the digging stopped and the door was pulled up.

Havid climbed up first. Conner quickly followed. They found themselves in the kitchen of a small farm house. Unlike the house in the city which had a dirt floor, the farmhouse had a wood floor. The flooring had been pulled up to get access to the covered trap door. A man and a woman, presumably husband and wife, stood across the room. The wife held a shovel. The man was missing his right arm below the elbow. The bandages indicated it might have been a somewhat recent wound.

"Welcome," the man said uncomfortably. "My name is Dane. This is my wife, Laura."

"Thank you," Havid said. "May I?" He took the shovel from Laura and started putting the dirt back on top of the trap door.

"I am sorry that we did not answer the first ring," Dane said. "It is the first time we have ever…done this."

"No worries," Havid said.

"It had always been my pa," Dane said. He glanced at his arm. "We were both fighting the Thellians. He took an arrow and killed him right away. I lasted a bit longer."

"I was there, too," Conner said.

Havid snapped up straight and gave Conner a stern look. He wished he had talked to Conner about talking to the people who manned the tunnels. You weren't supposed to. It kept things safer.

"You're just a boy," Laura said.

Conner rubbed his face. He could not wait until his fine facial hair grew in thicker. "I'm old enough," Conner replied.

Dane nodded. "It was a horrible time. Never seen so much blood. So much death."

Laura patted him on the shoulder. "It's been tough for Dane. He and his father ran a smithy. Just over yonder."

"It's tough to pound steel with just one arm," Dane said.

Havid tapped the last of the dirt and set aside the shovel. He pulled a handful of coins from his pocket. Dane took them with his good hand, turning them over, showing Laura. She raised an eyebrow.

"It's a little more than normal. But we'll need some supplies. A horse if you have one."

"No horses. I have an ox and a mule, though."

"Hunting supplies is all I need," Conner said. "A bow. Knife. Warm blanket or two."

Laura stepped forward. "Dane, you help this man put the floor back in. You know how it goes. You, come with me. We'll go to the shop, and you can pick out what you need."

Conner followed Laura outside. It was the middle of the night and the moon hung low on the horizon. There was plenty of light to see, as there were no clouds in the sky. Conner glanced back over his shoulder at the city. The castle was clearly visible, lit up from the torches that lined the walls. He wondered what Elissa was doing. His heart ached now more than ever.

"Leaving the city for good?" Laura asked. "I know I'm not supposed to talk to you guys, but I've never done this before. Dane's Pa always did it. He had told us about it and swore us to secrecy. But it's hard not to ask, you know? The bells have been ringing and the trumpets blaring. You have anything to do with that?"

Conner just smiled and shook his head.

Laura shrugged her shoulders and pushed open the door to their shop. It was cold and dark inside. The furnace had not been going for some time, but the smell of coal and fire still hung in the air. She lit a couple lamps to give them enough light to see by. She made her way to the back of the shop and began looking through stacks of finished knives. "What kind of knife do you need?"

"Hunting," Conner said. "Skinning, cutting, that sort of thing."

Laura found one and grabbed a matching sheath hanging from a nearby peg. She handed both to Conner. "Thank you."

"Need a bow?"

"Of course," Conner said with a smile.

Laura disappeared into another room before coming back with an unstrung bow in hand. It was taller than the bows that he had used, and it was a bit heavier, too. Conner took it and studied the bow from tip to tip, holding it by its grip. Since it was unstrung, he quickly strung it. He pulled the string back to his ear, testing the tension.

"It's very stiff," Conner said. "I could shoot an arrow very, very far with this one."

"It was Dane's," Laura said. "He made it himself. For hunting. No please, keep it."

Conner had tried to give it back. He could not take another man's hunting bow.

"He cannot…" her voice cracked. "He will want you to take it."

"Thank you. The knife, the bow. They are more than what I could expect."

"You said you were there," Laura said. "North. With the Thellians."

Conner nodded. "Yes, I was there."

"He isn't the same since he came back. When they left, he was marching behind the king. It was all pomp and circumstance! They were marching together. He and the king were only a few feet apart. Knights in their armor were right next to him. They were waving, and everyone was waving back. I was never so proud of him. He worked hard, really hard. Sometimes all night long to get his work done. He was such a good man." Her voice trailed off. "They started coming back in small groups. Some on foot. Some on wagons. The king came first. On the wagon. So stiff and cold he looked. They rode right by us since we are on the road leading to the main gate. I sat in the window of the barn and looked down and could see the king. I knew he was dead before everyone else." She buried her face in her hands until she could stop sobbing.

"And Dane had not come home, yet," she continued after composing herself. "I knew he was dead. I just knew it. But more kept coming down the road. Ones and twos and sometimes ten or fifteen in a group. I held out hope that he would come. Every moment of every day I watched from the barn. Until I saw him. He was alive. He was hurt, but he was alive." She took in a deep breath and continued. "But like I said. He's not the same. He can hardly work. He can do some things, and he's trying to do more. But not like he was before."

"It changed us all," Conner said. "In many ways."

"You kill a man before that?" she asked.

Conner nodded. "I did. But I had to. It was like war. I didn't like it. But if I didn't, someone would have died. Might have been me. That's like war. Someone always dies. It's either them or me."

"You're too young to talk like that. It changed you, too, huh?"

Conner looked at the bow to distract himself from his own thoughts. He had grown up. He was no longer the innocent boy in the woods who lived off the land. He had killed. He had murdered. He could not shake the face of Neffenmark from his vision. Or the first one. He even remembered his name. They had called him Jon. And he had held Brace Hawkden in his arms when he died. Their eyes had all lost their life as he watched. He had seen it leave them. He had seen the instant they had died. And he knew a little of himself had died each time as well.

Then he thought of Elissa, Queen Elissa. He unstrung the bow and gripped it tightly. "Maybe we all needed to grow up a little bit. There are things in the world that I could never have imagined before I marched off to war. I could have lived my life as a simple woodsman, never leaving the forest. I could have lived my life pretending the rest of the world didn't exist. But it does. I have seen death. I have seen treachery. I have seen the ships of the Taran Empire. They are not here to trade with us. They are here to conquer us. We all have our jobs to do. Sometimes it's to live, and sometimes it's to die. We have to live our lives with what was given to us. We can't dream about what's not there. If we do, then we become victims of history."

He turned and walked quickly out of the shop.

Laura did not follow. She could not follow. She felt sorry for Conner and cried for him. And she hoped that he was wrong. She touched her stomach where the baby was growing. She could not imagine such a life as Conner described. What a sad and pitiful life would be if that was all that there was.

Chapter Thirty-One

Conner kept the fire low to keep spying eyes from seeing him. He had dug a deep pit so that the flames could not be seen from a distance, but the light of the fire still lit up the trees and bushes around him. He had a rabbit spitted across the fire. It's skinny body sizzling in the heat of the fire. Darkness had fallen some time ago, and he had waited to stoke up the fire until darkness hit. He debated whether to light the fire in daylight or nighttime. The fire at night was easier to see, but also easier to hide. It was tough to hide smoke during the daytime as it rose above the tree tops, which made it easy to see from a distance. Regardless, if someone got close enough, they would smell the smoke of the fire or the scent of the cooked rabbit.

He pulled off a chunk of steaming hot rabbit meat, checking to see if it was fully cooked. It was still slightly pink, so he rotated the rabbit on the spit. It would not be long. His stomach grumbled its hunger, especially since the smell of rabbit meat filled the forest.

At the sound of a stick snapping, Conner leaped up, holding his knife in front of him. His eyes had been on the fire, so his vision was very much impaired. He grumbled at his own stupidity. This was another reason to have the fire during the day. It would not destroy his night vision.

The shadowing figure of a man appeared from the darkness of the trees.

"I hope I did not startle you."

Conner relaxed and lowered his knife. "Sir Marik! No, of course not."

Marik walked up to the fire and lowered his hands to the flame to warm them. "Fall will soon be upon us. The days grow shorter and the nights grow colder."

"It has been a long summer," Conner said, sitting back down on the ground.

"That it has," Marik said. "Is the rabbit almost done? I am famished."

"Almost," Conner replied. Then he asked, "How did you find me?"

Marik gave Conner a sly look. "Really? I am a master ranger. The best in the land. You did a fine job, though, hiding your tracks. It took all my best effort to follow you."

"Have you come to arrest me?" Conner asked.

Marik took a long stick and prodded the fire. "There is no reason to."

"I can think of one pretty good reason," Conner said.

"Things have changed a bit since you left."

"Is that good or bad?"

"Some good. Some bad. Queen Elissa will be sitting upon the throne and will rule the kingdom. All the lords have sworn fealty to her, so at least for now, she is safe."

"That's great news!" Conner said.

"Yes. Now comes the bad news. Neffenmark had a treaty with the Tarans. The Queen will not support the treaty and has kicked the Tarans out of the city. The ships left for Taran this morning. I do not know how that will go over with the emperor. He may choose to ignore us, or if he happens to be in a bad mood, he may decide to invade us."

"Let him come!" Conner said. "The knights will repel them!"

Marik shook his head. "There are no more knights."

"What?"

"In a rash moment, the queen's first order of business was to stop the feuding between the Royal Guard and the knights. So she essentially disbanded both of them. At first, we all thought it was just something she said in the heat of the moment, but she has followed through. The knights are no more. The Royal Guard are no more."

"How can that be?"

"Oddly," Marik said with a raised eyebrow. "It may just work out. She has not stopped the squire's training. In fact, she has expanded it.

She removed the restriction of noble blood. Anyone can join, now. I think if this were to have happened a year ago, there would have been a revolution. The knights would have revolted, and it would have been messy. But everyone saw you. They saw that someone without noble blood could still fight like a knight and have the honor and courage of a knight. Maybe the separation of the noble and the common people was not such a good thing. Maybe mixing us together can actually make us a better kingdom. The battle with Thell hurt us badly. Emotionally, physically. In all ways possible. Maybe this is a way for us to start up anew."

"A queen on the throne and no more Karmon Knights," Conner said thoughtfully.

"It's a strange new world. That is for sure." Marik took a chunk of meat with his knife and blew on it until it was cool enough to eat. "Good rabbit. Juicy and tender."

"If you didn't come to take me back," Conner asked. "Then why are you here?"

Marik smiled. "You asked me if I came to arrest you. I did not say I didn't want to take you back."

Conner shook his head. "I cannot go back."

"You are needed. We need good soldiers right now. Once word gets out that the Karmon Knights have been disbanded, it will be a sign of weakness. I could see Thell trying to take advantage of this and send their army south. Even Taran could march upon us. And with the way we kicked them out, I would not be surprised if they did!"

Marik took another chunk of rabbit meat and added. "And I think she will need you, too."

"Elissa?" Conner asked. Then he shook his head. "No. It's time for me to move on. She is queen, now. I would just get in her way."

"Not at all," Marik said with a strong shake of his head. "We can use someone like you. She can use someone like you."

Conner shook his head. "No, I am going to Taran to find Master Goshin. He left so abruptly." He looked up in the sky where the star lit up the sky. "He was so strange and mysterious about the star. He believed it meant something. I need to find him."

"Do not run from us, from Queen Elissa. Master Goshin can figure out this star thing on his own."

"I am not running from anything. I never fit in the castle. I was always the odd one. Between the fancy courtiers and silk shirts and dancing. It's not me. I was born and raised in the woods. That is who I am."

"You should come back, just to say goodbye."

"No. I need to just go. I don't want to make this any harder than it needs to be."

"It doesn't need to be hard at all! Just come back. She will not like it that you left without saying goodbye."

"She is the queen. She is ruler of the kingdom. I am sure she has more to worry about than just me."

Resigned to defeat, Marik let out a long sigh. "Okay. But do you have enough supplies? A bow? How about a horse."

Conner shook his head at the mention of a horse.

"It's a long ways to Taran on foot," Marik observed.

"I'll be okay."

Marik stood up and walked back out into the darkness. A few moments later, he came back, leading a white horse.

"Lilly?" Conner asked. "Won't Elissa miss her?"

Marik shook his head with a smile. "No. Not all. In fact, it was her idea."

"She knew I wasn't coming back," Conner said.

"She wanted you to," Marik replied. "But yes, she knew you wouldn't come back."

Marik handed the reins of Lilly to Conner. "Take care, Conner."

"Leaving already? I have more than enough rabbit for the both of us."

Marik pointed to the northeast. "I'm on my way to Thell. To finish the job that King Thorndale started. Not the war, but the peace treaty. Our kingdoms have no reason to be at war. So hopefully I can convince them that."

"A lot of blood was spilled," Conner said.

"On both sides," Marik replied. "With Neffenmark gone, hopefully, we can start the peace process fresh without outside influence."

"Speaking of Neffenmark, how much did Sir Brace tell you about what was going on?"

"Not many details. Pretty much what you know is what he told me. Neffenmark was the catalyst to it all. And the Tarans were involved, but I have no idea to what extent. It is not a coincidence that Neffenmark had a treaty established before he took the throne. That was his endgame. I just don't know what the Taran's endgame is."

"Invasion?"

Marik shrugged his shoulders. "There is no reason for them to. We are no threat to them militarily or otherwise. We do regular trade with them and they with us."

"I'll keep my eyes open in Taran."

"And watch your back, too."

Marik stepped forward and gave Conner a big hug. "Take care, Conner. And safe journeys."

Conner watched Marik disappear into the trees. He felt a big hole open up in his heart. He would miss Marik. And Elissa. But he knew leaving was the right thing to do. He just wished he knew why.

***

Prince Tarcious stood at an open window in the tallest spire of the emperor's palace. The late summer breeze was blowing in his face, bringing the slight scent of salt from the Gulf of Taran. The entire city was below him, spread out for miles. But his focus was not on the city, it was on the naval vessels that were moored just off the coast. He took deep breaths to control the anger that was burning deep inside of him. He could feel the edges of the power as it sat deep in his gut. It wanted to come out, to explode out, but he knew it couldn't. He knew he couldn't let it. It was all a part of the discipline. To have the power, one had to control it. To control it, one had to have the power of discipline. It was a vicious cycle that he was just beginning to master.

He closed his eyes and searched out behind him for the presence of his visitors. This was practice for when he really needed it. Once he honed the skill, all of the skills, there would be nothing that could stop him. But that would take time. And patience.

After the second deep breath, he could feel them. He could feel their heartbeats and their breathing. He could sense their minds, even though he couldn't peek into them. Someday, maybe he could. But that would take more time and more patience. There were two of them. One had a heartbeat and breathing that was normal. The other was huffing as if he had been running all day. And his heart was pounding. Once the prince focused on the heart, the pounding became so loud that he could not hear anything else.

"Admiral Hester," Prince Tarcious said. The stale, musky scent of sweat reached the prince's nose. "You are afraid."

"I come as ordered," the Admiral said. He was a career naval officer, having risen up through the ranks of deck hand to ship's captain. Now he was in charge of a large portion of the fleet. He had pushed and shoved and stepped on others to get to his position. He was afraid, but he was doing his best to not show it.

"Explain why you are here," Prince Tarcious demanded.

"The Karmon's broke their treaty," the Admiral said as steadily as he could. "They forced us to leave."

Prince Tarcious spun around and screamed, "Forced! No kingdom forces you to do anything!"

"We had not yet established the garrison, your highness. Most of my men were still on the ships, awaiting orders. They were not allowed to disembark." The admiral waited for a response from the prince. When he got none, he added, "They had us outnumbered. We had no choice. If it came to fighting, they would have slaughtered us."

The prince let out a low growl. "Neffenmark. He will not enjoy what I have in store for him."

"It wasn't him," Admiral Hester said. "It was Queen Elissa Thorndale. It was by her orders that we were sent home."

"The queen? You are listening to the queen?"

"She is in charge. She has the throne. Neffenmark is dead."

The prince was about to explode in anger, but those last words of the Admiral froze him. That was not expected. "What happened?" he asked as calmly as he could.

"Murdered," the admiral replied. "In his chambers. By a boy."

"A boy? Did the fat oaf not have guards?"

"It seems that he was one of his guards," the Admiral said. "It seems that Neffenmark has a penchant for beating up women and this particular guard did not like it. It is actually oddly coincidental."

"Oh?" the prince asked with a raised eyebrow. "I believe in many things. Coincidence is not one of them. Tell more about this boy."

"I know little about him, only what I could gather from talking to the castle's servants. His name is Conner, and he trained with the Knights for some time, even though he could never be knighted as he is not a noble. But the servants talked quite a lot about a time when he bested their best squires in a tournament. No one knows where he came from. Some small village I supposed. He just appeared the day the princess returned from being kidnapped. It seems he had a hand in her rescue. After that, he was given the title of being her Champion. It is some honor that Karmons can bestow upon one of their own."

The prince lifted a hand, and the Admiral stopped speaking. "Yes, yes. I am familiar with their silly honors. So this boy saves his princess not once, but twice. Both times interfering with well laid out plans. I do not find that coincidental. I find it maddening."

A confused look crossed the Admiral's face. "They say that the kidnappers were Thellian. It is what caused the king to march his army north."

The prince laughed loudly while he walked away from the admiral and towards one of the large open windows. He looked out at his city, and his gaze fell upon a large structure at the exact center of the city. The arena was empty, as it was still midday. But by evening, it would be filled with screaming, bloodthirsty fans.

"You say he trained with the knights?" the prince asked.

"Yes."

"And he bested one of their own?"

"No, one of their best squires."

"But he is good with the sword?"

"The servants I talked to thought he was the best swordsmen they had ever seen. But that's just coming from the servants. He saved the princess from her kidnappers and killed Neffenmark. That's all I know for sure. Everything else is just what I heard from the servants I was able to talk to."

"I think I have a plan for this boy. If he is even half as good as you say."

"Yes, your highness," the Admiral said with a bow. "Would you like me to return to Karmon and find him?"

The prince smiled, his back still to the admiral. "Oh, that won't be necessary. I have others for that purpose. I do have a plan for you, though."

"I'm at your disposal."

The prince closed his eyes as he envisioned the spell. He had spent many long hours memorizing this new one. He had practiced it a couple times on a small rodent. But never on a human. The words of a language long forgotten left his lips as his mind replayed the words over and over. He said them slowly, even though he had them memorized. They needed to be just in the right order for the power within himself to be released. As soon as the last word of the spell left his lips, he could feel the hot sensations of the power leaving his body. It started deep within his gut, warming him at first, and then turning him blazing hot. If he were to be stopped at this point, the spell would implode upon himself, so he had to finish it. He did not think about the scrolls that described the demise of many sorcerers who had perished because they could not complete the spell. He only thought about the power being released.

And then it came out of him almost like a sneeze. The power released in one instant was immediately followed by a sudden loss of all energy. The prince fell to his knees, exhausted. But he heard the screams behind him and knew that he had been successful. He turned just in time to see the last of the green cloud of poisonous gas dissipate. The admiral was on the ground, kicking with convulsions, his mouth open and releasing a piercing scream. Every spot of exposed skin had blistered, especially his face. He was barely recognizable as a human as the poison did its work. His eyes bulged out from the pain. His lips cracked and bled. Skin blisters grew and popped. The instant of the last moment of his life was as painful as could be imaged.

The prince smiled at his own power and the pain that he had inflicted upon the admiral. He wanted to stand, but he was still too weak. His mind still worked, so as he watched the last twitching of the admiral's legs, he considered his situation. With Neffenmark gone, his ability to gain access to the castle was now gone. There was always the obvious option, to send in legions of centurions to assault the castle. But he knew that option could never work. First, the assault would be expensive. He knew the might and courage of the Karmon Knights. Maybe they weren't as good as their reputation, but he had lost too many battles to the barbarians from the north to take anyone lightly. It would take too many men away from the other wars that they were fighting. He could not let their armies be stretched too thin. But most importantly, he could not let a battle happen that would cause the destruction of the castle. It needed to remain intact.

"Your power continues to grow."

Prince Tarcious turned towards the shadows where the voice came from. "Your work is incomplete," the prince growled with an angry voice. "Neffenmark is dead. The admiral failed in his task as well. You can see how I think of failures."

A tall and thin man stepped from the shadows. "Unlike the Admiral, I do not fear you."

"You should," the prince said. He tried to feel the power, but it was gone. He was exhausted almost to the point of collapse. If he even tried to force himself to tap the power again, it would consume him.

Hibold strode aggressively towards the prince, his cloak wrapped tightly around his body. "Your attempts at tapping into the ancient skills are impressive. But you are still weak. I can see it in your eyes. Your shoulders hang lower. You are hunched over like an old man."

The prince straightened himself up.

"Your master teases you with the power," Hibold added. He pulled a long jagged-toothed dagger from the folders of his cloak and held it out, pointed at the prince's chest. "I could kill you right now. You couldn't even stop me physically if you wanted to." He put the dagger back into his belt after a long moment. "But I won't. We serve the same master, and I don't think he would take it kindly if I killed his pet project." Hibold's eyes sparkled, and a smile grew on his face. "And I wouldn't get any ideas about stabbing me in the back, either. I don't think the master would take it too kindly if you killed me. I'm sort of a pet project, too."

The prince did not like the thin man who stood in front of him. But Hibold was willing to get his hands dirty, and that was one thing that the prince could not do right now. Until he was able to wrestle complete control from his brother, he needed to not draw attention to himself.

"I have a task for you," the prince said.

Hibold bowed low. "As always, I am at your command."

"Neffenmark was killed by a young Karmon by the name of Conner. Find him and bring him to me."

"You ask me to find a needle in the haystack?"

"You are resourceful. I am sure you will be able to accomplish this simple task. You have spies throughout the empire and beyond."

"Very well," Hibold replied.

"Now leave me," the prince ordered. "I must rest."

About the Author

Brad Clark grew up in the modestly sized city of Grand Rapids, Michigan, but now resides in a small town in the southwest corner of Michigan. He works as a software engineer at a local family-owned software company.

Reading and writing has always been his passion, but the stories that were jotted down into piles of notebooks never made it beyond a chapter or two. But after much nagging from his wife and kids, he broke down and published his first novel as an e-book. His love for the fantasy genre started when he was a young boy and had never left. That love for swords and sorcery grew into an idea for a story, and that story become his second novel, Knight Fall, book one of the series of books called the Champion Chronicles.

As much as he has a passion for reading and writing, Brad is also an avid road bicyclist and runner. Springtime is running season as he prepares for an annual half-marathon. Summer, though, is his favorite time where he can spend hours in the saddle, riding his bike on quiet back country roads.

With five kids, two still at home, writing is purely a hobby, a way to escape from the business of life. His stories come from his love of the genre and from his heart. Whether the stories work for the rest of the world is not why he writes, he writes because he simply wants to put his dreams on paper. He never wants his writing to be work, he only desires it to be a fun hobby and hopes that others can share in his stories.

You can follow Brad on Twitter @booksbybrad or visit his website at www.booksbybradclark.com.